FLOYD'S
Tire Mart

FLOYD'S
Tire Mart

Max Taylor

Library of Congress Control Number: 2007908222
ISBN: Hardcover   978-1-4257-9411-8
                   Softcover   978-1-4257-9407-1

To order additional copies of this book, contact:
Xlibris Corporation
1-888-795-4274
www.Xlibris.com
Orders@Xlibris.com
42350

To Linda:
For her love, help and encouragement

INTRODUCTION

The homes on Shady Lane were built on stilts. They were shaded by huge sycamore trees along the northern banks of the Meramec River. They were built as summer homes in the late 1940s for the new middle class. The carpenters, electricians, plumbers, and auto workers who had come home after the war had new expectations. They demanded and received higher wages for their work.

St. Louis summers are hot and humid. The new middle class wanted to escape the heat the way the rich had done. The developer of Shady Lane promised concrete roads and sidewalks. He left the state with the money after the last lot was sold. The homes were built by the owners one weekend at a time. When at last all the homes were complete, they numbered twenty-seven. All but six hovered ten feet off the ground on twelve-by-twelve inch posts sunk into the sandy clay soil. The others were perched atop concrete block walls.

The Meramec River came out of its banks and washed out the road. The homeowners had a meeting to discuss how the road should be paid for. The meeting ended without a plan but with resolve to meet again. The second meeting ended in a fistfight with no plans to meet again. The fight left bad blood among the homeowners and the cooperation that had made the dream of a summer home cooled by a soft breeze coming across the water, refreshing a man in a lawn chair as he sipped a cold beer in the shade, began to unravel.

Then the cost of air-conditioning dropped. Shady Lane began its decline. One by one, the summer homes were sold and became the full-time residences of those who had fallen on hard times.

CHAPTER ONE

Al Creed stood on the screened-in back porch of a small house built on stilts on the edge of the Meramec River. Al Creed bought his home with the help of a GI loan. He had big plans. He would not only bring the house back to its original charm, he would add on new rooms and a two car garage. Al's big plans never came to be.

Al puffed on his first cigarette of the day and waited for the coffee to boil. Leaning in the doorway between the porch and the kitchen, he stared blankly through worn and torn screens toward the river, subconsciously hoping for something of value to float by, something that would improve his life in some large or small way.

It was three thirty in the morning and Al had not gotten enough sleep to recover from the ten or fifteen beers he had poured into his ample gut just four hours before.

The river glowed in a black and white world and small chunks of wood floating by showed sharply on the reflected light off the water.

The coffee pot made its first perks and Al couldn't wait. He poured himself half a cup of thin coffee and went back to his watch.

A Greyhound bus would be pulling into St. Louis in a couple of hours, and he would be face to face with his fourteen-year-old son, his only son, a son he hadn't seen in ten years. He should be happy. A few hours ago, he was. He was celebrating his son coming home to live with him. People patted his back and drank to his good luck.

Now in the quiet, colorless pre-dawn hours, fear took a grip on Al's mind and body. He was tense and had to force the muscles in his shoulders down and back, and in a moment they were pulled up tight again. What should he say? The boy's mother was gone without a trace. Rayleen was a whore; anything might have happened to her.

Al knew she was a whore when he married her, but she was so pretty. When Rayleen took a shine to Al, he dreamed she would change and love only him. Al was not a handsome man. Never had any woman half as pretty as Rayleen showed any interest in him. As much as he hated her for what she had done to him, Al couldn't help but feel grateful for the good times. Never had life looked so promising as it did when he first married Rayleen. How proudly he had strolled with Rayleen on his arm.

What a fool he had been. He could see it plainly now; he saw it plainly then; he just wanted to believe that a woman that handsome wanted him and him alone. The signs were all there—the way she suddenly threw herself at him when just days before she wouldn't acknowledge his presence; the way she avoided him and chastised him for any public displays of affection; the way she insisted on making love only in the dark. Any fool could have seen; but any fool only sees what he wants to see, that's why he's called a fool. Al had come to this conclusion long ago, but that didn't stop him from beating himself up on a regular basis with these same thoughts and regrets. And now it was all fresh again and churned over and over in his mind. What would the boy look like? Would he look like her? If he did, would Al turn away, unable to stand her presence in front of him?

The coffee was ready now. Al filled a Thermos bottle and a fresh cup and descended a flight of wobbly steps to his old pickup truck. The drive from Arnold, Missouri, to the bus station in St. Louis would take an hour if traffic was good.

Al is the day shift manager at Floyd's Tire Mart for this week. The day shift manager unlocks the pumps and turns on the lights and helps one of the boys roll out and stack close to a hundred tires in random displays around the building and lot. At the end of the day, the night shift manager and one of the boys roll them back in and stack them in the tall, neat columns necessary for the limited space available. The process takes about forty-five minutes if it can be accomplished non-stop. It produces a heart rate that sends stabs of pain across Al's chest.

Skip Boman is the night manager this week, and although it is universally agreed that the night man has it worse for having to do all that moving and stacking after working a ten-hour shift, still the day shift guy has to start doing jumping jacks no sooner than his feet hit the floor was Al's argument. Al hated jumping jacks and pushups. The Army used such things on new recruits who couldn't follow instructions. Al had trouble following instructions.

Al turned his anger on the tire-stacking ritual. He was tired and his gut protested the coffee and beer mixture and was not at all happy with the extra stomach acid Al was producing. Damn them tires! Rolling them out and in every day. Al listed in his mind all the reasons why this waste of energy should be stopped or at least put off until later in the day. It was a well thought out list; Al went over it and refined it every morning when he was on days.

The drive up South Broadway into the city was going better than expected. If he didn't get a ticket, he would be at the bus station early. Al worried about getting tickets, and for good reason. He ran at least one red light or stop sign every time he entered the thick part of the city. "They put the damn things everywhere," he would say. "They got so many signs and lights, you don't see 'em until it's too late."

Today it was going well. The only light he had not seen until it was too late was green. If it had been red, he would have blown through it anyway because he was well on the other side before he saw it at all.

Byron Creed sat with his forehead pressed against the window as the Missouri countryside slid by. The bus driver said they would be in St. Louis in about an hour. Byron hoped the bus would crash and everyone on board would die. Maybe a bridge would collapse and the bus would plunge to the bottom of the river. That would be better than coming here to live with some man he didn't know.

The Denver police were a bunch of lazy bastards. They gave up looking for Rayleen in just a couple of days. She could be hurt up in the mountains, but they didn't care. They wouldn't even talk to Byron about the search. All they ever said was that they were doing all they could. "If that was true, they would have found her, and I would be at home in bed now and not in Missouri on this damn bus."

Byron felt like he wanted to cry. He hadn't cried—not when Rayleen didn't come home the first day. He was sure she would show up; she always did. Even after three days, Byron expected her to come dragging in with some big lie to explain where she had been. When she didn't come home on the fourth day, Byron went to the police. They seemed to blame him right off for not coming to them sooner. What good would that have done? All they did was fill out some papers and ask about relatives. They didn't even try to find her; all they wanted to do was put me on a bus to somewhere—anywhere. Once I was gone, they could go back to writing tickets and eating donuts. Byron's eyes began to tear up; but he fought back the emotion, wiggled in his seat, and looked around to make sure nobody saw him start to cry.

Al made good time and didn't get a ticket. The bus from Denver had not arrived yet. It was on its way and on time according to a not-too-friendly woman behind the ticket window.

Al found a seat and began to rehearse his first few sentences. Don't ask about Rayleen; he's probably still upset. If you don't ask, it's like you don't care. Well, you don't care, that's true; but it would be hateful to let the boy know that. Ask him how the trip was. Nineteen hours on a bus. How do you think it was? Tell him you're glad to have him come live with you. If that's true, why didn't you ever write him or call him or go see him? Don't start off telling him lies; he'll see right through you. I can't tell him the truth—that I hope his mother is dead and I would have killed her myself if I ever got my hands on her.

Al felt his blood pressure increase and his stomach would stand for no more stress. He would have to find a restroom without delay.

The bus was due in a few minutes, and Al didn't want the boy to be standing alone with no one there to meet him. But if he didn't go now, he might mess his pants, and that wouldn't make a very good first impression.

When the bus came to a stop at the St. Louis station, Byron kept his seat while the other passengers filed off. They were in a hurry to get to where they were going. Byron stared out the window at the uninviting, decaying city landscape. When the bus driver informed him he would have to exit the bus, he forced himself to his feet and trudged slowly toward the door. He collected his small suitcase and entered the bus station lobby. There were very few people around. The crowd that had just minutes ago left his bus had already met their rides and melted into the city.

Byron wore a bewildered look. His dark brown hair was plastered to his head in spots and sticking straight up in other places. He was five foot ten, tall for his age, and slightly built, more from bad eating habits and diet than from genetics. Wearing a black motorcycle jacket that was too big for him and blue jeans and black canvas tennis shoes, he stood motionless holding a suitcase that contained clean underwear, a toothbrush, socks, a comb, two t-shirts, and a pair of black dress pants that were almost new but too short.

Seconds ticked by and Byron felt the eyes of the bus company personnel scan him then look away. The sound of a door closing on the far side of the lobby drew his attention to an old man coming out of the restroom. The man saw Byron and headed toward him. This can't be him, Byron thought. This man looks to be a hundred years old. Maybe this is someone that works for my father and was sent to pick me up. That's what it is. Al Creed runs a big truck stop and can't just take off any time he wants. So he sent this old man that's probably the janitor to come and get me.

Byron studied the janitor as he lumbered across the room. His face is tanned and hangs loosely around his eyes. His eyes seem sad and dull. The face could be that of a retired boxer; the nose is flat and the cartilage twisted a little to one side. He is a large man, every bit six feet tall, maybe more. His shoulders are wide but droop with fatigue and regret. His left foot curls in at the ankle and the outside edge of his work boot shows excess wear. He limps when he walks; the left arm swinging higher than the right, keeping a balance with his shifting weight. His body is thick from head to toe and he wears a uniform with patches on the ball cap and shirt that reads Zephyr. Byron assumes Zephyr is the name of a deer from Africa that is the mascot of the truck stop his father manages.

When the man came to a stop directly in front of him, he looked even larger and uglier than before. Then in a voice that sounded like the growl of a large dog, he said, "You must be Byron. I'm your dad. You can call me Al." The old man sticks out his hand to shake and it is covered with callouses and blood-filled fingernails.

Byron reluctantly accepts the handshake and stares in disbelief. The ball cap on the old man's head is crumpled and crooked, exposing thinning gray hair around the edges. The old man is smiling at him with ugly yellow teeth. Byron has a sudden urge to run, but the old man is still shaking his hand with a tight grip. "Hi," said Byron. His hopes were sinking faster than a bus headed toward the bottom of a river. The old man is still pumping his hand and seems intent on doing so for hours to come, as if this would make up for the years he didn't care.

Byron pulled away and Al realized his mistake. "Sorry about that. I just don't know what to say," Al said.

Byron was shocked by the low pitched growl of Al's voice. "What's wrong with your throat? You got a cold?" he asked.

"No, that's just the way I sound. Come on, we got to get going. Want me to carry your suitcase?"

"No, I can carry it."

Al felt awkward about asking to carry the suitcase. It was a tiny little thing and surely the boy could carry it okay. He just wanted to try and be nice. That's all. "Okay then, let's get going," he said.

Byron sat quietly as Al wrestled the old pickup down the city streets. Every few minutes, Al would point out something of interest and Byron would look in the direction indicated but saw nothing that he considered interesting. "You ever go to a doctor about your throat?" he asked. He couldn't quit thinking about Al's voice. Nobody he'd ever met talked like that.

"Yeah, I seen one once," Al said.

There was a period of silence. Byron waited for Al to continue. Finally, when he could hold it in no longer, he blurted out, "So, what'd he say was wrong?"

"Oh, he didn't know for sure. He wanted to do some cutting though. That's all they want to do these days. When I was a boy if you went to the doctor, he'd give you some pills or a shot to fix you up. Not now. Cut, cut, cut, that's all they want to do. They get more money for cutting than for pills."

Byron considered Al's thoughts on doctors, not sure if the old man was making sense or not. He looked blankly through the windshield as the conversation dried up, and the drive to where they were going was taking forever. He was pulled from his trance when he noticed Al blow past a red light like he didn't even see it. Byron started to bring it to the old man's attention but thought better of it. After all, this was St. Louis, not Denver. Maybe things were different here. He didn't want to appear to be a stupid kid. Best to say nothing. The old man lived here and he had to have seen the light. There was probably going to be a lot of new stuff to learn.

"We'll pass by the station on the way home. I guess you'll want to get some sleep. I have to go in and open up, but I'll take you home first," Al said.

"Okay." Byron sat up a little straighter and peered down the road waiting for the station to come into sight.

Herman Kepler, one of Rayleen's boyfriends, had given Byron a ride in his eighteen wheeler once down to the big truck stop on Interstate 19. Byron remembered how impressed he had been with the sheer size of the place. There must have been twenty or thirty pumps, five huge bays big enough for whole rigs to be pulled inside. There was a fancy restaurant with little bitty jukeboxes on every table, and right next door was a gift shop that had everything you could ever want.

Herman Kepler helped Rayleen get a job there, and Rayleen said she would get Byron a job there bussing tables, and when he was older, pumping gas and diesel and parking rigs for the drivers while they ate dinner.

Rayleen only worked there two weeks. She said somebody was stealing her tips. Herman Kepler said he heard the register was coming up short. They had a big fight about it, and Herman Kepler didn't come around anymore.

"There's Floyd's up ahead on the left," Al said.

Byron leaned forward for a better look in the gray dawn light. There up ahead, a long, low building that looked old and tired. There were no bays, no restaurant, no gift shop; there were only six pumps on three islands running parallel to the highway and the building.

"I'll get you a job there in a couple of years," Al said.

Byron slumped back in the truck seat, saying nothing. He wanted to scream out, Who the hell want to work there, but thought, What's the use. He was going to have to live with this old bastard for a while; no use starting a fight the first day.

The truck turned off the highway just before a bridge. The road was gravel and mud, full of potholes. Al swerved the truck from one side of the road to the other, dodging the largest of the holes. The road ran along the edge of a river and was covered by a canopy of huge sycamores. Houses lined the road on both sides, each one poised atop twelve inch-by-twelve inch posts at the corners and down the center.

"Why are all these houses up in the air?" Byron asked.

"This old river comes out of its banks every so often," Al said.

Byron at once wished he had given the question a little more thought before he spoke. The old man must think I'm dumb as a hammer. Oh, who cares what he thinks.

Al pulled the truck in under a shabby looking place on the river side of the road and turned the motor off. "This is it," he said.

The last of Byron's dreams and hopes were shattered. The big, two-storey house with pillars in the front and a big green lawn that Byron had expected to come with the job of manager wasn't to be.

"I'll go up and unlock the door. Wait till I get in before you come up. These damn old steps might not hold both of us," Al said.

Byron waited as instructed and did a slow turn taking in his new environment. The river bank was scarcely a hundred feet from the back of the house. Not a blade of grass grew anywhere; mud and gravel seemed to coat everything. Most every house within sight had a car or truck in some state of disrepair hovering on top of concrete blocks. The smell of dead fish and mildew was thick in the air, but amazingly became normal after just a few minutes. The sycamore trees towered over everything, refusing the dim light entry so early in the morning.

"Come on up," came the voice of God with a cold.

Byron, with all he owned in the world packed in his little suitcase, ascended the stairs. The handrail was no comfort at all, being rubbery to the feel. The stairs led to a second porch with a doorway to the kitchen. Byron was somewhat relieved to find the interior much cleaner and brighter than the outside.

Byron was used to moving. In Denver, he and Rayleen moved often. Rayleen had trouble keeping the rent paid, and her various boyfriends and shifting jobs created the need to move in a hurry, sometimes in the middle of the night. A few times they lived in real nice apartments, but these never lasted and they would drift to run-down, old buildings in bad neighborhoods.

Byron surveyed the kitchen. Clean, fresh paint, linoleum floor. The floor felt a little spongy and sagged in the middle, but all in all, it was much better than his last address.

"I got to go and open up the station. You get some sleep and find yourself something to eat and I'll be back at about four thirty," Al said. Byron was still holding his suitcase standing in the kitchen. He heard the gravel pop and the motor struggle till Al was gone from hearing.

Byron missed the mountains. He'd only been to the mountains on a few occasions and had never gone skiing or horseback riding or camping or anything else everyone else seemed to be doing in the mountains, but they were always there waiting. He could look at them every day and make plans for the days he would spend up there—the days when he was older and free to do whatever he wanted. The air here was thick and wet. The sky was blocked from view, and the house was wobbly and liable to fall to the ground if he jumped up and down.

Byron still had not moved and let his self-pity run its course. Then, when he could think of no new reasons why he hated this place, he decided to take a look around to see if he could find some.

Byron wandered around the house, interested to see if he had a room of his own. There were two bedrooms, a bathroom, and a living room. The largest of the bedrooms belonged to the old man. His clothes lay in several small piles on the bed and on the floor. A flannel shirt hung on the back of a chrome kitchen chair. A cheap watch, a leather belt, and some loose change cluttered the top of an aged, darkened dresser. The belt showed its running battle with the old man's gut; the holes were stretched and puckered to the last one.

The smaller bedroom had a freshly made bed, a lamp on a wooden night stand, a chest of drawers, and a chrome kitchen chair. The furniture in his room matched all the furnishings in the house; they all had the same chipped paint, missing knobs, sagging spring, tired look.

The bus trip and his uncertainty had taken its toll. Byron's curiosity willed him to explore, but the cool clean sheets pulled at him with magnetic force. He decided to test the bed for firmness, but dropped into darkness before an accurate judgment could be made. When he awoke, the sounds of his new world drifted through an open window. Birds were singing, children's voices squealed their disappointment with one another, an outboard motor buzzed faintly, then louder, then faintly again.

Byron lay still, piecing together the events that had brought him to this time and place. After a moment, with his confidence restored, he began a search for food. The refrigerator and the cabinets were well stocked. Rayleen had been bad about not keeping enough food on hand, and Byron was used to eating whatever was available, and liking it. Now, with so much to choose from, he felt unsure of what to do and went to the old reliable bologna and bread. With a sandwich in each hand, he descended the rubbery steps to explore his new environment.

In the full light of day, color revealed itself where there was only gray and black before. Pink seemed to be a popular color; there were pink houses and pink cars scattered among the green foliage and brown mud. Byron circled the house, stopping at the water's edge in the backyard. As far as he could see up and down the stream, there was a clean mud bank five yards wide sloping to the water. On the other side of the river, the trees and underbrush seemed to grow right out of the muddy brown water.

The sound of angry voices drew his attention farther downstream than he could see. A curve in the river hid those responsible for the foul language that was being broadcast across the water. Like a moth drawn to a flame, Byron drifted down the bank of the Meramec toward the source of the commotion. Two young men about Byron's age, wearing nothing but cut-off blue jeans and tennis shoes, stood at either end of a small aluminum boat. One was tugging toward the river, the other pulling back.

"I'm not puttin' this boat in," said one.

"No one's asking you to," said the other.

"Yeah, well if the motor quits, you won't be able to swim back with it alone. The current's too swift."

"I'll take it upstream and if it dies, which it won't, the current won't matter."

Byron had moved close enough to see and hear clearly. He peered around the edge of a huge sycamore trunk, enjoying the show and his bologna sandwich. The boy on the downhill end of the boat had the advantage of gravity, and despite the efforts of the other, inched closer and closer to the river.

"That's it. I give up. You're the stupidest asshole I ever saw. Anyone that goes out with a fucked-up motor and no paddle is an idiot."

"I fixed the motor and it won't quit, and I'd have a paddle if you hadn't lost it."

"I didn't lose it, you did, and you couldn't fix a fart in a bowl of chili."

Byron let out a laugh at the chili remark, although it made no sense to him. Both boys lost interest in the boat and turned and stared at Byron's head sticking from the side of a tree. Byron timidly waved a bologna sandwich at the now frozen figures.

"You spyin' on us?"

"No, just watchin' to see who'd win."

"What's your name?"

"Byron Creed." Byron stepped out into the open.

"Is Al Creed your old man?"

"Yeah," Byron said with no enthusiasm.

"You want to go for a boat ride?"

"I can't swim."

"You ain't gonna learn no younger."

Growing up in the Denver area, it had been common to engage in a fight every time he moved to a new residence and met with the established ruffians of the locale. These boys had not challenged him yet, but it was coming—he was sure of that—and he didn't want to be out in a boat when it happened.

"Some other time maybe," Byron said. He moved closer to examine the boat and motor. "You guys live here?"

"Yeah, that's our house right there," said the boy who claimed to have fixed the little outboard motor. "We're the Coal brothers. My name's Dwayne and his is Dwight. We're twins."

"No shit," Byron said.

"What's that supposed to mean?" Dwight asked.

"Nothing. I just mean you look like twins."

Dwayne and Dwight were five feet seven inches tall, with brown eyes and shaggy brown hair. They were darkly tanned and well muscled in the way young men, who spend their summers swimming and boating all day, every day along the river, develop. Byron was an inch or two taller with longer, thinner limbs. In his past fights, he had been able to stand back and jab. If he could land a couple of light blows, and if his opponents were able to get in a couple of licks, the fight would generally end in a draw. Since the only reason for the fight was because he was new, there was little desire by either opponent to continue.

"I don't like it when people make fun of us," Dwayne said.

"Who's making fun?" Byron said.

Dwayne began taking in short gulps of air and puffing his chest up and down. His eyes took on a wild look, darting from side to side. The color darkened in his face and the muscles in his jaws began to flex and twitch. Byron readied himself, shifting his weight, putting his right foot back so he could transfer his power to a right cross if and when Dwayne charged.

Byron glanced at Dwight, hoping they wouldn't both come at once. Dwight wore a bored expression and then a smile. "Knock it off, Dwayne," he said, "he ain't buyin' it."

"Were you?" Dwayne asked, beginning to laugh. "If I'd had to keep that up much longer, I'd have passed out."

"Did you see him get set for you?" Dwight asked. "If you had come running in, he was going to clean your clock."

"Yeah, I saw him. You know what, though, I forgot to do my crazy laugh."

"Yeah, you did forget that. Show him your crazy laugh."

Dwayne started puffing again and let out a loud maniacal laugh that tore at his voice box and left him red-faced and coughing.

Dwight laughed until he started to cough too, but his was entirely natural. "You ever see anything as stupid as that in your whole life?" Dwight asked, pointing at Dwayne.

Byron shook his head, a smile on his face. These boys were going to be fun to hang out with, he thought.

Ten minutes later, the boys were cruising up the Meramec with Byron in the bow.

"What's it like in Denver? Did you have a horse?" Dwight asked.

Byron shook his head.

"What'd you do for fun?" Dwayne asked.

"Not much. I moved a lot. Never got to know anyone very well."

"What grade you in?" Dwight asked.

"I'll be a freshman in high school."

"Us too. Hell, boy, you've come to the right place. The one thing we know how to do is have fun," Dwayne said. "We'll take you around in school to meet everyone. You'll have to punch a couple of guys out, but that won't be no problem."

Byron gave a knowing nod.

Dwight was at the motor and guided the boat out of the channel and into a wide slough. A short distance up the slough, a tree hung over the water with a thick rope descending from an upper limb. The bank was bare at the base of the tree, with natural steps formed by the roots. Dwight killed the motor, and in an instant the brothers rolled over the side and were gone. Byron felt a moment of panic just before the boys resurfaced. Dwight and Dwayne swam to the bank and scrambled up the rootwad steps.

Byron sat very still in the bow of the now drifting jon boat. Dwayne hooked the rope swing with a tree limb left handy for just that purpose. Pulling the end of the rope to its farthest point, he straddled a large knot tied at the end. With a rebel yell, he swung through the air and at the highest point of the arc over the water, let go with his hands, falling backwards and letting the rope knot under his thighs pivot him into a double back flip, hitting the water feet first.

Dwight caught the rope on its return swing and launched himself out over the water. He hung by his arms below the knot, holding his legs up until the arc took him high enough to extend them. Then at his highest point, he swung his body horizontal and let go with his hands. Arching his back, he seemed to drop in slow motion, piercing the water in an almost splashless dive.

Byron applauded the Coal brothers' performance. "That was damn good," he said.

"Hell, that ain't nothin'. We'll have you doing some stuff by the end of the summer," Dwayne said.

The brothers swam back to the boat, positioning themselves on opposite sides, and on some unspoken signal, they pulled up and over the side into the boat in one smooth motion. Their hair lay flat against their heads, water glistening on their tanned skin. With bright eyes and big smiles, the Coal brothers looked at Byron expectantly.

In the world of young men, a certain amount of respect was necessary in a group because of the natural tendency of the strong to dominate the weak. Byron knew he could decline this unspoken challenge but was thrilled by this all new lifestyle of cut-off shorts and motor boats and circus tricks. He decided he not only needed a little respect from these two, but wanted a lot of respect and would be a full-fledged member of these Meramec River rats.

"You won't let me drown, will you?" Byron asked.

"Hell, no. Your old man got any beer in the house?" Dwayne asked.

"I think so."

"Well, there you go. All you got to do is learn to swim before Al figures out we're drinking his beer," Dwayne said.

Both brothers thought that was funny and giggled and punched each other in the shoulder.

Byron was drawn into the silliness of it all, and without another word, produced a large pocket knife and began cutting off the legs of his only pair of jeans. The Coal brothers were suitably impressed by his bold actions. The blade of the pocket knife was very sharp and whistled through the blue denim.

"Look how sharp that knife is," Dwayne said.

"I see it," Dwight replied.

"Did you put that edge on that knife?" Dwayne asked.

"Yeah, an old Indian showed me how," Byron answered.

"Your ass," Dwight said. "You mean like a cowboy-and-Indian Indian?"

"Yeah, he ran a little two-pump Texaco station close to where I lived."

"Did he wear Indian clothes?" Dwayne asked.

"No, he wore jeans and boots like normal people."

"Did he show you how to scalp people?" Dwayne asked.

"No, but he could do birdcalls real good, and he was going to show me how."

"Let's hear one," Dwayne said.

"Oh, well, I never got taught before we moved."

Dwayne and Dwight exchanged shocked looks. "What," Byron said, "you don't believe me?"

"Oh, we believe you about the Indian," Dwight said.

"We just can't believe what we're hearing," Dwayne said. "You never got taught. Is that what I heard you say?"

Both brothers lowered their heads and moaned softly. Dwight looked up and said, "Damn, boy, I thought we were ignorant. You're making us look good." Dwight punched Dwayne in the shoulder and the punch was returned without hesitation, as it had been a thousand times before. The Coal brothers began to laugh then, and although no one was exactly sure what they were laughing about, they were feeding off each other and had to look away to regain control.

Byron sensed there was some mental illness in the Coal family, but they did have fun.

Dwight gave a pull on the starter rope and the little jon boats outboard came to life. When the boat was maneuvered into place, Dwayne scampered up the bank, retrieved the tree limb the boys used as the rope catcher, and was back in the boat nimbly. The jon boat picked up speed as they headed out to the main channel. Dwight tossed a small pile of yellow nylon ski rope over the head of Dwayne into Byron's lap. "Take out that sharp knife of yours and cut off a couple of feet," Dwight said.

Dwayne tied one end of the new piece to his stick and the other to the belt loop at the back of Byron's new shorts. "We'll get out into the strongest current. When we get there, you get out on the river side of the boat. Dwayne will hold you up with the rope stick. All you have to do is lay on your stomach and throw your arms forward one at a time like this," Dwight said and demonstrated the movement. Dwayne, not to be outdone, mimicked

Dwight's arm movements. A shoulder punch was exchanged, and the brothers suddenly went quiet and turned their attention toward Byron. The message was clear: Are you going to do it or not? No words were spoken until the spot in the middle of the channel was reached.

Dwight pointed the bow upstream and the outboard puttered at just above idle, holding the boat in one place. "What now?" Byron asked. Byron knew the answer was going to be to get in the water, but he was unable to make that decision on his own. The Coal brothers said nothing. They smiled cruelly at Byron, enjoying his fear.

Byron gazed around, judging the width of the river to be two hundred yards. He dipped his hand in for a temperature check; the surface was warm but turned cold just a few inches down. All three boys knew he was stalling for time. "We can take you home now and come back when you're older and not so nervous," Dwight said.

Byron knew he had to act now. If the offer to go home came again, he would weaken. He stood at the bow facing upstream. He took one last look around like it would be his last, then stepped over the side. The cold water sent a shock wave through him like he had never experienced. He came to surface screaming like a girl.

The Coal brothers rolled around in the boat punching shoulders and laughing. Dwayne lived up to his end of the bargain; he kept enough tension on Byron's tether to keep his head above water.

Byron flapped awkward, splashing water everywhere. "Okay, just hold still a minute, I'll hold you up," Dwayne said.

"Now just lay on your belly and start moving your arms," Dwight said. Byron did as instructed. He tossed his arms forward and the current of the river pulled them back. The boat picked up speed and water pushed his arms back faster.

"Now start breathing with bigger, slower breaths," Dwayne said.

Byron soon fell into a rhythm, became over confident, and sucked in what was surely a gallon of river water through his nose. Dwight stopped the boat while Byron composed himself.

"You need to kick your legs too," Dwayne said.

"You had enough?" Dwight asked.

"No, untie me. I want to try it by myself," Byron said.

Dwayne pulled Byron toward the boat and slapped at the tether line with Byron's knife. Byron disappeared for a second and resurfaced a few feet farther from the boat.

"Head downstream. We'll follow you," Dwight said.

Byron began flapping his arms forward as he had before.

"Now start kicking your legs," Dwayne said.

Byron put all the movements together and then he felt it—the mystery was solved. He could feel his movement across the water; he was swimming; and he was swimming at a fast pace.

"Okay, slow down and make your strokes count for more," Dwight said.

Byron took Dwight's advice and slowed to a slow rolling stroke that he felt he could maintain for quite some time. He swam on down the river with a strong current helping him along. His strength did not hold up to his expectations. He had swum only another twenty yards and he was exhausted.

Dwight was well aware that Byron would burn out quickly. He and Dwayne were great swimmers, but most people weren't. Byron was doing pretty good by the Coal brothers' standards. They had seen people do mighty stupid things in their fifteen years along the Meramec River. Some folks go crazy if they just fall in waist-deep water. They start flapping and gasping for air and their head's not even been under water yet.

Dwight swung the bow of the boat across Byron's path and killed the motor. Byron was happy to grab hold. "That's good enough for the first day, Tarzan," Dwayne said. "By the end of August, you'll be racing me and Dwight across the river and back."

Byron hooked an elbow over the side and tipped the boat dangerously close to coming over. "Hold on there, Tarzan," Dwight said.

"You need to learn some boat etiquette," Dwayne said.

"Well said, old chum," Dwight replied.

"Thank you, Godfrey," Dwayne said.

Byron worked at regaining his breath and was amused at the brothers as they assumed the characters of rich aristocrats. "Would you be so good as to show this fine young fellow how to properly enter a jon boat?" Dwight said.

"I should be delighted to," Dwayne said. Dwayne rolled backwards off the boat and came up next to Byron. "You gonna live?" Dwayne asked. Byron, still breathing hard, nodded his head. "Okay, lower yourself until your mouth is just above the water, then kick both legs together like a scissors and pull up at the same time. When you get your butt up high enough, just twist around and sit down. But wait for the folks in the boat to get set for you."

Dwayne then demonstrated the movement and was back in the boat dripping and smiling, proud of his skills. Byron kicked and pulled up and down, testing his coordination. "When you get ready to come in, say 'Coming aboard' and that lets people know to get placed to counterbalance you," Dwight said.

"Our dad was the best skier in the state. He showed us all this shit before we ever started school," Dwayne said.

Byron stopped his bobbing and was startled by the word "dad". He had a dad. Confusion circled his head and flashes of his mother played like a slide show in his mind. She was not a good mother. She was a poor planner, but he missed her. She had booze and men ahead of him, but he missed her. She could be wicked and mean and say and do terrible, unforgivable things, but he missed her. The emotions that had been held in check for so long poured out in long sobs and flowing tears. Dwayne and Dwight looked at each other with disbelief. Byron cried on. He felt humiliated bawling in front of his new friends and had he been anywhere else, he could have turned and walked away. But he could not walk away and the tears and sobs would not stop.

The brothers sat quietly looking anywhere but at Byron. Byron was grateful he was not being ridiculed and he felt he should provide some explanation. "My mom didn't come home one night. No one's seen her or heard from her in four weeks. Everyone thinks she's dead."

Dwayne and Dwight at once reflected on their own loss. Their father had been a hero to them in the way that boys see their fathers when they are still too young to see their flaws. Dwight's and Dwayne's eyes began to tear up as they identified with Byron's sorrow. When Byron was able to take a couple of deep breaths and blow his nose into the river, Dwayne broke the silence.

"Hey, we can't sit around here crying all day. Let's go get a few of your old man's beers."

CHAPTER TWO

Al paced and smoked and sipped on a lukewarm paper cup of coffee he didn't want. Cigarettes and coffee took the place of meals out of habit rather than desire. His day was almost over and he would be going home to spend the evening with his son once the tanker truck arrived and was unloaded.

Floyd's Tire Mart was located on a long, straight, flat section of Highway 67 just a mile north of the Meramec River. The long driveway without curves made it easy for cars and trucks to swing up to the pumps. Then, with a full tank of gas and a clean windshield, they could get up to speed before swinging back onto the highway.

Al leaned his back against the cool metal of the above-ground gas tank. The day had been warm and sunny, but the black asphalt drive turned warm sunny days into hot foot burners even this early in the spring. The huge above-ground tank had a fresh white paint job. Halfway up the side, the big blue letters read: Floyd's Tire Mart/Best Prices on Tires. Above that, in even larger letters, the Zephyr logo was painted in bright red across the side of the tank. At the other end of the drive was a matching tank full of ethyl. Stretched from the white block building to the light poles above the pumps were red, blue, and yellow triangle shaped flags. The flag strings zigzagged back and forth over the drive a dozen times. When the wind blew, the flapping of the flags became annoying in short order.

Al had hung the flags himself. He had also contributed to the painting of the building, a fact that galled him when he thought about it. Managers were supposed to manage, not paint.

The sound of a tandem dump truck downshifting through the gears grabbed Al's attention. A new red Ford rolled to the pumps. Al recognized the truck as belonging to Pete Bradford. This was his second fill-up today. Rock hauling was going strong. The new section of Interstate 55 was coming and the profitable work for dump trucks would set up a man for life. Pete was one of many drivers with new trucks these days. A man with a good number at the quarry could run all day long every day.

Al ground out his cigarette with his toe and pitched his now cold coffee on the drive. The tanker truck was in sight bringing five thousand gallons of ethyl. After climbing on top of the tanker, breaking the seals, and verifying that the tanks were full, Al's day would be over. Ten hour or more days if necessary, dragging your sorry ass up and down the drive, burning in the summer, freezing in the winter—how many more years could he take. Those thoughts occupied Al as he climbed the ladder to the top of the truck. Manager—huh!

From his perch on the tanker truck, the sound of the driveway bell and squealing brakes pulled his attention back to the pumps. Six more new tandem dumps were topping their tanks so they would be ready to roll the next day. Damn place looks like a dump truck showroom, Al grumbled to himself. Al hobbled along unsteadily across the top of the tanker. He broke the thin metal strips that proved the tank lids had not been opened since the truck left the refinery. He lifted the lids and peered inside to see that each compartment was full.

As he went about this routine chore, Al thought about all the new tandems on the drive and how one of them should have been his. He saw himself at the Ford dealer showroom ordering a new truck to be built to his exact specifications. He would order the F-650 with the 10 speed transmission and the 292 motor, with the extra large oil pan and dual oil filters. He would get Goodyear tires even if it came with Firestones. He would pull them off and put the Goodyears on, and he would get air-conditioning, and the cab would be painted bright red, and the dump truck bed would be black. And he would get some mud flaps with a picture of that little Mexican guy with the two pistols in his hands shooting in the air. Then, when he had made out his order, the salesman would say, "We could save you a little money if you want to drop the air-conditioning or go with a smaller motor."

Then Al would say, "I didn't come here to save money; I came here to buy a dump truck."

Al smiled at himself as he climbed down from the tanker. He knew it was foolish to keep reliving the same daydream, and when his foot hit the asphalt the dream was gone. Maybe it was the gas fumes he was breathing on top of the tanker that took him to his new truck dream. Maybe it was a combination of fatigue and gas fumes. Either way, he had this pleasant vision every time he checked out a load of gas.

His work day was over and he headed home. Al parked his pickup under his house, turned the motor off, and sat frozen. He dreaded facing Byron in a way he couldn't understand. Was it guilt he was feeling or just the newness of the situation that made him want to avoid the boy? The old hatred of Rayleen resurfaced. In an instant he saw her as she was, and he saw the deceitful smirk on her face. What if she turned up and came here for the boy? The thought sent new shockwaves along his spine and he unconsciously gripped the steering wheel so tight his hands began to cramp.

Al counted to ten and when he mouthed the word ten, he opened the truck door and climbed out. When he came into the kitchen, he was surprised to find nothing disturbed. A walk to the bedroom and the bed showed the boy had taken a nap or at least laid down. He was probably out exploring.

A sudden fear caught Al's thoughts. He had not asked the boy if he could swim. What if he fell in the river and was carried downstream? Hell, the boy was here less than a full day and you already let him drown. What would folks think of you? She had him for ten years and as bad as she was, she didn't let him drown. What do you care what folks think? It's not about you, it's about the boy.

Al was feeling guilty again, this time for thinking about his reputation instead of his boy's death. "Damn it," he said out loud. He shook his head to clear the thoughts, then went outside. The buzz of an outboard motor caught his attention. Out in the middle of the channel, a jon boat with three people aboard slipped downstream. Al hurried back up the steps and grabbed a pair of binoculars he kept handy for just this purpose. There he was, in the bow of the boat, shirtless and wet. The other two were Dwight and Dwayne Coal. Al had been a good friend of their father, Dry Coal. That's what everyone called him because of his everlasting thirst.

The boys were drinking something. Al adjusted the focus. They each had a sixteen-ounce can of Schlitz in their hand. Al chuckled to himself. "Well, the little bastards. Wonder where they got the beer." He put the binoculars down and made a quick check of the refrigerator. His last three beers were gone.

*   *   *

Byron crept up the wobbly steps as quietly as he could just in case the old man was asleep. It was just past dusk and unlikely he would be in bed that early, but old people sleep a lot so there was a chance.

When he entered the kitchen, he could see the back of Al's scraggly gray head above the recliner in the living room. "Gunsmoke" was on the television and seemed to have Al's full attention. Byron let the screen door between the porch and the kitchen slam just hard enough for Al to be sure to hear him come in. He wasn't sure what to expect from the old man. He was sure he would notice his beer gone and would have something to say about that. Let him bitch all he wants; I didn't ask to come here.

Byron decided to take a defiant attitude, although for the first day things had gone much better than he could have imagined. The Coal brothers did know how to have fun and had taken him in as one of their own. They even helped him improve his swimming skills, which were pitiful at the start of the day. The boat riding and beer drinking were pleasant surprises he would never have guessed could be so much fun. Byron had tasted beer in the past-warm, half-empty bottles cast aside by lustful drunks on their way to Rayleen's bedroom. He had not seen what all the fuss was about.

This time, riding in the bow of a boat in the late afternoon sun with a warm breeze drying his hair and shorts, the world was at peace and the cold can of beer slurped brazenly in front of anyone who wished to see caused Byron to sit a little straighter in the boat, holding his shoulders back and his chest up.

"Where you been?" Al said without turning around.

"Out on the river. I met some guys and we went swimmin' and boatin'," Byron said.

"And drinking," Al said.

Al still had not turned around to face Byron.

"Yeah, we had a beer." Byron made it sound as if it were no big deal.

"You mean you had three of my beers—my last three."

Byron studied the back of Al's head, trying to get some sense of the old man's mood. He could tell nothing from his voice; he sounded pissed off all the time. "Yeah, well we had to drink your beer because I just got into town and haven't had time to buy any."

Al came up out of his chair and covered the distance between them with such quickness Byron was stunned. Al had a menacing look on his face and towered over Byron within easy striking distance. He maintained his scowl for only a few seconds and then let out a gruff laugh and went back to his chair shaking his head. "If you're going to smart mouth me, boy, you need to be farther away when you do it. Get your supper. It's in the oven. If you hurry, you can get in here in time to see old Matt Dillon slap leather with this back-shooting card shark."

Byron hesitated for a moment, not sure the storm was over. Inside the oven, he found a large bowl of beef stew and three buttered biscuits. "Can I eat in there?" he asked.

"Sure, I do all the time. Now be quiet. I've been waiting for two weeks for Matt to plug this bastard and I don't want to miss it."

Al stared at the TV considering his handling of the beer incident. "Those boys you met, they didn't happen to be the Coal brothers, did they?"

"Yeah, Dwayne and Dwight."

Byron balanced his bowl of stew on his knees and dipped his biscuits into the broth and slurped them down with a concentrated effort.

Al studied the boy. He had to shift his eyes only slightly to appear to be watching the television if Byron looked his way. The arch of his neck, the shape of his chin, the way he held himself, that smile . . . there were parts of Rayleen sticking out all over the boy.

Byron caught Al's eyes. The stew was good. He had not realized how hungry he was before he started eating. If the old man wants to look at you, let him get his fill, Byron thought.

The gunslick gambler just backhanded Miss Kitty, then pushed her to the floor. He laughed as he pushed through the batwing doors with a saddlebag of money taken from the Long Branch. His laughter stopped as he stepped into the sun and there, only some twenty feet away, stood Matt Dillon. Matt began his gunfighter walk and with each step, the flash of hands and the boom of six-guns became more absolute.

Al gave up his study of Byron and focused his attention on Matt Dillon's right hand. The gambler had had his way in Dodge with Matt out of town, but Matt showed up early. He wasn't to be back until the next day, but here he was, and the gambler would pay with his life. The bad guy went for his gun and fired. He missed. Matt's gun hand came up slower and his aim was from the eye, not the hip, and he never missed.

Al let out a sigh and went back to studying the boy. There was a lot that reminded him of Rayleen. He didn't know if he could stand to be reminded of her on a daily basis. She had left a mark on his heart that would never heal. The good memories were so good he thought for a time he could get over his bitter hatred of her, but it wasn't to be. The daily challenge of life, the loneliness, the financial failure needed to be put on someone's shoulders, and with righteous indignation, Al placed his woes on Rayleen.

Was she dead? Was she decomposing in a ditch next to a dirt road? Al toyed with the image. In one picture, she was old and haggard and weary and wearing a sad expression of guilt and remorse. Then she was young and beautiful and wore an expression of cool serenity where evil could never lurk.

"Them Coal brothers are a wild pair," Al said.

"You're damn right they are," Byron said, blowing bits of biscuit across the floor.

Al smiled weakly and shook his head. "Well, I guess I should find out more about you." Al paused to gather his thoughts. "I know you drink and cuss." Al paused again, letting the air turn cool for one long second. "That's a good start, but what else you got?"

Byron enjoyed a good chuckle and bounced his head up and down, unable to speak without spraying more biscuit bits. Al waited patiently for him to swallow his food.

"What else you want to know?" Byron asked.

"Well, do you smoke?"

Byron nodded sheepishly.

"I'm not paying for 'em," Al said. "You hear the way I sound? You'll sound the same if you don't stop now." Al fumbled with his shirt pocket and plucked out a Winston. He placed the cigarette in the corner of his mouth and lit it with a chrome lighter. The repetition of the act was so ingrained that the brain need not be engaged. "But if you're going to smoke 'em, you gotta buy 'em. I'm not paying to have you killed." Al considered this a reasonable stance. He didn't want to start laying down hard and fast rules without knowing the boy better. "You got any other bad habits?"

"I don't think so."

"You look like you're hard on your clothes." Al glanced at look at Byron's shorts. "Weren't those pants damn near brand new?" he asked.

"Yeah, they were, but now they're damn near brand new shorts." Byron had stopped shoveling stew just long enough to make his reply. It was two spoonfuls later when he understood that he had just smart mouthed the old man again.

Al sat rigid as his cigarette smoked in his fingers. The hand had been on its way to his mouth when time stood still. Byron smiled weakly in Al's direction and went back to shoveling stew. Al now comprehended the job he had ahead of him for the first time. The weight of the responsibility paralyzed him.

Byron pulled his attention away from the television and noticed that Al still had not moved a muscle. Is he having a stroke or something, Byron thought. "You're okay, aren't you?" he said with genuine concern in his voice.

Al came out of his trance; his spirit renewed. The tiny spark of compassion that drifted across the room inspired a new resolve. The slight quaver Al heard when Byron asked if he were okay—just a little quaver that Al himself did not consciously hear—but his soul did and knew it for the truth. The boy had no one else and his deep down fear that he would be alone in the world came through, and Al heard it and was now determined to make up for his past selfish neglect.

CHAPTER THREE

Al asked very little of Byron; Byron asked very little of Al. The summer of '62 slipped by peacefully. The days were hot and slow; the nights were soft and thick. It was just after dawn, when the shadows of the sycamore trees are driven back toward the shore, the river is still, and the green water reflects the pink sky and nothing mars the surface but the nimble water spiders. They tiptoe across a pink mirror, leaving no wake or ripple.

Byron, Dwight, and Dwayne had motored miles upstream in the dark. They were determined to squeeze every last second of freedom from the last days of summer vacation. They drifted silently now in the early light, each absorbed in his own thoughts. School would start Monday; they had only today and the weekend left of what seemed like forever back in May.

Byron leaned over the bow, letting his hand dip in the water. Dwayne sat at the stern, resting an elbow on top of the motor. Dwight sprawled sideways on the metal bench looking at the sky. "This was the best summer I ever had," Byron said. No one responded. There was no need. The twins had had their best summer too.

Since Byron's arrival, they had not had a single fight with each other, an unusual situation. Both brothers were perplexed as to why Byron's presence changed the chemistry of their relationship, but it did.

Byron twisted to face the brothers. His persistent clumsiness inside the boat jostled them from their thoughts. "When's your brother getting out?" Byron asked.

"Some time next year," Dwayne said.

"You don't know any more than that?"

"You're dealing with the State. They never do what they say they're gonna do," Dwight said.

"So he's real tough, huh?"

"As tough as they come," Dwayne answered.

"He beat the hell out of three guys at the VFW dance one year," Dwight said.

"You think he'll go back to stealin' cars?"

"Sure, he's real good at it," Dwayne said, the family pride evident in his voice.

"You gonna fight Bobby Poley?" Dwight asked.

"If I have to," Byron answered.

"Oh, you'll have to. He'll sucker punch you if he gets the chance. You got to be ready."

"How come he don't mess with you guys?"

"'Cause he knows he'd have to fight us both," Dwayne said.

"And because Clay would break both his arms when he gets out," Dwight said.

"Both his arms?"

"Yeah, that's what Clay tells guys that really piss him off. He says he'll break both their arms between the elbow and the shoulder so that they won't be able to wipe their own ass," Dwayne said.

"Has he ever done it?"

"At least once that we know of," Dwayne said.

"Maybe I could tell this Bobby kid that Clay was a friend of mine and he'd leave me alone," Byron said.

The brothers looked at each other, thought for a second, shook their heads and said, "Naw," in unison.

"Dwayne will think of a plan. He's the smart one," Dwight said.

*　　*　　*

Brent Darby became a bus driver six years ago. His only child, Cliff, a senior at the time, played on the boys' basketball team. The team would have to forfeit a game if a driver couldn't be found. The team's regular driver, old man Simmons, had decided to die without giving notice.

Brent Darby worked a small farm. He fought an ongoing battle with high planting costs and low harvest prices. It was a losing battle. Driving the school bus meant he could fight on a little longer.

Brent watched the kids on his bus grow up these past six years. He knew their nature as well as their parents or better. His ears were trained to each voice, and the whispers and squeals of the girls played harmony to the shouts and barks of the boys.

Brent was a small man, slim of build, and just over five feet tall. Like many small men raised on the rough side of the tracks, he had made a habit of measuring the pugilistic worth of other men quickly and accurately. His first look at Byron Creed put a smile on his face. Now he understood why the energy level on the bus crackled with anticipation. The smaller children found it almost impossible to whisper, and the words "fight" and "Bobby" drifted forward to the driver's ear. Brent Darby began to whistle a happy little song softly so that only he could hear it. Bobby Poley needed his butt kicked. Perhaps today was his day.

Bobby Poley had always been bigger than anyone his age. He stood over five and a half feet tall when he was in the sixth grade. Now in his second year of high school, he was almost six feet tall. He enjoyed his role as a bully; he thought of it as the natural way of things—the strong take from the weak because they can. Bobby snatched lunch bags from those who could not protest, those already on the edge of pubescent exclusion, those with less than perfect skin or clothes or hair or posture, those already labeled as whiners. He would take a bite of an apple and put it back; he would finger a peanut butter and jelly sandwich, belittle its owner, and toss it out the window to be run over by a passing car.

Brent Darby had put Bobby off the bus twice in the previous year and was certain he would have to again. This being the first day of a new year meant he had to let Bobby ride until he could show cause to have him removed.

Brent checked his mirror, and at the far end of the bus, up against the backdoor, Byron Creed stood hunched over, his head and shoulders bent forward, matching the curve of the back wall. There was something different in his look. He was holding a large, brightly wrapped box he didn't have before. His shoulders were drawn up and his head tilted down. He looked smaller, weaker. He had on a jacket and gloves that were not part of his attire when he boarded the bus just minutes ago.

Brent pulled his attention back to the road. Bobby Poley's stop was coming up. The doors of Bus 73 opened up; Bobby Poley came up the steps. There were seven kids to be picked up at Bobby's stop; Bobby always entered the bus first. Bobby Poley halted at the top of the steps. He looked toward Brent Darby, but not at him. He looked past him out the window on the opposite side. There was nothing to see; he was just taunting. The other six kids began grousing. Brent Darby was forced to speak. "Move along, Bobby."

Bobby remained where he was, still pretending to see something of interest out on the street. Then, after a second had passed, he turned down the aisle, giving no indication he had seen or heard Brent Darby. He headed for the back of the bus, his bus, to his seat—the last seat, where he could stretch his legs across the seat and hold court and rule the bus with an iron fist. Brent Darby felt the sting of the insult and his foot bounced nervously on the clutch pedal. He watched Bobby in the mirror. The doors did not close, the bus did not move, the excited chatter that had filled the bus before was now subdued and nervous.

The sun was coming up into the windows, much brighter now, and Brent examined Byron Creed more closely. The box in Byrons arms covered his chest from his chin to his waist. Nothing that large could have been brought on the bus without Brent's approval. The sudden realization that the box was empty and fake, put a smile on Brent's face. He began whistling his favorite Cole Porter tune, "Anything Goes". The box he held was wrapped in red and white striped paper. The paper sagged from the corners and was loosely tacked in a hasty, poor job of wrapping. The sleeves of the blue jean jacket Byron had on lay flat and empty against the sides of the box he held. The brown jersey gloves extending from the sleeves had no life, and it was too warm for gloves. Brent Darby slipped the gearshift into first gear, but still the bus did not move.

Bobby Poley stopped halfway down the aisle next to the Coal brothers. Bobby was giving Byron Creed a hard stare. Byron would not meet his eyes and looked at the black rubber mat on the floor. Dwight and Dwayne began to punch each other in the shoulder. Bobby gave them a glance. They were nut cases, he thought. He'd deal with the Coal brothers one at a time some day as soon as Clay went back to prison.

"Hey, butthead, that's my seat," Bobby Poley said. The bus got very quiet. Small heads twisted on tiny necks. The very youngest sat the closest to the driver and with little variation, the age and size of the kids progressed evenly toward the back of the bus. The very back seat belonged to whoever could hold it. The Coal brothers were suspiciously out of place.

Bobby calculated his moves. He would approach within kicking range. He was taller with longer legs. He would tower over this guy with his hands on his hips, and if he doesn't cower at once, I'll grip the corner of the bus seat in each hand and lean back and kick the shit out of this prick. He won't be able to dodge or block. I'll have him trapped against the wall. The plan came together quickly, unconsciously.

Bobby scanned the bus, looking for something to eat. He had been stealing candy bars from Marsha Webster for so long that it had become a payment or tribute. Marsha was a booger eater, among her other bad habits; and because of this, she was teased constantly and complained about it constantly and was ignored.

Still the bus had not moved. Bobby was enjoying the drama. He had snubbed old man Darby and apparently had him so mad he couldn't drive. Bobby reached across Marsha Webster, brushing her breasts with the back of his hand, never too proud to get a cheap feel, even off Marsha. She had matured over the summer and didn't look as creepy as she had before. He rummaged through her lunch bag, taking one of two Hershey bars she almost always packed. Bobby filled his mouth with chocolate and with great stage presence, slowly turned his attention back toward Byron Creed.

Byron forced himself to take slow, deep breaths. Byron was worried he wouldn't be able to attack a total stranger. Fighting this Bobby guy seemed unnecessary at first even though the Coal brothers had assured him he would have no choice but to fight or crawl. Now that he had seen Bobby in action, he felt no moral code was being broken by setting him up.

Bobby Poley strutted down the aisle. He decided he was not going to wait; his plan changed instantly. He would come to a stop, grab the seats, and kick the prick in the nuts without saying another word. Brent Darby watched intently in his mirror. There was no traffic on this road and he had his own reasons for not pulling in the "Stop" sign and closing the door and proceeding on his route.

Bobby knew old man Darby was watching and would have him thrown off the bus for this, but he didn't care. His mom was on the school board and would get him back on again.

Byron would not look up. He was sure Bobby would see in his face that all was not what it seemed. Byron held his fists tightly against his chest. The fake package held in place with empty coat sleeves and taped on gloves was starting to come undone. Byron watched a pair of size eleven brogues plant themselves just out of his reach.

Bobby Poley made his first move. He took hold of the seat backs on each side. Then the motor of the bus roared and Brent Darby released the clutch. Bobby Poley held tightly to the seats, the floor moved beneath his feet, and his posture matched the carved wooden figures that adorn the bows of sailing ships of old. Byron Creed, wedged firmly against the curved back door, shot a rigid right cross out of the red and white striped package and into the oncoming fat nose of Bobby Poley. His head snapped back, dragging his neck and shoulders with it.

Brent Darby hit the brakes and Bobby Poley took flight. Wide eyes and open mouths watched Bobby drift by. He seemed so relaxed, not pawing at the air or trying to get his feet under him. He floated high in the air past the freshman and a little lower, past the sixth and seventh graders, and came in for a landing next to the third graders.

Brent Darby put the bus in neutral, set the brake, and turned in his seat. "You back there, take a seat. No standing on the bus. Bobby, there's no lying in the aisle. Take a seat."

Bobby mumbled an insult at Brent but could not be understood. "Don't smart mouth me, Bobby." Then his tone changed and he was now overly compassionate. "You know, I don't want to make a report of this, but if I have to, I will. You just can't sleep in the aisle. If you're tired, you should try and get to bed sooner. Now find a seat and quit all this horseplay."

Marsha helped Bobby into her seat. She gave him a handkerchief for his bloody nose. He tried to talk but couldn't put the words together. He seemed drunk and confused. Bobby told Marsha his neck hurt and that his mother kept a cow in their living room and that he had to get home to feed it. Marsha said she would feed the cow and not to worry about it. The other kids within earshot giggled, but Bobby didn't know why.

The Coal brothers left their seat and joined Byron in the last two seats. Shoulder punches between the three continued all the way to the high school.

When the story reached the high school office, the principal, Mr. Armstead, started an investigation. He summoned Brent Darby to his office for an explanation as to why the incident wasn't reported. Brent Darby did a poor job of acting confused as he tried to remember whether anything unusual had happened on his morning run.

"That may be why Bobby Poley was in the aisle on his back," Brent said.

Mr. Armstead looked over his glasses unamused. Brent Darby met his gaze unflinchingly. Mr. Armstead sighed, a signal of his defeat. He could only ask Mr. Darby to pay more attention. He had the authority to fire as many bus drivers as he chose; he also had the responsibility to replace them. Not an easy task. The hours were irregular, the pay was poor, the responsibility was great. Brent Darby could navigate a bus over snow covered back roads as good as any and better than most. And he almost never missed a day of work.

"I'm going to suspend this new boy. His name is Byron Creed. Don't allow him on the bus," Principal Armstead said.

"Are you sure that's necessary? I didn't see him hit Bobby. Maybe Bobby just fell," Brent said.

"Mr. Darby, don't treat me like a fool and I won't call you a liar. Now that's fair, isn't it?"

CHAPTER FOUR

A l Creed had little to say about Byron's two-week suspension from the bus. In fact, he felt more than a little fatherly pride. So the boy can handle himself against a bigger bully. Good for him, he thought. He kept these thoughts to himself. Wouldn't be good to encourage the boy to fight. It could get out of hand. So in his typical short and sweet manner, he said, "Dammit, boy, would you try to get along."

Al traded shifts to stay on nights so he could drive Byron to school. It was up to Byron to find a ride home or walk if he had to. "It's only four miles," Al said.

Weeks and months went by without trouble. Byron made a convenient friendship with a boy named Doug Kearn. Doug had a car. Doug was a senior and no self-respecting senior would be caught dead hanging out with a sophomore. Doug had little self-respect and few friends. He was a straight A student and a teachers' pet, but he was not happy. Doug thirsted for more out of life. He had only a year of high school left and would have no interesting memories or stories to take with him to college if he didn't begin to break some rules.

Byron offered to help. He convinced Doug that the Coal brothers would also be willing to help. This proved more difficult than they thought. Doug got on their nerves. He talked a lot, he used big words, and he gave the definition of the big words he used without being asked. He made bad jokes, each one having to do with the size of his dick or the size of your dick. He laughed at his own jokes even when no one else did.

Dwight and Dwayne made their feelings known. "He's a jerk," they said in unison.

"He has a car," was Byron's brilliant defense. Byron won his case.

Dwayne laid out a plan to skip school and go to the zoo. "He's the smart one," Dwight said.

Doug drove a '56 Ford. It had a 390 engine in it that smoked a lot and ran poorly, but the mufflers were loud and the heater worked fine. The radio had a reverb unit attached, and it sounded like you were in a cave. The boys thought that was cool.

Doug was a nervous wreck. How did he get into this? He was certain the police would recognize them as truants at first sight. He had never driven into the city before. He had no idea how to get to the zoo, and if he found the zoo, would he be able to find his way home before they ran out of gas? "I only have half a tank," he said.

"That'll be enough," Dwayne said.

"You think the school will call our homes to see why we're not there?" Doug asked.

"They might," Dwayne said.

"Well, then, what'll we do?" Doug asked.

"Well, then, we're caught."

Byron and Dwayne were in the back seat enjoying Doug's dilemma.

"Maybe we should go back now and say we had a flat tire and then we'd only get a tardy," Doug said.

Dwight was the voice of reason. "Doug, just relax. It's a sunny day. I'd say it'll probably get up to fifty degrees. It's a weekday. We'll have the whole zoo to ourselves. You just can't pass up days like this in December. You want to see the monkey jack off, don't you?"

"I don't believe you about the monkey."

"It's the truth. And when you see him beatin' his meat, it'll be like you watching yourself in the mirror," Dwayne said.

Byron and the twins enjoyed a big laugh and punched shoulders. Doug reddened, became embarrassed and angry, and came to a decision. These young punks think they're so smart. I'm not going to be expelled for their sick entertainment, he thought.

Twenty-five minutes later, after three wrong turns, Doug turned off the engine in the almost empty zoo parking lot. "I told you we'd have the place to ourselves," Dwight said.

At the edge of the lot, Doug turned back to lock the doors of the car. Byron and the twins argued about what to see first. The engine came to life, and mufflers roared as Doug spun pea gravel into the air. The boys watched silently as the smoky old Ford left the lot and disappeared into the St. Louis traffic. "I told you he was a jerk," Dwight said.

Dwayne wouldn't listen to anyone once he set his mind to do something. He raised the outer glass window and stepped over the short wall. Mr. Moko ignored his arrival. The chimps' cage was closed off with glass at this time of the year. The winter season had begun, and the chimps needed to be protected from the cold. The glass enclosure surrounding the cage was inside the rail, the rail that kept the average visitor out of range of the potentially dangerous reach of an agitated chimpanzee. Dwayne was not the average visitor.

There was very little supervision at the St. Louis zoo in December. Dwayne felt completely at ease with his rule-breaking behavior and stood about three feet from the bars. Byron and Dwight made several arguments about this not being a good idea. Dwayne wouldn't listen to anyone once he started to do something, and this was something.

Dwayne had heard of Mr. Moko's propensity to change the act in the middle of a show and cause small children to ask their mothers, "What's wrong with that monkey, Mommy?" This, along with other aggressive and defiant behavior, had shortened Mr Moko's stage life.

In Dwayne's slow cooking brain, the story was not as captivating as the story of a woman and a donkey in a bar in Mexico. Still, if true, he had to see for himself. With a mimicking movement of the procedure, Dwayne hooted and squealed at Mr. Moko to no avail. Dwayne was on a mission. Byron and Dwight chuckled in amazement at Dwayne doing a charade of a sex starved monkey and making what he thought would be monkey love sounds.

Mr. Moko finally gave him a look. The weathered chimp was clearly the king of his small environment. He sat at a right angle to the bars that separated him from freedom. On the other side of those bars, Dwayne was making a fool of himself, and Mr. Moko showed his disgust by ignoring the pubescent, hairless human.

Dwayne would not be dissuaded from his goal. His movements became more exaggerated, his hoots and squeals louder and longer. Mr. Moko raised himself to his feet and took several slow steps toward Dwayne and paused, looking him in the eye. The small red eyes of the chimp showed no emotion, but his attitude was clear to anyone who cared to notice. Life in a cage was bad enough, and aggressive behavior was not rewarded. These things were well within Mr. Moko's powers of comprehension.

Mr. Moko casually looked around. Byron watched his eyes. Behind those eyes there was a mind at work. Two small female chimps in another cage huddled together, embracing each other as small children do.

Mr. Moko scanned his perimeter once again. No one else was in sight; no old people, old people who chatter and point and bring the keepers every time a stink log is thrown into a crowd, the keepers who bring the food and lock the cage. No keepers were in sight. Mr. Moko urinated on the floor where he sat. Dwayne saw this as a sign that his actions were going to bring about the desired effect.

Mr. Moko began circling the small puddle, slapping his hands on the concrete floor. Mr. Moko's circles widened with each revolution until he was slapping the metal walls that surrounded him on three sides. The screaching and banging became louder and louder and sent a primordial shiver down the spine. Then to everyone's astonishment, Mr. Moko slurped up the puddled urine and ran to the back wall, leaping high against it. He rebounded from the wall with twice the speed he had approached it. In a startling display of speed and cunning, he was in the air hitting the bars with hands and feet thrust forward grabbing steel. The hands and feet pulled Mr. Moko's chest to the bars with a thud, his head fit neatly in an opening; and he spit a rigid stream of liquid into Dwayne's awestruck face. Mr. Moko's left arm made a snatching thrust at Dwayne's head, and had Dwayne not whipped his head back in reaction to his eyes being sprayed with monkey piss, Mr. Moko would have had a handful of hair in his powerful grip.

Dwayne shouted every possible monkey insult he could think of. He mixed in all the curse words he knew. The monkey insults mixed with the curse words often made no sense at all. Dwayne wiped his eyes with his t-shirt. He would stop his verbal insult on Mr. Moko and all monkeys in general just long enough to cough and spit, then would start again on what he was going to do to get even with Mr. Moko.

Mr. Moko understood that his missed grab at the hair was the only opportunity he would have to bang this young brat's head into the bars; so with his rage spent, he waddled to the wall at the far end of his cage, turning himself half away from the bars, where he sat and pretended to pout. His head would slowly rotate toward Dwayne every ten seconds, his eyes patiently measuring the distance between Dwayne's head and the bars just on the chance that his tormenter would foolishly move within arm's length.

Byron and Dwight were rolling on the ground, rolling on cigarette butts, rolling on peanut shells, rolling on flattened paper soda cups. Dwight was crying and gasping for breath, holding his stomach. "That's . . . that's . . .

that's the smart one," he said. Dwight was barely able to get the words out and when he finally recovered enough control to shout it out, he and Byron went into another spasm of gut wrenching laughter. After five minutes of this, both boys tried in earnest to regain control of themselves. Their stomachs were becoming painful and their lungs gasping for air.

Dwayne had climbed back over the rail. He was still spitting and wiping at his face with his t-shirt. As he did so, he looked at the ground for a rock or a bottle or a stick to throw at Mr. Moko. He could find nothing. The smell forced Dwayne to remove his shirt and t-shirt, which he pitched into the bear pit in an effort to extract some revenge on the zoo in general.

The temperature never reached Dwight's prediction of fifty degrees; and Dwayne, with only a blue jean jacket, became cold. With Dwight leading the way, they cursed Doug Kearn while they walked and hitchhiked toward home. The journey home took five hours. All in all, it was a great day.

CHAPTER FIVE

F loyd Barnett made the hour and twenty minute drive from his home to the station five days a week. He liked the time alone to think and plan. On the way in, he would set goals for himself and his business; on the way home, he would examine his successes and failures. His father, a successful businessman himself, had put up the money to get him started, but that was all. Floyd repaid the loan and ran the station as he saw fit. He saw himself as a football coach. He had a good team and he knew it. That was where he took his pride, not so much in putting the team together, but in recognizing what he had and keeping it together. "How many mid-level managers have ruined good teams nobody knows. They don't keep records for that sort of thing," Floyd would say.

Floyd re-opened the old gas station/diner without the diner on June 1, 1962. Floyd, a man described by some as fidgety, had good reason to be fidgety on that day. The day started with forgotten keys. The newly hired workforce stood around with their hands in their pockets while Floyd broke out a rear window to get in. Floyd became fidgety and began chain smoking. Floyd was a square-built man of five feet eight inches. His eyes were dark and bright. He wore his black hair in a butch-waxed flattop. He had a constant five o'clock shadow, but he smiled a lot and his customers liked him.

The next surprise was a small, rusty Eagle Stamp sign that blended in with the old spark plug and battery and tire signs so well that it was not noticed, but many a customer noticed before the sign could be removed.

Signs continued to plague the man. A large, hand-lettered sign decorated with balloons placed at the edge of the road, promised free popcorn; but the popcorn machine wouldn't pop.

Floyd had happily greeted, serviced, and collected from the very first customer at Floyd's Tire Mart. And he beamed with joy and self-satisfaction. He cleaned all the glass, checked the oil, and aired up a low tire. The customer, a small woman of ill temper, paid her $2.00 for the gas. Then she ordered two bags of popcorn for her two small, dusty boys that were wrestling in the back of the dusty Ford Falcon station wagon. Floyd explained and apologized for the broken popcorn popper but received a cold stare. Next she demanded her Eagle Stamps and was not happy with Floyd's apology and accused him of fraud. Floyd refunded her a dollar of her purchase to make up for the two cents worth of Eagle Stamps and the penny's worth of popcorn he had cheated her out of. She showed her displeasure with a tire chirping exit that sent the dusty children tumbling to the tailgate.

The day continued on in this manner and Floyd became more fidgety. Around noon that first day, in the middle of the continuing opening day confusion, Floyd filled the tank of a remarkably clean turquoise green Rambler sedan. The woman driver, known to everyone as Miss Maples, looked to Floyd to be a hundred years old. She paid for her gas and without invitation suggested Floyd fire one of his newly hired employees. She motioned for Floyd to stick his head in the window so she could speak softly. "You need to fire that one," she said, pointing to a small, greasy looking man fueling a Cadillac.

Floyd said, "Huh." Floyd always said Huh.

"That man over there. He ran the pump for a while, then he reset it. Now you watch, he'll collect a dollar for probably five dollars worth of gas. That's his sister or cousin or girlfriend driving that car, I'll bet," Miss Maples said.

She turned out to be right about the man she had pointed out and continued to be right about every employee Floyd hired from then to now. Floyd valued her opinion so much he made sure each new hire fueled her car at the earliest opportunity so she could pronounce judgment.

CHAPTER SIX

Ike Williams had just begun his first day at the Zephyr gas station known as Floyd's Tire Mart. Al Creed showed him the basics of the job—how to work the pumps, how to make change with the chrome changer, where to wear it on his belt so it wouldn't scratch the paint, how to address the customers with a "Yes, sir" or a "Yes, ma'am" or "What can I do for you, sir?" It was an important part of the job. Floyd would not tolerate pump jockeys with a bad attitude.

Ike had handled a few cars alone and felt he had things well under control. The first of what would be many dump trucks pulled onto the lot. The dump trucks were different; they required a different level of service. Most of the drivers were in a hurry. Some wanted their oil checked every time they came in; some never wanted their oil check and didn't like to be asked. Others had constantly low tires that should be replaced; but that would mean losing up to a dozen loads, so the tires were aired up twice or three times a day for weeks at a time.

Floyd had small stepladders by the pumps for cleaning the windshields of the dump trucks. Some of the drivers ran charge accounts and just signed for their gas. Others used credit cards. Most paid cash.

Art Grump was a long time customer with an ornery sense of humor. When his truck pulled next to the pumps on Ike's first day, all the other pump jockeys moved off out of sight where they could watch the show. Ike approached the truck a little apprehensively. This was his first dump truck and he wasn't for sure where the gas tank would be. Art Grump, a thin, gray, wiry little man, climbed down from the cab and started right in on him. "I haven't got all god damn day. Get this truck filled up. Check all my tires. Ninety pounds, no more no less. Check that oil and if it needs any; I've got some in the cab. Clean that windshield inside and out. Don't scratch the paint, you little jackoff."

"Yes, sir," Ike said.

Ike was dumbfounded by this assault. He looked around to see if anyone else was witnessing this. There was no one in sight.

Art Grump started in again as Ike put the pump in the thirty gallon saddle tank below the step cab of the truck. "I'm part owner of this place and I don't like skinny little jackoff punks dragging ass when they should be humping and happy to have this job."

Ike went about his duties as the assault continued. "I've had three assholes like you fired this past year, and you'll be next if you don't show me some respect."

Ike suddenly felt a shot of adrenalin course through his body. Just as old man Grump, as he would later come to be known, was starting in again, Ike stood up from the tire he was checking, turned to face Art, and said in a clear, controlled voice, "Fuck you."

Art jerked up his arms and began pumping them up and down as he coughed and laughed until tears ran out of his eyes. Behind the glass inside the building, a chorus of laughter broke out. Art was laughing and coughing so hard he had to lean on the doorframe for support. Al and Skip and Floyd, each with a cigarette and a cup of coffee, came rolling out of the door spilling hot coffee as they whooped and bellowed and pointed in Ike's general direction.

Art Grump was a seasoned resident among the dump truck crowd. At the age of sixty-six, he didn't drive for a living anymore, but was always on the lookout for a truck he could buy cheap and sell high. "I was running out of names to call him," he said, holding one arm to his side to keep his stomach from protracting too hard. "You got a good one there," he said to Floyd.

Floyd was beaming. He loved a good joke more than most. He was terrible at telling a joke, and everyone avoided him when he had a new one to tell. His grin was ear to ear and his unshaven face was flushed. Floyd would be telling this story for the next two weeks. "He did okay, didn't he?" he said. Floyd ran a family friendly business and wouldn't tolerate bad language or poor service in front of the customers.

Art Grump had first pulled this stunt three years before when Skip Lurch was hired. At that time, Skip was fresh out of the army and ready to take on the world. Floyd liked his attitude but wasn't sure he could deal effectively with some of the rough crowd that came into the station. "Everyone needs gas," Floyd would say. "You think murderers get their gas from the moon? No, they get it at the gas station." He would let that statement soak in, then turn and point to the pumps.

Art volunteered to test this new assistant manager for backbone, and that's how the tradition was born. Skip passed his test easily. He had come after Art and chased him into the building, where he had to be saved by Floyd. "If anyone gives you that much trouble, just tell them to get off the lot," Floyd said. Those were his words of instruction at the time. He didn't want his men sucker punching the customers on the driveway even if some did need it.

Ike was reminded of the episode by every dump truck driver in the county for months to come. The story was told and retold with the usual embellishments and exaggerations.

The eleven full- and part-time employees of Floyd's Tire Mart made up a diverse and interesting crowd-hustlers, bartenders, middle managers, high school boys, and one ex-dump truck driver. Ike was the youngest man on the payroll. He learned quickly the art of a good sale. Tires were profit, but gas paid the bills, and there was plenty of gas sold—fifty thousand gallons a month. Cars and trucks rolled down the driveway all day long. They also came in waves, and the rule was: Sell tires, but man the pumps. "If you piss off someone at the pumps, that's a set of tires you're not going to sell," Floyd would say.

The big wave comes in the morning rush from six thirty to eight o'clock in the morning, car after car, truck after truck. Trucks get two cents a gallon discount; cars get every piece of glass cleaned. Trucks have their oil and tires checked more often. Cars have pretty girls with short skirts. In the summer, it's hot, boiling hot on the black asphalt. The heat bakes the bottom of your feet. In the winter, the constant wind of passing traffic whips at your face and blows up under your jacket. The men wear longjohns, a sweatshirt over the longjohns and insulated vests over the sweatshirt, the company shirt and pants over that, and an insulated nylon jacket. Floyd provides brown jersey gloves when it's zero or below, but they quickly become soaked in gas and oil and are useless.

Ike was grateful to have this job. He was sixteen and in desperate need of a fast car. This was his first week of summer vacation following his junior year in high school. He wanted to go back to school in the fall with a muscle car, a car that would smoke tires at will, a car that would make the girls and guys take notice.

Brad and Leon had recommended Ike for the job. They each had over six months experience and were no longer considered new hires. Brad and Leon were classmates. Ike hadn't known either of them well in school. Fox was a large high school with nearly four thousand students enrolled. Only in the last semester had Ike said more than a word or two to either boy. Thanks to a computerized classroom assignment program that placed students of similar learning capacity in the same classes, Ike found himself at a table in music appreciation class with Brad and Leon on either side.

The meeting had been tense at first. Brad and Leon were greasers and Ike was perceived to be a suckie. Those were the two categories that all students were obliged to choose from. If you did not make a conscious choice, someone else would.

Brad and Carl suspected that Ike was part of a suckie group. Ike's manner of dress, while only slightly different from their own on most days, leaned a little more toward the Beatles than Elvis.

The teacher in the music appreciation class allowed for quiet conversation so long as it didn't overtake the music. After some probing, Brad and Leon decided that Ike was okay. He had probably been mislabeled and could be saved.

That weekend, the three young men climbed out of Leon's '57 Chevy in front of the J.C. Penney store where Ike would buy his first pair of brogues—brogues, short for brogans. Only the J.C. Penney brand of brogans would do. The brushed suede leather, ankle-high work boot was the signature shoe of the greasers. The brogues signified defiance of authority. In the high school handbook, it read that heavy-soled work boots were not to be worn as part of a proper dress. They also sent a message that the wearer wore the shoe not only for their campy style, but to add extra weight when a kick was delivered to the head of anyone who needed it.

Ike looked great in his new brogues. Standing at five eleven and weighing one hundred pounds, wearing tightly tapered silver iridescent pants, the size ten a half boots looking like snowshoes made the perfect picture.

From there on, the three boys would form a muscatel-like alliance. Working part time at Floyd's was a great job for a high school boy on the way up in the working world. On days when the three boys worked together, it was non-stop horseplay. The water bottle squirt was a favorite with the customers. Ike's crotch area stayed wet most of the time. The alcohol and soap combination burned like hell if it got into your eyes, so the rule was anywhere but the face. The plastic squeeze bottles, small enough to fit in a rear pocket of your royal blue Zephyr pants, had about a ten-foot range when fully charged. Tire gauge dropping was another workday pastime. Having the chrome gauge snatched out of its Zephyr plastic pocket protector was particularly frustrating for Ike, who failed to get a blocking hand in place most of the time and so developed the strategy of holding one hand over his pocket protector with its whole array of ink pens, tire depth gauge, and air gauge, whenever Brad or Leon were close by.

Floyd, if he were there, would put up with the silliness to a point. Then with a few stern words, he would bring things back to an acceptable level. The customers for the most part loved it. It was something real in their artificial days. Floyd encouraged his employees to know their customers by their names and always use Mr. or Mrs. unless the customer said differently.

Mr. Nolte was a Ford man; a trusty and economical Falcon was his car of choice. He would always veer off the highway at a slow rate of speed and refuse to downshift from third gear, slipping his clutch unmercifully up to the pumps.

Mr. Kramer was a Chevy man. The beige '62 Impala fit his needs. He never had his oil checked. He would say, "If you get it changed when it needs it, you don't need to check it."

There were Buick men and Dodge men and even the occasional Peugeot. Try to find the gas cap on that.

Most loved to talk about their cars, the rock-haulers loved to talk about their trucks. No truck on earth pulled harder, started easier in any weather, or delivered more cost-free miles to its owner than the one you were standing next to on any particular day. Dinah Shore loved her Chevy, Tennessee Ernie Ford loved his Ford, and Joe Citizen loved his car.

CHAPTER SEVEN

The top of the scarred old wooden desk lay covered with money. The room was dark except for the light of a green metal desk lamp. Al sat hunkered over the money and the tickets and the other paperwork necessary to calculate the day's sales. Al punched in numbers on the electric adding machine. The machine clicked and clicked. The ribbon was old, and Al could barely read the numbers; but he could read them, and he'd be damned if he were going to change that ribbon. On the floor by his feet, a brown paper bag contained three, sixteen-ounce cans of beer. Three empty beer cans circled the adding machine.

From his position at the desk, Al could peek through the Venetian blinds and look into the showroom. A window to his left with more blinds allowed him to peek out onto the driveway.

Al's thoughts drifted to Sarah Belle Hicks, his sixth grade sweetheart. If only he had pursued her harder. Her daddy owned the sawmill. Often when doing the mundane work of counting money and entering figures in the books, he would daydream about what had been and what could have been. It was not that entering the day's receipts was a things of ease; it was just the opposite. The job of reading the pumps, subtracting the previous day's numbers, entering the gallons, multiplying the profits by four and six cents per gallon (for regular or ethyl), and coming up with a final figure for gas, oil, tires, and miscellaneous, and then making that figure match perfectly with the amount of money taken in was at the very limits of Al's education—a fact he didn't want to share with a sixteen-year-old know it all.

Ike had just started a week ago and was making almost as much money as Al. The thought simmered in Al's subconscious all day and was still jumping out while he struggled with the books. It's just not right. Floyd should pay these boys less or pay me more. The thought played in his mind like a song you hate but can't stop humming.

Ike wasn't a bad kid; he was just too much—too much smart answers, too much mischievous charm, too much salesman of the year. Al tried not to like the kid, but that was hard to do. The kid took a lot of abuse and didn't complain. He learned quick and was even a lot of help. The fact that a sixteen-year-old with a week of experience was making nearly as much money as the assistant manager wasn't right. Al felt trapped.

Al pushed the demons out of his mind as best he could and went back to fighting the numbers. The driveway bell began to ring again. Al punched numbers into the machine. The bell was still ringing—ding, ding, ding, ding—as each set of tires crossed the black rubber hose encircling the pumps. All peeked between the blinds and looked out to the drive. Four cars. If it were another night with a different boy, Al would get up and go help. Tonight, Al popped the tab of his fourth Schlitz and thought, Let the hotshot hustle.

Top quality service was expected and given at Floyd's Tire Mart. Ike knew the standards he was expected to keep. Floyd paid top wages and wasn't too hard to get along with. Ike was happy to have this job and on days when he worked with Leon and Brad, there was so much fun he would almost have done it for free.

The new shiny dump trucks were a sight to see in the bright afternoon sun, but the hotrods that came out at night made Ike's heart race. Fords and Chevies rumbled roughly next to the pumps; their large carburetors and high loab cams begged for gasoline. Open headers released each cylinder's explosion with a sound wave you could feel in your chest. The young men who drove these fire breathers wore greasy jeans and had dark lines in all the creases of their hands and under their nails. Ike listened to their talk of retarded timing or a flat spot in the carburetor. He didn't know what they were talking about, but he knew he wanted to be one of them.

Floyd didn't like the hot rodders hanging around unless they were spending money. He did, though, enjoy selling tires to people who could burn through a pair in a month or so. But they couldn't hang around; it upset the moms and dads with carloads of kids to see rough-looking young men standing next to thundering cars winking at their daughters. Floyd made more than a few mad with his policy of no loitering. Some of these river rats, he would say, come in, buy a fifty cent quart of oil, and think that gives them the right to work on their cars in the driveway for the next forty-five minutes. Floyd wouldn't stand for it.

Ike had a gas nozzle in all four cars and was skipping between the pump islands like a seasoned veteran. Two were fill ups, one wanted $5.00, the other $3.00. Ike was in position to watch the $3.00 while doing the windows on the $5.00; then jump to the $3.00, do the glass, round the trunk just in time to catch the nozzle at $2.90, collect the money, get back to the $5.00, finish her off at full volume, collect, then clean the glass on both fill ups before the pumps kicked off.

Ike could see Al peeking through the blinds. He should have come out to help but was probably on his third sixteen-ouncer by now and in a bad mood about the tickets. Every time a quart of oil or a wiper blade or a headlight was sold, a ticket with a carbon had to be hand written and put in the drawer in the showroom.

In the frenzy of battle, with tires being changed while gas is pumped and radiators are boiling over, the sale is made with the well-intentioned salesman, mostly Ike, forgetting to do the paperwork.

Al punched numbers into the electric adding machine until all the tickets were gone. Now with one last press of the Total key, he would be finished or would have to start again. Al raised his tired head from the desk and leaned back in the swivel chair. Al wasn't a praying man, but he often hoped with all his might for luck. Tonight, for some reason, he would go mad if the numbers didn't match and he had to go through them again. Al took another gulp of beer to give the luck he was hoping for a chance to arrive.

What to do about Byron. There was a question that made itself at home in Al's brain. Al was sick of this question too, but here it was back again. The moment his mind was free to daydream about his own future and the few pleasures he might expect, what to do about Byron came barging in and took control.

"He's been suspended three times and the principal's promised to expel him on his next violation," Al had said to Ike earlier in the day. Why did I tell Ike about my problems with Byron? I don't even like the kid. Al brooded over the situation.

The bell went bing, bing, bing, bing again. The rhythm of the bell binging as tires crossed the rubber hose told a man of Al's experience what was happening on the drive. The bell's serenade, accompanied by a large variety of exhaust notes, painted a picture of driveway activity.

A dump truck was pulling out. Sounded like one of the Lurch truckers. They were water haulers. There were three of them, the old man and two boys.

The boys would stick a water hose into the hot, glass packed mufflers. The water would make the hot fiberglass rigid and it's sound absorbing qualities severely diminished. The truck now pulling across the bell had a crackle to its exhaust. Yeah, I bet that's one of the Lurch boys making a late run for a good customer.

What to do about Byron. "Damn," Al said, just loud enough for his own ears to hear.

The bell began again. The squeal of brakes, the whine of a diesel shifting down through the gears, the ding, ding of eighteen wheels crossing the hose—a scale dodger, Al thought. Over the road trucker with too much weight or messed up paperwork going around the weight scales out on the interstate.

I should go help, Al thought. Two more cars crossed the bell, their quiet mufflers whooshing hot air as they floated on soft suspension up to the pumps.

What to do about Byron. Damn.

Al took two more quick slugs of beer and hit the key marked Total. The machine clicked and clicked, then gave out one last burst of miraculous mechanical calculation and stamped out a number in red ink. Thirty cents difference in the two final totals. Al breathed a sigh of relief and produced thirty cents from his own pocket.

Ike Williams manned the pumps at a high level of efficiency. Like anything else, pumping gas can be done by slobs leaning against your car picking their nose or by trained professionals like the men at Floyd's Tire Mart. Ike took pride in his job. He skipped across the islands and hurdled the pump hoses in fluid motions that rivaled sport stars in grace and efficiency. Windows were cleaned, mirrors were polished, gas nozzles were pulled like Colt .45s and slipped into hidden access points behind the tail lights, behind the license plates, behind chrome fins, behind blank squares of painted metal that released from the inside. There was only a fifty percent chance the driver would release the painted metal flap without being reminded. This slowed the process and frustrated the pump jockey. But nothing rivaled the locking gas cap for killing momentum.

Al came out to help, hoping it would take his mind off his problems. "Was that one of the Lurch boys I heard?" Al asked.

"Yeah, that was Gerald."

"What's he doing out so late?"

"Didn't say. He was in a hurry, though," Ike said.

Al took over the fueling of a Buick wagon. "This a fill up?" Al asked.

"Yeah, and he wants his oil checked," Ike hollered from across the drive.

The nozzle was in and pumping. Al began cleaning glass.

What to do about Byron. Damn, Al thought. "Have you seen Byron tonight?" Al croaked out across the hood of the Buick.

"Yeah, he was through earlier with the Coal brothers," Ike replied. Ike was checking a pickup truck's tires.

"Did he say where he was going?"

"No, he don't talk to me except to cuss me."

"It's the same with me," Al said.

CHAPTER EIGHT

The treetops looked like bushes growing out of a brown mirror. The Meramec had been at flood stage for three days. She would not crest and begin her fall back to obedience for two more. Byron Creed and the Coal brothers cruised slowly down the middle of Orchard Street on an aluminum flying carpet. The ten horse outboard propelled the flat bottomed boat effortlessly past the second storey windows and rooftops that jutted out of the water in neat rows. Dwayne opened up the throttle on the little outboard a bit more and began weaving between houses, swinging to the backyard of one and then back to the street before swinging back again.

The light of the full moon and the sharp eyes of youth served well as each marveled at the spectacle of this exotic new world. Everything was the same—the same street signs, the same trees, the same rooftops, the same Pepsi sign. Still, everything was different. The full moon cast deep shadows, the light coming off the water turned floating debris into crocodile heads, and the homes they recognized only made it all the more unfamiliar like a fever dream.

Byron was unsure he could find his way back if he had to. The fear was exhilarating. He begged to drive the boat and Dwayne conceded, but only after strict instructions. "Keep her running along under these trees. You see the way the treetops make a tunnel. Stay in the tunnel until I tell you to turn."

Byron sat at the stern with a tight grip on the throttle, following orders to turn toward the Pepsi sign or turn away from the power lines. The object of their moonlight ride was treasure, stolen treasure, a boatload of treasure.

Byron didn't see himself as a burglar; he was just helping himself to some stuff that would just go to waste if the river got it. It would be washed downstream or to the muddy bottom, no good to anyone.

Dwight's constant moving around in the small boat became unnerving, but to say anything would only bring about an opposite effect.

Dwayne spoke in whispers about what might be in each rooftop they passed. "I bet this one has a big color TV."

"We ain't putting a color TV in the boat, dumb ass," Dwight said.

"You see if we don't, dumber ass," Dwayne answered.

Byron tried to stay out of these brotherly arguments. Any suggestion of his, either directed to both the brothers or him, would raise the ante of the fight between the two. The fighting of Dwayne and Dwight had been a constant since Byron had known them. A fight could break out with no warning. If the brothers went at it in the boat and turned them over, Byron shuddered at the thought. Each brother had beaten the other several times, but neither was dominant and the outcome was decided by the brother who wanted to win that particular fight the most.

Their mother, Loretta, had always been nice and good from what Byron could see. She tried hard to keep the boys in line; but given their identical age, ability, and temperament, she could not stop the fights, which were likely to break out any time.

Byron twisted the throttle of the little outboard and the sudden acceleration turned both the brothers' heads. "You want to go for a swim?" Dwayne said. Dwight's expression said he agreed with his brother. Byron slowed the motor and the quiet surrealness of the adventure returned.

They were several miles upstream now, in less familiar territory. "Swing out toward the channel," Dwayne said. All was dark along the usually brightly lit shoreline. Two lights sat on top of the water up ahead.

"Head toward those lights. Let's see what that is," Dwight said.

As they came closer, they recognized the white globes with the blue-winged horse on each side. It was the tops of two gas pumps at a Mobil station. The boys marveled that the lights were still working and all around was dark. The sight thrilled the boys for some unknown reason and all three looked at each other with large grins.

Several snakes crossed the bow; one even tried to come in the boat, but Dwayne routinely grabbed it, swung it around his head, shook it at his brother, and tossed it back to the brown water, laughing like a lunatic the whole time. When the show was over, he began laughing for real until his stomach hurt. Byron felt sure he would never have this much fun again.

The sighting of the Mobil station gave Dwayne his bearings and he directed Byron into the flooded backwater. "There it is. You see it?" Dwayne said, pointing into the distance. "Turk's. Turk's sold everything that anyone might need on the river, from worms to spark plugs. This could be a gold mine." That was the way Dwayne explained it to Byron, a once in a lifetime opportunity.

Turk had been slowly losing his mind for the last ten years. He had owned and operated Turk's Bait and Tackle for as far back as anyone could remember. His location on a small peninsula created by a sharp bend in the river offered a gently sloping ramp good at high water and low. He also offered gas, beer, soda, ice, fishing licenses, sporting goods, and all things required for a good time. Everyone knew Turk; everyone liked Turk; and then one by one, he threatened or attacked one old friend after another until there were none left. Most of the incidents involved only curse words and hot tempers. The others escalated to pushing and bottle throwing. No charges were filed. His old friends just stayed away. His last victim, a man named Owen Bahr, was threatened with a shotgun for sleeping with the woman Turk called his wife.

Clara and Turk were never married. People said they saw a change in Turk right after she died. He forgot things; he remembered other things wrong. His final friend he accused of sleeping with his wife. He forgot Clara had been dead a full year when Owen moved there. He forgot they were never married. He had a clear picture in his mind of their wedding day.

On the day of his death, Turk had gone to Floyd's for new tires. Turk leaned against a stack of tires, breathing heavily. He carried 400 plus pounds on his five feet, eleven inches frame. The walk from his truck to the tire changing room took his breath away. He lit a cigarette.

Al worked up a sweat trying to get the new six-ply truck tires on the wheels. The tires had been on the bottom of a large stack for a long time; the inner edge of the tire called the bead was warped and wouldn't take a grip. Al slammed the tire against the wheel over and over until it hooked and the changer could get a start and peel it into place. Turks heart pounded more than normal; he sucked in large drafts of air, but still could not catch his breath. He leaned on a stack of tires for support. Old dreams came into his mind, anger began to build, but he wasn't sure why. Now he remembered. That's the man he had seen dancing with his wife. His blood boiled. He looked around the room. A small lead hammer lay on the bench. He would bury that hammer into the back of this bastard's head. Turk lunged for the hammer and his world went dark. He never felt a thing when he flopped to the floor.

Al saw Turk begin to go down but couldn't stop his fall. He looked into his eyes and felt sure he was dead. Still, he thought he had to do what he could. He rolled Turk on his stomach and worked his arms over his head and back to his sides. He hollered for help as he went about the only thing he could think to do.

"Turk's dead. Are you sure?" Dwayne had said. Dwayne took interest right away. He got a wild look in his eye when he was thinking about making a move on something.

Byron wasn't sure why he felt the Coal brothers would be very interested in this news; he just knew they would.

"When did this happen?" Dwayne asked.

When told the day and the time, Dwight also caught on and made a poor attempt at the crazy look.

The river had come up suddenly, much faster than anyone had predicted. The Coal brothers paid attention to such things. When their father, old Dry Coal, died, he didn't leave much for the boys except some good memories and a couple of jon boats. The boys had loved their father and tried hard to please him. But when he left them, they drifted toward an easy life that offered quick profits and excitement.

Byron was reluctant to go along. He had never before set out to steal. He had stolen. His conscience wouldn't let him deny the truth of that, but that was different. He was eight years old, and if a nickel plated Zippo lighter with the Marine Corps insignia gold plated on the side is left from the night before on Rayleen's night stand, well, it had to be taken. He received a whipping for stealing it but would never admit to having it. He would still have it today if someone hadn't stolen it from him. That was the easy way out for him—the fact that he wouldn't steal anything unless it fell into his lap.

Dwayne took only a few minutes to explain. The river was still rising. "If we don't get it, the river will. That's not stealing. That's salvage."

It was a good argument. Byron couldn't deny that and didn't try very hard.

Turk's was right up ahead. The shape of the bluff and the silhouette in the moonlight gave Dwayne his exact location. Byron followed orders to slow to a crawl and not make any noise. Dwayne climbed onto the porch that usually stood twelve feet off the ground and fifty feet from the river bank. The boys were dressed in their standard river attire of cutoff jeans, sockless tennis shoes, and t-shirts.

Dwayne climbed over the rail and stepped into knee deep water. He wasted no time gawking and pried open a window with a little crowbar. Once inside, Dwayne opened the door. Dwight and Byron stepped into the cold water.

Byron waded directly to the gun cabinet. A small padlock on a sliding door was no match for Dwayne and his crowbar. The top shelf of the glass cabinet was full of cheap pocket knives, red and white bobbers, hooks, line, batteries, flashlights, and all manner of shiny temptation. There were three blue pistols that were displayed on a middle shelf just above the waterline. Dwayne awarded himself first choice. Dwight was about to protest when Dwayne and Byron each grabbed one. All three were Ruger target .22s, two of them with six inch barrels and one with a nine inch barrel.

Dwight would randomly tear up at odd times, and it was best not to say anything. The last pistol unclaimed had the nine-inch barrel. The longer barrel and larger adjustable sights made it less desirable to the Coal brothers. "What's wrong with it?" Byron asked.

"Too hard to conceal," they said in unison.

Byron traded with Dwight. Dwight was happy again.

Byron was thrilled with his new pistol and bragged he would be a crack shot.

The boat was loaded with outboard motor oil, shotgun shells, pocket knives, cigarettes, whiskey, and other spirits of all colors and flavors. Dwayne pleaded with Dwight and Byron to take only the most expensive items and the things they could sell the easiest. The boys could not control themselves and Dwayne gave up and joined the feeding frenzy.

The flashlights were Dwayne's idea. He laid out the plan like a field general. "The first thing to be done," he said, "is gather all the flashlights old Turk carried, put batteries in them, and place them all around the room. With both hands free, we can carry more loot faster."

Byron and Dwight both agreed that Dwayne was a deep thinker.

The raid was a complete success. The ride home was slow and quiet. The boat was loaded to capacity. Only two inches of freeboard separated victory from disaster. Dwayne took the motor in hand and steered a backwater course that brought them right next to their tree house. Byron and Dwight were both amazed to realize their location. The trip had been so far inland; they had recognized nothing.

It was a pure stroke of luck that the water and the floor of the tree house were a perfect match. With the bow of the jon boat sitting on the floor of the tree house, they were unloaded in no time. Dwight objected to the idea of climbing up and down to the tree house with arms full of loot. Dwayne explained, in an unkind way, that the loot was already in the tree house and that to get it out meant dropping it to the ground once the river went down. "Dumb ass."

The tree house was a twelve square foot room with roof, walls, windows, and a door. A small porch with rails hung on one side. It belonged to the Coal brothers. Their father and brother had built it together the summer ole Dry was killed.

The tree house was on quarry land so far back up a tangled slough that no one but other kids ever came around. Clay had made sure that anyone that entered the tree house uninvited paid a price. When Clay was away in prison, Dwayne and Dwight took over the job of running off trespassers. As far as they could tell, no one came around. Dry had told the boys that the quarry had bought this lumber to keep in storage. So as a loyal employee, he would help them store it on their own property up in their own tree.

Clay had only been back to visit the tree house once, the day he got out of prison. He looked at it from the ground for just a few seconds. "I remember it as bigger," he said and walked away.

Clay was happy and funny like his father in the old days, but now he wasn't the same. He worked hard at being the same, but everyone could tell he wasn't. He had a hard, intense look in his eye whenever anyone disagreed with him. He shoved both his brothers to the ground on separate occasions and hovered over them ready to deliver a knockout blow if challenged further. Dwayne and Dwight learned to walk softly around Clay.

Loretta didn't escape Clay's temper either, and in a moment of clear thinking, Clay realized he must avoid her or suffer forever the shame of striking her.

Clay left most of his things in Loretta's house but slept there or ate there only when Loretta was away. She continued to wash his clothes and make his bed.

The Coal gang sat around their loot like star-struck children around a Christmas tree. The loot would be safe in the tree house, to be sold or consumed as needed by the outlaw gang. Beer, potato chips, beef jerky, soda, whiskey, chocolate candy was passed out to the delight of all. Byron was the first to puke but was able to get to the rail in time. Dwayne lost his stomach on Dwight's shoes, the sight and smell of which pushed Dwight's control over the edge and he joined Byron at the rail.

The gang slept in the tree house until noon the next day.

CHAPTER NINE

Clay Coal was home from prison. His time at the University of Advanced Criminal Science was well spent. He majored in wealth redistribution. He stood six feet and one inch tall. With brown hair and eyes, he looked like a larger version of his twin brothers. He weighed 190 pounds, all of it muscle and bone. He had the crazy look in his eye; and when he turned on the crazy look, he made you believe it. He graduated summa cum laude in the art and history of auto theft. Old timers there could hot wire a steam engine and told him how.

Cars since their invention have been a favorite target of the short-hours, long-pay crowd. Clay was a rising star in the business.

Getting the car was the easy part. Getting the papers for it took a crooked lawyer and judge. While he had not reached that level of sophistication just yet, he felt confident he would. The cars he stole now went to Arkansas and were dropped off with little fanfare.

The barn where he left the stolen car had a clean return car registered to Baxter Construction, a phony company that offered an easy alibi for travelers. If he were pulled over in the stolen car, he was on his own. Clay had a fake driver's license and a good line of bullshit. He never put different plates on a stolen car. Doing that would tip the cops faster than anything.

Clay would cruise the shopping center parking lots watching for Corvettes, the car that always has a market. A shopper with a bag of milk and eggs always went straight home. The name on the mailbox would be the car owner's ninety-five percent of the time. "Write the name on a piece of tape and stick it to the visor," Whistler said. This was the method most recommended at Jeff City.

When pulled over, you're always asked if this is your car, the old timers said. Always say No and no more unless asked. When the cops run the plates, they're going to ask you whose car it is. You'll have the name, along with some boring story—this being your brother-in-law's car and him being sick with the flu, and "I think I'm coming down with it too. Anyway, I've got to go get my sister 'cause she won't ride on my motorcycle. It's a Harley. You ever ride on a Harley? How much is this ticket gonna cost? I hope it's not more than $50.00. I'm gonna catch hell from my sister about this."

Never overplay your hand. Just answer questions that are asked and look distressed over whatever traffic violation you're receiving. This had been time-tested and worked almost always.

When he first began his studies, Clay thought it might not be a good idea to take training in the car theft business from guys in prison. Their presence proved there was a flaw in their plans, but on the other hand, his plans fell short of his expectations. He thought he'd never be caught.

Clay preferred to work at night and take the cars from the owners' driveway or garage. If everything went well, the stolen car would be parked in a barn in Arkansas before the owner realized it was gone. The Baxter Construction car Clay drove home was left on a parking lot near Highway 67 and would be picked up by someone else. A few days later, Clay would receive an envelope in the mail with $800.00 in it.

Whistler was the oldest man in the cellblock. At sixty years of age, he was still a dangerous man even in the hand-to-hand world of prison. Whistler picked Clay out for recruitment. He could tell in one look who would be an asset and who would be a liability inside or outside the walls. Whistler still had five years to go on a twenty year sentence for murder. He never would discuss the murder; he would just say, "Dead men tell no tales," and squint one eye and say, "Aaargh," like a pirate.

Clay delivered his first car to the barn one week after his release and tried to deliver two a month in cold weather and three or four a month in the summer when the pickin' was easier.

Most people left their window down in the summer; and although getting a door open was not that hard, you were exposed there next to the prize and for a few moments even a fool could tell what you were doing. On the other hand, if the door was unlocked, you could approach your target, time your entry, and be under the dash and out of sight even with people walking through the parking lot. Then, when you sat up in the seat, the car started and you were gone.

CHAPTER TEN

Lowell Maynard paced restlessly in his work area. There were three bodies to be prepared, but Lowell could not get started. An old man, toothless and gray; a middle aged woman with her surgical wound loosely closed; and a middle aged man with fragments of windshield glass glittering in his face—all lay nude and uncovered on the tables in the embalming room.

Lowell passed back and forth among the bodies, not seeing them, his mind in other places and other times. He returned to his desk and stared down at two photographs lying next to each other. One was of himself at age fifteen; one was of Byron Creed which he had taken with a telephoto lens. The resemblance was amazing.

Lowell started his work several times, but was drawn back to the pictures again and again, each time amazed and startled by the resemblance.

Lowell Maynard was a very successful man. His success was due to long hours and careful attention to detail. The Maynard Funeral Home was free and clear of all debt. Lowell Maynard was comfortable. He had a wide range of interests. He could work a room; he could talk sports, religion, politics, or life and death. He was at home with a hotdog at a Little League game or in a church basement handing out compliments on the newest quilt being sewn.

Lowell had made himself knowledgeable on wide variety of subjects. Should he happen to be caught in a conversation where he was ignorant of the basics, he would find the information and arm himself with enough facts to appear brilliant upon his next encounter. When it came to spreading bullshit,

Lowell's only rivals were traveling tent show preachers, luxury pre-owned car salesmen, and democratic congressmen.

Lowell could work a room; and when the time came to provide the last customer service anyone would ever need, his quiet confidence and incredible knowledge on so many subjects induced people to think that he must know his own business better than anyone.

Lowell's wife, Margaret, was a small woman, just barely five feet tall. When she was young, she had a small, sweet, doll-like face, small breasts, and proportionate hips. She gave Lowell two daughters, Holly and Molly, who were now sixteen and nineteen. The girls took after their father in height and stature and carried their mother's facial features. Lowell was pleased. He needed a quiet, well-groomed family to complement his funeral trade. People expect their deceased loved ones to be prepared for burial by solemn, professional, caring people. That type of person must live a nondescript life with a nondescript family.

Lowell could have made a living with a less than perfect image, but he didn't want just a living; he wanted money, lots of money, and he had worked hard to get it. Smart business decisions, a quiet, well-groomed family, and a gift of gab had made him wealthy by small town standards.

Margaret was excellent at the duties of raising daughters. She spent her energies on them without hesitation. Lowell demanded no less. After the birth of their first daughter, a slow, steady drift took place. Lowell was concerned with the details of his trade. He hated to pay wages that could be kept in his own pocket. Lowell kept his own books, did the hair and makeup, did his own maintenance inside the embalming room. Lowell worked on and perfected new methods of adding efficiency to an old trade. Small pumps and hoses littered the shelves and countertops. Lowell worked on faster and cheaper methods of replacing bodily fluids in a constant search for ways one man could accomplish the work of three. The need for efficiency overshadowed his thoughts on most occasions, protecting himself from his own unhappiness.

Today, he could not apply his energies to the technique or technology. Again and again he found himself staring at the picture of Byron and dreaming an impossible dream of a father and son relationship that was perfect in every way. In his mind's eye, Byron and Lowell would be fishing on a quiet lake, making small talk about sports or business. The conversation would not be insightful or profound; the father and son would just be so happy in each other's company, nothing else mattered.

That was just one of many idyllic scenes that rotated around in Lowell's private world. There was the ballpark scene where Lowell and Byron are cheering for the home team and in their enthusiasm, embrace each other as the winning run is scored. Lowell's personal favorite is where he turns over the keys to the business to Byron after years of working side by side. In this version of the Lowell and Byron Show, Byron is fascinated by the business and is a tremendous help to his father, eagerly learning all he has to teach and expanding his knowledge until he is ready to assume the responsibility of carrying on the tradition of excellence.

The business must be passed on. He must find a way to kill Al Creed. A sudden burst of air erupted from Lowell's mouth. "Hah," he said, amused at himself for planning a murder over a boy he couldn't be sure was his; a boy he thought he would never see. Just months ago, he had gone about his life almost never giving this boy a thought. Now he was consumed by too many thoughts. The out-of-sight, out-of-mind approach that he and Al Creed had both been guilty of employing could not go on. But murder? Lowell laughed at himself again. No, not murder. Be patient, he thought.

His thoughts drifted back to a dark night almost fifteen years ago. It was a Saturday night. He was driving past Turk's place after dropping off some papers to a grieving family down the road when Rayleen ran in front of his car. She was a large framed girl with large breasts barely contained in a button-down sleeveless blouse. She had climbed in the passenger door before Lowell could say a word. She had a wild look in her eye, the way women get when some man has crossed them.

"Get me out of here," she said.

Lowell hit the gas and gravel pinged off the underbelly of the car. Rayleen looked back toward Turk's several times until the lights of the beer garden were out of sight. She had thrown herself at a man and he had ignored her; and when she would not give up, he embarrassed her. She had been spurned for the first time ever and did not want to start down that road.

Rayleen recognized Lowell for who he was. His big Cadillac car smelled of formaldehyde and money. She could see him peeking at her open blouse and toyed with him, pretending not to notice as she giggled while she spoke. Lowell had asked if she needed help and where she could be taken. Rayleen only gave vague answers and suggested that they get some Amaretto liquor at the bar they were just about to pass. Lowell gave Rayleen $20.00 for the liquor. She raced back to his car full of life and fun. Another button on her blouse had somehow come undone. When she got in, she slid over to his side and left the door open so that the dome light would stay on and Lowell could get a good view of the promised land. Rayleen kept the change from the $20.00.

Lowell would relive that night many times. There was the moment Rayleen suggested they stop for Amaretto. If he had hit the gas instead of the brakes, yes, that was the moment—hit the gas, take her up the road, and drop her off. Hit the brakes, get drunk, and screw.

Lowell looked at his watch. He must get to work. He glanced around his room, looked at the bodies again and again. So many of his days were spent to build something. To just sell it off or close it down was unthinkable. No, it must be passed on and cared for in the manner it was built. If not, then his time on earth was wasted.

Lowell thought about his time on earth. He saw far too many young corpses to think that there was any certainty in the time a person is allowed. He had no illusions of a long and happy old age. Death comes when it comes, and few have sufficient warning.

A plan began to form in little bits and pieces—a plan to claim Byron as his son. The plan needed time to work itself out, but a plan was forming and Lowell let it form, encouraged it to form.

CHAPTER ELEVEN

"So you were related to old Turk," Dwayne Coal asked.

"He was my wife's cousin," Lowell Maynard replied in a stiff, don't-ask-me-any-more-questions kind of way. Lowell Maynard sat uneasy in the middle of a jon boat sputtering through the back water of the flooded Meramec River. The sun was warm and reflected off the silver boat, burning Lowell's tender white legs without his knowledge.

The news of Turk's death was a welcome relief in Lowell's image important life. The old man had never asked for anything and never showed up at the home, but he was a loose cannon that would eventually hurt someone or get himself murdered by some river rat as looney as himself. Either way, Lowell was bound to be dragged into it as his closest relative.

Lowell wanted to settle his estate as quickly as possible. Turk had flood insurance and had filed a claim before his death. No settlement would be made until the water returned to its banks. Lowell wanted to make sure the old bar and tackle shop was a total loss. He inquired at Zeigler's, a small grocery store on the edge of Sycamore Village. Two men were recommended to him. The two young men sitting in the bow and stern of the sixteen foot jon boat had come highly recommended.

Dwayne and Dwight Coal exchanged a quick look when Lowell Maynard approached them with the idea that they take him to Turk's tackle shop. In an instant, the brothers read each other's mind. "I don't know," Dwayne said. "If we get out of the channel, you don't know what you're going to run into."

"Well, son, I know the river, and if you can follow simple instructions, we'll be all right," Lowell said.

"You said you'd give us $10.00 a piece. I guess for that kind of money we can take a chance," Dwight said.

"You boys don't happen to have a chainsaw, do you?" Lowell asked. The idea of a chainsaw caught Lowell at the last minute. His plan was to just open some doors and windows and make sure as much merchandise as possible was ruined or lost to pad the claim. Everyone knows you have to claim twice as much as you hope to get. Lowell could use a little pocket money. And it wasn't like he was doing anything wrong. That was the self-serving rationale that propelled this adventure.

The deal was made and they were on their way. Lowell looked closer at the Coal brothers as they churned up the channel toward Turk's. Their hair was long and stringy; they wore cutoff jeans and cheap tennis shoes without socks. Lowell could only imagine what those shoes smelled like at the end of summer. They seemed dull and simple. Lowell wished he had offered them $5.00.

When the trio reached Turk's, Lowell asked one of the boys if he would mind wading inside with him. "I don't want to get out of this boat for no amount of money," Dwight said.

"Don't look at me. I'm not goin' in there. There might be snakes in there," Dwayne said.

"Look here, boys, I'm paying top dollar for your services. I think you should get hold of your fears and do the simple task I'm paying you for."

"We agreed to bring you here. We never said we'd get in that backwater," Dwayne said.

The Coal brothers had a god-given talent for looking pathetic and wistful. One was less than half as good without the other. Together they bounced off each other and the result was slightly less than an Oscar winning performance.

Lowell could see these two were too stupid to argue with and decided to take care of the situation himself. Lowell had worn an old pair of Bermuda shorts just in case. He removed his tasseled leather loafers and his black nylon socks and emptied his pockets, placing the contents in his shoes and sliding them under the seat. The water was only slightly colder than he expected, but he persevered. He stepped out of the boat onto the landing at the top of twenty feet of stairs submerged in the water.

Dwight reversed the little motor and moved slowly away.

Lowell fumbled with keys until he found the one that opened the door. Dwayne and Dwight Coal both saw Lowell put his wallet inside his shoe under his seat, but focused looks in opposite directions disguised the fact that they followed his every move out of the corner of their eyes.

"Don't you shut that motor off," Lowell said. "I don't want to take a chance she won't start again."

"Don't you worry about that. I'll keep the RPM's up so she don't foul the sparkplug up on us," Dwayne said.

Lowell made his way into the shop. Bottles and boxes and bobbers and lures floated on the surface and he cut his way through the debris, catching a hook here and there. He moved slowly around the shelves and displays of river necessities. Most of the contents were ruined or gone. He had only a vague idea of what had been there before the water turned everything into brown slime. He inched along in the waist deep brown water, his tender feet feeling every grain of sand or pebble or stick on the floor.

Turk had been sick for several years and was a poor record keeper even before he went mad. Lowell suspected he would have a hard time collecting much insurance money if there were an examination of the contents. He was determined to make sure nothing was left and to try for the maximum the policy was worth. As he waded around in the store, he stepped gingerly, acutely aware of anything coming into contact with his feet that might be a snake. As he moved around, he would fake a stumble and rake everything within his reach off a shelf into the water.

Lowell looked back to the Coal brothers to see their reaction to his slapstick fall. Dwayne and Dwight smiled knowing smiles and said nothing. Lowell felt like he may have misjudged these river rats. They possibly weren't as stupid as he had thought.

"Hand me that chainsaw," Lowell said. Dwayne did as instructed without comment. "I guess you're wonderin' what I'm doin'," Lowell said.

"No, we know what you're doin'," Dwayne said.

Lowell looked back and forth between the brothers. Both sat stone still with barely perceptible smiles. Lowell pulled on the chainsaw ten times with no good result.

"You got to put the choke on," Dwight said.

Lowell began to get an uncomfortable feeling about the brothers. They watched him like a black snake watches a baby bird.

The chainsaw came to life and Lowell looked for weight bearing studs and slashed away at them. He had remained dry above the waist until his untrained hands began wrestling the chainsaw. The saw dipped into the water after bouncing off walls and ceiling. Lowell managed to keep the motor above the waterline, but the chain sent a spray of water and floating debris into his face and eyes. The mixture of tree bark, seed heads, dead insects, and hundreds of other particles of nature in rapid decline had a tendency to irritate the eyes.

Lowell pushed the saw away from himself and grabbed at his face with both hands. The saw gurgled for a moment, then went silent and sank to the floor. Lowell wailed in a muffled tone with his hands clutched to his face.

"That reminds me of something. I can't remember what." Dwight said.

"Fuck you," Dwayne said.

Lowell splashed water in his face and ground away at his eyes. "That's it. Let's go. Bring the boat in," he said.

Dwight didn't respond. The brothers sat as motionless as before.

"Bring the damn boat in," Lowell said. He now saw the foolishness of his plan. How stupid could he be to risk his life for a few thousand dollars. "Let's go. Bring the boat in," he said again.

At last Lowell's vision cleared enough to look in the direction of the idling outboard. "What the hell are you waiting for? Bring the boat in."

"Dwayne thinks this trip is worth more than $10.00 and he's the smart one," Dwight said.

Grins were exchanged between the boys. Dwight began his wild eyed lunatic act that had never failed him before. "Aaah, hah-hah-hah-hah-hah-hah-hah-haaa! You the carp."

Dwayne was all set to chime in with his own brand of insane, river folk gibberish until he heard Dwight call Lowell the carp. "What the hell was that?" Dwayne shot Dwight a sharp look that was easily interpreted to mean tone it down, you idiot. Lowell didn't pick up on it.

"We're just poor old country boys, Mr. Maynard. We don't know much, but we know enough," Dwayne said. He pulled his lips back tight across his teeth and laughed a sinister laugh and snorted planned snorts between breaths of laughter. Dwight jumped in with snorts and laughter of his own, trying as always not to be outdone by his brother.

Lowell said nothing and looked stunned by the theatrical display.

Dwayne suddenly produced Lowell's wallet and pulled out a thick wad of twenties from inside.

"You boys better think about what you're doin'. You'll go to jail for this," Lowell said.

"We don't think we's gonna go to jail. You know why?" Dwayne said.

"No, you tell me why. Is robbery not against the law around here?" Lowell asked. He felt the anger rise in himself and was sure he could throttle both boys at the same time if he could get within arm's reach of them.

"No, it's still against the law, but only if someone complains. We don't think you'll complain," Dwayne said.

"Hell, you may even be able to add this money to your claim, and furthermore not be out no money at all," Dwight said.

Dwayne gave his brother the look again. Furthermore? What the fuck you doin'? The thought was sent telepathically. Dwight received the message loud and clear and sent back "Eat me," with a tilt of his head and the words muttered out of the side of his mouth.

"That's right, Lowell," Dwayne said. He put a little extra effort into the pronunciation of Lowell. "We think this is money well spent on your part. You think this is the first time this river come out of its banks. Dealing with insurance companies is an art form, and my daddy was Rembrandt. Why, you just ruined an expensive chainsaw that belonged to my daddy and had great sentimental value. Naw, you're not going to complain. And unless you promise not to complain, you're going to have to swim and hike out of here."

"Then when you do go running to the sheriff, we're gonna tell him that you was tryin' to put a dick in our butt," Dwight said. "Dwayne, show him your honest but stupid look."

Lowell looked at Dwayne and was forced to admit to himself that the boy did look honest and stupid.

"When word gets out about charges like that, they'll never go away. How's that gonna affect business, Lowell?" Dwight said.

Dwayne counted out the money—$247.00. "Now that's gonna seem like a bargain when you consider what it could have cost you." Dwayne divided up the money, giving his brother $122.00. Dwight took note at once that Dwayne was coming out $3.00 to the advantage, a detail he would discuss later. Both boys rolled the bills into tight little wads and shoved them down the front of their shorts and into their underwear.

"You ready, Dwayne?" Dwight asked.

Dwayne reached into the bottom of the boat and came up with a Pepsi bottle held by the neck. "I'm ready. Are you ready, Dwight ?"

Dwight displayed his own bottle for Lowell to see. "I'm ready."

"Mr. Maynard, have we come to an agreement on price?" Dwayne asked.

Lowell's temper bubbled a few seconds more and then he did some rapid calculation on the distance to shore, then the walk up the long gravel road to the blacktop, and then possibly—no make that probably—injuries he would receive from pop bottles swung by healthy teenage boys, and then the story in the paper of alleged homosexual behavior. He pondered the situation for almost four seconds. "I think $247.00 is a fair price for the wonderful services you have provided me here today," Lowell said.

"I'm glad we got that worked out. You just pick up that chainsaw and I'll come over and pick you up," Dwight said.

Lowell bristled at the idea of putting his head under water. Not that he couldn't. He had held his breath the longest at his cousin Ellie's swimming pool on the Fourth of July in 1935. That water was clear; you could see your feet. Aunt Judith would throw dimes in the pool and he and his cousins would dive for them. Lowell made good money diving for dimes. He sat down one day and worked out the numbers and concluded that he could make $1.80 an hour if he could dive for dimes at a steady pace. That was good money in 1935.

Lowell's thoughts came back from cousin Ellie's and he plunged his head into the chocolate water of the Meramec. He opened his eyes like he was looking for dimes and there was nothing but orange blindness. He came to the surface and sucked for air too quickly. Parts of the entire state of Missouri and Illinois and possibly other states were sucked into his lungs.

Dwight and Dwayne shook their heads. Lowell coughed for the longest time. Dwight said, "When you get done coughin', climb in the boat." Dwight ran the boat in as close as possible and reversed the motor at the last moment to keep from running Maynard down. Lowell bent back in horror but recovered enough to climb in the boat. Dwayne and Dwight leaned the opposite way to counterbalance Lowell's weight as he awkwardly climbed into the aluminum life raft.

No sooner had Lowell settled into his seat than Dwayne rolled off backwards without a word and disappeared into the swollen waters of the Meramec. Lowell looked at the water, expecting Dwayne to break the surface at any moment. The surface was still. Dwight worked the motor with unconscious precision, holding the boat in one spot. Lowell watched the water on both sides of the boat. The brown surface displayed ripples and sharp lines that flowed away as far as you could see. He glanced toward Dwight to get a reaction from his face. Dwight looked bored. As strange as that seemed, Lowell was sure that was the expression Dwight wore.

Lowell heard the water splash and turned to find its source. The chainsaw slammed into the bottom of the jon boat and Dwayne launched himself back to his seat on the bow in one fluid motion. Dwight backed the boat up just enough to cut sharp and full throttle the three of them out into the channel. Lowell felt the wind in his face and suddenly felt the thrill of being one of the boys. He thought back on what Dwayne had said about this being a bargain at $247.00 and now that it was over and they were headed back, he had to agree.

Lowell arched into the wind and tried to think of a reason to stay out a little bit longer.

CHAPTER TWELVE

B ud Browdy and Martha Skaggs both attended Festus High School in 1947. Bud was a senior; Martha was a freshman. Bud was a star player on a state championship team; Martha was a skinny, plain girl from a poor family. Bud played four positions, including pitcher on the school baseball team; Martha paid no attention to baseball before seeing Bud play the game. He was the best anyone had ever seen. He was sure to be a professional baseball player. They say the Cardinals sent a scout to take a look at him.

Martha studied Bud from afar. She fell in love with him and dreamed that someday he would love her too. She could hold on to the dream as long as she never met him. If she were to be introduced to Bud she would see in his eyes at once that he was not interested in her, and she would be crushed. She could not take that chance. She avoided him if she could and never looked straight at him if he could see her. She went to the home games and cheered until she was hoarse.

Bud's father worked for the railroad. Bud was the oldest of three boys. His mother did laundry every day, so it seemed. Bud matured early. He had to shave daily during his last year in high school. He was a tall boy, six feet, three inches. He had speed and agility. Bud went away after graduation. He spent three years in the minor leagues with the Detroit Tigers farm system. It didn't work out. Bud joined the army in 1951 and went to Korea to fight the communists.

Martha left home after graduation for no reason other than she felt it was the right thing to do—give her poor parents one less mouth to feed. She moved in with a widow aunt in St. Louis and went to work at the VA hospital.

Martha held on to her small town style. Her hair and dress remained simple and conservative. She wore only a touch of lipstick. Nature would not let her hide. She had filled out and had become an attractive young woman. She had several suitors but none of them measured up to her dream and they felt her disapproval and went away.

Martha faced the reality that she would never see Bud again. It was time to earn a living and see what fate had in store, but a part of her wanted to believe they would meet again some day. And what if they did? Would she run and hide as she did as a child? No, she would say hello and ask about his family, relive a high school memory, make up a lie: I heard you married. Who is the lucky girl? she would ask. He had to be married or engaged. She wouldn't allow herself to believe him to still be available. No man so handsome and intelligent and fun to be with could remain single with so many conniving females on the hunt.

The Korean War continued long past the six months most people thought it would take to kick the crap out of a bunch of little Jap look-alikes. The veterans hospital in St. Louis put Martha to work the day she applied. She rode the bus to and from her aunt's house. Overtime at the hospital was plentiful; she took all she could stand.

The wounded men lay side by side in crowded rooms and in the halls. Many were bandaged so completely they became the same. Martha finished her shift as a practical nurse at midnight. She walked down the street to the all night diner and had some ham and eggs, then went back to the hospital to roam the wards and sit with injured boys.

Tonight she peeked in and out of the rooms looking for a boy, any boy, who couldn't sleep and needed someone to talk to. "How you doin'?" she said to a boy who was crying softly in a half sleep.

The boy pulled himself back to the present and was embarrassed that this pretty girl had caught him at a weak moment. "I'm doing okay," came in a trembling voice behind the gauze.

All the boy's head was bandaged except his right eye and mouth. Martha pulled a stool close to the bed where she could talk in quiet tones. "How long have you been here?" Martha's lips were only inches away from the bundle of cotton gauze that contained the boy's head.

"I don't know." The voice was weak, not weak from loss of air but from loss of spirit.

"Well, it don't matter. The thing is, you're here. I know you're all busted up, but you survived when a lot of others didn't. I wish my man was here right now. I don't care if he was all shot up; I'd rather have him here and alive and know he would stay alive and know that he was going to get well and that we were going to get married. That's the way your girl will feel. I know it."

"I . . . I . . . I don't have a girl," the bundle of cotton replied.

Martha stopped stone cold as if she had been struck by lightning. She slowly moved her hand across the surface of the covers and lightly patted his private parts. "Honey, once word gets out about what you're packin' down there, I don't think that will be a problem."

The single eye followed her eyes. A slightly constricted chuckle followed by a cough rumbled out from the cotton ball. His lips pulled back in a reluctant smile.

"I'm sorry, honey, that was unfair of me to take advantage of you like that. I tell you what you can do. You can get yourself a handful of tit if you want." Martha leaned in so the boy wouldn't have to stretch.

"Maybe later," the cotton ball said.

The two shared a muffled laugh. "When was the last time you wrote home?" Martha asked. The sounds of the barely living and the newly dying made a chorus of noise in the background like bullfrogs on a pond.

"It's been awhile," the cotton ball said.

"Then nobody knows you've been hurt?"

"I guess the army told them." His voice was unsure and newly concerned.

"Well, even if the army told them, it's not the same as hearin' it from you," Martha whispered. "Let's write a letter."

"I don't write many letters," the boy said.

"Well now's a good time to start." She opened a drawer of the boy's bedside table and brought out a pad of paper and a pencil. "Who do you want to write to?" Martha asked, trying hard to keep the mood light.

"My mother, I guess."

"What's her name? No, first off, what's your name?"

"Scott Vogel."

"Well, Scott, I'm Martha," she whispered to a spot of cotton where his ear would be.

Several boys groaned as a muscle spasm or a nightmare jolted their sleep. The squeaking wheel of a cart being pushed out in the hall became louder then faded away.

"Well, we'll just start this out Dear Mother. Now what do you want to tell her?"

"I don't know. I don't know how to talk in letters," Scott said.

"I can fix that," Martha whispered. "You see, I know magic and what I can do is bring your mother here in the wink of an eye." Martha closed her eyes and snapped her fingers. "Okay, she's here. She's right on the other side of that curtain and she can hear everything you say. But she's not allowed to answer you or let you see her. That's the rules of magic. So go on and talk to her and I promise she'll hear you."

Scott moved his eye slowly away from Martha and toward the end of the bed where a curtain on a metal frame served as meager privacy. He smiled faintly. "You say my mother's on the other side of there?"

"Well I believe she is. Let me see. Miss Vogel, you over there?" Martha stepped to the end of the bed, poked her head around the corner, mumbled a few words, and nodded her head up and down as she stepped back. "She's there all right. She's just waitin' for you to tell her somethin'—anything. She's so desperate for news, anything you want to share with her would be fine. She said she'll be back tomorrow and the next day and all the days to come so you don't have to tell her everything today. Just what you want to share right now."

"Okay," Scott said. He continued to look at the curtain. The make believe world where she stood waiting for him to speak did make it a little easier.

"Hi, Mom, I'm okay." Scott choked up and couldn't continue. He was embarrassed to be crying in front of this pretty girl and the humiliation he felt for not being stronger only drove his despair deeper and into more uncontrolled sobs.

"I'm going to look around and see if any of these other men need anything. I'll be back in a few minutes."

The use of the word *men* had not been by accident. Martha stepped away from the sobbing cotton ball and moved through the canyon of white curtains and beds toward the hall and began her own soft sobbing. She had seen too much; she needed to get away. But she needed to stay. Tonight was not a good night, but there had been good nights. She wrote hundreds of letters. Her writing style was conservative and neat.

Martha walked to the end of the hallway and dabbed at her eyes with a small towel. She had become hardened to the ugliness of young men torn apart and suffering, but she refused to fault herself for crying once in a while and feeling. What else makes us human? she believed. She had become better at holding it in until she could reach the hallway and she was much faster at recovery. She took pride in that, but she refused to harden herself any more than necessary. She had seen others who had, and they were empty and dull. It's okay to cry, she would silently lecture herself. It's okay to cry; just get it out and move on. Those were the rules Martha forced herself to conform to.

Martha washed her face and crept so quietly back to cotton ball's bedside that he wasn't aware of her return. "Let's try this again," Martha said, her mouth close to his ear, if he still had an ear.

"Okay," Scott said.

Martha managed to get a four page letter out of Scott before he fell asleep. She was going home now, her strength gone, her emotions on the ragged edge.

A voice carried down the long hallway that led to the main entrance. She knew that voice. It's Bud. Her mind exploded with happiness, only to be doused with elementary thinking. If Bud is here, he's hurt.

Martha began to quicken her pace and within a few steps she was running, still hearing that voice. It must be him. He was talking about baseball. She rounded the corner and there he was—Bud. It is Bud. He sat in a wheelchair, both hands and both feet in small balloons of white gauze.

"Bud," Martha gasped.

Bud turned from his conversation and took notice of the pretty girl who seemed about to jump out of her skin. She looked at his bandages with disbelief. Bud felt compelled to say something. "Frostbite. They say I'm gonna be okay," he said, giving Martha his big grin.

Martha threw herself at him and pressed her mouth to his. Bud did not pull away. Martha had to at last when she needed air. "I hope you all get well soon," Martha said. She scanned the room and acknowledged three other young men wearing the same pajamas, sitting in the same wheelchairs, with the same hands and feet bandaged. "I hope you all get well soon," she said again, then turned and ran for the door like the devil himself was chasing her.

Bud turned to his companions, wearing his biggest grin, and said, "This happens to me all the time."

CHAPTER THIRTEEN

B ud Browdy should have been a baseball player. People who liked Bud said so. Bud heard it over and over. Those fools don't know a good player when they see one, he was told almost daily. His hands and feet still caused him problems. He lost his little toe on his left foot; he had no feeling in two fingers of his right hand.

The retreat of the 7th Division started on December 3, 1950. The damn Chinese entered the war and never gave the boys any rest. The long march and the intense cold still occupied Bud's dreams. Many of his comrades lost more than a toe. Bud considered himself lucky and was glad to be out of the army.

Bud worked for Hansom Lumber as a yard man, loading trucks and unloading trucks. A green '38 Ford panel truck stirred a memory. This one was freshly painted and in good condition. The last time he'd seen an old wagon like this it was sitting on blocks and converted into a chicken house. How the years had passed, he thought. His back hurt today more than most days—that dull aching stiffness that inspires you to twist your head around all day long.

Bud carried two-by-twelves's one at a time from the rack to the panel truck. Hansom's Lumber Yard had been his last stop after two failed businesses. Old man Hansom, the son of the founder of the store, hired Bud as a favor. Bud had accumulated a large debt at the store before his roofing business went under and Hansom withheld $10.00 a week from his pay and didn't charge him interest. Every year Hansom deducted $1,000.00 from the debt as a Christmas bonus. Bud was grateful. The arrangement had kept him from filing for bankruptcy.

Bud's debts were repaid. Seven years had flown by. He was free and clear.

The two-by-twelve's Bud carried were sixteen-footers. The weight alone made the job harder than most, but the length added gut wrenching torque. He carried the lumber on his shoulder across the yard. He slid the last board in place and circled the old truck like a prospective buyer, letting the memories flood his mind. Martha's father had turned one just like this into a chicken house and it sat in their front yard.

Martha had been coy after their first meeting. She came to his bedside like she did all the boys and wrote some letters for him but never explained that kiss. Rumors spread among the boys that she was an easy screw. Bud didn't want to believe it, but too many guys knew a guy that knew a guy that screwed her.

Martha kept her distance and Bud pretended not to be interested in her. Then word spread that she quit. Some of the boys said she got caught screwing a guy in the shower room and was fired. Bud didn't believe that either. He found out where her final check was to be mailed and was amazed that it was close to his own boyhood home in Festus. When he was released a few weeks later, he looked her up. A battered mailbox matched the address he was given. A washed out gravel driveway led to a rough old house surrounded by a bare dirt yard. The house had a small front porch covered with rusty corrugated metal sheeting. All the walls of the house leaned a little.

Bud felt sure he had come to the wrong place, but then Martha came out the door. She wore men's overalls and a cotton shirt. The denim overalls were worn white in the knees and around the pockets. Her shoes were leather saddle oxfords with the strings missing and the soles coming off. She saw the stranger in the yard and was about to ask his business when recognition hit her. She was delighted and Bud was delighted that she was delighted. Then she became aware of her clothing and turned for the door, but she was unable to make her escape. Her father came out, followed by her mother and her three sisters and her two brothers. The whole tattered looking group stared with open mouths at the stranger in the yard.

Bud had a dozen long-stemmed roses in a white box with a red ribbon tucked under his arm. He shifted around for what seemed like eternity until Martha's father spoke.

"If you're here to sell somethin', you're wasting your time and mine."

"No, I . . . I . . . uh, came to see Martha," Bud said.

Now even the youngest boys understood, and the older girls began to whisper and giggle. Martha couldn't just leave him there, as much as she wanted to go change. She walked out to meet him with the whole family watching.

"These are for you," Bud said.

Martha opened the box and breathed in the sweet aroma and then to everyone's shock, kissed Bud on the lips. Her sister squealed and her brothers covered their eyes. Martha's parents gave each other questioning looks. "We were just about to have supper. Won't you join us?" her father said.

The table was small and crowded. Martha's young brothers squeezed their chairs up close on both sides of Bud. The meal consisted of cooked cabbage and cornbread. Bud had never in his life sat down to a meal without meat. He felt sure he could have eaten the entire table of food alone.

"Would you like some more?" Martha asked.

"No thanks, I'm full," Bud said.

That evening they kissed and hugged on the porch swing. The moon placed a spotlight on the yard; the old truck glowed with a soft light reflected from faded gray paint. Chickens flapped in and out of the driver's side window.

Martha confessed to her high school crush; Bud remembered her as a quiet, mousey little girl always in the back of a crowd. They talked till dawn.

Bud was eager to tell Martha at supper about seeing the old truck that day. He was sure it would stir her memories too. They had been married now for eleven years, but that night on the porch swing was their sweetest memory.

A flatbed backed up to a rack on the other side of the yard. A load of four-by-four posts had to be stacked. Bud stretched his back and went to work.

CHAPTER FOURTEEN

Bud Browdy awoke hours before daylight. He wanted more sleep but his mind refused to rest. He left Martha to her envied slumber as quietly as he could. At the kitchen table, he shuffled envelopes containing bills like a deck of cards. No clear strategy for paying them came forward, so he put them aside. Just a couple of months ago, he could pay his bills and even had a small savings. That was before, before he accepted an invitation to join the Reform slate and run for sheriff.

Bud shook his head in disbelief at his own actions. He thought back on how it all came about. William Brace and Thomas Sorage had come into the Jury Room. The Jury Room was the name of a bar/restaurant across the street from the courthouse in Hillsboro. The place was frequented by a diverse group of people who did business at the county seat. Bill and Tom were regulars. They both had successful law practices and liked to tip back a few at the end of the day and discuss how the world could be a better place if they were in charge.

Bud's part-time job as bartender at the Jury Room allowed him to take part in the discussions three nights a week. Then one evening the three of them decided to take over the world. Bud, always the voice of reason, convinced the two attorneys they might be a little too ambitious and would be happier in the long run if they started out by taking over the courthouse.

The plan was hatched. William Brace would run for prosecuting attorney, Thomas Sorage would run for presiding judge, and Bud would run for sheriff. The Reform slate would sweep cronyism and corruption out of Hillsboro.

Bill and Tom filled out the necessary paperwork at the last minute. The slate was on the ballot. William Brace made speeches to the Chamber of Commerce, Thomas Sorage made speeches to the Knights of Columbus and the Elks, and Bud Browdy bought a staple gun and stuck a poster on every telephone pole and tree he could find. The posters proclaimed "BRACE, SORAGE, BROWDY" in bold letters and in small type read "For a Better Tomorrow."

Bud attended several rallies with his running mates but made only short, well-rehearsed speeches. The DeSoto picnic was a small, rural affair, and Bud was convinced to go alone. Bill and Tom wanted a day off and figured there wouldn't be enough votes there to matter. Martha had agreed to go with him but decided at the last minute that her sister needed her more.

Bud skipped his breakfast—a mistake. Hindsight truly is 20-20 he would later conclude. It had been a hot morning so early in June and everyone wanted to buy Bud a beer. He knew the hazard and did well at first. He would accept a paper cup of foamy, cool beer with a big smile, take a sip, let out with a big *Aaaah*, slap the man on the back, shake his hand, and ask for his vote. At the first opportunity, he would put the cup on a table or car hood and pretend to forget it was there while he explained to the folks the problems in the county and how the sheriff's department with a strong sheriff could turn things around.

One of Bud's miscalculations that day was underestimating his support at this gathering. These people loved him. The outpouring of affection and support was intoxicating. Every man at the picnic wanted to shake his hand and buy him a beer and talk about what a great day it would be when he was elected.

The time had slipped by quickly and the sun was at full strength. The brown wool suit coat was the second mistake of the day. It had seemed like the perfect compromise of dignity and common man affordability. In hindsight, he could see how the want of a nail could cost you a war. In this case, a day too warm, a coat too heavy, a shirt too wet, a beer too many.

Bud stepped up on the makeshift podium, which had been thoughtfully put in the sun so everyone could get a good look at him. The brown wool material across his shoulders and back pulled in the heat and held it there. He knew he should have taken it off after everyone had seen him wearing it, and now it was time for his speech and his dress shirt was soaked through. With his handkerchief in hand, Bud mopped his face and delivered the campaign speech of his life.

The sipping from the paper cups had a cumulative effect on Bud's empty stomach. He swayed in the heat at the end of the tent full of supporters. The crowd of onlookers seemed not to feel the heat—the women in their cotton dresses and the men in their short sleeves. How he envied them.

Bud's white dress shirt lay threadbare and thin against his ample belly and chest. Bud peeked under his jacket for the third time, each time hoping it would not look as bad as he remembered it, but it did. He might as well be naked. He had always thought the brown circles around his nipples were too large. Although he had no charts to go by, he was sure that if there were such charts, he would be in the one percent freak section. If he took his coat off now, no one would be able to focus on his speech. They would all wonder silently what was wrong with the picture. Then one by one, their gaze would fall on the huge brown spots on his chest. So the coat stayed on.

The words poured out effortlessly. The crowd applauded often. They couldn't get enough. Bud had completed the speech he had planned—his standard speech on law and order, the evils of drugs and gambling, and his long term plan to right these wrongs. But the crowd wanted more, and Bud was so thrilled with his reception, even with the sweat pouring out of him, he talked on.

Bud started talking to the crowd like a trusted friend. He started telling inside stories of things he knew or suspected. A few days later, the story of the speech was all over the local papers and was picked up by the St. Louis papers—the Post and the Globe. Bud read the accounts of the speech and was shocked. He knew he had rambled on, but the things he had said . . . He had named names and called the staff at the sheriff's office leeches just because they were related to the sheriff. He said he had evidence of graft. "Why on earth would you say that?" he thought out loud.

He had lost. Bud sat at the kitchen table with his head down staring at a cup of black coffee. The hard wooden chair offered little comfort for a tired body. The effort to lift the cup to his mouth seemed too much. His entire nest egg had been spent on the campaign. He could go back to roofing—that would pay the bills and get him caught up again for a few years. The thought of nailing shingles again pushed his spirits down to a point close to panic. He was too old to go back to roofing; he knew that. Roofing is a young man's job; and if you're going to do it as an old man, you need to stay with it over the years. To go back to it now would break him down in no time.

Walter Hansom had made it clear that if he took off to go campaigning, he would not be able to take him back. "The customer comes first," Walter told him. "You go out callin' the sheriff a skunk and you're going to drive business off. People will go down the road to avoid having to talk to you. You better think hard on this. You've done a good job here selling lumber and such. The customers, the contractors, and the home repair folks like you. You got a future here. You're only forty-four. In another ten years, you'll be assistant manager here."

Walter Hansom, a small wiry man in great shape at eighty-six years of age, thought everyone should be in great shape, and that they should work and work hard.

Bud still had his bartender job three nights a week. He was sure he could get more hours if he asked, but that wouldn't pay the bills. Walter had warned him. Now here he was broke, tired, and unemployed.

Bud gazed around the kitchen trying to think his way out of this mess. The shrill ring of the phone broke the silence. He didn't want to answer; he didn't want to talk to anyone right now. But Martha was sleeping. He jumped up and snatched the phone from the wall before it could ring again. "Hello."

"Yes . . . uh . . . is this Sheriff Walter Bud Browdy I'm talking to?"

"Yes, and who are you to be calling me this early?"

"I am sorry, Sheriff, to be so bold, but it was necessary. My name is Lowell Maynard of Maynard Funeral Home."

"Mr. Maynard, if you're calling to sell me a funeral plan, you're gonna get a cussin' like you never had before in your life," Bud said.

"No, no, no. This is about your future, Sheriff."

"Mr. Maynard, you keep callin' me sheriff. I'm not the sheriff and you know it. So stop it."

"You will be if you'll allow me to explain."

Bud felt a glimmer of hope—not real hope, just a speck of hope, the kind you have when you throw a small wooden ring toward a case of Coke bottles at the carnival. "Okay, I'm listening."

"Tomorrow night, Sheriff Wells will be doin' a live talk radio show with Willy Wally at KJCF. I have bought the next half hour for you, Bud. When Sheriff Dan Wells starts to leave the broadcast booth, you'll come bustin' in with an armload of books and papers and challenge Wells to defend himself against the proof you've got right there. Wells will bolt; I just know it."

"That might be true if I had an armload of proof," said Bud.

"That's the beauty of it, Mr. Browdy. They're running scared. You must have hit a nerve. They're sure you've got the goods on 'em. I heard it from a source right inside their camp. If you show up at the radio station while he's still on the air with Willy Wally, full of bluster and swagger shoving papers around, Wells will refuse to debate you. After he leaves, you'll have half an hour to sway the election. The farmers are your salvation, Mr. Browdy. The only reason you're not projected to win this close race is because it's so hard to get folks out to vote. You know how it is, a tractor needs a fuel pump or there's a new batch of piglets that need extra care.

"Now if you'll take my advice, as soon as Wells leaves, you'll forget about those corruption charges and the ugliness of the campaigning. You just talk to the people about how important it is for them to vote. Now Wally's a friend of mine and he can't afford to openly take a side in this election. He's got commercial time to sell, but he's on our side, and he'll ask you the right kind of questions. All you have to do is give honest answers. Wally will mix in some country music along with the hog prices and whatever else farmers care about, and they'll be listening. This is a popular show among these folks. All you have to do is talk about how great this country is and how good it's been to you personally.

"I was in the crowd at the church picnic last week. I was doin' a little campaigning of my own. You know there's a lot of old people at those things. Someone's going to have to bury them. Ha-ha-ha. Might as well be me. Anyway, you talk to the people like you did that day at the picnic and you can win this thing. Only don't drink any beer beforehand. Ha-ha-ha. Sorry, Sheriff. I mean Bud. By the time Wells figures out you were bluffin', it will be too late. The Willy Wally Show carries a lot of weight out among those farmers. If you fail to win, I'm the one out the $5,000.00 for the radio time and there won't be any trouble from Wells 'cause he'll just want the whole thing forgotten."

Bud thought about his next question carefully, but could not think of a careful way of asking it. "What do you get out of this?" he asked.

"Well, that's a straightforward question, Sheriff. Have you had your breakfast yet?"

"No."

"Well, why don't you meet me at the Country Kitchen for breakfast. We can work out some details and I believe come to an understanding."

Bud agreed to the meeting and went back to his chair. He tried to hold back the sense of hope that began to pulse up his spine. Defeat could suddenly turn to victory. He must not let himself get too excited. He didn't know this Lowell Maynard.

CHAPTER FIFTEEN

Only one other car, a black Cadillac, occupied space on the parking lot in front of the Country Kitchen diner. Bud stepped into a water-filled pothole as he climbed out of his older, faded, dusty Dodge pickup. He cussed softly and shook water from his foot.

Maynard was sitting in a corner booth looking at a menu. The place was all but empty this time of morning. It was four thirty and the rush wouldn't start for another hour.

Bud waved and threw a big smile at the waitress. He sat down across from Lowell without saying a word. Suddenly he was sorry he had come. He felt he was about to make a deal with the devil and give up his soul to win an election, if winning were still possible.

"Don't look so glum, Mr. Browdy," Lowell said. He thought better of calling him sheriff. He was a much more imposing man at close range. "Let's order our breakfast and while we wait I'll explain myself."

Bud suddenly began to think of himself as a prom date. If he let Maynard buy him breakfast, he would have to put out. "I'll buy my own eggs, thank you." Then he felt a little foolish because Maynard hadn't offered to pay for the meal.

"That's fine, Mr. Browdy."

"Call me Bud."

"Okay, Bud. Let me say right up front that I'm not going to ask you to do anything outside of the law."

Sally came over and took their order. After she had dropped out of hearing range, Lowell took a sip of his coffee and placed the cup down with a solid clunk on the table, an indication he was able to talk business. "I never got along with Dan Wells. He made problems for me on a regular basis. That alone would make me want to see him defeated."

"What sort of problems?" Bud asked.

"Oh, just small things like promising me a police car to stop traffic for a funeral here and there. If I made the request personally, along with a hundred dollar bill, it got done in quick order. If not, the paper work got lost and made me look like a fool. I can't leave one of my customers and his or her grieving family stuck at an intersection. I end up out there myself directing traffic looking ridiculous."

"I see," said Bud. "That still doesn't add up to $5,000.00."

"No, probably not to most people, but I've got another favor to ask of the new sheriff. You see, Sheriff . . . uh, Bud . . . when you become sheriff, you'll become privilege to a lot of secrets. You know, like a priest or a doctor or a funeral director."

Bud didn't like the direction the conversation was taking. He didn't like secrets and he didn't want to hear one. "I'd rather not know what you're about to tell me, Mr. Maynard."

"It comes with the job, Bud. I'm telling you the truth. You can't escape it."

Sally brought their breakfast with a big smile as she cluncked down the large porcelain dinner plates like a veteran waitress with no time to waste. She refilled their coffee cups with well aimed sloshes tipped from her pot a foot above the cup. Both men had droplets of coffee splashed on the hand closest to the cup. Then she was gone.

Bud wiped the coffee from his hand, as did Lowell. Both looked around to see where the waitress had gone and made a mental note to sit back in the booth when she returned.

Bud buttered his pancakes and considered his situation. "If you tell me anything about a crime, I'm not going to keep it a secret," he said.

"Well, sure, I wouldn't put you in a position like that."

"Okay, then, let's have it. What do you want for your money?" Bud asked with a bite of pancakes in his mouth.

"Well, Bud, all I'm askin' you to do for me, if we can get you elected, is to take a personal interest in a boy that's headed for trouble."

"What boy and what kind of trouble?"

Suddenly this had caught Bud's interest.

"His name is Byron Creed. He lives down there on Sycamore Road."

Bud was familiar with the area—the raised homes, the old refrigerators in the yards, cars up on blocks. "So what's this boy done?" he asked.

"I'm not sure of anything specific, but I know he's running with a rough crowd and there's a lot of car stealin' going on that he might be involved in. If you could unofficially look into his situation, maybe let him know you're watchin' him, he might be able to outgrow his bad behavior."

Bud poured more honey on his hotcakes and let the information and the honey soak in. So this is how it begins, he thought. You go around telling everyone that'll listen what an honest sheriff you'll be and before you even get the job, you're makin' deals. He pondered on it a second more.

"Aw, crap," he said out loud, "I'll do it. But only to a point. This Byron Creed ain't gonna get away with much. But if you can pull off this radio thing and get me elected, I'll do what I can. And if that's not good enough for you, then we're done talking."

"That'll be fine. I trust you. That's why you're gettin' my vote," Lowell said.

Bud dragged his shirt sleeve across the honey cakes when he reached across the table to shake hands with Lowell. Lowell noticed the honey dripping from his sleeve but acted as though he didn't.

CHAPTER SIXTEEN

On his way home, the defeatism started to take hold again. His old truck swayed and squeaked up and down the narrow two-lane back roads of Jefferson County. The county was growing fast and the roads were falling behind. Many of them were old cow paths with a thin layer of asphalt busting up on the surface. In the early morning light, when everything along the road looks gray and tired, Bud reviewed the deal he had just made. I'll do what I can. That was all he had promised.

When Bud arrived home, Martha was at the kitchen table in her flannel housecoat and curlers. She beamed with happiness when she saw him; she always did. Martha was a happy person from birth. Bud counted his blessings every day. One look into her face could lift his spirit as nothing else would. Martha had total confidence in him and would refuse to listen to any possibility of failure on his part. She was sure he would be sheriff and that he would be a great sheriff.

Bud discussed the morning meeting with Lowell Maynard. He discussed everything with Martha. She would listen, nod her head at the appropriate times, smile, and tell Bud he would know what was best.

Martha was true to form on this occasion. Then she startled Bud with a simple question. "Why does Mr. Maynard care about this Byron boy?"

The simplicity of the question pushed Bud down to the lowest reaches of his ego. He wanted to be a sheriff, an investigator, and had not thought to ask the simplest of questions—what the boy's problems were to Maynard. And even more revealing, Maynard hadn't said why he was concerned. Now the whole thing seemed foolish and impossible. He would not be able to pull this off.

Martha put her hand on his shoulder. She could sense the loss of confidence the question had caused. "It probably doesn't matter," she said. Bud nodded his head. He wanted to go take a nap. He could work all this out later.

Bud's spirit was dragging the floor. For the first time he was scared. There was no escaping the future. It would come and he had to deal with whatever came. He was in it too far now to do anything else. The problem as he saw it now in a state of inadequate self-pity was impossible. If he wins, he temporarily at best escapes poverty until he's run out of office or must resign in shame. If he loses, he's doomed to poverty and shame right away. The poverty part is just a matter of speech, Bud reasons with himself. He knows he can always put food on the table unless he gets crippled or sick. It's just that he had always thought he could do better, not just for himself but for Martha. She had been so unselfish for so long, he just wanted to give her a little better life and make her proud of him. At this low moment in time, he wasn't sure he wanted to win.

For nine weeks, Bud had been telling anyone who would listen what a great sheriff he would be if he could just have their vote. Now it was close to the end and if he won, he would have to try and deliver on his promises. He didn't have a single friend in the sheriff's department and, in fact, had made many enemies among the deputies and with city hall in general.

What if he bungled the job so badly he cost people their lives? Would he ever be able to live with that? Bud had never dealt with this kind of uncertainty before. A nap. That was the answer. Just get some sleep. He could work this out with a little rest.

Bud stretched out on the old iron bed he and Martha shared. He didn't remove his boots; he just hung them over the end. The bedroom was filled with shadows and was cool and quiet at the back of the old three-room house. There were four rooms now with the addition of the bedroom; the new bedroom Bud had promised he would add right after they were married. The years went by and still no bedroom addition.

When Bud was finally able to make good on his promise and built their new bedroom, financial problems hit again and he was never able to find the time or money to completely finish the project. The drywall was in but had never been taped or painted. The floor was still plywood. Bud had found an area rug that all but filled the room, leaving only a few inches of bare wood around the edges. The rug was a temporary solution to bare feet on a cold floor and would only be needed for a couple of months, Bud had said at the time. Four years later, the rug was still there and looked the worse for wear.

Bud had not run new heat ducts to the room either and it was much cooler in the winter than the rest of the house. Bud pulled the bedspread over his upper half and stared at the ceiling of brown drywall, nail heads, and gaping seams. A mantle clock that had been in Martha's family ticked loudly on the dresser.

In the beginning of their marriage, Bud hated the loud ticking; but Martha loved the clock so much, which was a point of pride, and believed it to be very valuable. And since it was all she had brought to the marriage besides the clothes on her back, she was determined to use it and display it.

The nap didn't help. Bud awoke from a restless sleep. Martha was gone; she was off somewhere running an errand for somebody or helping a friend she had just met. Bud had long ago given up on trying to keep track of her. The notes she used to leave were jumbled with possible destinations, that changed to meet crises or fabric sales or sick kids or dogs that belonged to somebody else. Martha filled her days so completely that nothing new could be added without a cancellation of some kind. The only thing certain about Martha's whereabouts was that she would be home for the evening meal—a self-imposed duty she took very seriously.

Bud made himself a bologna sandwich and a cup of coffee and went outside. A walk around the old farm always soothed his mind. The ripe clover heads made a carpet over the old hog pen. The fence of rough cut lumber and rusting wire was on its side in several places around the pen. The small pond had been dried up for years and was taken over by the clover and wild grasses. Flecks of white clover blossoms covered the wet toes of Bud's cowboy boots as he strolled around the place, taking large mouthfuls of sandwich, to be washed down with slurps of hot coffee. He gazed on the relics of past lives.

Bud walked to the back side of the empty pond and examined the rocks stacked in neat rows—rocks dug out of the fields, stacked in small piles, then loaded on mule-drawn sleds and restacked to form the back wall of the pig pond. He tried to estimate the number of trips, the numbers of smashed fingers, the number of strained backs it must have taken to complete this task. Whenever he looked at this monument of hard work, it made him feel guilty for his own self-pity. The hard lives of those who had come before him made his problems look small.

The wind brought the sound of a hammer driving a nail half a mile away. The crack of the hammer from far away was part of the natural order of things on the ridge tops of Jefferson County. Like the woodpeckers' song, the hammer's crack had been a constant since before 1890 when the town of Blackwell was built. Somewhere on another ridge top, someone was trying to hold together the old homestead or start a new one; and would most likely fail or fall far below expectations.

The county was growing, but no one was getting rich as far as Bud could see. Small farms were drying up at an ever increasing pace. Those who couldn't see what was happening were doomed to suffer the most. Bud considered this thought for a moment and believed he had uncovered a new universal truth. He brightened with his discovery. A moment passed and he had to admit to himself that his deep thought of adapt or die was the oldest truth of all.

Bud swallowed the last of his coffee, feeling better about himself. A moment ago, he was a wise old scholar thinking important thoughts about the truths of life. A moment later he was a fool re-inventing the wheel. This sort of setback should have made him feel worse, but he laughed at himself for being profound and all knowing. He laughed at himself the way a man in a barrel going over the falls must laugh at himself. No one made him climb in the barrel; he put himself there and bragged that he could go over the falls unhurt. That man must laugh at his foolhardy decision just before he goes over the edge. Bud laughed at his own foolhardy decision. He was about to go over the edge now and there was nothing to do but laugh at the fool who willingly climbed in the barrel.

Bud walked back to the house with a renewed energy. Somehow he would survive whatever the future would bring. He willed himself to survive.

The boy is his son. The thought raced forward from some unknown recess in his brain. Bud knew at once he was right. Byron Creed must be Lowell's son; that's all it could be.

I can do this job. Bud's confidence soared.

CHAPTER SEVENTEEN

The day had arrived. Bud rose with the sun. He read and reread the newspaper accounts of his now infamous speech at the DeSoto picnic. One newspaper described his speech as a call to arms. Bud was unsure of what that meant, but he kind of liked it. Bud never lied to himself about his public speaking ability. He just assumed he would get better at it. He never did. If he wrote out a long speech covering all the information he wanted to discuss and then tried to memorize it or even worse, try to read it to an audience, he was sure his droning, monotone voice could put a hamster to sleep. He would think of something else. He didn't have to be at the radio station until six thirty that night. Plenty of time, he assured himself.

Martha made him a huge breakfast of eggs, biscuits and gravy, and sausage. Bud would not eat again until after this radio thing was over. He normally had faith in his stomach behaving itself under stress, but this was a different kind of fear. His mind shifted again. Index cards. He would use index cards with short reminders in large letters. He made himself a note. His mind raced with thoughts of possible foul ups. So much counted on this radio thing. Would he freeze up? Would his brain go into neutral and refuse to budge?

"You'll do fine," Martha said, sensing his worry.

"You always say I'll do fine. You said I'd do fine when I got into the roofing business."

"Well you did too. That company should have stood behind the shingles they made. That wasn't your fault."

"You said I'd do fine in the asphalt business too."

"Well, if a man's partner borrows money against the equipment and skips town with the money, I guess you could say the man should have picked a better partner. Maybe you just trust people too much. That's probably not a good trait to have as a sheriff, but you'll do fine."

Martha wasn't offering anything new in her show of confidence, but Bud appreciated it just the same. This was his last chance at success. He couldn't fight back from failure again. Each time had taken its toll; and if he failed here, he would end his days working long hours at low wages just to pay the bills. Martha deserved better than that.

Bud rallied his spirits again and studied his note cards, each with the opening sentence of a thought he believed in. One card read: The Deputy's Thankless Job. With this opening, he would expand on the rich history of the deputy's job in Jefferson County. Many of the men on the force today were great grandsons of men who chased robbers, bears, and Indians not so long ago. Like their fathers and their fathers' fathers, they do what needs to be done with little fanfare and meager pay.

On another card was written: The Men and Women Who Work the Land. On this subject he would discuss the farmers' role in this county and country. He would promise a sheriff's department that recognized the problems of farmers and rural America.

On another card: In God We Trust—to lead into how that played a part in our lives.

There were eight more file cards with the opening line on gambling, drugs, corruption, Mafia infiltration, money management, prostitution, and bravery; and he would finish off with the men and women who gave their lives in the last war and the ones fighting at this very moment to hold back the spread of communism. This he would put his heart and soul into. With a pleading voice, he would beg the voters of this great land to go vote for a sheriff who would not let the Red Chinese take over Jefferson County.

CHAPTER EIGHTEEN

Bud drove slow on his way to the radio station. He wanted to time his arrival to the last minute. He had no intention of standing around waiting, thinking, and worrying. That would be too much. He listened to the Willy Wally show on his way to get a feel for this disk jockey friend of Lowell Maynard. He didn't know Maynard and wasn't sure he liked him, yet here he was trusting Maynard's judgment of this Willy Wally guy. Maybe you trust people too much, Martha had said. Bud had to agree with her. Here he was again putting his fate in other people's hands.

Lowell Maynard climbed out of his black Cadillac as Bud pulled up. "You ready?" Lowell asked.

"My throat's so tight I can't swallow," Bud said.

"You'll do fine," Lowell said as he handed Bud a stack of folders.

Bud gave him a confused look. "What?" Lowell asked.

"Nothin'" Bud answered.

"These are the same kind of folders used in the sheriff's office. They're packed full of scrap paper. This one on top has a copy of last year's fuel invoices. Let about half of it show. Old Dan Wells will know exactly what it is at first glance. My insider tells me he's been over billing the county for gas ever since he took office. Are you a poker player, Sheriff?"

"I've played a few hands."

"Well, this is the biggest bluff you'll ever try to pull. Good luck."

"What if old Dan calls my bluff?" Bud asked.

Lowell hesitated, then answered, "He won't. I've made it my business to study human nature. Wells knows he's dirty; he just didn't think anyone had the goods on him, and he was right. What I've given you is nothin' but window dressing, but his own guilt will make him believe he's been caught."

Lowell lit a cigarette and patted Bud on the back, a gesture Bud didn't appreciate and made it known with a sharp look. "Sorry, Sheriff. I know you don't care for this sort of thing, but what you've got to keep in mind is that this is politics and your last chance of winning this election. There is no tomorrow."

Bud let that sink in. Lowell was right. He couldn't pull this off with a halfhearted effort. With a nod of his head and a resetting of his shoulders, he started toward the door. When you're playing shortstop and a worm burner comes to your off-glove side, if you think for a moment you could miss it, you will. Bud had never doubted his ability to make the play. This was no different. He kicked in the door of the radio station like he owned the place.

It was a small building, with the sound room behind a glass wall. Bud pushed opened the door where Willy Wally and Dan Wells sat with headphones on about to conclude their interview. At this time of the day, Willy Wally would give the farm price report in between country music songs. Bud slammed down the pile of folders on a desk. "I've got some questions for the sheriff," he said.

Wally was aware of Bud's upcoming time slot but was visibly confused by Bud's interruption. "Well, folks, Bud Browdy just walked in the studio and seems intent on a debate with Sheriff Wells. What you say, shall we shift gears and do a political discussion on the upcoming election, Sheriff?"

Dan Wells glanced at the stack of folders on the desk. The fuel invoice caught his eye at once. "I'd love nothing better, Wally. If Mr. Browdy would have worked this out with my campaign manager, that's exactly what we would do. But I have other commitments." Dan Wells knew full well that Bud could make all the charges he wanted and it would be construed as campaign talk. On the other hand, if he were to try to answer these charges without knowing what Bud had, he might end up looking guilty as hell.

"I demand you debate me right now and own up to the corruption I've uncovered in the sheriff's department," Bud said as he pounded a fist on the stack of folders.

"You're not in a position to demand anything," Dan Wells said, trying to regain his control of the situation. He made a deliberate move with his gun hand to his hip, just fast enough and close enough to make one wonder if he were reaching for his gun. This move had served him well at debates with speed limit violators and drunk teenagers. It had no effect on Bud.

All this talk went out over the airwaves and the listeners were enjoying every moment as Lowell had predicted. Lowell listened on his car radio. After several more charges and countercharges were exchanged, Dan Wells made a hasty exit from the studio.

"Well, folks, we had some fireworks going off here tonight. We're talkin' to Bud Browdy, who's runnin' to be your next sheriff. He's going to be with us for the next hour, so you might want to call your neighbors and tell them to turn on the radio. This is the Willy Wally Show and we'll be right back."

Willy plugged an eight-track cassette into a slot on his console and left his glass cubicle to meet with Bud and get him set up with a microphone and headphones in a small glassed-in room opposite his own.

Bud could see his own reflection in the glass. The sight of himself in the huge silly looking headphones added to his unease. He noted that Willy Wally's headphones were much smaller and sleeker and didn't make him look like a clown.

Wally scurried back to his control room and pushed a button on the console. "We're back and we're havin' fun like we always do here on the Willy Wally show. I'd like to thank one of our many sponsors, the good folks at Jack's Tack and Feed. Jack's Tack has just this week renewed their sponsorship of our show for another year and we're all happy about that. And to celebrate, Jack's Tack and Feed is giving away a one pound can of udder balm with every two hundred pounds of cattle feed you buy this week only. So go on over and take advantage of this offer and tell 'em I said hello.

"Okay, we're talkin' with a man who wants to be your next sheriff. Our guest tonight is Bud Browdy. Bud, how would you describe yourself to someone who doesn't know you?"

Bud's brain shifted to neutral. His subconscious focused on his reflection in the glass. He looked ridiculous. Precious seconds slipped by. It's radio, not TV. Say something, Bud's internal voice demanded. "Well, I'm about 6 feet 5 and weigh about 240 pounds if that's what you want to know," Bud said with a forced laugh.

"Well, that's a fine description of a man I'd vote for if we elected hay balers," Wally said. He pushed a button and a cow mooed a long, deep, sorrowful moo. "What do you have to say to that, Bud?" He gestured at Bud to speak into the microphone.

Bud tried to keep the anger out of his voice, but it trickled through. "Yeah, uh, yeah that's a nice cow sound you got there."

"Well, thank you, but enough about my cow. Let's get back to you. Let me ask you this—you have owned and operated several businesses in Jefferson County and you grew up on a farm in Jefferson County. Would you say that that gives you an understanding of the problems that both groups face in their everyday lives?"

"Yes, I do," Bud said. Bud felt better about the situation and was about to expand on his answer when Wally interrupted with another question.

"How would you do things differently than they're being done now?"

"I'd watch the money closer so there wouldn't be a need to increase the taxes we already pay." Bud settled into a shortened version of his proposed economic changes, changes that would free up money to be spent on improvements in other areas and without a tax increase. These included a bid process for the maintenance of sheriff department vehicles and a more efficient use of deputies such as catching bad guys instead of writing tickets. Bud felt comfortable again. His last line about tickets always brought applause when he spoke to a crowd.

"I understand you were close to declaring bankruptcy," Wally said.

White hot anger snapped Bud's eyes onto Wally. Wally smiled a benign smile and mouthed the words "trust me" toward Bud. "I'm sorry there, Bud, your microphone got cut off. Okay, we're all right now. I asked you about your close call with bankruptcy."

"I . . . uh . . . found myself in a difficult situation," Bud said, hoping to put an end to this topic. But Wally wouldn't let it go.

"Did you seek advice from financial people like, say, accountants and credit counselors?"

"Yes, both."

"And what did they advise you?"

"They said I should file for bankruptcy, declare all my debts, and start with a clean slate."

"But that's not what you did, is it?"

"No, sir."

"Is it true that you've worked two jobs for over seven years and paid back every nickle you owed?"

"Yes, that's true," Bud said.

"Well that's a rare thing these days," Wally said. "We got some music to play and a lot more questions to ask Mr. Browdy. That is, if he can stay. I understand you've got a meeting tonight to discuss a charity baseball game featuring the St. Louis Cardinals," Wally said.

Bud hesitated, then decided to go with it. "Yes, that's true, but I can stay a little longer. I'm enjoying this so much."

"Well that's great. We'll be right back," Wally said and pushed a tape into a slot.

Bud removed his headphones and went for the door that separated his large hands from Wally's skinny neck. The door was strong; the lock was heavy duty; Willy Wally was a seasoned veteran.

Lowell Maynard entered the building full of enthusiasm. "It's going great," he exclaimed.

Bud was about to put his shoulder into the locked door when he saw another target. "That's not the way I see it," he said through clenched teeth.

"Okay, I can see you're upset," Lowell said as he backed outside to the parking lot with Bud striding toward him. "That talk about your money problems just shows what an upright man you are."

"You should have cleared it with me first," Bud said.

"You would have said no."

"That's right."

"Well it's done now and it came over great."

Bud hesitated. "Great, huh?" he said, beginning to cool.

"Yeah, great. You've got a voice for radio. You sound warm and sincere."

"Really? You got any more surprises planned?"

"No, that's it."

"What was that about the St. Louis Cardinals coming to play a charity game?"

"Don't worry about that. That was just to make people listen a little closer. When they hear the words St. Louis Cardinals, they think of the team they love, they think of baseball, they remember you were a great high school player, and subconsciously they associate you with the Cardinals—and they love the Cardinals so they love you," Lowell said.

Bud gave him a perplexed look.

"It's called subliminal messaging. They used to sell popcorn that way," Lowell said.

"What the hell are you talking about?"

"Don't worry about it. Just go back in there and talk the way you would if you were fishin' with an old friend."

"What about the Cardinals?" Bud asked.

"The game was cancelled due to a scheduling conflict. We'll try again next year. That's what you'll say if you're elected, but first you have to get elected."

Lowell went in the room and spoke to Wally. Wally backed off his badgering style and let Bud lead the way. The next twenty minutes, Bud spent reading from his cue cards and talking with his heart. He believed everything he said. It was no trouble at all to explain what needed to be done to fix the county, the state, the country, and it all came spilling out like it had many times before in a barber chair or on a bar stool or in the lumberyard. Things were simple after all. Good leaders leading smart, motivated people could accomplish anything.

The words floated out with patriotism and courage and God mixed in, and at the end, a heartfelt plea to get out and vote—call your neighbor, call your grandpa, call your son or daughter and ask them to please go vote. "It don't matter who you vote for," Bud said with a tired but soothing voice. "The point is to vote. Our soldiers in Vietnam are dying at this very minute so that you can. That's all I've got to say tonight except if you're happy with the way things are, vote for Dan Wells, but if you'd like to see a change for the better, vote for me, Bud Browdy."

Willy Wally plugged in the show sign-off tape. The Willy Wally song played in the background and Bud stared at the needles bouncing on the console. It was over; he had pulled it off; the rest was up to God and the voters.

CHAPTER NINETEEN

Martha lay comfortably and warm in Bud's arms. Their bedroom began to brighten in the early dawn. Only their breathing and the ticking of the clock broke the stillness. Today they would vote; tomorrow life would be different.

Bud stirred to improve the circulation in his arm. Martha clung to him, afraid he might be getting up. "What's wrong?" Bud whispered in her ear.

"Nothing's wrong. I just want us to stay here as long as we can."

"I know what you mean. I was thinking about what I was going to do if I lose, and it scares me a little. Then I think about what I'm gonna do if I win and it scares me worse." Bud laughed and Martha laughed and then it was quiet again.

A pleasant half hour passed before Martha spoke. "Bud."

"Yeah."

"Can we adopt a baby?"

CHAPTER TWENTY

The rural vote turned out like never before. The Reform slate won a narrow victory. Bud Browdy became Sheriff Browdy. Martha Browdy became the sheriff's wife.

CHAPTER TWENTY-ONE

The gravel roads along the banks of the Meramec River were deeply shaded by towering sycamores. The air was still and moist and held the smell and taste of the river; an invisible curtain engulfing all those willing to partake of its pleasures. The aroma combined damp soil, dead fish, and decomposing vegetation—the smell all newcomers are advised they'll get used to, and do—a smell that cannot be mistaken or confused with any other, a smell that invokes memories in those returning to the river's banks after a long absence like the farmer forced to the city upon his first re-visit to the country driving past a well used pasture, his brain picking up the signal and putting a host of memories in motion, the subconscious deciding which ones to bring forward.

Clay Coal had some memories. He cruised slowly down Sycamore Road. He had the top down on his '61 Chevy. The warm moist air washed over him like a friendly spirit. He thought of his father. What would old Dry have to say about this? he thought. Behind the turquoise blue Chevy convertible there was a matching turquoise fiberglass speed boat. Whooeee, that's what he would have said. He would have run his hands along the lines of the car and the boat, stepping back for a side view, then running forward to lift the hood, then running to the outboard motor to inspect the prop, talking, always talking.

The old man could find something good to say about everything. She's a fine lookin' boat, he would say. Old Dry told the owner of every boat he ever saw, She's a fine looking boat, no matter what its condition. He would point out how solid the transom was made. Never seen one like this break, he would say, if that were true. You could turn this lady on a dime, if that were true. He could find some advantage that your boat had over all others and help you lighten your cooler one beer at a time.

Clay glowed in the memories for a moment. He shook it off. He turned on the radio, punched at the buttons, found nothing to his liking, and turned it off. He spit out the window and increased his speed. He had no time for daydreaming. He had to put this boat in and check it out, then he had to bleed the brakes on his car—he was having to pump the hell out of them to get it stopped—he had to steal a Corvette and drive it to Arkansas tonight, then turn right around and come back. Clay didn't like to sleep away from home; he felt too vulnerable in a strange bed.

The car and boat were his only visible signs of prosperity. He slept in a cramped and dirty trailer; the trailer perched on concrete blocks overlooking the yard at Tri-State Salvage. The wrecked or abandoned cars that carpeted the six acres of oily mud had all come from the local county, but the owner thought Tri-State made his business sound bigger. Clay paid no rent. His presence stopped parts thieves from plying their trade. He hid his money in coffee cans buried under the trailer. Three concrete blocks stacked to look like a support pier under the trailer covered the hole where the money was buried.

Clay gave Walt Doran, the owner of Tri-State Salvage, cash. Walt Doran gave Clay a paycheck. When Clay felt he was due a raise, he gave Walt Doran more money.

Clay's parole officer was very happy with Clay's readjustment to society. He noted with mock surprise that Clay received a raise. "You should be proud of yourself," he said.

"I am."

Shirley's tavern offered a ramp that would put him on the stretch of water where he could open her up without worry. The parking lot was all but empty. Shirley's old Pontiac and a Ford Falcon were close to the door. The ramp was clear and there were no empty boat trailers parked off to the side.

Clay swung around and lined her up with the ramp. His Chevy had a 3-speed transmission with the shifter mounted on the column. He put the car in reverse and began pumping the brakes. After half a dozen quick pumps, he had enough brake to start down the steep ramp that led to a deep hole.

Shirley came out on the second storey deck of the tavern. "Clay, is that you?" she hollered.

"It's me," Clay said. He had the boat far enough in now that he could see it was starting to lift off the trailer. He turned off the motor and set the emergency brake.

"You goin' for a boat ride?" Shirley hollered.

"Yes, I'm going for a boat ride." Clay tried to keep his annoyance out of his voice.

Shirley liked Clay the way a maiden aunt thinks of her nephew as the son she never had. His father, old Dry, had been a long time friend and steady customer. She had watched Clay grow up. She gave him strawberry sodas on the house when he was young.

Clay shoved the boat off the trailer and hopped on the bow as it slid away.

"You want me to move your car?" Shirley hollered. Shirley had suddenly become concerned about losing a ramp fee.

"No, I'll be right back," Clay shouted over the buzz of the outboard. He slipped her in gear and gave her full throttle. The bow arched for the sky and white water churned at the stern. Then she planed off; only the propeller remained in the water. She could fly. Clay cut the wheel back and forth to get a feel for her as she screamed up the river. Would she slice sideways in a clean, controlled manner or would she dip and hop. Clay put her on a straight line and eased the throttle forward, listening intently to the outboard's voice. There it was—a misfire. He eased her back, then accelerated again. There it was—a sputter that he could feel and hear. Maybe just some varnish in the carburetor, he thought. Open her up, Clay's inner voice said. Run her till the fresh gas washes out the gunk.

Down the river he flew. The surface was calm, the channel was wide, the air like a warm blanket on a cool night. The shoreline slid past. The boat was not moving. It stood on its propeller, its bow defiant, and the shoreline on both sides slid past, and a strip of blue sky dotted with tiny white clouds rushed overhead. Clay eased off and the bow slowly, reluctantly deepened its slice.

What would old Dry say to that? Clay turned to the seat his dad would have occupied if he were there. "What do you think of that, old man?" he said. "Whoooeee," he sang out, and some kid somewhere on the shore heard him and sang a whoooeee back to him. Clay laughed with delight. He turned to share the laugh and found no one.

CHAPTER TWENTY-TWO

Byron Creed whacked a sycamore ball with a stick. He carried the stick at his side like a sword. He pulled it from its imaginary scabbard and stabbed a couple of guys. Then the stick became a bat again and he hit a rock. He missed two more rocks and pitched the stick into the weeds. He walked his loose-jointed walk and kicked at anything in his path.

Byron was on his way to Murray's to buy cigarettes. The warm weather would be gone soon, and this walk would become even more tiresome in the cold. Day after day, since his expulsion from school, he made this walk. The buzz of a big outboard motor caught his ear. He could see small pieces of the boat through the trees. That might be Clay Coal, he thought. Although he was interested, he would have to tromp through some tall weeds to get a better look. He decided he didn't need to know that bad.

Byron fantasized about getting to know Clay better. Clay would take a liking to him and they'd be good friends; and Clay would show him the easy ways to steal a car, although at every meeting he had ever had with Clay, Clay had shown him no friendliness at all. In fact, he had shown him something close to scorn.

Byron carried on with his fantasy as he kicked a Texaco oil can down Sycamore Road. Clay and him would go to the bars every night. They'd drink beer and tell jokes and pat pretty girls on the butt. And if anyone didn't like it, they'd kick the shit out of 'em. Byron had begun to think of himself as a bad ass. His problems at school had all been fight related; he never did any homework; and he never brought a book home. He sat quietly in class or slept. He picked up enough to maintain a solid D minus average.

His problems were like those of a TV gunfighter. There were boys who would not stop until they could pick a fight with him. Byron had perfected the art of the sucker punch; and since he always struck the first blow, he was seen as the one who started the fight. Being the new kid in school and the kid who punched out Bobby Poley put a large target on his back.

Al didn't throw as big a fit as Byron had expected. He took the news of Byron's expulsion with tired resignation. "You'll have to get a job. I ain't buyin' you cigarettes either," Al said.

Byron had worked out a deal with Murray, the owner of a mom and pop IGA store up on the highway. He would come in and clean the storeroom, carrying the cardboard boxes, paper, and crates out to the dumpster, in exchange for a pack of Winstons. Murray wanted his storeroom cleaned every day so he would not pay two packs for two days' worth of cleaning. Byron had to pick up and sweep whatever was there for one pack, so every day he made the mile and a half walk to get his smokes. Al laughed heartily at Byron's deal for cigarettes and knew Murray was having a good laugh too.

A green Dodge pickup pulling a small ski boat bounced down Sycamore toward Byron. He didn't recognize the truck or the boat. That didn't mean anything; people came from all over to run the river when the water was high. As the truck came closer, Byron could see that the driver and passenger were girls. On impulse, he stepped in front of the truck and stuck out his hand in the universal sign language for stop. He had let his hair grow long to match the style of the Coal brothers. He wore cutoff shorts and a gray, long-sleeved sweatshirt and dirty tennis shoes. Black plastic sunglasses lay crooked across his face.

The girls in the truck giggled at the spectacle in the road. "You girls gonna put that boat in the river?" Byron asked as he approached the driver's side.

"Is that any of your business, sweetie?" the driver said. She was older than Byron. He thought maybe twenty. The passenger was younger—closer to Byron's age.

The truck started moving again and Byron trotted alongside trying to keep a conversation going. "I'm the road tax collector and it'll cost you fifty cents to come down this road," Byron said.

The girls giggled. "You look more like a scarecrow," the driver said.

The truck picked up speed and Byron jumped onto the running board. "For a ride in your boat, I'll forget about your taxes for today," he said. He climbed into the bed of the truck and hopped onto the running board on the passenger's side, startling the other girl as he had planned. "What's your name?" Byron had his head in the cab and the girl slid across the seat with a shriek, followed by a laugh and a bright red blush.

The girls looked to be sisters. They wore their hair in tightly pulled ponytails. They both had the same full face, slightly puffy. They had good complexions and thick legs. They smelled of flowery perfume and baby powder.

"Can you back up a trailer?" the driver asked.

"I'm the international trailer backer-upper champion for the last four years," Byron said, showing a very solemn face.

The younger girl gave the statement much more credibility than it deserved. Byron and the driver waited patiently while she came to a conclusion. "Oh, you are not," she said. But it had taken too long. A good laugh was shared by all.

The Chapel sisters, Cindy and Becky, were from Wisconsin. Their father's job brought the family to St. Louis. They had always lived along a lake and Cindy, the older one, said she could run a boat in her sleep. The problem was, she couldn't back a trailer. The boats she had grown up on were always in the water all summer long. The opportunity to learn had never come up. The ramps along the Meramec were often steep and narrow. If a wheel slipped over the edge on either side of the ramp, it might drop as much as twenty-four inches before finding a home among the limestone chunks. The ramps were lined with almost square chunks of white spearheads the size of a toaster.

Cindy Chapel followed the silly boy's directions and parked her truck behind Shirley's tavern, with Byron still riding the running board. "Give me $3.00 and I'll go pay your ramp fee," Byron said.

Cindy considered that this silly but kind of cute boy might run off with her $3.00, but if he did, it was just $3.00. He didn't appear to be wearing underwear under his cutoff shorts, she noticed and handed him the money. "You want me to move the truck?" she asked.

"No, I'll line her up. You just take the straps loose. All except the bow line."

Byron paid the $2.00 ramp fee and bought three packs of cigarettes. "That's Clay Coal's car on the ramp, isn't it?" Byron asked.

Shirley gave the boy a closer look. "Yeah, that's Clay's. It's a beauty, ain't it. The boat matches perfectly," she said with a hint of pride. "You know Clay Coal?"

"Oh, yeah, me and Clay are good friends. His two little brothers, Dwayne and Dwight, and me hang out. And I've been over at their house a lot. I'm almost part of the family, you might say."

"They're good boys. You know, one time I had a drunk in here that was cussin' and threatenin' everyone and he grabbed me by the hair and slung me around when I tried to make him leave. Well, I got on the phone and I called Clay." Shirley looked around the bar to make sure no one was listening, a wasted motion since no one else was there. "He came over, walked right in, went straight to the troublemaker, a big guy too, without even asking if he was the one. He took him by the arm, twisted it till it popped. I heard that. And he shoved him out the door." Shirley leaned a little closer and lowered her voice. "They say Clay broke his other arm and kicked his teeth out. He never came back, I know that," Shirley said. She locked her eyes on Byron, waiting for him to dispute any part of her story.

"Yeah, he's somethin'," Byron said. Shirley seemed satisfied and went back to her stool at the other end of the bar.

The two girls had the boat loaded with life jackets, skis, and a cooler that had been in the back of the truck. "We're all set," Cindy said.

Byron strolled around the boat and trailer like a pilot making a final inspection before takeoff.

"Who owns that convertible on the ramp? Is he coming out to move it?" Becky asked.

"That belongs to Clay Coal. He's a friend of mine. That's him on that blue boat that just went by." Byron pointed in the direction the boat was last seen. The buzz of the motor could still be heard in the distance. "He'll be back in a second. Let's have a beer while we wait." Byron tried to act like his drinking of a beer was the most common and natural thing to do.

"We don't have any beer," Cindy said.

"We have some Cokes," Becky announced. Becky was falling for his bravado.

Cindy felt like poking Byron with a pin for trying to act so grownup and manly. "If you're good friends with this guy, he wouldn't mind you movin' his car, would he?" Cindy asked sweetly.

Becky looked at Byron with high expectations and Byron took the bait. "No, he wouldn't mind."

Byron strolled jauntily with a Coke in his hand and a smile on his face and three packs of cigarettes stuffed in his pants pockets. It's been a great day so far, he thought. Things were finally going his way. He made a silent plea to God that Clay had taken the keys, but God did not do last minute requests for self-destructive teenage boys on that particular day. The keys sparkled in the sun, a tiny chrome plated piston and rod dangled from a chain attached to the keys. Like a cat looking at a wounded bird, Byron went into a trance, his focus on the keys. Then much to his amazement, he was in the car. He set his bottle of Coke between his legs and looked through the windshield at the girls waiting at the top of the ramp. His heart rate increased. He ignored the clear warning his body was sending.

The younger one liked him; she couldn't hide it. Byron anticipated being in the back of the boat with her, maybe getting a feel or two while big sister wasn't watching.

Byron looked the controls over. The emergency brake was set. The shifter looked and felt like it was in reverse. He pushed in the clutch slowly and felt the brakes pop as they took the weight of the car and trailer. He had plenty of motor; Byron knew that. He had seen Clay burn rubber on several occasions. A 327 cubic inch V8 made all the power he would need.

Byron turned the key and the car came to life. The deep rumble coming from the dual exhausts pumped his confidence. You could pull ten boats up the ramp with this motor, he thought. He pulled at the shift lever and it didn't want to release. He pulled harder and it moved to neutral. "Now put her in first." Byron fed himself simple instructions and you could see his lips move if you looked closely. "Now give her some gas, let out the clutch slowly until the motor takes the weight. Now release the brake and give her some more gas." And the motor died.

The car was in third gear and slowly began to succumb to the pull of gravity. As each piston pumped through its cycle, the car drifted closer to the river. Byron stabbed the clutch in for a restart, but that caused the car to fairly leap toward the river. He let the clutch out, but now the shifter was in neutral. He stomped on the brake and the pedal went to the floor. The car slowed, but only slightly. Clay had been meaning to bleed the brake lines for some time now, but since it only required two quick pumps on the pedal to make the brakes perform, he kept putting the matter off.

Byron had both feet on the pedal now and with both hands gripping the steering wheel, pushed with all his might. The brown water rushed over the trunk and into the back seat. The white vinyl interior reflected the light well and could be seen as much as eighteen inches deep before it faded from view. As the backseat filled, the river played its part and now was not content to let the car come to her. She pulled it with a sucking current. Byron released his grip on the steering wheel only when his head was about to go under. He swam to the ramp and turned in time to see the headlights and grill disappear.

Out on the river, the blue boat that matched the car that was there only five seconds before was coming at him as fast as it would run.

Byron heard gravel being sprayed and turned in time to see the green Dodge pickup fishtail down the road, the loose boat behind it bouncing half off the trailer.

Shirley came out on the deck overlooking the river. She had missed the whole thing. "Hey, where're your friends going?" she hollered.

Byron gave her a look without replying. He turned his attention back to the boat coming at him full throttle.

Shirley looked around the lot, clearly perplexed. "Where's Clay's car?" she asked. Now she took note of Byron's sweatshirt stretched out of shape and limp with water dripping from the sleeves. She brought both hands to her mouth and her eyes became big. She looked to the water at the end of the ramp, willing the car to come back. Bubbles came to the surface; the car did not.

Clay pointed the bow of the boat to a spot on the bank covered with smaller, softball size limestone chunks. Still coming on at full throttle, he turned off the key thirty yards out. He climbed out on the bow and as the fiberglass bottom scraped to a stop on the rocks, he leapt off, his attention acutely focused on Byron Creed.

Byron backed up the ramp a step. He looked toward Shirley and noticed some new onlookers—two old men, skinny old men with draft beers in their hands watching the show. One of the old men even had a camera around his neck. Byron felt betrayed by humanity. These onlookers were no better than the crowds at the gladiator things, he thought. Then he saw them as witnesses and was grateful for their presence.

Clay was only a couple of steps away now. Byron readied himself to block Clay's first blow. Clay had not said a word as he approached. He came right up to striking distance and brought a looping, overhand right fist aimed at Byron's nose. Byron saw the punch coming and for a millisecond was sure he had it blocked. Byron's left arm carried the weight of sopping wet cotton; and as he continued to learn throughout his life, timing is everything.

The fury hardened fist of Clay Coal found its mark. Byron felt nothing. The light of day was simply gone. As his head bounced on the concrete ramp, the day reappeared and an incredible pain radiated from his face. Byron rolled to his side, his hands to his face. Clay put the toe of his tennis shoe into Byron's solar plexus. Byron could not breathe. His muscles were locked in a trauma induced cramp that would not release.

Clay was cocking his leg for another, perhaps fatal, blow, his rage setting no limits, when he heard his name screamed by a woman with panic in her voice. He saw Shirley shaking with fear, not for herself, not for Byron, but for him. Clay huffed and stomped in a circle, looking to the spot where his car had gone under.

Byron had all but passed out from the lack of oxygen when his muscles relaxed and he sucked at the air and the muscles tightened, but not as tight or for as long as before. He gulped at the air and looked for help. The old men were milling about talking to each other and slurping their beer. Then they turned and went back inside the tavern. Shirley was still there but had her face covered with her hands and did nothing to help Byron breathe.

At last the air began to flow and he took deeper breaths and the muscles hurt a little less than before. But he began to cough and the coughing stabbed him with pain. He spit blood into his hands. His hands were already covered with blood from his nose and split upper lip. This was new blood rising in his throat. He was bleeding inside; he was dying and no one cared. Byron's thought brought on a terrible depression. He was alone in the world and being beaten to death in front of a crowd and no one cared.

Clay Coal looked out toward the horizon, his anger under control. The hours he had spent piecing that car together and the hours of sanding and readying it for paint, finding the perfect match for the boat . . . his thoughts drifted back to those long hours. His anger began to build again, but he pushed it down. There was nothing more to do but deliver an ultimatum to Byron Creed. Clay scanned the shoreline for a rock. He picked up a rectangular shaped chunk of white limestone the size of a mailbox. He carried it above his head with both hands. He stood over Byron with the rock poised, his arms began to tremble, and a look of pure hate crossed his face. With a war cry on his lips, he pulled the rock down and struck the ramp inches above Byron's head with a hollow thud.

I'm alive, was Byron's first clear thought. "You got two weeks," Clay said. "You get me $2,000.00 in two weeks or I'll crush your skull just like that. But first I'll break both your arms so you won't be able to cover up. You'll just lay there like you are now and watch it coming." Clay was down on one knee now speaking quietly through clenched teeth.

Byron sensed it was over and without considering the consequences, blurted out, "Don't you have insurance?"

Clay's left hand snapped a short jab to the exact spot he had hit before. Byron was stunned and made squeaking sounds into his hands. "Two weeks," Clay said. He walked up the ramp and went into the tavern.

Byron remained on the ramp ten more minutes. His spasms decreased and he pushed himself to his feet. The sweatshirt felt heavy and clammy against his skin. He pulled it over his head and wiped at the blood on his face, then dropped it where he stood. He pulled the wet packs of cigarettes from his pockets and dropped them to the ground. He took a step and stopped. He took another. An hour later, he was home in his bed wishing for the comfort of sleep.

CHAPTER TWENTY-THREE

Al was on his way to the refrigerator to get the last beer. The 16-ounce Schlitz were on sale, so Al had brought home three six packs just a few days ago. He was slightly bemused to see only one left and tonight was "Wagon Train" night, and Al wasn't sure if one can would be enough to save the train. Tonight was about Indians, not one of those misunderstood foreigner shows where the foreigner saves the train at the end. Al hated those episodes. It had almost gotten to the point where all Al could find to look forward to anymore was "Wagon Train," and when they did one of those learn-about-the-foreigner shows, it was a big letdown. Not tonight, though; there was Indian trouble. Not those misunderstood Indians either. These were just bad Indians, the kind that's the most fun to kill.

Al was on his way back to his chair when a speck of fire caught his eye out the window. Down by the river, he saw Byron in a lawn chair next to a small campfire. Al thought maybe he ought to go down there and talk to the boy. He had heard of the car sinking and of Clay Coal's threat but had not confronted the boy about how he was going to pay for Clay's car. Al didn't take the threat seriously. He knew Clay, and he knew Clay to be a dangerous brawler, but he didn't see Clay as a murderer.

In the background, he could hear Ward Bond hollering orders and Indians were screaming as they ambushed some poor foreigner.

Maybe he should go down there and sit by the fire and tell the boy things ain't as bad as they seem. Clay will cool off and the car will get paid for somehow.

The Indians were making sounds like coyotes and probably getting ready to attack again.

If Byron's still there after wagon train, I'll go talk to him, Al thought. That seemed like a reasonable plan, so Al hurried back before all the Indians were shot.

Byron added small sticks to the flames. The air was crisp and Byron was underdressed. He was perched on the edge of an aluminum lawn chair, his knees pressed tight together, his hands stretched toward the heat. He had not put on his heavy coat as Al had told him to; he wore his black leather jacket with the zippers going sideways and the wide belt around the waist. He had always looked good in this jacket. A glance in the bathroom mirror on the way out of the house had confirmed that, but now he was cold and would not go in for his heavy coat. He would have to pass by Al and Al would say somethin' and he would say somethin' and the shouting would start again.

The fire only warmed Byron's hands and he began to chatter his teeth unconsciously. The wind blew up the back and out the collar of his imitation leather jacket. The zippers had failed first. The jacket was just a few days old when the zipper on the cigarette pocket jammed, and when Byron pulled harder on the small chain to force it, the chain pulled off. After a few weeks, all the zippers were broken. The pockets that were zipped closed when they broke were made useful by cutting the fabric just above the teeth of the zipper, and this provided a pocket and preserved the beauty of the zipper. Only two of the snaps still worked, one at the top and one at the bottom. If he squeezed his shoulders up too quickly, the split vinyl around the collar would pinch his cold sensitive neck like the claws of a crab. The breast pocket was torn at the lower corner and white filler material pushed its way out.

The jacket had been a Christmas present from Rayleen. She had been out all night on Christmas Eve that year. Byron had waited up wrapped in a blanket on the sofa watching television. The heat had been turned off and the refrigerator was empty. Rayleen had received a check from Al the day before and hadn't been seen since. She was going shopping, she said. She was going to buy presents and food and fix a real nice Christmas dinner.

From his position on the sofa, Byron could watch the fuzzy picture on the TV and see out the window to the street without moving his head. As the hours passed by that Christmas Eve, he never changed the channel or moved from his warm spot, but stared at the TV screen and out the window at every pair of headlights that came by. His eyes would follow the headlights until they were out of view, then drift back to the TV screen. Finally, he fell asleep.

He woke to a sound. He listened intently. A thump shook the apartment, a man laughed a loud hard-edged laugh, Rayleen cursed at him, then laughed her drunken laugh. They stumbled and bumped against the wall coming up the steps. The door banged open and they tumbled to the floor. They were tangled with lust and rolled clumsily.

"We have to be quiet. We'll wake up Byron" Rayleen said.

"He needs to learn about sex someday," the man said.

"Oh, you're awful," Rayleen said.

It was almost daylight. His mom had a man with her. He looked like all the rest, loud and clumsy with watery eyes. "I got you a nice present, honey," Rayleen said, and she pitched him a brown paper grocery bag. The bag landed on the sofa and fell to the floor. Rayleen and the man stumbled into the bedroom and closed the door.

Byron looked from the bedroom door to the bag on the floor. There was no bright colored paper of Santa Claus or snow with sleds or Christmas trees—just a Kroger bag with the top rolled down like garbage going out to the can. Byron could hear sounds coming from the bedroom, so he pushed himself out of his blankets and turned up the volume on the TV. On his way back to the blankets, he snatched the bag from the floor and dumped out the jacket onto the sofa.

Byron had begged for this jacket for months. He had made a million promises about what he would do and things he would not do if he could have a leather jacket like this one. One touch and he knew this was plastic. He put the jacket on and stared back at the TV. All the promises he had made to get a leather jacket were off now; he would do what he wanted when he wanted; all deals were off.

Byron's thoughts drifted back to the present. He pitched a few more twigs in the fire. The twigs were rapidly consumed and snapped and popped as they burst into flames. Above the sound of the fire, he heard footsteps approaching from behind him. His mind jumped to a picture of Clay Coal approaching with a knife. He spun his head around. It was Dwayne. The collar of the jacket jabbed Byron's neck deep enough to produce a drop of blood. God damn it. Byron ripped at the snaps and slammed the jacket into the fire.

Dwayne seemed not to notice that his friend had just taken off his jacket and pitched it in the fire. "How's it goin'?" he asked.

"Great, just fuckin' great," Byron said as he watched the black plastic melt and catch flame.

Dwayne waited for the jacket to all but disappear in the fire before saying anything. "You know Clay's crazy. He loved that car."

"Yeah, I know."

Byron pulled his chair closer and hovered over the small fire. The vinyl shell of the jacket blazed hot and put off noxious smoke. He coughed violently after inhaling a lungful of his former prized possession. "Have you seen him lately?" he asked, still peering at the flames and hacking in between words.

"No, but Dwight did." Dwayne squatted down close to the flames and waited for Byron to direct the conversation.

"Where'd he see him at?" Byron asked.

"Comin' out of Murray's. He had a pint of whiskey he was sippin' on. When Clay drinks whiskey, he gets mean."

"He already said he was gonna kill me. How much meaner can he get?"

"I don't think he'll kill you, but he'll bust you up until he gets his money," Dwayne said. "Does Al know what's goin' on?"

"Not yet, but he's bound to find out."

"You think he'll come up with the money to get you out of this?"

"Naw, he'll just yell at me and call me stupid, and then he'll call the cops and tell them Clay's made threats and then try to force Clay to accept $35.00 a month until the debt is paid. And all that time I'll have to work in some goddamned seventy cents an hour job."

Dwayne poked at the fire and considered Byron's predicament. "What's wrong with that? It's better than getting your arms busted."

"I'll tell you what's wrong with that. I don't wanna be no damn busboy or car wash jerk. You get started doin' that kind of crap work and that's all you'll ever do. And besides that, I don't want to ever hear another lecture from that fat old fart in the house. I'll take care of this myself, and I'm not going to do any crap work to get the money." Byron stared off toward the horizon, not looking at the outside world at all but looking at the world he created in a daydream. "I'm gonna pull a heist, pay off Clay, and have money left over. I may decide to travel after that. I don't have to stay here in this dump forever. I may just go to Canada and be a logger."

"It gets cold in Canada," Dwayne said.

"Hell, it's cold right here," Byron replied.

"It's not so bad if you have a jacket on."

The joke broke the somber mood and Byron gave Dwayne a shove. He rolled down the riverbank laughing almost to the water's edge. Dwayne hopped to his feet and moved back to his spot next to Byron. "You really going to do a heist?" he asked, squatting at the fireside.

Byron put on his most serious face and nodded his head slowly.

"Wow," Dwayne said in an airy whisper that rose to the level of a normal voice.

Byron swelled with pride in his new found career path. Dwayne had never looked at him with this kind of admiration; this was the way he wanted to be seen. He had made the right choice. Up to the moment he had voiced the words, his mind was undecided about pulling an armed robbery. Now with Dwayne's reaction so positive, he knew this was the right thing to do. One good heist and all his troubles would be over. He could tell Al and Clay both to kiss his ass. No one would be running his life but him.

"I won't have to take no fruit carhop or dishwashing job. I'll just move around, pull a job when the money gets low, then move on." Byron's mood rose from the ashes and although he wasn't sure how he was going to do it, he knew he would. There was no turning back. How hard could it be? You just point a gun, demand money, and leave, he thought.

"Who you gonna hit?" Dwayne asked, his excitement showing in his wide eyes.

"I can't tell you." His tone reflected the seriousness of the job ahead of him. In truth, he had no idea of the who, what, or how. He would figure that out later. It was enough right now to glow in the respect of his friend.

"You're going to tell me about it after it's over, aren't you?" Dwayne asked, a little pleading in his voice.

"I don't know. Maybe." Byron wanted to milk his position of power for as long as it would last.

"You're going to need a getaway car. Where you going to get that?"

"I'm working on that," Byron lied. He hadn't considered his escape yet. He was still thinking of who to rob.

"Banks are good to rob," Dwayne said. "There's always money in them, and when you rob a bank, you're a bank robber, not just a robber."

There was sound logic in Dwayne's thinking. A bank might be the way to go. "Like I said, I can't tell you any more right now. This has got to be kept quiet, you understand."

"Sure, I understand. I can tell Dwight, can't I? He won't say nothin'."

Byron tried to show deep thought about the matter. He knew Dwayne would tell his brother—might as well give him the okay. "Okay, but that's it. Nobody else."

The bank robber and his assistant, the director of bank robbers, planned until the firewood ran out. The various disguises that might be worn became a large topic. So, too, was the shooting to be done, or the lack of shooting. Byron was on the lack of shooting side. He had decided to use the target .22

he had stolen from Turk's. He carefully explained the advantages of using a pistol as opposed to a shotgun, which Dwayne favored. Dwayne suggested the shotgun for its intimidation factor and its roar. His idea was to fire off a round right away to let people know you mean it.

"It takes two hands to handle a shotgun, and the only one I can get easily is Al's old double barrel, and it weighs a ton. If I have to drag that big bastard around, I won't have a free hand for the bag of money," Byron said. Dwayne could see he was talking to a much smarter kid than he had ever given Byron credit for being. "You think you'll have to shoot anyone?"

"Naw. People don't want to get shot. You just point a gun at them and they do what you say."

The talk stopped as the boys stared into the fire lost in their own thoughts. Dwayne broke the silence. "Where do they do the most loggin' in Canada? Maybe I'll come and visit you after you get settled."

"I didn't say for sure I was goin' to Canada. I said I might. I'm thinkin' of moving to South America. They say the girls are real good lookin' and they start fuckin' when they're thirteen years old, and their parents don't care because it's part of their culture."

"Man, I like that South American culture," Dwayne said.

Both boys giggled and grabbed at their crotches, drifting off for a second to their own hormone-driven, lame-brained sexual fantasies.

Byron couldn't tolerate the cold any longer and a new urge had come upon him. Al would be in bed by now, so it was safe to go in. Byron gave Dwayne one more warning to keep this quiet and started toward the house.

Dwayne ran most of the way home and woke Dwight up to tell him the news. Dwight had little interest in the details, but thought immediately of how he could use this information to impress Marsha Davis. He could tell her he was friends with a bank robber and predict the day a bank would be robbed.

"You can't tell anyone." Dwayne's voice broke through the fog.

"Yeah, right, something like this has to be kept quiet," Dwight said.

Dwight only caught bits and pieces of what Dwayne was saying. His mind drifted back to Marsha Davis's breasts and how she would gladly let the friend of a bank robber handle them as often as he liked.

The following day, the bank robber and his two planning directors worked out the details all afternoon. They walked the well worn path along Coal Creek. The boys carried their pistols and as many boxes of .22 shells as they could stuff in their pockets. The slough belonged to the Coal brothers as it had their father only because he claimed it. Old Dry Coal used the slough as his personal highway and playground. No one in the Coal family ever had a title or ever made a payment on Weber Creek, the official name, named because it cut through the back section of the Weber Quarry.

"Title," old Dry would say, "well that's just paperwork."

Only a few people who knew of this section of the river would venture in there. The local crowd had had too many bad experiences whenever they went exploring down Coal Creek. People say old Dry Coal stretched lines draped with fishing net just under the surface to snag and tangle a propeller. People say it's happened too many times to be an accident. The quarry turned a blind eye to what happened on Coal Creek because the Coals offered a secure gate to the site at no cost.

Byron took a long steady sight on a chunk of bark the size of a quarter. The water exploded, the bark disappeared. "Good shot," Dwayne and Dwight said in unison.

With an almost endless supply of ammo and firing into the water so you could see where your shots were going, the Coal brothers became proficient at hitting bottles, turtles, driftwood, light bulbs, pigeons, and similar sized items that might be found floating in the backwater slough where the boys went to play.

The three boys shot box after box of stolen .22 shells down the barrels of stolen .22 pistols. Byron was the most accurate with the demon chaser, the name he had decided to bestow on the Ruger target pistol. Demon Chaser had a 9-inch barrel and an easy pull target trigger. Byron used two hands and was laughed at by his fellow bandits for shooting like a girl. Dwayne and Dwight preferred the one-handed shoot from the hip cowboy style that the Duke used.

Byron's shooting style gained approval when he began to hit bottle caps, water spiders, and the heads of softshell turtles that sunned themselves on the logs that clogged the banks.

"That's good shootin'," Dwayne said. "I know what you could do—you could shoot out a light at the bank if they don't move fast enough. That'll show 'em you mean business and that you're a good shot."

"No," said Dwight, "if you're going to take a shot, might as well get some use out of it. You should shoot the telephone off of someone's desk. That way they can see what a good shot you are and you might mess up the phone lines so that they can't call the police."

"That ain't gonna mess up the phone lines, you idiot," Dwayne snapped.

"Well, who made you a fuckin' phone expert?" Dwight came back.

Byron needed to play his role as arbitrator. He couldn't let this argument escalate when both boys had guns in their hands. "I ain't gonna shoot at all. I'm just going to grab some money and go. I'll have a mask on and coveralls and no one will be able to tell if I'm a man or a woman, young or old. For all they know, I might be an escaped lunatic that just killed eight guards. I won't have to shoot anything."

The Coal brothers looked at each other and back at Byron with amazement. For a bank robber that was only just getting started, Byron had it all figured out.

Last spring when they had first met Byron, he didn't seem very smart. He couldn't even start an outboard motor, he couldn't swim, and he didn't know nothin' about cars. How did he get so smart so fast? As is often the case with twins, they both had the same thought at the same time. They were able to communicate that thought with just a look.

"Maybe after you pull your first job, you could start a gang," Dwight said.

"Yeah, maybe, if I decide to hit larger banks that have so much money in 'em I can't carry it all by myself. Then we might start a gang," Byron said.

The blood flow picked up pace in the Coal brothers' veins at the prospect of money and fame. Clay Coal had a name—a name recognized all over the county as someone not to cross. Being Clay's brothers had its rewards, but the boys wanted their own reputations. Clay might take off and leave at any time or maybe even go back to prison. The boys were well aware he was stealing cars, and if he got caught or had to run, his name would fade fast. They needed their own names.

"We need a name for the gang," Dwayne said. Dwayne's mind was moving fast at the moment. Byron had given the okay to be part of his bank robbers' gang and images of wealth, girls, cars, girls, swimming pools, and girls splashed in rapid order like a slide show projector gone out of control.

"How about the Sputniks?" Dwayne said.

Byron and Dwight gave him blank looks. "The what?" Dwight said.

"You know, that thing the Russians put in space. Listen, we could talk in Russian accents and call ourselves the Sputniks; and the cops would be lookin' for Russian spies, not handsome young American boys."

Byron had to admit the idea made good sense.

The boys fed .22 shells into the 10-shot clips with practiced speed. Nothing larger than a postage stamp had a chance of survival if it moved on the surface of the backwater. Catsup bottles were plentiful, for reasons much debated along the firing line by the Sputnik gang.

Dwayne said, "Everyone eats catsup. Why shouldn't there be more?"

"Everyone eats mayonnaise, too. How many mayonnaise jars do you see?" Dwight asked. Dwight was becoming less tolerant of Dwayne's know-it-all attitude.

"That's because mayonnaise jars don't have a tight cap like catsup bottles."

Dwayne was reloading when Dwight snatched his favorite Cardinal baseball cap off his head. He pitched the hat between his brother's feet and Dwayne knew in a heartbeat what was on Dwight's mind. He had just opened his mouth to warn him not to do it, when Dwight began blasting away at the hat. Dwayne jumped back as bullets peppered the ground near his feet.

Dwayne called the hat his lucky hat for reasons unknown. Dwight, in his reckless zeal, emptied his pistol into the once proud symbol of the St. Louis Cardinals. The echoes of the last shots were fading to nothing and the slide was locked back on the now useless piece of metal and plastic. Dwight pointed the pistol and squeezed the trigger harder, but it was useless and it made him feel foolish and embarrassed. Byron had no intention of trying to mediate this situation and stepped aside.

Dwayne looked from his hat to Dwight and back. He fed one last shell into his now full clip and snapped it home into the handle of the 10-shot Ruger pistol. Dwight had that "uh, oh" feeling in his stomach. This was in no way a new situation. He remembered now that he experienced the same twist in his guts the moment he stepped into the air from the highest point of the railroad trestle over the Meramec. He had done it on a dare and reveled in the attention he received a week before and a week after he made the jump. But at that moment when he stepped into nothing and began his plunge toward the swirling green water below, that "uh, oh" feeling was just like the one he had now.

Dwayne didn't really care about the hat. He had decided it was time to move on with his image. Hats messed up his hair, and good looking hair seemed to be important to girls. The hat was going to go to the trash soon anyway, but according to the rules that governed behavior between fifteen-year-old twin brothers raised on the river without a father and trying hard to live up to their renegade brother's reputation, something had to be done about it.

"I will shoot you in the ass if you run," Dwayne said.

Dwight was on the verge of running before Dwayne warned him not to. Now that Dwayne had said he would put a bullet in Dwight's butt, Dwight knew he would. That was part of the code of the Coal men. Once you say you'll do something, you do it no matter how stupid. Old Dry Coal had lived by the code. Clay followed suit and the twins were determined to live up to the tradition.

Byron watched with mixed emotions. He didn't know what would happen next, but he was energized by the situation. Dwight was wearing his new brogues, an unusual thing—new brogues were a prized possession worn only with your good clothes. Everyone had a pair of old brogues to tromp around in. Brogues, unlike tennis shoes, looked great right out of the box, the signature look of a bad ass when worn with tight fitting, tapered, iridescent silver slacks. Any color shirt or sweater topped off that look.

"I'm going to shoot a hole in one of your brogues," Dwayne said.

Dwight became indignant. "These brogues cost a lot more than that stupid hat."

"That's not your decision to make. You take off a shoe or I'll shoot it right now." Dwayne's pistol hung loosely at his side, then whipped forward and a shot cracked through the air. A crater of black river soil the size of a quarter appeared at the edge of Dwight's left shoe.

Dwight wobbled on one foot as he started untying his shoe. Dwayne's shot was fast and reckless, clearly showing he was willing to accidentally shoot his brother in the foot. He would be sorry and he would swear he didn't do it on purpose, and that would be the truth, but Dwight would still have a toe missing.

Dwight held the sacrificial shoe as he began negotiations. "One shot through the toe," he said.

"Two shots through the toe," Dwayne said.

"One shot at the cuff."

"One shot through the toe," Dwayne said.

"Two shots through the cuff."

"Done," Dwayne said.

Dwight pitched the shoe toward Dwayne. He wanted Dwayne to be sure of his shot. Dwayne was careful not to damage the boot too badly; he placed his shots high up around the ankle bone area so that pant cuffs would cover the holes. Dwayne was thinking ahead to a time when his own brogues might be dirty, at a time when he might need to borrow and do a switcheroo on Dwight.

The fight was over. Dwight hopped on one leg as he laced his ventilated shoe back on.

Dwayne was careful not to empty his pistol. He took a shot at a light bulb at the edge of the water on the opposite side of the creek. His snap shot went low, splashing muddy water over the target. On most occasions, Dwayne would fire several more quick rounds to get the bulb before his companions did. But the tension was still there like a magnetic force vibrating between the brothers.

Byron stayed where he was and pretended to examine the function of his own pistol—Demon Chaser. When Dwight had his shoe on and his gun reloaded, he swung the gun up and took a shot at the light bulb, using the two-handed girlie method he had made fun of Byron for using. The bulb exploded. Dwight was congratulated.

"Good shot. Hell of a shot. You could join a carnival with shooting like that. That was the best shot made today." Dwight soaked in the praise and everyone relaxed and went to burning up ammo like it was free.

The talk turned back to bank robbing.

"So, are you going to shoot the phone or not?" Dwight asked.

"No, I don't want to waste a shot in case I have to blast my way out," Byron said as he swung the long barreled pistol up to the firing position and with three quick shots exploded a trio of baby food jars bobbing on the water.

Dwayne and Dwight needed no more convincing and began to burn up shells using two hands to steady their aim. The boys blasted on until it became so dark they were having trouble reloading. The flash of the muzzles was a new source of amusement and several attempts were made to fire so fast as to keep a solid rope of fire exiting the barrels. When the last round was fired, they headed home.

CHAPTER TWENTY-FOUR

B yron wrapped his pistol in an oily rag and hid it in the floor joist under the house—Al's house. He never referred to it as home except by accident. Al's rules, Al's chair, Al's everything at Al's house. Byron hated Al's house.

The refrigerator contained a half empty carton of milk that was well on its way to becoming buttermilk. Byron sniffed at the carton and put it back where it was. There was half a can of pork and beans still in the can next to the milk. The top layer of the beans had a crusty look. The light coming from the refrigerator was all that illuminated the pungent smelling kitchen. Byron seldom used more light than was necessary. He didn't want to look at the dishes piled in the sink or the mess on the floor where he had spilled soup several days ago. Al had demanded that Byron clean the kitchen three days a week. Like everything else Al demanded, Byron refused. The battle to see who could live in the filth the longest was in its fourth week, and Byron had no intention of giving in.

Byron dug deep into the cabinet under the sink. There, behind the Comet, behind the dish soap, behind the plastic bucket was a large can of mixed fruit in heavy syrup. Byron and Al both had taken to hiding canned food all over the house. Byron suspected that Al kept a stash behind the seat of his truck. He tried to make a raid on what he thought would be a goldmine of Al's favorites, but Al never forgot to lock the truck doors.

In the living room, Byron sat in Al's chair, eating out of the can and dripping heavy syrup down his chin. It was Sunday night. Al worked from

8:00 a.m. to 8:00 p.m. every other Sunday and wouldn't be home until 8:30 p.m. at the earliest. If he sat in his truck and finished off a six pack of tallboys, it might be 9:30 or 10:00 p.m.

Byron thought he heard a car door slam. It couldn't be Al, it was only seven o'clock. Clay. The specter of Clay Coal lurking just outside the house rattled Byron right down to the bone. He went to the window. Across the street, the Bakers were carrying in groceries. It was a false alarm. He relaxed. The fear was over for the moment, but it would return. And one day, or one night, Byron would be looking into the cold, mean eyes of Clay Coal.

Now, now was the time. To wait any longer was not going to help at all. Dwight and Dwayne were sure to have told people of Byron's plans to rob a bank. They couldn't have kept a secret like that past the first day they heard it. The longer he waited, the more people were sure to know. Now. That was the word that hammered in his brain. Now. No more waiting and talking about getaway cars and Russian accents.

The plan wrote itself. Rob Floyd's. Take the bicycle trail. Wear coveralls. Cut through the field. The bike trail was all downhill on the return. He could fly on that trail. No car to steal. No bank to case. The job could be done at night. Banks don't stay open at night. The benefits of robbing Floyd's continued to mount. The mixed fruit in heavy syrup never tasted better. He sat like an Indian in Al's big recliner in the dark. Byron was amazed he hadn't thought of this before. This was perfect. Taking Floyd's money was even better than bank money. It would all be in small bills and Floyd was an asshole.

Byron had the sudden realization that this was destiny. A calm came over him. This was a sure thing. Nothing could go wrong. You don't have to worry about a bike not starting. You don't have to steal a car. You don't have to get rid of a car. You don't need to worry about fingerprints on the car door or the steering wheel. This was perfect. The cops won't have a clue.

Byron felt relief. Doing the bank job, for all its glory and its possibilities for huge sums of cash, seemed silly now when compared to this sensible plan that required much less thought. The whole car theft stuff had been a heavy burden. Byron had to admit to himself he was a terrible driver. He remembered the time just before Rayleen went missing when he and Ricky Blake, a short-time friend, stole a 47 Studebaker pickup. Those were the good old days. There were only four wires going to the ignition switch; the starter engaged when the clutch was pushed to the floor. Anyone with a pocketknife could steal that truck in two minutes.

Byron smiled and gloried in the memory; but as the memory played on, the frozen fear he had once experienced began to move through him little by little. His arms and legs tensed and his breathing became shallow. He relived the grip he had had on the steering wheel as the truck slid toward a drop off of a hundred feet or more, the confusion he felt as he pushed harder and harder on the brakes and nothing happened just like Clay's car. Then the tiny amount of friction created by hard rubber tires skimming over an icy mountain road brought the truck to a stop only inches from going over the edge. Byron and Ricky had both been screaming as death looked to be at their doorstep. Moments after the truck came to a complete stop, the boys were still screaming.

Byron shook himself to bring his thoughts back to the present. There was going to be no car to steal or drive. He shook himself again. No one knew about the stolen Studebaker. After their near death experience, the boys abandoned the truck where it sat, too shaken to try to back it up.

Now that the proper course of action had been established, Byron felt sleepy. He crawled into his bed with his clothes on and quickly fell asleep.

CHAPTER TWENTY-FIVE

Bud Browdy kissed his wife good-bye. Martha beamed with pride and waved to him until he was out of sight. He drove his old truck for the last time. Tonight when he came home, he would be driving the sheriff's car.

It was the first day on the job and Bud felt like a kid on the first day at a new school. Sheriff Wells had not been helpful at all in making the transition. He would not meet with Bud; and Bud, on advice from the newly elected prosecuting attorney, didn't push it. He was gone now and that's all that mattered.

Bud would meet his staff and deputies. "Slow and easy," Bud mumbled to himself. His fear of failure raised its ugly head. "Slow and easy," he repeated to himself.

Bud walked into the sheriff's office with high expectations and had them crushed at once. The place was empty except for a single girl at a paper-strewn desk in the back of the big room. The office was located on the second floor of the old Hillsboro Courthouse, a traditional building set in the town square. The interior colors were government green and dingy white. The whole building screamed "Don't Try and Change Me." The twelve-foot high ceilings were bordered with ornate plaster cornices of the chipped, yellowed, and missing variety. The walls showed where doors used to be with raised plaster outlines applied by a carpenter who was almost good enough to be a drywall finisher. The county had to cut costs where it could.

Bud introduced himself to the timid, brown eyed waif surrounded by books, files, and telephones. Millie Skaggs was rattled and said so. "I'm rattled," she said.

Bud picked up one of the phones that was ringing and informed the caller that if it wasn't an emergency to call back in half an hour. "Where's your help?" Bud asked.

"They walked out. They had it planned."

"Where'd they go?"

"They're gone—quit. They had it planned. I seen 'em whispering over there." Millie pointed to a corner of the office where a small kitchen table supported a coffee maker and styrofoam cups. "They come in this morning, picked up their paychecks, cleaned out their desks, and left."

"Why didn't you quit too?" Bud asked.

"I don't have another job to go to," Millie said.

"But they did?"

"I think so. They didn't tell me. They hardly ever talked to me."

"Why's that?"

"They was all related to Sheriff Wells and they was all fat and I'm skinny. With women that's enough," Millie said.

"If you had had another job to go to, would you have quit too?"

"Does this other job pay more than this one?"

"No," Bud said.

"Well then I'd stay."

Bud nodded his understanding. "How long you been here?"

"Three months."

"Have you got a pretty good grasp of how things are done?"

"No."

"Would you be able to hire a new staff of talented people?"

"I doubt it."

"I see," Bud said. "Do you know who would?"

"Rhonda would. Rhonda Long. She's the office boss at the revenue office," Millie said.

Bud was starting to believe he was wasting time with Millie. "Would she leave and come to work here?"

"For a typewriter, she would," Millie answered.

"A typewriter—just a typewriter?"

"No, it has to be an IBM Selectric."

Bud felt that lost feeling coming on. He had felt that way once in Korea when he became separated from his patrol and lost his sense of direction. The impulse is to start walking, but without a clear idea of what direction to take; it's a mistake. "Why would this Rhonda Long leave the job she has now?"

The phones were ringing all over the room. Bud answered one. "Sheriff's Office," he said and experienced a small thrill at the sound of his voice. "No, we don't do that here. You need to call the license office."

Millie concluded both her calls with, "I don't know. Could you call back tomorrow?"

"Now back to this Rhonda person," Bud said.

"Rhonda's not happy at the assessor's office. She's a go-getter; she says the other girls are lazy and she has to do all their work. She'd come to work for you if you let her hire the staff and get her the typewriter."

"Where am I going to get an IBM Selectric?"

"You have to order one from the company. They're brand new. High speed electric—they do all the typing for you." Millie picked up the phone. The ringing continued. She tried again and it stopped.

Bud listened as Millie did a poor job of explaining to the caller what forms needed to be filled out and how to proceed with their complaint, which seemed to center around a neighbor's tree that was about to fall on a chainlink fence.

Bud left Millie to her world of incompetence and entered his private office. His temper began to rise as the minutes ticked by. He sat at his desk and surveyed his new environment. The small office matched the rest of the building in neglect. Several large file cabinets stood opposite his desk. The lone window to the outside presented a view of the dumpsters at the corner of the parking lot. The desk was the gray metal government issue type with a plastic wood top. The drawers were all half out and empty. What to do first. He leaned back in the well-worn swivel chair and tried to think.

Of all the possible things that might have happened on this first day, this had never occurred to him. He was cursed. Bad luck was a frequent guest at his table. The chair popped and he almost went over backwards. The near fall snapped him from his self-pity. As bad as the campaign had gotten, the thought that the entire staff, save one, would quit perplexed Bud. Someone else was behind this; that was for sure. But that would have to wait.

Bud left the office with, "I'll be right back," tossed over his shoulder. Millie only blinked her acknowledgment as she attempted to keep two phone conversations going at the same time.

Rhonda Long was a large woman with a no-nonsense confident stare that dared you to dispute whatever she had just said. She had been married and widowed twice to men who lacked the fortitude to maintain her pace in life. Rhonda liked things to run in an orderly way. To live like she wanted to live required steady concentration on detail and no wasted time on leisure.

Rhonda's first husband, Roger, lasted only four years. She blamed that on herself. At the age of thirty, she was probably too young and foolish to pick a good man. Her second husband, Herbert, was a good choice. He just plain wore out and died. Herbert could work a sixteen-hour day for weeks at a time, take one day off, and start again. Rhonda matched him hour for hour. Many of their neighbors made mention of the fact that the two of them both worked full-time jobs yet never seemed to rest at home. The lawn was perfect, the paint on the house fresh, the cars waxed to a glow. There was always something to do. That's the way Rhonda saw it, and if you didn't see it that way, you wouldn't last long as an employee or a husband.

Bud wandered the halls looking for the revenue office. He was having a hard time getting from here to there. The old courthouse had gone through many renovations. Some stairways did not go to the fourth floor; some did not go to the basement. Elevators stopped at places that could not be reached by stairs; stairs went places that could not be reached by elevators. And every transition from stair to elevator was at the other end of a long hallway.

Several people tried to be helpful with directions, but they only confused him more. Bud wandered around the courthouse for ten minutes, feeling more and more desperate with each wrong turn. He knew he was being observed as he backtracked through the halls, and although he couldn't hear the giggling behind the doors, he was sure that the sheriff being lost in the courthouse was too much fun to ignore.

Rhonda Long busied herself with paper pushing as she stood at the business window facing the hallway. When Bud arrived, she recognized him at once and had a good idea of why he was there. "Well, Sheriff Browdy, you makin' the rounds in the courthouse today?"

"No . . . uh . . . uh, not just yet. I . . . uh, I'm looking for a woman named Rhonda Long."

"Well, you found her. That's mighty good police work for the first day."

Bud didn't mind the jab. He was quickly impressed with this woman who looked him right in the eye with a knowing smile. She knew why he was there and intended to have some fun with it. That much was apparent.

"You think I could talk to you in private, Miss—or is it Mrs. Long?"

"It's Mrs. And we can talk right here. I'm the only one in the office until ten o'clock. No use paying girls to sit around and paint their fingernails," Rhonda said as she squared and stapled stacks of pink and green carbons.

"I see. Well, I'll get straight to the point. I'm in the market for an office manager and your name came up as a possible candidate."

"You're up the creek without a paddle, aren't you, Sheriff?" Rhonda put her most concerned look on.

"Well, you see . . . ," Bud started to say.

"You don't have to make anything up, Sheriff. I'm on your side," Rhonda said. "I was happy to see that bunch go. I got wind of their plan late last week. 'Course you can't believe everything you hear, but then when I heard Pete Batters was involved, I thought maybe there was something to it."

"Pete Batters? Who's he?" Bud asked.

"He's a big shot businessman around here. He has an insurance business, a surveying business, a title company, a couple of used car lots. He does a lot of business with the county. Some say Sheriff Wells sent too much business his way. Some say that Batters and Wells plan on going back to their old ways after you fail and Wells gets re-elected."

Bud pursed his lips and tilted his head as he absorbed this new information. So it wasn't over. He had won the election, but Wells and his friends were going to try to bring him down. The slimy lowness of it strengthened his resolve.

Rhonda Long hammered the stapler with the palm of her hand. "So they walked out on you," she said.

"All but Millie."

"You know Millie can't do what you need up there." Rhonda motioned at Bud's office on the upper floor.

"She sent me to see you."

"She did? Well bless her heart," Rhonda said.

"She said you might be persuaded to leave this office and come to work for me."

"Sheriff, you're in a tight spot, but I'm not gonna rub your nose in it any more than I have to. Here's what I need from you—total control of the office. You back me a hundred percent of the time where the paper work is concerned; I back you a hundred percent of the time where the sheriff work is concerned. And I need an IBM Selectric."

Bud rubbed his jaw. He felt certain this was the bull secretary he needed to cover his back and keep things on track, but this typewriter was something else. "Why is this typewriter so important?"

"Because it can do more work than two lazy office girls and I want one, and if I don't get it now, I never will."

"Well maybe we can get you one after . . ."

"No, not after," Rhonda said. "I've been in government long enough to know later never comes. It has to be now."

"How much does an IBM Selectric cost?"

"I don't know, but it's a lot more than you got," Rhonda said.

Bud sensed she was working toward a solution in her own sweet time. "Maybe you know where I could get one," he said.

"As a matter of fact, I do."

"Well, where would that be?" Bud leaned a little closer so the conversation couldn't be picked up by a passerby.

Rhonda produced a business card from her purse. The card read: Truman Polk, IBM Sales and Service, District Manager.

"I happen to know that Mr. Polk is going to trial in a few weeks on a drunk—driving charge."

Bud pulled back from the window a little and looked into Rhonda's eyes with surprise. "I understand what you're saying, Miss Long."

"Call me Rhonda."

"Okay, Rhonda, but I think you've misjudged me. Nice meetin' you, Rhonda."

"Nice meetin' you, too, Sheriff."

Bud stalked off feeling insulted and frustrated. When he returned to his office, Millie was in tears from her efforts to field questions that seemed so complex there could not be an answer. The phones had stopped their nerve-stretching squawk for the moment and the office was still, except for Millie's sniffles. Clearly a command decision had to be made and Bud felt the weight of the office for the first time.

Millie dabbed at her nose with a tissue, not aware of Bud's return. She picked up the receiver of a phone that had just begun its ring and dropped it back.

"You sure that wasn't important?" Bud asked.

Millie started a little at the sound of his voice, but without looking up said, "I don't care."

Bud chuckled softly. Millie heard him and smiled weakly and blew her nose. "The deputies are waiting for you down in the basement," she said. Bud nodded and began his search for the lost stairway.

The deputies were a diverse lot. There were old timers whose fathers and grandfathers were deputies, and there were mid-life career changers who started out as rent-a-cops and then migrated to the deputy ranks over time. And there were fresh faced world savers just out of police school.

Winning the deputies to his side was a major priority that had to be met head on. Now that he was aware of a plot to bring him down, Bud needed the deputies' help more than ever. The night shift men were still on the road and he would have to repeat everything he said to this group later.

The oncoming shift gathered in the basement of the courthouse. There was no room in the sheriff's office to accommodate the thirty-five officers of the night shift. The senior deputy called the men to order and introduced the new sheriff. Bud took the podium and looked out at the faces staring back at him. The least senior man had years more experience behind him in police work than Bud did, and knew it. Bud had braced himself for this moment, but now felt incompetent to lead these men.

Bud stammered and stuttered, trying to give the speech he had in mind, but his thoughts were cluttered so he changed course. "I'd like to ask each one of you to give me a short description of your most memorable arrest."

The group shifted in their seats while exchanging glances and eyes rolled between obvious partners. Bud stood his ground and laid his gaze upon everyone in the room. "You, what's your name?" Bud asked, pointing to the front chair on the right.

"Deputy Larry Pratt," the man said.

"Please to meet you, Deputy. How long you been on the force?"

"Too long, sir." The answer was given with a straight face and it brought on a general chuckle from the group.

Bud leaned across the podium with an equally straight face. "You're fired."

The chuckles stopped. Deputy Pratt held Bud's penetrating stare. Seconds ticked by. "Ha-ha-ha." Bud broke into an exaggerated smile. "Ha-ha-ha," he repeated until he had everyone in the room laughing. "Okay, that was fun. If you all are finished playing, I got a lot to learn in a short time. Mr. Brown, we will continue with you. Can you tell me without any jokes what you learned on your most memorable arrest that might be of benefit to me as I embark upon this mission."

The next hour was filled with one story after another. Each man had several stories of his own and several had stories he had heard from his father or grandfather. In the early days, Jefferson County deputies were part-time jobs that fell to men with the best horses. In those early days, most of the men in the county were eager to earn a little whiskey or tobacco money and go for a ride. The job of choosing the right man came down to how good a horse he had. The sheriff couldn't provide horses and a man with a poor horse becomes a burden. In those days, the sheriff went out on every case, only calling for deputies for such things as bear hunts and Indian raids when more than one man was a necessity. As times changed, even the burden of serving court papers to an ever increasing county demanded full time men.

Deputy Pratt, it turned out, was a third generation deputy. His grandfather raised fine horses and would sometimes loan an extra horse to a man known to be a good shot. "Grandpa was no fool," Deputy Pratt said. His father followed in the footsteps during the Depression. It was a steady paycheck when others were out of work for long periods of time, and it was an exciting time to be a deputy, with telephones, radios, and squad cars all making their appearance in a twenty year period.

Larry Pratt's daddy drove one of the first brand new cars ever purchased by the county for the express use of the sheriff's department. Clinton said he knew he wanted to be a deputy sheriff the moment he saw his daddy park the car in front of their house. Deputy Pratt's great granddad, Simon Pratt, was crippled in the line of duty. Every man on the force knew the story by heart, but they listened intently as Deputy Pratt retold it to the new sheriff.

It seems the regular jailer had left in a hurry to be with his wife's first birth. Simon Pratt took over the job of feeding the prisoners and got a little careless. Sam Richards was allowed to stand too close to the bars as Simon pushed his plate through. Richards, a small wiry petty thief, grabbed the unsuspecting man's arm and pulled him into the bars and held him tight against them. Richards ordered Simon to hand him the keys, which were within Simon's reach. Simon declined. Richards broke every finger one at a time, each time demanding the keys. Simon declined. Richards then pushed his elbow backwards against the bars until it was broken. Simon would not give him the keys. Richards continued punching and kicking Simon until he wore himself out, when Simon pulled away and rolled across the floor out of his reach.

The room fell silent as each man, including the new sheriff, imagined himself in the same situation. When the sheriff at that time, a man named Fletcher, came in and saw what had happened, he never said a word to Sam Richards about his bad conduct, but he did give him a long look. And in his eyes, Sam Richards saw that his fate was sealed. What Sheriff Fletcher saw when he looked at Richards through the bars was a copperhead. He'd killed many a copperhead but he never enjoyed it. Sheriff Fletcher took Simon Pratt to Doc Hamby. The doctor did what he could, but Simon was too busted up to ever have use of his left arm again. A few days after the incident at the jail, Sam Richards was being moved to a more secure location and was killed by Sheriff Fletcher as he tried to escape. The story of his escape attempt was never fully told. No one ever asked.

Deputy Larry Pratt told the story of his grandfather's honor and courage with subdued pride. The jail keys hung on a peg within easy reach of Simon's right arm, and with his left arm pulled through the bars and the fingers being broken one at a time, every man there considered, would they have grabbed the keys? The term "Grab the keys" became a taunt at any deputy unwilling to do the most in his power to do the job right. To Grab the keys was to take the easy way out.

Larry Pratt wasn't sure why he had a sudden liking for Bud Browdy. Maybe it was the clumsy way he tried to explain things. Maybe he saw something that said you could trust this man to cover your back. Maybe it was the humble sincerity of the simple questions he asked and the confidence he showed in the answers he received from his new employees. The way he talked to the men was like they were volunteers, only there to help out their neighbors. He didn't ask one question about his men's qualifications. The fact that they were there and were willing to follow his lead seemed to be enough.

At the end of his meeting, Bud had won over most of the deputies to his side. The stories the deputies told were old and worn out to everyone but Bud. The enthusiasm he showed toward the men made each man feel like he had a new friend in the sheriff. Bud's praises and appreciation made them all want to help and shelter this friendly pilgrim entering Indian territory.

Bud returned to his office feeling better about his situation. Millie informed him that there had been thus far no matter needing his immediate attention. Bud returned to his desk and was caught off guard again by the broken chair. This time he went over backwards. Millie heard the commotion and hurried in. "You okay?" she asked with a wide-eyed expression.

Bud maintained as much dignity as possible from his position on the floor and in his deepest, official sheriff's voice said, "Yes. Would you try and find the arrest record of a man named Truman Polk?" "He sells typewriters."

CHAPTER TWENTY-SIX

B ud Browdy shoved open the heavy courthouse door and tasted the night air. The end of his first day was here at last. Bud felt he only had two or three nerves left to stretch. If every day is like this, I won't last two weeks, he thought. He slid into the driver's seat of a brand new Cadillac DeVille. The door closed with a satisfying thump and all was quiet. The soft velour seat melted as his weight reshaped the foam rubber core. Bud let out a long sigh, a long deep sigh, a sigh so deep he made no effort to inhale. His mind reasoned that it was up to his lungs to do their own work; his brain was too tired. He studied the dashboard with unfocused eyes. The car had more knobs and buttons than any he had ever driven. Then with the addition of all the police gadgets, it was all but overwhelming.

Good old Dan, Bud said to himself. He had bribed or begged or extorted the county into buying him a Cadillac for his sheriff's car. And now look who's driving it, Bud thought. He giggled silently. Old Dan had it outfitted with lights on top and lights in the grill, dual spotlights on each side of the windshield, and radio antennas arched over the trunk. Three different radios hung off the dashboard. The standard factory radio had a foot operated button that changed the stations. The citizen band radio had a microphone of its own. The sheriff's department radio had a microphone. The state highway patrol radio had a microphone. All three were clustered together and their coral cords dangled beneath the dash. Toggle switches operated four different sets of lights and two sirens.

A broad grin stretched across Bud's face as the problems of the day faded. He turned knobs and flipped switches until he thought he had her figured out.

On his way home, he pushed the gas pedal to the floor and listened contentedly to the 500-cubic inch motor dig deep for horsepower. He took note of the speedometer and laughed out loud. Who's going to tell me to slow down—I'm the sheriff, he thought, and kicked her into passing gear again. She handled pretty good for such a big car. The suspension was too soft for any serious high speed pursuits, he thought.

The thrill of the drive didn't last and his mind recounted the day's events. How quickly he had traded a drunk driving charge for a typewriter. What would be next, a murder charge for a color TV? Bud would have called any man a liar who would have predicted such a thing. How will I know when I'm doin' wrong? Bud thought. Of all the worries and concerns he had before his election, his ability to know right from wrong had never concerned him.

Martha was sitting at the kitchen table talking on the phone when Bud walked in. "Bud's home. I'll talk to you later," she said. She hung the phone on the wall and smiled her pride at Bud. Bud smiled back as he must. To do otherwise would cause Martha to fear for the worst and be sure Bud was holding back some terrible secret that she would find out only too late.

Martha moved about the kitchen in a haphazard manner, never coming to a stop, only gliding by a pot for a peek or to the fridge for some milk, in constant motion that ended with a plate full of meat and vegetables served with a huge glass of milk.

Bud watched and listened in wonder as Martha chatted away about the number of people who called to give their congratulations. He accepted his food with pleasure and filled his mouth and nodded and grunted at the appropriate spots as Martha talked on. She had arrived back home only yesterday after a weekend visit with her sister. Her sister Margaret was the proud mother of two little boys and a new baby girl. Martha was sometimes full of life, hope, and happiness after a visit to her sister's house and sometimes not. The playing with and caring for her niece and nephews made her happy and would ease the pain of being childless like a shot of whiskey to a drunk. Only sometimes the same shot would leave her hopeless and forlorn. This was a good visit. No doubt his election victory had taken her focus away from being a mother for now, only to return next week or the week after.

Even when Martha was at her lowest, she seldom complained. The meager lifestyle Bud had been able to offer had always been accepted with gratitude and good cheer. The only thing she longed for was a child, and that he had not provided.

The first years of their marriage had been uncertain financially, with jobs and careers and businesses that didn't work out, and money always in short supply. Martha understood, and she was willing, as a good partner in life, to wait for her turn at happiness until a good house in a good neighborhood and a steady income made their way into their lives.

When they began to try in earnest to start a family, she was still patient and optimistic. The second year of trying began to weaken her faith. Bud had enjoyed the extra effort Martha had put into their lovemaking. She seemed to will herself to become pregnant by intensifying her passion. Bud thought the fact that they might have a baby was icing on the cake. As the months flew by and still no baby, Martha began going to doctors. She went to St. Louis and she went to Kansas City. She cried like a baby when Bud refused to go with her to St. Louis and produce a sample of sperm at the clinic. Bud had never seen her cry before and vowed never to make her cry again. He went to St. Louis and did what was asked. The results were positive, which only made Martha cry again.

Bud had secretly thought he might be the one to keep Martha from the children she loved. As a young man, brush hogging the field one day, he had stood on the fender of the tractor to relieve himself. While scanning the fence line, his water stream splashed a spark plug and the jolt had knocked him to the ground and left him sore for quite some time. The results of his sperm count put that fear to rest at last, but now Martha carried the blame alone. She was the failure. Martha stopped crying three days later and never cried again. The trips to her sister's sometimes left her blue, but she carried her pain quietly and didn't blame doctors or God for her barrenness.

CHAPTER TWENTY-SEVEN

Rita Coal turned off the lamp next to her bed. She slipped between the cool sheets and looked into the darkness, waiting for her body heat to warm her spot. She slept on her side of the double bed; Dry slept on her right side. She moved her arm to where he would be on the chance that he might be there. Gone almost nine years now, Rita still searched for him in the darkness where anything is possible. Why did he have to go? She needed him so badly. The boys needed him. She couldn't bear to see another son sent to prison. Why is the eternal question that has no answer. Why? Why? Why? she asked in the dark.

She remembered what a beautiful night it had been. The stars seemed so close. There must have been thirty ski boats nosed into the sand on the Illinois side of the Mississippi River. A long, flat stretch of sand that lay just below Crystal City made for a perfect beach party. It was the Fourth of July in 1955. The members of the Meramec Yacht Club were in high spirits. Huge bonfires spread dancing amber light across the white sand. An abundant supply of driftwood fed the fires.

Groups of men in funny hats and checkered Bermuda shorts and cut off white painter's pants and flip-flop shoes discussed boats and sports and unions and the army and the government. Groups of women with scarves on their heads and one-piece bathing suits and towels around their waists and sandals on their feet discussed husbands and kids and the value of a driver's license. Teenagers around their own fire far enough from the parents to not be heard discussed their mothers' and fathers' archaic rules and the pitiful lives they were forced to endure.

The sleek and graceful fiberglass boats beached side by side created a wall of color—pink and white, aqua green, and white, red and white, blue and white—some with canvas tops with bold stripes. In a few hours this place will be empty and desolate but now it's a carnival.

The teenagers had exploded their last bottle rocket; and after a full day of sun and skis and hotdogs, a pleasant fatigue washed over the party. A few packed up to leave, but most wanted a little more time around the tribal fires. The good times had exceeded what should have been an adequate supply of beer. Old Dry Coal, never one to shirk a responsibility, took up a collection and volunteered to make a beer run.

Rita Coal stood around the women's fire and watched as her friends proved they could still jitterbug like they used to. Their laughter floated across the sand in high pitched waves and the husbands and the kids shook their heads. The women were happy. They felt they had a right to be happy; their men had won the war and had good blue collar jobs, their children went to good schools, and their homes were as good or better than the homes they grew up in. They had followed the rules and the rules had worked and they were proud of themselves.

Rita Coal was not a handsome woman. She was small and bony, her face was sharp of feature, her eyes were small and dark; she carried the heart of a saint. She herded Dry in the right direction whenever necessary and without harsh words. He trusted her and she gave him a loose rein. She could turn a dragon to stone with a mean look; but when she smiled, the dark eyes had a light in them that sparkled like a dewdrop in the sun.

The tugboat blew its horn. The horn blew again and again. Eight barges, two across, four deep being pushed by the tugboat Memphis Pride came abreast of the party. All heads turned and all understood at once the tragedy that was about to unfold in slow motion. Old Dry's boat lay in the path of the barge—stalled and helpless. Dry had installed what he called Steak and Shake lights on his boat, a string of white lights that circled the boat in a continuous parade of flashes. Everyone on the beach knew whose boat was about to be crushed. The captain of the Memphis Pride reversed his engines. It would do no good, but at the inquiry he would be able to say he had done so when asked what evasive measures he took to avoid the collision. Old Dry had cut across his bow and had his boat continued to run, he would have cleared the path of the barge with a hundred yards to spare. Did the carburetor clog? Did the magneto fail? Did the fuel line kink? No one ever knew. When an outboard fails at the wrong time, it's no different than an airplane motor's failure in its absolute repercussions.

The captain of The Memphis Pride shut down his engines now and an eerie silence preceded the collision. The party on the beach could hear the starter grinding away on old Dry's boat and the outboard came to life for a moment, but died. Dry had waited too long to abandon ship. There was no hope now of swimming to safety. The leading edge of the barge overshadowed the boat. Steel and fiberglass rubbed against each other and the boat was pushed sideways in the water; its buoyancy refusing to submit. Then the Steak and Shake lights were gone. Rita knew in her heart that Dry was dead.

Rescue boats were sent out and circled the barge. Pieces of the boat popped to the surface, but old Dry Coal was never found.

Dewey Bazler, who was there that night, retells the story once a year on Christmas Eve; and the rough and tumble crowds that gather in the riverside bars along the Meramec River cry like babies.

CHAPTER TWENTY-EIGHT

Byron Creed shifted from foot to foot, leaning against an oak tree, looking down on the lights of Floyd's Tire Mart. The dry leaves crunched excessively to Byron's way of thinking. A few feet away, a bicycle leaned against another tree; its front wheel pointing downhill on a tractor road. The two-track trail ran along the ridge top on the west side of Highway 67. From this point going south, the tractor path went downhill all the way to the river.

Byron unzipped the front of the brown duck coveralls he wore. The effort of pushing the banana seat bike up the long hill in the dark had overheated him. In his back pocket, the handle of Demon Chaser slapped his butt. The long barrel of the pistol kept it from setting deep in the pocket. Byron was forced to keep one hand on the gun and push the bike with only one hand, a job more difficult than he had anticipated.

Byron checked his watch. It was nine forty-five. Skip would be counting the money and adding the tickets at the desk. Ike Williams would be stacking tires. Byron had studied the route he would take across the field to the edge of the highway. The lights of the gas station would be his beacon. He needed to be crossing the highway just before the lights went out. The field was overgrown with thick red sumac, small cedars, tall weeds, and large sticker bushes. Large tentacles from the sticker bushes reached far out from the bush. Byron had laid out a path in the daylight. The field could be crossed, but it was a zigzag path and a wrong turn could send you up a box canyon of long thorned sticker bushes.

The Coal brothers had supplied the coveralls and the ski mask. Byron had expected a dark blue or black ski mask. Instead, he had been supplied a white one with red and green Christmas trees circling it in a repeating pattern. He felt the mask wasn't sinister enough. He wore brown jersey gloves so he would leave no fingerprints. He had planned to wear leather gloves but had apparently lost another pair, the pair Al said were the last ones he was buying if he couldn't hold on to them any better than that. Fuck Al, Byron thought. I'll buy my own gloves from now on.

Byron began his approach. There would be no turning back, he counseled himself. The last tire was rolled inside and stacked. Ike Williams leaned on the stack watching the clock. Five more minutes and he could turn out the lights. He hoped he had cleaned his last windshield for the day. The rumble of a dump truck brought him to the door. Ike sighed with relief as it went on down the road. A movement caught his eye and he saw a man in coveralls coming out of the field and crossing the highway. Something about the man's gait, the loose limbed stride, tweaked Ike's brain, but he wasn't able to understand its meaning. Only teenage boys and drunks walk like that, he finally concluded; but while he was studying the situation, Byron was covering ground.

Byron pulled at the eye holes in the ski mask as it contracted up his face. Ike was watching him approach. He had to hurry now. If Ike became suspicious and stepped inside and locked the door before he could get there, he would be forced to turn and run with nothing. Byron broke into a run, holding the pistol in the back pocket with his right hand and pumping the air and pulling at the mask with his left. The thick insulated coveralls made him feel as though he were running in a foot of water.

Ike was hypnotized by the spectacle and only when it was too late, realized he was about to be held up. Byron had the gun out now and backed Ike into the building. Byron's heart pounded with excitement and fear. The laborious dash had added to his heart's workload. His gun hand vibrated and the brown jersey gloves could not find traction on the black plastic grips of the pistol. Ike had backed to the doorway that led to the office. Ten seconds had elapsed when Byron remembered his part. "Money," he said, using the foreign accent he had practiced.

Ike appeared frozen with fear and Byron felt a jolt of confidence. He suddenly thought he would not pay Clay Coal any money; he would keep it all and go to Mexico. He wasn't sure why he would go to Mexico; it was just what you did after a holdup. "Money," he said again.

Ike heard the demand for the second time and remembered where he had heard that voice before. It was Boris Bentenoff the Russian spy from the Rocky & Bullwinkle show.

Now Byron's confidence began to sink. This wasn't working. In his mind, Byron had rehearsed the chain of events over and over. He would point the gun, say the word *money* in his foreign accent, Ike would go to the office, get the money from Skip, come back, hand him a bag of money, and he'd be gone across the highway and into the sticker bushes. He'd cross the field, climb the hill, get rid of the clothes, jump on his bike, ride down the trail, go under the bridge, stash the money, and be home and in bed before the cops even showed up. This was taking too long. Ike wasn't moving. Byron hadn't practiced saying anything besides the word *money*. He needed to make something happen and quick. He fired a shot into a stack of tires next to Ike and repeated his practiced word. This time the emotion of the moment overcame his voice control and the tone was much higher and shakier.

Al appeared in the doorway, Byron visibly jolted at the sight of him. This was Skip's night to close, he was sure of it. Damn it, he thought, another foul up that's not my fault. Al had heard the word *money* on the first try and froze in his chair. The desk was covered with papers, cash, lamps, ashtrays. Al's mind raced around the office for a weapon. Nothing. An umbrella in the corner offered a brief promise, then faded. He could see Ike standing rigid by the counter, but only the lower half of the robber. The gun was not visible, but Al assumed he had one. The crack of the pistol brought Al to his feet. Not sure why he was walking toward danger, he just did. Ike was out there and he couldn't let him face this alone.

The second demand for money on the heels of the gunshot sounded strangely familiar. "Byron?" Al said.

Ike looked around. "Byron," he repeated, and the goofy walk and the voice came together in his mind. "Byron?" he said again.

Byron swung the pistol back and forth covering his retreat and took a step backwards. "Byron, is that you?" Al's voice grumbled.

"No," was the response that leaked out of Byron's throat before he could stop it. Now he swung the gun faster back and forth. The length of the barrel made the pistol handle twist in his gloved hand, the cotton fabric unable to create friction on the plastic grips. Crack! went the second shot. Al clutched at his side. "Shit," Byron said.

Blood poured from between Al's fingers. Al knew in an instant that he was not hurt bad. He had been shot before and he knew the difference. "Damn, boy, have you gone crazy?" Al said.

Byron hadn't moved. He still held the gun pointed at Al. Al looked away from his bloody right side where the small caliber slug had cut a crease into the fatty tissue of his love handles. "You gonna shoot me again?" Al asked.

Byron lowered the barrel of the pistol, turned, and ran out the door. Ike and Al stood for a second and watched Byron disappear into the darkness. Ike turned and reached for the phone. "Don't!" Al barked. "I'm okay," he said in a softer tone.

"You don't want an ambulance or the cops?" Ike asked.

"No, I don't," Al shot back. "It's just a scratch. I'm fine." Al went back to his desk and put a stack of paper towels used to clean windshields to his side. Ike followed him to the office and pulled a chair to the desk. Al checked his wound again and replaced his paper towels. "Don't say nothin' about this," he said.

Ike studied Al's movements and expressions as he tended to his side. He didn't appear to be in terrible pain. Ike had seen him stomp and cuss over a smashed finger several times so this must not hurt too bad. Al popped the tab of a 16-ounce Schlitz. Ike didn't wait to be asked. He just reached over and popped one too. "Where will he go?" Ike asked.

"I don't know. Some empty cabin on the river, I guess. He'll stay gone a couple of days. Then if he don't hear anything about this, he'll come home."

Ike took a long draw on his beer, lit a couple of cigarettes, and handed one to Al. As he puffed on his own, Ike considered the situation and gulped more warm beer. He began to relax. He had not realized how tense the attempted robbery had made him. Now as the adrenalin rush wore off, the long day took its toll.

"Look here, Ike, I know this is asking a lot and I haven't gone out of my way to be nice to you, but I need some time to work this out. If I turn him in, he'll be ruined forever," Al said.

"Won't they help him?"

"Hah!" The sting in his side reminded Al not to laugh so heartily. The innocence of youth always brought a smile to Al's face. The young people today lived in a world of supermarkets and central heat; they believed most problems can be solved in an hour or less, the way Ben Cartwright did every week. "No, they ain't goin' to help him. They'll just train him how to be mean."

Al took a gulp of beer before continuing. "Right now, Byron's just stupid. He goes to jail, he'll come out mean and stupid." Al pulled himself to his feet and lumbered across the showroom floor to the breaker panel and shut off all the outside lights. Ike remained at the desk gulping the beer in short intervals as he sorted out the events of the last five minutes. Al came back to the desk and lowered himself cautiously, letting out a final grunt of air as his butt made contact with the chair. Al studied Ike's face for clues to his thoughts. "You gonna keep this quiet?" he asked.

Ike returned Al's direct stare and nodded silently. "What you gonna do when he does come home?"

Al was relieved by Ike's apparent sincerity and worked a cigarette into his mouth. "You got one burning," Ike said, pointing to an ashtray. Al grunted his acknowledgment and lit the fresh one anyway. "Are you sure you don't need a doctor, 'cause if you up and die on me, I could end up in a lot of trouble."

"Yeah, I'm sorry I got you dragged into this shit. I gotta try and get through to the boy one more time. I've been a crappy father."

Ike was still. Al's confession landed in his lap and he didn't know what to do with it.

Air leaked from the tire changer as it had all day. A moment ago, it wasn't heard; but now it seemed loud and demanding of attention in the stillness of the room. A car used the driveway to turn around and the hose bell broke the trance.

"How are you going to get through to him if he won't listen?" Ike asked.

"Well, I'll have to make him listen. He turns and runs every time I try to talk to him. I need to tie him to a chair and make him listen."

Ike watched Al's face for a sign that he might be hurt worse than he claimed. When Al said he would tie Byron to a chair, his eyes suddenly brightened and Ike could tell an idea had just taken shape.

CHAPTER TWENTY-NINE

Al drove himself home. The potholes of Sycamore Lane seemed deeper tonight. He held the stack of paper towels against his wound. He parked his truck and slowly climbed the stairs. He lit a kerosene heater he kept on the back porch. He went to the refrigerator and grabbed a six pack of tallboys and took his post.

Al leaned his wooden chair back against the wall and stared out onto the river. The kerosene heater glowed efficiently in the corner. The heat moved across the floor in steady waves that baked the fabric warm against Al's legs, sending chills of relief up his spine.

The river was a place of eternal fascination like looking into a fire. Al's far off stare toward the river brought him the relief he needed. Six, sixteen-ounce cans of Schlitz just cooled his thoughts.

Al began making a list in his mind, his plan not fully formed, but his thoughts kept returning to the supplies he would need to make it work. Like a camper going out into the wilderness for a long stay trying to anticipate every possible need. Canned goods of all types—vegetables, beans, fruit, canned meat. Nothing that can't be eaten cold. How much? Enough for two weeks? No. Enough for two months? No. Enough for six months. That's it. It's not like it will be wasted. You can bring it home when you let him out. When he sees all that food, it'll send the message that you're serious. He's not completely stupid. If you give him only a couple of weeks' worth, he'll calculate that as his release date pretty quick. No, give him food by the case. That'll send a message.

Christmas would be here in two more weeks and Al pictured that in his mind for Byron's release. It was bad enough to lock your son up, but to keep him there over Christmas was more than Al could do. Christmas was still a special time to Al. The memories of his youth generated soft pictures of happiness and well being, of poor children huddled around a pitiful Christmas tree decorated with slips of colored paper glued into chains, tops of tin cans tied with a string hanging from the branches twisting in the lantern light. Young faces eyeing presents wrapped in newspaper with bows and ribbons saved from Christmases past and saved again for Christmases to come.

Al's plan to deal with Byron was crazy, his rational side told him again and again. His desperate side would not budge from the notion that desperate times require desperate measures. Al had been wrong in his life many times. That was made abundantly clear to him every day. The long hot summer or the cold wet winter days at Floyd's filling brand new tandems that should have been his, airing up the tires on new trucks owned by men half his age with only a third of his experience.

There was no denying that Al had made some wrong decisions. That's the thing about deciding. Half the time you don't even know you've made a decision until after you've made it. The other thing about decisions is that they always seem right at the time. Al pondered this. Nobody sets out to make a wrong decision, he thought. Why the odds alone should get you right half the time. Al pushed the mathematical part of this inner discussion out of his conversation. Doing math on paper was hard enough; working out numbers in the head will drive you crazy. That was a phrase his father would say from time to time as he struggled with the home finances. Al found this to be true in his life also.

Al's thoughts drifted back to the present when his pants leg began to burn his skin. Would Byron be warm enough? Would he have sense enough to find shelter? Sure he would. Cold forces even the simplest of creatures to seek heat, he thought.

Al drifted into darkness. After a few minutes, he was awakened by his own snoring sounding like a lion's roar in the quiet night. He rubbed the back of his neck with his left hand to work out the kinks and touched his wound with his right. The area around the wound was naturally sore, but he was relieved that it wasn't more sore than it should be. He checked his watch. Two o'clock. Three hours sleep was possible if he could fall asleep right away. There was a bottle of whiskey under the sink. One or two good swallows should put him out.

Al went down on his knees and pointed a flashlight at the bottle of bleach in the back corner of the storage space under the sink. Reaching over a variety of cleaners, brushes, oils, additives, and a plunger, he carefully raised the bleach bottle straight up. The bottom of the plastic bottle had been removed and a pint of bourbon whiskey appeared. The last twisting stretch required to reach the whiskey pulled at his gut muscles and Al felt his wound reopen. He fell to his face, unable to catch himself with his hands. He fell in under the sink, pushing bottles and cans and making a general racket as he went down.

Al returned to his chair by the heater and moved it a little closer. The wound was throbbing again. He had a sudden chill quiver through his body as he considered getting up and getting a blanket, but that meant rising from the chair again. He gave it considerable thought, and there were lots of advantages to having a blanket, but then again pushing your weight straight up to a standing start—no make that a sitting start—that took more commitment than Al felt he could spare at that moment.

Al poured a shot of whiskey down his throat right from the bottle. The liquid fire burned a path from his lips to the bottom of his belly. That should do it, he thought. One more swallow just to make sure.

Al stared out toward the river, still visible under a small moon. Would Ike keep his mouth shut? Would Byron do something stupid again before Al could put his plan together? Where was Byron right now? What would he be doing? Would he come home and pretend he knew nothing? Will he run? Where would he go? Back to Denver?

An escaped beer keg glowed in the dim light of the moon, bobbing along on the black water. Will it make any sense to do the thing he was considering? One more swallow and maybe all these questions would be answered.

Al leaned back in the chair and let his eyes close, but the darkness wouldn't come. His stomach rumbled its unhappiness at the lack of food. He had not eaten since lunch. Three o'clock. Two hours would get him by. All he really needed to do was go in and unlock all the pumps, help Ike get the tires out, and then he could come back home and go to bed. That was the plan. Go in, open up, come home, go to bed, get some good sleep and think this through. He looked at his watch again.

Al slumped into a head bobbing sleep and the snap of his neck catching his head as it drifted back past the point of balance became part of the dream. In the dream he was a boy again. He was running barefoot across a field chasing after his older brother Daryl. The wet grass dripping with early morning dew soaked his overalls from the knees down. The shoulder straps bounced up and down on his bare shoulders as he chased after Daryl. Then in the dream he was locked in a chicken coop and Daryl wouldn't let him out.

Al was often trapped in a chicken coop. Whenever life became too much to handle, he would dream of the chicken coop. That was the part where he was unable to separate fact from fiction. Did that really happen on some farm when he was a child? Did Daryl really put him in a chicken coop and not let him out? He might have. That sounded like something Daryl would do. But Al could not remember. In the dream he was behind wood slats crying to be let out. Daryl wouldn't open the gate. "You can't follow me anymore, Alvin." Daryl was the only person who always called him Alvin even though his name was Alfred. "Alvin, Alvin, you're too young to go with me. I got grownup stuff to do. You're too small." The feeling of terror shaking at the wall of the chicken coop, screaming to be freed, promising anything to be freed. That was it, to be free, willing to say anything to be free.

Byron was going to jail; that was undisputed fact in Al's mind. Not for what he had pulled tonight, but for what he would surely do. He had to get through to him what it would do to his soul to be in jail. The fear of captivity ran deep within Al. The dream with the chicken coop bars had been a recurring event since his teenage years whenever stress tortured his sleep. In times of sadness or death in the family, the dream comes when there's nowhere to run.

Byron must feel what captivity would be. He needs a taste of what a long term prison sentence would do to his mind. He needs time to think about how foolish the things he's doing really are. He needs to feel time minute by minute, counting the seconds on a countdown that never ends, a countdown that someone else controls.

Why not let the county handle it, he argued with himself. That was a debate that had been playing throughout the night. No, he'll make friends with people that think the way he does. No, the county can have its chance if this fails. Hell, they may get both of us. Al chuckled at himself for only a moment. The joke was too close to the truth.

Sleep came again for only a few hours. Al awoke stiff and cold in the early morning light. He was late was the first startling thought that twanged his nervous system like a guitar string. He shot up from his chair and fell back again on the numb legs that had lost circulation. He felt cautiously, probing his skin around the bullet hole. The wound itself seemed no worse. The bandage was soaked and he had lost more blood. He tried again to rise and this time stayed on his feet and hobbled into the kitchen. He stopped at the bathroom and examined his wound in the mirror. It was crusty and ugly, with bruising covering the area between the entry and exit of the .22 caliber slug. He washed the injured area with a hot washcloth. There were no more clean washcloths to be found, so he folded a t-shirt so it covered both holes and taped it in place with a role of masking tape.

Al checked his watch again. He wasn't late. He had read it wrong. It was 3:30, not quarter past 6. He let out a sigh of relief. He returned to his chair and finished off the whiskey.

CHAPTER THIRTY

Byron Creed crashed through the brush in a confused panic. He was running over the top of small cedars, the sticker bushes raked at his hands and face, the gloves and ski mask were snatched off by a million fish hooks attached to long willowy branches. Byron started to retrieve the lost apparel so as not to leave a trail then remembered they knew who he was; a trail didn't matter. Maybe they didn't know for sure. He could swear it wasn't him. How could they prove it? He found his way to the bicycle and stripped off the coveralls. The air was a pleasant 45 degrees and his run across the field and up the hill had overheated him to the point of torture. The cool relief allowed him to think.

What to do? Where to go? He sat on a banana seat bike in the dark in the woods with Al shot and the police on his heels. Then he started to pedal. He pedaled down the two track fire road at a leisurely pace, mostly coasting. He had ridden this fire road many times, knew every bump and twist, even in the moonlight. The parallel ribbons of dirt glowed slightly out in front of him as it wove its course toward the river. The ride was all downhill; the trail was smooth.

Byron pulled back on the apehanger handlebars and slumped on the seat and let the bike carry as much speed as it could. He was no longer in a hurry. He was just enjoying the sensation of the ride. His problems were behind him for the moment. He could not think of anything but the control of the bike plunging down the hill in the dark. The bike shook its head, the rear wheel skittered over rootwads growing into the road. The turns were banked. Byron was in a groove. He had come down this hill many times and always received a thrill from the challenge of pushing to go a little faster. Now the thrill was back. Byron had meant to ride this at night at least once in his life but had never seemed to find the right time. Now he regretted putting it off for so long. Because of what happened tonight, he thought, this might be the last ride he would take for some time.

The last sweeping turn is just ahead. The twin lines of light disappear as they arch away into the darkness. Byron is carrying more speed now than he ever did in daylight. Yet he pumps the pedals two more times and vows not to touch the brakes before setting up for the curve.

The bike dives into the night with reckless abandon. The bank of the curve is high and smooth and Byron leans left. He feels the bike climb the bank, the centrifugal force holding its own against gravity. He must lean further and trust the tires won't lose their grip. One more moment. He bursts out into the moonlight again, cutting back to the right to set up for the jump and he's up. The stingray bike with the armed robber on board leaped from the darkness into the moonlight to drift down the hillside. Like a ski jumper, Byron stands on the pedals leaning forward catching air with his chest, hanging in the night sky for blissful seconds only to be pulled back to the earth.

The landing was good. Byron's trajectory was perfect. His angle of descent couldn't have been better. The bike simply wasn't up to the task. The frame snapped like a pretzel. The crankshaft Byron stood astride plowed itself deep into the soft clay. The front wheel and the handlebars became a separate unit. The ground slapped him in the face, the rear wheel tangled in his feet arched over his back, taking Byron with it. Byron's face slapped the ground and he was chewing dirt. Up in the air he tumbled, still tangled with the frame, seat, and rear wheel. He hit the ground again, his left arm twisted behind him. His momentum was such that he bounced once again before coming to a stop. Then it was over. The frogs returned to their croaking, the crickets played their song, and the rear wheel of the broken rocket ship went click, click, click, click.

When Byron returned to the conscious world, two hours had passed. The headache was dull and throbbing. He raised his hands to smooth his head, but his left arm screamed No! Byron lay in a root wad twisted and ugly. The effort to get to his feet took another twenty minutes. When he had walked a dozen steps, he paused and winced in pain as he tried to swivel at the hips and look back at the landing sight. He stutter stepped around to take one last look at the scene.

That was one hell of a jump, he thought. If only someone had seen it. He wished the Coal brothers had seen it. Even Clay. It took a lot to impress Clay, but a jump like that would do it. He was certain of that.

Wincing in pain, he stutter stepped around again and hobbled toward home. The trek took forever. Each pothole, every stick became an obstacle to be avoided. Any misstep on his shaky legs was sure to cause a fall, and a fall could not be tolerated. The arm hurt the most, followed by the head, the left knee, and the left ankle. As the night wore on, the knee and ankle moved into second place in the pain race. Both had swollen to an alarming size. The tears flowed freely down his cheeks. He wasn't crying, he reminded himself. Crying is when you whimper or whine. Byron wasn't making noise, but the water ran out of his eyes cutting erosion ditches down his bloody dirty face.

Somewhere along the way, Byron became sick. He dropped to the ground and emptied his stomach. That was a long time ago. His watch was gone. His dizziness forced rest stops, and at each rest stop he passed out. He would awake at the bite of a bug or a rock pressing a point in his back. Each time when he awoke, the place looked the same—the same towering sycamores, the same reflection of the river, the same gravel road, the constant roar of the frogs. In the darkness he could not tell if he was making any progress.

When Al's house finally came into sight, the morning light was beginning to brighten.

Al Creed had spent the night in a wooden chair balanced on its back legs in the shadows of the back porch. He had a view of the river and he could watch the road. His wound throbbed but was bearable if he didn't move, so he didn't move. He stared at the river and blamed himself, then he blamed Byron, then himself more, then Byron more. The running battle continued through the night. Al wore the arguments out in his mind until he couldn't think about who was to blame any more. What to do became the question. He wrestled with that in the pre-dawn light.

Byron could see the speck of fire that was Al's cigarettes glowing with each draw. The failed robbery now seemed insignificant to him, but Al would still make a big deal out of it; he was sure of that.

Byron's strength was all but gone, and the pain consumed everything. Nothing mattered now but easing the pain. He pushed on.

Al looked at his watch as he had every ten minutes all night long. The specter hobbling toward the house was Byron—he was sure of that. Why he was hurt or how badly would become clear soon enough. With a deep sigh, he pushed himself from his chair to meet Byron at the door. He knew he was supposed to be concerned. He should race to Byron and see to his injuries with loving care. He just didn't feel that way. Byron had caused a lot of people a lot of trouble. He had used most everyone's benefit of a doubt.

Al reached the bottom of the steps just as Byron stumbled into the driveway. His good leg dropped into a pothole, one Al had asked him to fill, and he hit the ground. Al stood looking at him from the steps. He should go help his son up; he just didn't want to. He had given up another night's sleep for a boy who just wouldn't grow up. "Can you get in the truck?" he asked.

Byron nodded his head and made it to his feet and into the pickup.

Neither said a word as the Ford pickup wobbled down Sycamore Lane. Byron braced himself with his one good leg. His other knee had swollen to the size of his thigh. His good arm held his bad arm, and his head rolled around with little control. Al took a good look at the boy as he flipped on the defrosters. The fan motor came on with an irritating hum. Al slammed a calloused paw on the dash and the humming stopped. Byron sat straight up and winced in pain as he was pulled back to the here and now. "Sorry," Al said.

Byron heard the word but could not put it together with its meaning. What was Al sorry about? The light got hazy again and his head dropped back to its loose hinged bobble. Al lit another cigarette and by the flame of his lighter examined Byron's face. Blood had crusted around his nostrils and his split lip, both eyes were blackened in equal proportion. His parental responsibility momentarily overcame his frustration. He needed to find out what had happened to the boy and if anyone else was hurt.

Al slapped the dash. Byron jolted to attention with a howl. "Sorry, damn fan," Al said. "What happened to you?"

"I had a wreck."

"You wrecked another car?"

"No, a bicycle."

"A bicycle. You busted yourself up on a bicycle?"

Byron didn't reply. He wanted to tell someone about the length of the jump he'd made but knew Al wouldn't appreciate or understand. He was probably still mad about being shot and that wasn't his fault. The damn gun had a hair trigger. Where was the gun? He couldn't remember. He knew he had lost it but couldn't remember when or how. He closed his eyes and slipped into a half sleep.

CHAPTER THIRTY-ONE

Al pulled onto the lot at Floyd's an hour late. Ike had the coffee on, the tires out, and several cars being fueled. Ike normally didn't open the station himself; only the managers had keys. Al had suspected he might have a long night and not make it in on time when he gave Ike his keys the night before. The sight of Al brought relief to Ike. He had been able to keep up with the morning rush at this point but would fall behind soon without help. Al, feeling every bit his age, limped his shuffling walk up the drive. He had a newfound respect for Ike, who was putting himself on a limb and working his ass off to cover up all that had happened.

Even Al's thoughts were tired. He had to think very slowly. This was going to be a long day. That was all Al knew for sure. His bandaged wound was still leaking and he hadn't slept more than a couple of hours since receiving it. How many times had he said I give up trying to set the boy on the right path?

Al put the gas nozzle in a Rambler wagon. The windows weren't dirty but got the usual cleaning. The world was moving on at its normal pace, but Al was running in slow motion. He barely heard orders for gas and repeatedly put too much or not enough of the right octane in the wrong car. The events of the last two years came forward in random scenes of passion and violence. He couldn't give up; he knew that even as he wanted to. Life was hard enough, he thought, and Byron still showed no signs of maturity, but he couldn't quit. It just wasn't part of his makeup.

The Rambler wanted a full tank and Al was holding the nozzle on full volume when the air bubbles splashed gas back up the filler pipe and all over his pants. He was drenched from the waist down but didn't seem concerned. He only cussed his usual cuss words softly and moved on.

A spot of blood on his shirt was growing in size where the bullet had gone through. Ike watched as Al stumbled and mumbled all morning. Floyd would be here in half an hour. He would see the blood. A lie would have to be concocted on a moment's notice. Ike didn't believe Al could come up with a reasonable lie in his condition.

The dump truck drivers were coming in now and they were a crusty bunch who wanted their tanks filled and their tires checked quickly. Al wasn't keeping up. He shuffled and limped around in a daze. Ike finally convinced him to change his pants; he was a walking fireball ready to go off at the first spark. All the men kept spare pants in the office for just such an occasion. The trucks were backing up and impatience was building while Al shuffeled along with clean pants in his hands. He walked absentmindedly right into the tire room with its full length window and undressed.

Ike could smell the liquor on Al's breath. If he was drunk, he didn't show it, but he was slow and confused. He was having trouble making change.

Lowell Maynard was waiting his turn at the pumps twisting in his seat, checking his watch. The service was unusually slow this morning, and he considered leaving, but his tank was on empty and his windshield needed cleaning, a service that was fast going out of style. The real reason he always came to Floyd's was his chance to see Byron. He believed the boy to be his son. Byron's mother, Rayleen, had been a one night stand. Lowell Maynard did not go in for one night stands and that was his first and last. That night so many years ago still haunted him at least once a day and every time he came to Floyd's.

Now he remembered again. It was a Saturday night. It's always a Saturday night, he thought, when something like that happens. Rayleen never told Lowell that Byron was his son, but it was plain to see if looked for.

Lowell Maynard only did company business with Floyd's. It would not be good if his wife, Helen, ever saw Byron walk across the parking lot and recognized his gait to be the same as his. Women pick up on things like that.

Lowell's turn came at last. It was clear to him that if he wanted his windshield cleaned he would have to do it himself. He plucked a handful of blue paper towels from the dispenser and began rubbing at the bug guts that refused to let go.

There in the big window, Al Creed hopped on one foot in his underwear. He fiddled with his belt buckle, unable to get it to release. The heavy chrome changer clattered to the floor as it finally did. He tried to pull his wet pants over his shoes while standing on one foot. It didn't work. He did the one leg sideways hip hop right out the door, then onto the driveway. Al landed hard on the cold asphalt. He looked up at the sky, aware of the situation but unconcerned. He only grunted his standard cuss—"Damn it." Booze and sleep had been lost or gained in bad proportions. Al's body demanded rest. He could see Ike helping him up and hear the hose bell ring when a car rolled in, but it all seemed far away. He was lying in the driveway with his pants down around his ankles staring blankly at the sky and it all made perfect sense to him. As a youth he had dreamed that his mother was a Navy test pilot. The dream had been so strong that when he awoke, he had searched her closet for her flight suit. Now that dream was back and made perfect sense again, and there was Al—he could see himself as if he were on the big screen at the drive-in. He could see himself being helped as he stumbled toward the office with that Ike kid holding him up. What were they doing?

Al's mind raced through the fog for answers. He remembered the boys had teased Ike about being a good dancer. Al had always had a secret ambition to dance. Maybe this was a new dance step he was being taught.

Ike got Al to his feet as quickly as he could. The truck drivers would be coming to help as soon as they quit laughing. He had to get Al to the back office before anyone noticed the blood. Al seemed willing enough to go where he was being led. He even seemed to be skipping some polka step or something.

Al sat in the office chair in his underwear while Ike removed his shoes. He put his cigarette in his mouth and Ike slapped it to the other side of the room. Al slapped Ike on the side of the head with a reflex that could not be stopped. The strength was gone and the blow was little more than a love tap and only brought a chuckle from Ike. "Knock it off, you crazy old bastard. You want to blow us up? You're something, you know that? I'm doin' all I can to save your ass and you want to slap me in the side of the head."

Ike pulled and tugged at the gas soaked pants until they were off. He ran to the ladies restroom, which was the closest sink, and put the pants in the sink and turned on the water.

The truck drivers topped off their own tanks and strolled into the station full of coffee and cigarettes. Everyone had a comment and a smile. The story of Al's fall would be embellished with each retelling. The lies were already being tested for approval.

"I'd say he flew eight feet in the air."

"No, it couldn't have been more than seven and a half."

"Has Al ever done any long jumping?"

A chorus of laughter filled the air. Ball caps and canvas fedoras, flannel shirts and khaki pants, weathered, unshaven faces sipping black coffee, blowing blue smoke toward the ceiling.

"Where's Al at? I've got to hear what he has to say about this," Art Grump said.

Ike hurried to the office door and pulled it closed. "Uh, look men," Ike started out as he blocked the doorway. Art Grump gave Ike a hard look that he should dare to block his path. "Sorry, Mr. Grump, I know you can move me if you want, but Al asked me to keep people away. He's had a bad night and he's half drunk and, well, he's embarrassed about coming in drunk. And I got to take him home before Floyd gets here. If you guys could just wait a day or two till Al can come up with a story to explain his fall, it might save his job."

Art softened a bit. He craned his neck trying to get a better look at Al through the cracks between the Venetian blinds. "Floyd won't fire him," he said.

"He might. He's been pretty unhappy with Al lately," Ike said.

The drivers murmured among themselves about giving a guy a break and not being a rat. "Has this got something to do with that no good boy of his?" Art asked.

Ike just nodded his head. The murmur began again about teenagers and trouble.

Ike was out on a limb. He was telling more than he should, but he couldn't tell these men any more lies than necessary. "You okay, Al?" Art yelled toward the window.

The half open blinds showed the outline of Al's head lying on folded arms on top of the desk. He raised a hand and gave a shooing wave to the speaker that said go away and leave me alone.

"You sure you're okay?" another driver yelled out.

Al's arm came up again, his middle finger extended from a fist of split skin and grease filled fingernails. The room erupted in laughter. "Okay, well we'll leave you alone for now, but you ain't heard the end of this," Art said. The men chuckled again and began to drift back to their trucks.

There were other drivers now filling the belly tanks of their trucks and looking toward the station, aggravated at the slow service. Ike ran with all the speed he could muster in an effort to placate the grouchy drivers. When he had them filled up and their windshields washed and on their way, he started filling the Cadillac and then ran back to the office. When he returned, Al was slumped over the desk unconscious, a lit cigarette in his fist.

Lowell Maynard witnessed the whole spectacle. The man was drunk and making a fool of himself, and at this time of the day.

Rayleen had married Al just three months after their frolic in the back seat. At the time, Rayleen was seeing more than a few gentlemen and had no idea whose baby it might be. Many of the men still around today would give Byron a critical look, let out a long, low, soft whistle like they had just dodged a bullet, then walk away. Lowell made a mental note to call in a favor from his friend Sheriff Browdy.

The driveway was full again. Some cars were pulling off in disgust to get their gas somewhere else. Many of the regulars filled their own tanks and dutifully brought the money into Ike, who was on the phone for help.

"Is Al okay?" all the regulars wanted to know.

"He's got the flu and didn't get any sleep last night," Ike would say. He had the door of the office locked. He fumbled with the phone, mis-dialing numbers while answering questions and making change. He was in it now and couldn't go back. What if Al dies? Ike looked up the number for Mercy Ambulance, dialed part of the number, and hung up. He took a five dollar bill from a regular named Johnson and explained again about Al having the flu.

Ike ran back to the desk afraid Al might stop breathing. He gave him a vigorous shake. "Are you all right?"

"Go to hell," came a grumble from the face on the desk.

Ike took that as a positive sign. He went back to the phone and got Brad out of bed. "What do you want?"

"Get in here right away and get Leon to come too."

"I'm off today," Brad said.

"I can't talk now, but I'm in a fuckin' mess and I need help."

"What's wrong?"

Ike cupped his hand over the receiver and turned to the wall. "Al's been shot."

"Your ass!" Brad said.

"I'll tell you more when you get here. Hurry." Ike hung up the phone and went back to work. He had done all he could do for now. If Brad and Leon got here quick, the secret might be kept. If not, he would be up the creek.

Leon's 57 Chevy squealed to a halt with the two young men inside. The two boys half ran up the drive side by side in their Floyd's Tire Mart uniforms. They looked to Ike like the cavalry coming to the rescue. "Where's Al?" Leon asked.

"He's in the office. Help me clear the drive first," Ike said.

Ten minutes later, there was a break in the morning rush and the drive was empty. Ike lead the way as all three boys hurried to the office. "Help me get Al into his truck," Ike said.

"Where's his pants?" Brad asked.

"In the sink in the ladies room. He got gas soaked," Ike said.

Both boys immediately understood. Both had been splashed before. "Was it a Rambler?" Brad asked.

"I don't know," Ike said as he wrestled with Al in the swivel chair.

All three young men used all their strength to get Al out the back door and down the steps. After several attempts and drops, the best method for carrying Al's unconscious dead weight was hit upon. Leon had his head and shoulders, Ike had his legs at the knees on one side, and Brad had his hips on the opposite side. They carried him like a rug some thirty-five yards to the employee parking lot.

"Don't stop. We'll never get him up again if we put him down," Ike said, breathing hard.

"The tailgate's down," Brad said. And the boys slid him into the back of the truck feet first.

The constant ding-ding of the driveway bell meant people were driving away, some with full tanks no doubt, some just angry and going somewhere else. This was bound to get back to Floyd, and he would demand an explanation.

"We've got to do something quick," Leon said.

"Grab some tires," Brad said.

A mountain of worn out tires was piled just up a slight hill from the truck. Leon began rolling a stream of tires to Brad, who handed them up to Ike to be placed around Al's motionless body. The top layer of tires was placed in a way so as not to put much weight on the sleeping man's chest.

"That looks pretty good," Brad said.

"Okay, I've got to get him out of here," Ike said, climbing into the cab.

Leon and Brad stood side by side next to the cab door. "Who shot him?" they asked in unison.

Ike let the moment hang for a second. "Byron."

"No shit!" the boys said, again in unison.

"I got to go," Ike said as he started the truck. "Come and get me at Al's house in ten minutes," he hollered as the truck pulled away.

Brad and Leon were somehow energized by the news. Byron was not liked by any of the station pump jockeys. Al had convinced Floyd to give Byron a job right after he was expelled from school. The job only lasted four days and he was fired. Byron had a way of pissing people off without even trying. He tried to get out of work with what he thought were clever deceptions, his manners were bad, he felt working was for fools, and he thought he was smarter than everyone else. With the volume of gas being pumped at Floyd's and the hustle required to keep them moving, Byron's attitude earned him bad comments from his co-workers and customers alike.

Floyd fired him on the spot on his fourth day when he heard him tell a woman in a station wagon that her tires looked fine when she asked to have the air checked. In typical Byron fashion, he cussed everyone at Floyd's as he stomped off on foot. He was well down the driveway before he started the name calling and waving his middle finger in the air.

Ike pulled in under the raised house where Al lived. It was typical of the rest of the neighborhood—two bedroom bungalows with screened in porches. There was no way to get him upstairs to bed. The house was unlocked, so Ike stuck his head in the door and yelled Byron's name several times. He did a quick search of the small house and pulled several blankets off the bed. He went back to the truck and moved enough tires to cover Al with the blankets. He put the tires back to keep him hidden.

Leon pulled into the yard just then and they headed back to Floyd's. Brad moved in and out of the pumps and cars at record pace. He wasn't making any headway, but he was keeping up. Ike and Leon arrived back only ten minutes before Floyd turned in. He had a habit of parking right in front of the door so everyone and anyone that had a doubt as to who he was and what his position allowed him to do could take notice.

Floyd had a big smile on his face as he climbed out of his El Camino. The pumps were pumpin' and the boys were humpin'. It would be another record month, he thought. The fact that no tires were being installed gave him a moment's pause. Still, all was going well.

Al's flop in the driveway with his pants down in front of half a dozen cars and trucks would need to be explained. Ike worked his brain as never before to come up with a logical explanation. Brad and Leon were no help at all since there had been no time to talk while getting the morning rush under control.

Floyd walked back to the office carrying his sack lunch and his all but empty briefcase. The briefcase, a Christmas present from his wife, served as a snack case on most occasions. He snuffed out his smoke on his way out to the pumps to do some public relations work. He, himself, had no idea what PR work was, but he knew how to win customers. The average guy in the street likes nothing better than to see the owner, a man of wealth and means, fill his tank and wash his windows.

Floyd had noticed right away Brad and Leon were here on the day when Al and Ike had this shift. That fact alone gave little reason for him to be concerned. Al had the authority to call in extra help if needed. Still, Al was nowhere in sight.

Miss Maples had just pulled to the empty pump. She was one of Floyd's first and best customers. She unknowingly had the final say on the pump jockeys. She had confirmed the decision that Byron had to go several days after the fact. Floyd rushed out to greet her and do her bidding. Miss Maples was good for a set of tires every year. Her Ford Falcon only accumulated around three thousand miles annually, but Miss Maples liked new tires. She said they held the road better. Anyone who had found themselves behind Miss Maples on a curvy road knew that she really didn't need much holding power in her tires. The Falcon was seldom pushed beyond 35 miles per hour.

While the weather was being discussed, Floyd filled her tank. Miss Maples was fumbling with stiff old fingers over one dollar bills stuck in her coin purse when she noticed the new boy, Ike Williams, hopping sideways across the lot with his pants down around his ankles. The boy made three good hops before a headlong dive into the driveway. Floyd had turned just in time to see the final one-legged, crippled albatross dive come to a grating halt. Ike jumped back up, apparently unhurt, struggled with his pants, and ran back into the tire changing room.

Leon and Brad couldn't believe their eyes and stood motionless over a windshield half cleaned. "I think that boy needs a belt," Miss Maples said.

"What he needs is my size eleven shoe up his butt just to get his attention," Floyd said. Floyd reddened with embarrassment for speaking so crudely to Miss Maples. "Sorry about that ugly outburst, Miss Maples. I'll have to talk to Mr. Williams there."

"Don't go getting yourself worked up, Floyd. I seen 'em come and go for years now and that one's a keeper."

"Of course you know what you're talkin' about. You've not steered me wrong yet," Floyd said.

"Seems to me," said Miss Maples, as she paused to collect her thoughts. "Seems to me there must be something wrong with the trousers you're forcing these men to wear."

Floyd cocked his head trying to understand what the old woman was getting out. "How's that, Miss Maples?"

"Well, I hear your manager took a similar fall just an hour ago."

"Is that so?" Floyd said, his interest piqued now.

"Yes, it was all the talk at Big Bill's Café this morning. The rock haulers were busting a gut over the whole thing."

"Al fell in the drive this morning?" Floyd asked.

"That's what they were sayin'. I don't want to spread no lies now, so you give the story only the merit it's worth, but I heard the dump truck driver's say how old Al had his pants around his ankles and come out of the door just the same way Ike just did. Landed hard and Ike scraped him up and took him home. Wouldn't let no one else get near him."

Floyd studied Miss Maples closely as he listened. He was reading her lips as she talked, never once interrupting or saying Huh as he was given to do out of nervous habit. No one at the station knew if Floyd had a real hearing problem or if he just said Huh constantly to give himself time to think. The joke around the station, repeated regularly, was Floyd didn't have any trouble hearing when the price of tires was the subject.

"Well, you know I always appreciate your business, Miss Maples, and the advice you've given me has been a great help."

"That's quite all right, Floyd. How much do I owe you?"

Floyd had been staring at the spot on the drive where both his employees had just fallen, trying to visualize Al repeating the fall he had just witnessed. "What?"

"How much for the gas?" Miss Maples said.

"Oh, well, I . . . uh . . . let's see. It's $2.60 and that's a little over eight gallons, and I give you the same discount I give the rock haulers—3 cents a gallon—that comes to . . . just make it $2.35."

Miss Maples leaned out the window and spoke in a softer voice of serious concern as she handed Floyd the exact amount. "You know," she said, "if I were you, I'd forget about the pants as the problem. I'd look for a virus," she said with the exaggerated honesty of a soap opera doctor. "That's right, a virus. One that makes men want to go naked skydiving. Ha-ha-ha-ha!" Miss Maples bounced in the seat as she laughed an infectious laugh that made her eyes water.

Floyd got a big kick out of Miss Maples and would steal her jokes at every opportunity. Floyd, himself, was not often quick witted so he needed other people's jokes to hold his own around the station when everyone was saying something funny. He would repeat this often over the next few days until all of his good customers had heard it twice. Miss Maples got a big kick out of herself and cackled softly as she drove away.

The pumps were still jammed and Floyd hated to see a customer wait. He would pump some more gas and then get to the bottom of this.

Brad and Leon were scurrying from pump to pump in a most efficient manner, managing to avoid eye contact with Floyd. "What are we going to say?" Brad asked as he leaned across the windshield opposite Leon.

Leon rubbed at a stubborn bug on his side of a Crown Victoria. Neither boy recognized the businessman type as a regular customer and felt free to talk about the recent events. "We don't say nothin'. We only answer questions with 'I don't know'. Play dumb. That should be easy for you."

Brad ignored the insult that would normally have sent a squirt of soapy water toward Leon's neck. Brad could feel the tension in the air by the way Floyd had been watching them since Miss Maples drove away.

The only spare pants Ike was able to find were much too big in the waist and two inches too short. They would have to do. He threaded his belt through the loops and cinched it low around his hips. When he reappeared on the drive, every eye was on him. He had only the vaguest idea of what he was going to tell Floyd. In a desperate effort to do something quick, he had reasoned that if he did exactly what Al had done, and he wasn't drunk, it would make it look entirely possible that Al wasn't drunk either.

Floyd went to the office and looked over the books from last night. Everything looked normal. Gasoline sales were good, but no tires were sold. Damn, he thought, am I the only person who can sell tires?

The morning rush came to a sudden stop as five cars at the pumps all pulled away at the same time and no others pulled in. A completely empty drive that had been a flurry of activity just seconds ago left all three boys standing where they had collected for their last sale. Now they all turned toward each other like Hollywood gunfighters, each waiting for the other to make a move toward the door. This was the predictable ten to twenty minute break between the blue collar workers who needed to be on the job at 7 and the 9 o'clock crowd getting an early start. It was at this time of the morning that the first wave of the Floyd's Tire Mart Social Club would start to drift in. Retired dump truckers and small contractors with pickup trucks and two wheelbarrows looking to pick up work.

On one wall of the tire showroom, a large cork tack board hung covered from corner to corner with homemade for sale signs and business cards. All manner of goods and services could be found on the board at any given time. Boats, motorcycles, washing machines, cars, television sets, backhoe work, water hauled, wood cut, roofs replaced, and water heaters installed. They came in when they didn't need gas or tires to look over the board and strike up a deal with someone else looking at it. Gossip was exchanged, stories were told about a best friend's mishap on the job, about a high lift operator that knocked down the wrong building or a water hauler going too fast with half a load, something any idiot ought to know you don't do. And everyone standing in the showroom with a cup of coffee in one hand and a cigarette in the other swears that the first time they met the victim of the latest story, they could tell there was something wrong with him.

The three boys were all wanting that coffee and cigarette, but no one wanted to enter the showroom first. They could see Floyd standing next to the coffee pot looking out to the drive with short sideways glances. The first one in the door would get the questions directed at him. Floyd had a way of putting the hard eye on the young men who worked for him. The last thing the boys wanted to do was get caught in a lie to Floyd, for to do so was to damage your reputation among all the rock haulers and all the retired old men and all the hotrod driving young men and all the mothers of all the daughters you might some day get to go out with it if your name was good at Floyd's Tire Mart.

Ike reluctantly took the lead as the three of them shuffled in with their heads just slightly down avoiding Floyd's eyes.

"What the hell happened out there with you? What the hell were you doin' out there? Naked skydiving?"

Brad and Leon bent over with laughter. Floyd beamed with success at having said something that got the kind of reaction from this younger crowd of clever wits. All three boys thought the joke was fruit, as most of Floyd's jokes were, and usually they would have only chuckled softly to keep Floyd from total embarrassment, especially if there were members of the social club present. But at this time, each boy saw the opportunity that was presented and jumped on the bandwagon. The ridicule of Ike had a green light, and as long as they could keep the barbs flying, there would be no more questions asked.

Ike took the jabs good naturedly, waiting to see if another opportunity would present itself before he was interrogated by a hard eyed Floyd Barnett. Leon piped in. "You ought to sue those skinny fuckin' legs of yours for lack of support."

Floyd spun around with uncontrolled laughter. He loved being one of the guys. As a young man growing up, he made few friends in high school and was considered a nerd by the neat guys. Floyd's size and temper discouraged bullies from picking fights with him, but he never fit in with the neat guys. These young men he hired to pump gas were just the sort of charming, fun loving guys he would have loved to be part of twenty years ago. Now he could fill that void.

Brad and Leon chimed in with exaggerated, taunting laughter. "Howdy, boys, what's so funny?" Art Grump asked. Art had parked outside the bell hose and walked up unnoticed.

"You should have seen it, Art," Floyd said. He had to be first to tell the story. "Ike went hoppin' out onto the drive with his pants around his ankles. Then he hit the ground and rolled around."

"He did what?" Art said, giving the boy a slanted look and a knowing wink. "Is that true?"

"Well basically it's true. They're leaving out the part about me spilling gas on myself and trying to change pants standing on one foot."

"Okay, I can see that part of it," Art said. "It's the part about you rolling around on the drive with your butt showing that I'm worried about. Why, if my wife would have seen that, I wouldn't get no pussy for a month. She'd be dreaming of your skinny butt, your skinny baby butt, and wouldn't want nothin' to do with my big hairy butt." Art could say something that wasn't funny, but when he said it, it was funny.

Ike wished a dozen cars would pull in and break this party up, but the rush was over and he wanted to finish his coffee and cigarette. He absorbed the rough play and even pretended to start getting mad about the thing. That's what they wanted—to push him until he was steamed. That would make another story. He took two more draws on his smoke and flipped the butt out in his half finished coffee and pitched the cup in the trash. He spun so quickly he knocked a display tire off its perch. The tire rolled to the floor and in the direction of Art Grump, who not so nimbly sloshed hot coffee down his shirt getting out of the way. Ike stormed out to the drive to the laughter and owl hoots from inside.

Ike walked up the drive out of sight and sound of the party. The temperature was coming up; that gave him some comfort. Al was dressed warm above the waist and with the blankets, that should be enough, Ike tried to convince himself. If Al dies in the back of his truck, did you kill him or Byron? Ike wrestled with what to do, but in the end found it easiest to do nothing.

Ike began wiping down the pumps and working out the details of his lie. Floyd had still not asked about Al. Just say he felt sick and went home and that he told me to call in Brad and Leon. But he'll hear about Al's fall, he argued with himself. Yeah, he'll hear about it, but if he don't hear about it before you go home, you won't be in for two days. And by then, the stories about your fall and Al's fall will get mixed in and Al's fall won't seem so strange. And then you can just pretend to be mad and not talk to anybody about anything for the rest of the day. Ike felt better now that he had a foolproof plan in place.

Al felt the weight of the tires on his chest. His back was hurting and it was hard to breath. This was it; he was sure he was having a heart attack. He tried moving his arms and legs, but they would not move. Panic raced in his brain and he pushed again in his half sleep. He could not move; he was paralyzed. A cry of anguish hollered from deep within him and came rolling out of his open mouth. The sound of his own cry awoke him. It was full daylight now and Al recognized the look and the feel and the smell of old tires placed all over him. The panic receded slowly and Al worked an arm free and pushed the tire off his chest. His breathing was easier now and one by one, he uncovered himself enough to sit up. The relief of not being paralyzed caused him to utter a small but sincere thank you to his God.

After a few minutes, Al gathered his strength and crawled out of the truck and put himself to bed.

CHAPTER THIRTY-TWO

The old refrigerated trailer had been abandoned and empty for several years. The trailer was one of the first of its kind, built to keep beer cold for as long as necessary as beer shipments were delivered further and further away. Anheuser Busch began building refrigerated trailers during prohibition to help keep the company afloat until the madness ended. The trailers were smaller and had rounded corners, the shell was aluminum, and the metal work resembled that of an airplane wing. The interior had the same kind of look. Three inches of insulation separated the two skins. It was an icebox on wheels, but like many early products of new technologies, it was quickly surpassed by bigger and better refrigerated trailers.

Floyd acquired the trailer for free and used it for tire storage, but it proved not to be useful because there was nothing to nail to that would allow for racks to be built, and stacking tires on their side only guaranteed that the size and style wanted would be at the back on the bottom. Floyd had bought four newer trailers that had plywood sides where racks could be built and moved them up close behind the building so the employees wouldn't have to walk so far to roll up a new set of tires for a customer waiting. The older refrigerated trailer wasn't needed anymore, but wasn't eating anything.

Al talked Floyd into giving him the trailer for a hunting cabin, to be hauled out to a friend's land. Floyd saw this as a win/win situation and offered to let him do his remodeling where she sat and use his electric if he wanted to work at night. Al was enthusiastic about the project. He installed crude lighting and an emergency crapper for those times when it was pouring down rain.

Then the dream faded. Byron's trouble with the school and the law escalated. Time spent away from home in the woods had to wait and the trailer was needed for another purpose.

Al had his pickup truck loaded with supplies on the day he picked Byron up at the Jefferson Memorial Hospital. Byron had a hanging cast on his left arm and some sort of hinged brace on his left knee. The left ankle was covered with a white plastic boot.

Al carried several bottles of drugs and listened intently to well intentioned doctors about the kind of care Byron needed. Al assured them that Byron was going to get the treatment he needed. Al read the bottles out loud while driving down the road: For pain—1 every 4 hours.

Byron hadn't said hi or even looked in Al's direction. He knew there was a fight coming; he just wanted to get home before it started.

Al pulled a Schlitz tallboy out of a brown paper bag. He took a long draw and smiled. "Welcome home, son," he said.

Byron waited for the other shoe to fall—the shouting, the cursing, the threats, and the punishments. Nothing. Al drove down the highway without a care in the world. "You in any pain?" he asked, grinning from ear to ear.

"Some."

"You want one of these pills?"

"Wouldn't hurt," Byron said, accepting the orange plastic bottle.

"Open a beer if you want." Al motioned toward the bag.

"I'm not supposed to have alcohol with these."

"One swallow won't hurt you."

Byron finished off the beer and opened another. Al was still smiling. Byron thought he could hear the old bastard humming. The old truck rocked gently down Highway 67. It would be a forty minute drive from the hospital outside of Festus to Al's house in Arnold. Al doesn't want to talk, that's fine with me, Byron thought. He leaned against the door and relaxed and listened to the drone of the motor, the whish of the wind, and the roar of the tires and closed his eyes.

When Al pulled the pickup into Floyd's back lot, Byron was slumped against the door breathing deeply, oblivious to the waking world. Al unloaded the truck, leaving Byron where he was. He peeled open the big double doors at the back of the abandoned trailer. The interior was silver, smooth, and clean. Al had grand dreams for this aluminum cabin. Before all this mess came up, he had worked long hours and consumed many six packs turning it into a camping lodge. His plan had been to pull this baby into the woods and set it on some blocks on the edge of the Gasconade River. Logan Hanby, an old friend, owned land along the Gasconade and was eager for Al to set up a campsite on his ground. Another dream put on hold, Al thought.

Al piled blankets and jugs of water just inside the door. Up and down crude wooden steps he trudged with beanbag chairs, pillows, cases of canned food, and toiletries. The last of the gear was pushed in place and Al turned to get the boy. He had gone through a lot in the past three weeks, all of it his own doing.

Al opened the passenger side door slowly and let Byron fall into his arms. The limp body was much more work than he had anticipated to carry up the steps. He took a short run at the steps, but his momentum failed and he stepped back down. On the second try, a board broke and sent Al sideways down the steps after pitching Byron to a small landing outside the doors. Byron moaned softly but didn't move. "Sorry, boy," Al said.

Al got to his feet and crawled up on top of the platform. Picking Byron up by the arms, he drug him into the trailer and leaned him up against two of the bean bags. One last look inside checking the inventory of survival gear and he closed and latched the doors. The double doors were designed to accept a padlock, but Al would not put a padlock on the doors. He might have to get in there in a hurry. But Byron was locked in for sure.

Al stepped back from the door. There was still time. He could open the door, put Byron back in the cab, and be home in fifteen minutes, but he didn't do any of that. He looked at the latched double doors for a full thirty seconds and in that time reviewed all that had brought him to this point. Then he headed home with a brief stop at Ajax Liquor.

CHAPTER THIRTY-THREE

B yron Creed awoke cold and shivering. His back was warm. He was sunk deeply into a pair of beanbag chairs. He recognized the beanbags as the ones he often flopped on to watch TV at Al's house. The room he was in was brightly lit. A single bare lightbulb hung from a hook. The walls and ceiling and floor were metal, a silvery metal, and the light had nowhere to hide and was reflected again and again. The hunting cabin, he thought. He was in the hunting cabin, that old trailer that Al thought he could make into a weekend home.

Byron pushed himself to his feet. What was he doing here and how did he get here? He looked at the boxes of canned food and the gallon jugs of water and a sudden realization and a panic hit him at the same time like nothing he had ever experienced before. He hobbled to the end of the trailer and slammed himself against the double doors. They did not give. Byron slumped to the floor and sobbed into his good arm.

When Byron could cry no longer, his need for warmth forced him back to the beanbags. He pulled a blanket from a stack piled next to the bags and wrapped himself like an Indian and sat down. Hours passed by. Or was it only minutes? He couldn't tell.

Byron lay back in the beanbag chairs and searched the length and width of the trailer for the hundredth time, each time looking for something new to cling to that would take his mind off the situation. There was nothing. The sheets of aluminum plate overlapped down the walls and ceiling and floor every four feet and were held in place by line after line of roundhead rivets. He began to count the rivets, but he was unable to keep the line he was counting from overlapping with the line he had just finished. He thought he could just count one full circle and multiply that by the number of lines down the length of the trailer. Then he dismissed that idea altogether. What did he care how many rivets there were?

Ten minutes later, Byron began counting again and multiplied the lines and came up with the number 864. "So what," he said out loud just to hear his own voice. After a few minutes, he did the count again and came up with the same number, and for no reason he could figure out, he was pleased with himself.

He looked over the canned food. He found the can opener and opened two cans of mixed fruit in heavy syrup and slurped them down greedily. He unbuttoned his jeans and lowered his zipper halfway. The extra space was taken up quickly by his expanding stomach.

Al had cut a hole in the floor that had a 6-inch plastic pipe sticking through it. The pipe came up out of the floor 10 inches and was covered with a cap of the same material. The pipe went down through the floor into a 55 gallon steel drum containing water and anti-freeze. Byron had tried to break the pipe from its mooring in the hope of getting someone to hear a shout, but it was much tougher than it looked and he had no tools except the can opener.

Byron had figured out its purpose in only about three minutes, a fact that made him feel proud. He had put off its use as one more act of defiance. At this point, though, he began to see several flaws in his plan. His original idea was to hold it until he burst. When the police saw the mess, they would probably start beating Al the moment they saw him. This particular daydream offered Byron the most comfort—the vision of Al being beaten by cops with big sticks—but now several problems showed up as his stomach began to move things along unconcerned with what the brain of a sixteen year old wanted.

Another disturbing thought plodded its way toward consciousness. If he waited too long and lost the battle on his clothes, or on the floor, the stench would make him puke and the combined odor would be unbearable. He would be forced to clean up the mess and try to bury it under his clothes until Al came back. But suppose Al gave in and released him due to the stench? Suppose he didn't. Do you really want to live in a can of shit? And if that were the case, then no one would suffer but him.

There seemed to be a pattern here. Maybe he was the cause of all his own problems. Maybe he didn't think through what could go wrong when he did things. No, that wasn't it. He was just having some bad luck. Things would get better. That's all it was—bad luck. That could happen to anyone. He just needed to wait this out, put Al in jail, and go on with his life. Al would be gone and he would have the house to himself with no one to tell him what to do. He would be a car thief. Easy money, fast cars, girls everywhere. Again a nagging thought formed in a small wrinkle of a warm, well fed, blood flow portion of his slowly expanding brain. And that minute, needle point of electricity moved its way along miles of nerve endings, a maze too complex to comprehend, and slammed into the frontal lobes just above his eyes. What if he were to get caught and thrown in prison?

Byron's mind suddenly cleared. Like a fog covered windshield with the defroster on high, the thick grey mist which shadowed his world evaporated, and all things became clear. But no, Byron shook his head and suppressed the thought. His plans were made. His career was set. Car thief. He was too smart to get caught. The tiny spark of electricity charged neutron glowed once more faintly and went out.

Byron's stomach muscles made themselves known with authority that could not be ignored. He made his way to the pipe, disillusioned at the failure of another good plan.

Byron lay on the floor in a fetal position. His crying had stopped. He stared dully at the lightbulb hanging on the wall, and when he closed his eyes he could see the bright glow on the inside of his eyelids. He hated Al more than he ever thought he could. His teeth were set tight together as he thought of how he would enjoy beating Al with an ax handle, the way it would sound as the wood struck flesh and bone, the sinking thud, the shot of pain Al would receive, the feelings of total dominance he would have as he peppered Al about the head and shoulders. The thought added the only comfort Byron could feel.

When the rain first started, Byron was relieved and excited. The constant silence was wearing on his nerves. In a way he didn't understand, being alone with his thoughts for so long with nothing to take his mind off his failures was maddening. He thought the rain would help him sleep, something he had been trying to do constantly, but couldn't. With no way of telling time of day, his sleep habits had become jumbled. The first day after being tossed in the trailer, he knew he had slept most of that day away. He was sure of that. Because of that, he was sure he was up most of the next night, the night that he was sure this was a joke and that someone would open the door and have a big laugh at his expense. But there was no big laugh.

The rain was soothing at first as Byron tried to sleep again. He tossed about for what seemed like four or five hours. The first few drops were the pleasant sound of well being, of knowing water was coming down on a cold day and you were under shelter, the sound that's born in our brain's memory of primitive people appreciative of the very basics of shelter. Now the rain was coming harder in slashing sheets that roared up and down the roof of his cell.

Cell. That was the first time he had used that word in his thoughts. Until now, this was a trailer. Now in that flash of thought, it was a prison cell and always would be. Byron realized now that the doors weren't going to fly open any time soon. The constant predictions by the old man that he was going to go to jail if he didn't change his ways replayed in his mind. So this was Al's idea to show me. "His ass is mine," he thought out loud. But as soon as the image of Al being arrested and put in jail came to Byron, he knew he was lying to himself. He couldn't put the old man in jail—not just yet. But he better come soon, and I mean real soon. That was it. He was not going to press charges cause you're obviously fuckin' crazy—that's what he would say. But what if Al still doesn't open the door? Then I'm going to press charges and your ass is going to jail. That's what he would say. Byron planned his conversation with Al over and over in his mind.

The rain had been coming down hard for some time now and the pleasant sound had become deafening. Byron lay on his side on the blankets on the floor with his knees drawn up tight to his chest and held his ear tight to the pillow on the floor. The constant noise was something that drove prison inmates to near insanity, or so he had heard. When Clay had first come back from prison at Jeff City, he talked about it. He hadn't given the idea much thought, but now he could see how a loud, constant, unrelenting roar of rain could make a person become agitated and quick tempered. In fact, Clay always seemed agitated and quick tempered. Maybe he wasn't like that before going to prison.

Al finished his paperwork, turned out the lights, and locked the door at Floyd's Tire Mart. He shuffled his way to the parking lot and started his old truck. The temperature was dropping and the warm truck would feel good after his talk with Byron. The rain had stopped, but his clothes were damp and he felt chilled. He zipped up his jacket and turned up the collar and made his way slowly in the dark to the side of the trailer. A small door in the side of the trailer opened from the outside. The door was originally designed to store a two-wheeled hand truck that hauled cases of beer from the trailer to the customer. The opening to the inside was only ten inches high by twenty-two inches wide and had a latch like a refrigerator door that snapped it tightly shut.

Al popped the handle and the door dropped open. "You awake, boy?" Al said and waited a few seconds for an answer.

"When's this going to be over?" Byron asked. His voice was distant.

"That's up to you, son."

"I'm ready to get out now." Even as he said it, he knew he was wasting his breath.

"I wish that was true, son." Al's voice was as rough as ever but sounded weak.

"Okay, just tell me what the fuck I have to do to get out of here." Byron's voice echoed through the little door in the side of the trailer.

Al was sure he was going to go into a fist pounding, wall kicking fit. "If you're going to talk like that, I'm leaving." Al raised himself from the stack of old tires where he sat and closed the little door.

"Wait," Byron said.

Al heard his voice, but he didn't move or answer. He wanted to be sure Byron was ready to listen. He tilted his head and strained his ears to hear.

Byron dropped to his knees to get his face closer to the little door. "Wait," he said again.

As the door opened, Byron and Al saw each other eye to eye. Neither one could see more than the center most portion of the other's face. The reflected light off the silver metal on both sides gave each face an eery glow.

"What do you want me to say? You want me to say I'm sorry? Okay, I'm sorry. Now what else?"

"You need a plan. You can't just keep going the way you are, boy. You want a cup of hot tea?"

"Hot tea?" Byron said in disbelief.

Al had been drinking two pots of coffee a day for as long as Byron could remember. In his mind he could see Al on the screened in porch watching the river go by. In the winter, he had a kerosene heater by his side, and in the summer, a rotating fan. But always a cup of coffee in his left hand and a Winston in his right.

"I switched to tea for a while," Al said. "You know how many millions of people drink tea?"

Byron just blinked.

"Well, it's a lot. I know that," Al said.

Byron suddenly remembered that he was uncomfortable in his position down on the cold floor that smelled like black rubber. "Open the door, Dad," he said in a smooth even tone.

Al jolted inside. He had braced for this moment. He knew his son like he knew himself. They were of the same blood. Al knew enough about genetics to be sure in his own mind that Byron truly meant what he said. The temptation was tremendous to go raise the latch on the large double doors. He sat motionless staring at the gravel under his feet waiting to hear what Byron said next.

"Are you going to let me out?" Again the same relaxed voice of someone seemingly unconcerned about the answer.

"Not just yet," Al said, still staring at his shoes. Tense frozen seconds slipped by.

"What kind of plan?" Byron asked.

Al fought back tears. He was sure this was a turning point. "A plan for life," he said. He poured the tea from his seasoned thermos bottle into a paper cup slowly, letting the last words hang in the air for as long as possible.

Byron's knees protested with authority now and he was forced to break the field of energy now flowing evenly back and forth between their eyes as they were locked in a timeless stare, neither showing any malice toward the other. Byron sucked in a deep breath and said, "I gotta get a blanket." His face vanished from the little door.

Al started bouncing his knees up and down to try and bleed off the shot of energy this moment had just created. His jubilation subsided just as quickly as he scrambled his mind to remember what he had decided the plan should be.

Byron moved back to the opening after laying several blankets down and stretching out on his stomach. He reached through the opening and took the tea from Al. He took a sip and grimaced as he set the cup down and looked back at Al, who was lighting a cigarette.

"Well, boy," Al said, and stopped to collect his thoughts. "You gotta have a high school diploma first."

Byron's nerves came alive but frustration and anger were about to overtake him once again. Al could feel it too. Byron choked back his anger. "What day is it?" he asked.

"It don't matter."

"Well it does to me, God damn it!"

"If you start carrying on, I'm leaving." Al took a sip from his cup, forgetting it was tea when his mouth was set for coffee.

Byron chuckled through his tears. "Good stuff, ain't it?"

Al fought back a laugh and forced himself not to start feeling sorry for his son. It was too late now to bail out. He had to see this through to the other

side. "Here's the way this is going to work. I put you in there to give you a
taste of what you have to look forward to. I'm not going to tell you how long
you've been in or how long you have left. That's part of the understanding
you have to learn."

Byron was comfortable now on his stomach with a blanket folded under
his ear. The energy level had dropped just as quickly as it had risen. Resignation
had taken over. The three or more days and nights he had spent locked up
had sent him into nothing less than tantrums. His desire to put Al in jail was
as strong as ever, but he just listened to the terms of his confinement with
distant sadness.

"From what I've been hearin', you'll be probably be sent up for six years
your first time," Al said as he fumbled for a cigarette. He pulled out two, lit
one with his lighter, and lit the second off the first. He handed a smoke to
Byron, who quietly accepted it. Al stared off into the darkness for a second to
collect his thoughts. "Most first timers don't do the whole six years. Course
you won't know for sure you'll get out early, so you need to get to the idea of
not being able to control the time."

"Can I have my watch?"

"No, that would just give you something to cling to. You'd count the
hours and the days and tough it out until I opened the door."

"When you gonna open the door?"

"When you've learned enough to pass your high school diploma test."

"How am I gonna do that in here?"

"Read this," Al said as he slid a book through the small passage.

Byron examined the book in the harsh light of the bare lightbulb. It was
one of a set of encyclopedias that had set on the book shelf in Al's home
unopened since its arrival.

The old man has lost it for sure, Byron thought. The binding crackled
as he flipped through the pages of the book labeled Volume A. "What am I
supposed to do with this?" Byron dropped the book to the floor.

"Read it," Al said.

"That's it? If I read this book, you'll let me out? That's gonna keep me
out of prison?"

"Probably not."

Al popped and snapped in several joints as he rose from the stack of tires
he had made into a chair. He needed to stretch and pace. He was on shaky
ground where his plan for Byron's release was concerned. His theory of forcing
the boy to think and read in order to bring about the colossal change necessary
seemed less brilliant now than it had before.

"I'll bring more. When you read each one, there'll be a test. If you pass the test, you get another book."

Byron's face disappeared from the opening. His reaction came as no surprise to Al. The cursing and the kicking on the walls of the trailer made only muffled thumps barely audible ten feet away.

"I'll kill myself."

Al had closed the pigeon hole door and was walking away when Byron made his claim. He could not let the boy have this as leverage. It would never end—the halfhearted attempts leading to more serious threats of murder and suicide. Somehow he has got to be strong. He walked the few steps back to the door and casually opened the latch. "I'll be really sorry if you do. You've got a chance here to look deep inside and decide to be more than you are. If you want to die, nobody can ever stop you." Al closed the door and walked up the driveway toward the truck. He had begun to sleep in the truck seat several hours a night, keeping a vigil on the trailer that high wind or electric fire or some other natural catastrophe wouldn't kill the boy.

Byron reached for the book, intent on only looking at the pictures, a sort of vow he made to himself. He would glance through the book looking at the pictures and that's all. He would not read anything and would not learn anything. The moment this thought ran across his mind, he knew it was a stupid thing to think even if he didn't say it out loud. Now the battle had to be fought again. It was better to be lazy and stupid than learn and prosper. No, that wasn't right. He wasn't stupid. It was just that he knew all he needed to know and didn't want nobody telling him what to do. And lazy? No, he wasn't lazy. He liked sports, didn't mind running when necessary, but going to bed early so you can get up early to work at some two-bit job? That was fruit. And I'm not going to do it. His mind was set. He closed the book.

The days passed and Al settled into a pattern of work, short naps at home, and hours spent in the cab of the old truck. The motor jiggled the seat in a steady rhythmic pattern produced by the idling six cylinder. The heater blower still needed the occasional slap, but it ran on and on. Al surrendered to his guard duty as his own punishment for failure at fatherhood.

When Rayleen left with the boy, he never went after him. He felt the weight of his guilt. He had not sent the boy birthday or Christmas cards. He didn't go see him, didn't try and bring him back even though the boy had liked his father a lot.

Al reflected on Byron's progress, or lack of. The "A" book took two tries twenty-four hours apart. Al was sure Byron had not really expected a test and he failed it the first time. His protests were mild, all things considered, and the tests were unscientific. Al asked only three questions. He would open the book at about one-third of its thickness, announce the topic being written about, and ask Byron to tell him all he could about that subject. If anything Byron said matched up with what the book said, it was a right answer. Byron got three wrong answers the first test.

It was truly amazing how smart he could be when pressed. The second test a day later had an opposite result. This brought some degree of hope that this whole mess might somehow turn out right. He couldn't hold the thought for long; he had gone too far; he had to let Byron out. He wondered if he would be better thought of by a jury if he kept the boy locked up twelve days or four days. Would it really matter? If it didn't matter, then he should stick to his plan. The boy is at least reading, something he never did before. If he can handle two books a day, I'll give them to him. That settled the argument in his heart for now.

Al leaned up against the door and put his head by the half open window. With his worn out leather boots up close to the heater vents, he went to sleep. He had to start his shift in two and a half hours.

It was on the third day that Byron broke down again. The constant sleeping, the high sugar content food he was eating—canned mixed fruit all he wanted, canned corn, corned beef, crackers, soda—Byron's metabolism was hitting on all eight cylinders. His energy level had never been higher. There was nothing to do. His body shook out of control with sobs of self pity. His heart and will were broken. He gave up. And then a moment later, he was doing calisthenics. Then, without warning, he was balled up on the floor again bawling and completely confused as to exactly why he was crying. Then the self pity would evaporate and the growing muscles of a young man moving into his physical prime demanded work, and shadow boxing and pushups and situps became a timeless and worthy goal unto themselves.

Byron's injuries healed at a rate to match his enthusiasm for his own ability. Years of bad food, poor sleeping habits, and a lackluster attitude toward physical fitness vanished in a matter of days. Byron more than ever found himself in need of measuring time. The sore and expanding muscles he built needed time to heal, but only enough sleep and inactivity to repair and no more. He knew that eight hours of sleep was considered optimal. He must find a way to know when hours and days passed. He stared at the ceiling for the hundredth time, examining every square inch, and then he saw it, a crooked rivet. With the edge of the can opener, he pried until he could attach a string to the rivet. He tied the can opener to the end of the string. Holding it against one wall, letting it go, and counting One Mississippi,

Two Mississippi until it came to a stop established twenty-six minutes. Now he had a clock. Rounding the twenty-six minutes to thirty minutes to allow for the minutes that passed when he hadn't noticed that the pendulum had stopped gave him time. A mark on the wall for every thirty minutes sixteen times gave him an eight hour day.

Byron decided to exercise the full eight hours then sleep until he was fully rested, then start the clock again. At the end of the first hour he was exhausted and frustrated at the failure of another good plan.

CHAPTER THIRTY-FOUR

Byron tried to sing Christmas songs but gave up after only three lines of three different songs. He realized he didn't know a single song all the way through. The western television show "Cheyenne" had a great song, but he could only repeat the first two lines over and over—"Cheyenne, Cheyenne, where will you be sleeping tonight, lonely man Cheyenne. Cheyenne, Cheyenne, where will you be sleeping tonight?" This lasted through about twenty renditions and then he sat silent again.

Byron pressed his ear lightly against the cool metal wall of his cell. The whishing sound of his own heart was reassuring. The encyclopedia lay close to his feet. He eyed it suspiciously. He couldn't give in. He was nobody's slave to be forced to do things he didn't want to. Al had no right to lock him in here. This wasn't fair. The argument in his mind that he should expect fair treatment from others while pursuing a life of crime was the same fight every criminal in the world had to fight and win if he wished to continue in his chosen profession.

Byron flipped open the hard cover of the letter "A" encyclopedia with the toe of his sock covered foot. Then he closed it again. In the daytime, he would sit and pout and stare at the ceiling unconsciously counting the rivets in the aluminum sheet metal that was his world. He had discovered in bright sunlight small specks of light showed around the edges of the double doors when he turned out the light. This was somewhat of a victory. He took any little victory he could get. He was not going to submit. Was this midday sun, early morning sun, or late afternoon sun? No way to know. He would try to keep track. Every two hours or thereabouts he would turn out the light and peer through the total darkness searching for the pinpoints of fire that connected him to the outside world. The plan was to stay awake as long as light could be found and try to sleep the whole time the specks were gone.

Each arrival of the stars in Byron's constant darkness meant daytime and a day closer to getting out. The number of days Al intended to keep him there was unknown, but there had to be an end to this, and every day was a day closer no matter how you looked at it. The ability to count days helped put boredom in order.

Byron reached for the book, intent on only looking at the pictures, a sort of vow he made to himself. He would glance through the book looking at the pictures and that's all. He would not read anything and would not learn anything. The moment this thought ran across his mind, he knew it was a stupid thing to say even if he didn't say it out loud. Now the battle had to be fought again. It was better to be lazy and stupid than learn and prosper. No, that wasn't right. He wasn't stupid. It was just that he knew all he needed to know and didn't want nobody telling him what to do.

And lazy? No, he wasn't lazy. He liked sports, didn't mind running when necessary, but going to bed early so you can get up early to work at some two bit job? That was fruit. And I'm not going to do it. His mind was set. He closed the book.

Al had supplied him with a large variety of canned goods and Al knew his eating habits. He had provided most of the food Byron normally ate. There were twelve cans of mixed fruit. The number of cans, along with Al's knowledge of Byron's eating habits, told Byron Al intended keeping him there twelve days. Al had always scolded him about eating all the canned fruit. What if Al knew he would eat it all in three days and still hold him longer. What if Al was going to lecture him on only eating a can every three days? As he had often said in the past, "A can of God damned mixed fruit ought to last a couple of days between two people."

Al's idea of eating was to fill up on corned bread and beans and top it off with two tablespoons of mixed fruit in heavy syrup. He figured if him and Byron both would only eat their fair share of the treat he so seldom got as a child, each should have it always available. The fit he would throw when there was none left. "I went shoppin' just two days ago. I bought six cans of mixed fruit in heavy syrup and now it's all gone."

Byron had his own responsibilities. He had friends over when Al was at work or at the bar and these people liked mixed fruit too as much as the next guy. And the proper way of serving mixed fruit was to supply each guest with a can, a spoon, and a can opener. Byron had tried to explain the logistics of this absolute duty on several occasions, but Al wouldn't listen. None of this was his fault. There it was. This wasn't his fault and that was that. And he was right back where he started. "Cheyenne, Cheyenne, where will you be sleeping tonight? Lonely man, Cheyenne dah-da-dah, dah-da-dah, dah-da-dah."

Byron began to count the rivets in the ceiling again. As the count reached 178, his mind began to drift through his life. Like a leaf falling from the top of a large tree, his thoughts touched on a branch for only a moment, then moved on, sailing freely with no intent, just moving ever downward.

The stillness began to put pressure on his lungs and when at last he could bear the loneliness and quiet no longer, he would hurl a can to the far wall and breath easier as the sound waves loosened the weight of the air that lay upon him like too many quilts.

The rain began again. The rise and fall of the rain's intensity increased Byron's pulse despite his best efforts to remain calm and steady. When a stronger wave of rain came down, the noise traveled the length of his cell like a train down a track. The noise rolled over him and brought him a heightened sense of solitude. He wanted more than ever to turn to somebody, anybody, and say Wasn't that somethin' but there was no one there; there never had been. He was completely alone in here or out there.

Byron let himself sink into dark depression. He felt he deserved the luxury of total despair, but when next he woke he couldn't help but be optimistic. He could no more control his youthful exuberance than his hunger and thirst, and his despair came with fatigue and left with rest.

Byron hadn't been starting his clock for some time now and he felt he would be making faster progress with his incarceration if he could get back to documenting time. With each mark on the wall, hours and days must dwindle down to the final few. He turned each new mark, the mark of another day, into a formal ceremony. He would march from end to end a few times, then formally square himself in front of the wall waiting to receive its mark. Then with a long, dramatic drum roll produced from his tongue, he would make the mark. Then there was wild cheering from the crowd and Byron waved and bowed and thanked the academy for its support and the academy members for their votes.

Now the marking ceremony was over and another day must be endured.

The little door opened with a clatter. Byron couldn't help but be happy to hear Al's voice rumble his greeting. "You awake, boy?" he asked. There was always a hint of humor in his voice when he made his same greeting every time.

"What do you care?" Byron said.

"Well, I got a cup of hot coffee here if you're awake. If not, I'll just throw it out."

"I'll drink it," Byron said as if he were doing Al a favor.

"Gettin' much reading down?" Al asked as he handed Byron the paper cup.

Byron didn't answer. He accepted the hot liquid and slurped it greedily. He sat with his back against the wall. Al could only see his ankles and feet.

"Son, you're a tough one, I'll give you that. You can take pain as well as anyone I ever saw, but all that's going to get you is more pain."

Byron thought about the statement for a moment, and decided it didn't make any sense. "Shut up," he said.

Al ignored the remark and continued on with his planned conversation. "You know it occurred to me that I never asked you what you wanted to be."

Byron saw this as a small crack in Al's resolve. If he could convince Al he had a new game plan, he could get out.

"Well, what do you want to do?"

"I want to be an album artist."

Al widened his eyes and tilted his head in an effort to let the information flow to his brain unobstructed. When at last he had formed an understanding, he gave Byron a sympathetic look. "I didn't know you could sing." Sudden hope raced its way along the outer edges of Al's brain. What if the boy had a great voice, a natural talent? It wouldn't be the first time that troubled youth and talent went hand in hand. Al's mind raced to the day in the near future when he would meet Johnny Cash with Byron at his side. Al's happy little daydream was dissolved by Byron's voice.

"No, I don't want to sing on albums; I want to draw the pictures on the cardboard covers the records come in." He had come upon this idea in an instant as he thought of what talents he had, and he remembered that he doodled well in class and could draw a car that looked really cool.

The sudden rise in hope in Al's heart deflated just as quickly as it had arrived and despite his intentions not to ridicule the boy, he let out a long sigh that voiced his thoughts on Byron's future profession.

Byron took Al's sigh as another slap in the face. "Well, someone's got to do it," he said.

"Yes, I suppose that's true. Son, unless there's an album cover drawing school somewhere that will teach you the trade and give you a diploma or a certificate that is recognized, that is recognized by the album cover drawers' union, well it ain't gonna happen."

"You don't know that," Byron said.

"I don't know a lot of things, but this ain't one of them." Al paused. That had sounded good as he thought it, but hadn't come out so good.

Byron noticed the awkwardness of the statement, too, and was going to sneer something about Al's English skills, then decided what's the use. "If all you want to do is make fun of me, why ask?"

"Because I want to know, that's why. Maybe I didn't try hard enough to get you settled when you come here. Well, I'm trying now."

"By locking me in a tin box, you're trying to help?"

"Yes. If you could walk away right now, would we be having this conversation?"

"No."

"Then I guess my plan's working."

Byron rolled away from the opening, picked up the closest thing in sight, and hurled it to the farthest end of the trailer. The bang of a tin can of mixed diced fruit in heavy syrup striking the double door of the aluminum cave reverberated for several seconds.

Al pushed himself to his feet. The stack of tires he was perched on had begun to pinch off the circulation in his legs. He fumbled for a cigarette and waited for the tantrum to play out.

After the flash of temper had dulled, Byron examined the can of mixed fruit. He was relieved to see it hadn't split. He paced in his stocking feet, his rage returned, and he wanted to kick the walls. But without shoes on, he feared his feet would suffer for no gain. So he began to cuss and spit out every dirty word he could think of in combinations never before used except at sea during violent storms spoken by men more experienced at weaving hate and fear and disgust into a single sentence.

Al walked in small circles, rubbing his legs and puffing on his Winston. As Byron spewed his venom, Al heard his name mentioned quite often. He chocked back a laugh at the poor use of perfectly good cuss words cast about and mixed with threats and accusations that didn't have a hint of credibility. He chuckled again at the absurdity of the situation. What would Ward Cleaver do if Wally or the Beaver said things like that to him? He would send them to their room and then go up and have a talk with them after supper. "Well, I'm right on track," Al said out loud to himself.

"What?" Byron said. Byron had come back to the open door.

"Nothing. You done cussin' for a while?"

"Maybe."

"Well, let's get back to talkin'. We got to do a lot of talkin'. That's what Ward and the Beaver do—talk, talk, talk. So if my plan's gonna work, we've got to do less cussing and more talking."

"Your plan?"

"Yeah, my plan to turn your life around. If this album artist thing don't work out for some reason, what you gonna do then?"

"What do you care?"

"I care enough to go to jail for what I'm doin', and I don't want to go to jail."

"You let me out right this second and I wont' say nothin'" Byron said.

"That's a fine gesture on your part, son, but that don't solve the problem."

"What problem?"

"Okay, let's add 'em up." Al held up a cracked and calloused hand with black and blue fingertips spread wide apart. He touched the fingers together as he listed possible problems. "You're sixteen years old and a high school dropout."

"So what?" Byron spat.

"Don't interrupt. If you interrupt me after every one of your problems, we'll never get this done." Al looked back at his fingers to find his thoughts. "You're sixteen and a high school dropout. We got that one. You like to drive, but you don't have a car so you steal one. That could cause you a problem. Course if you had a car, it wouldn't help much 'cause you don't have a license 'cause you're too lazy to read the book and pass your test."

"I could pass it."

"Don't interrupt," Al said, pushing a finger into the pile. "Then there's the money thing. You like money. You like to spend it. You don't like to work for it, but yet you got money all the time. I think that's a problem. That's going to bite you in the butt. You hate everyone because you're full of self pity. I'm going to run out of fingers before I'm half finished."

"Go fuck yourself," Byron screamed.

"I guess we're done talking for the day," Al said as he closed the little door.

CHAPTER THIRTY-FIVE

Money wasn't everything. Floyd knew that. He had a wonderful family, a loving wife and two handsome children, one of each. Money wasn't everything, but it's a good thing. That was one of many mangled or made up quotations Floyd loved to hurl at anyone within his reach.

The money was rolling in, the tires were rolling out, the men were happy and good at their jobs. The station looked like a winter wonderland. The face of the old stone block building had a hundred coats of white paint on it, the last one only a few weeks ago. The whole placed sparkled because of fresh paint and elbow grease. The white steel lamp poles in the middle of each island were candy cane striped with red paper ribbons.

Floyd strolled the driveway from end to end admiring his men's handiwork. From the corners of the red tile roof, yards of Scotch pine garland draped with silver tinsel hung in uniform valleys across the front of the building. The huge picture windows were criss-crossed with black electrical tape to replicate smaller windows, each shaded at the same corner with spray can snow. The telephone poles received the garland treatment as well, and stacks of tires wrapped in silver foil laced with red ribbons bordered each side of the showroom door. Giant candy canes hung from poles at every opportunity. Inside the showroom, a throne was built for Santa's arrival. Empty boxes wrapped in the bright papers of the season surrounded the throne. Santa would make his appearance on the last Saturday before Christmas and the kids would come to see him, and the parents would come to see their children on Santa's lap, and the cars they drove would need tires someday.

Floyd continued to be amazed at his own success. He had taken this rundown abandoned old gas station and turned it into a thriving enterprise. Floyd's Tire Mart was known by word of mouth all over Jefferson County as a good place to buy tires, a place that had what you wanted, sold them at a fair price, and got you out fast. Floyd was pleased that he wasn't arrogant enough to think he had done it by himself. The men were the key, and he had the best. Floyd would sometimes sit at the window in the office for hours at a time just watching the men greet the customers. Everyone got a smile. Regulars were greeted by name. Jokes were passed on. Kids got suckers from bright plastic buckets placed at each island. The men and the boys in this group were like a balanced football team. Everyone had a different job and did it well.

Floyd still had to laugh when he recalled the time he overheard Bill selling a pair of retreads. The customer asked Bill, "Are these retreads all blackwalls?"

"The retreads are all blackwalls."

"You got the right size?"

"We got the right size."

"You know I had some recaps go bad on me one time."

"You can get some that go bad on you."

"How do they wear?"

"Oh, they wear."

"How's the price on these? A good price?"

"Yeah, they're a good price."

"Well, you sold me."

"Good. Go see Al. He'll fix you up."

Floyd loved to tell that story.

As much as Floyd was blessed with success, he felt something was wrong. That thing with Ike flopping in the driveway was replayed over and over in his mind. The story of Al falling in the same manner earlier that morning didn't make sense, and yet it did. The whole thing smelled of lies and deception. If Al was drunk, he might have to be fired, a decision he didn't want to make. If this was the only time that something like this happened, that would be one thing, but if this was one of many occasions and only the first he had heard about, that would be a different thing again.

Floyd didn't like thinking about firing Al, although from a strictly business point of view Al could be replaced with a younger man who didn't growl at everyone. Al treated the customers with the same respect and courtesy as expected, but when he hobbled over with a look of pain and disgust on his face and said, "Fill her up?" it came out so rough and deep that some people took it as a challenge. Overall, Al had been a good assistant manager. Should he say something to him or just let it fade away? He knew Al was unhappy with his salary, but that was a matter of economics. The fact that he was paying Ike nearly as much just proved that Al could be replaced. Al could make more money only by working more hours. That was all there was to it.

Al was already working sixty hours a week. How could he work more at his age and condition? That's not my fault, Floyd thought as he strolled back to the tire room. Still, his men were the best and he wanted to give each man a piece of the pie this year—some kind of bonus. Floyd parked the idea in the back of his mind for later consideration. He walked past a Buick station wagon that looked unstable, jacked too high on a single floor jack. He made a mental note to himself to tell Ike not to put them up too high, just enough to get the wheels off. Ike was learning fast. He had sold this Buick the best they had.

The rhythmic whish and clang and groan of the air powered tire changer filled the room. For many of Floyd's customers, the spectacle of men peeling stiff rubber donuts off of heavy steel rims was part of the new tire experience. Floyd never tired to separate the customers from the show. Men, women, and children would watch in mouth-open awe. The old rags were peeled off and good riddance. The new shiny black rubber snow tires had deep sharp treads, treads that would push a family up a long steep snow covered driveway. The memory of carrying groceries up the drive on foot was still fresh. The tires were hammered, bounced, and cussed into place and mom and dad and the kids were happy again.

Next to a Buick, a Mustang sat on jack stands waiting its turn. With all four wheels missing, it looked silly and useless. It was, after all, just stamped metal and cast iron. But with a new set of rubber, this car would take its owner to her part-time job or to her night classes or to the movies or anywhere.

Floyd recognized the emotional connection people had with their tires and instructed his men to talk as much as possible about tire construction and design. "Educate them and move them up a grade." Raised white letters were a hot seller and made a better profit. The sports car crowd loved them. Even some of the pickup driving crowd wanted them. Floyd shook his head and smiled. Putting fancy tires on pickup trucks. Next thing you know, they'll be putting electric windows in them. Floyd didn't really think it would ever get that far, but he liked to say it to start conversations that would eventually lead back to tires.

Bill Miller was one of his top salesmen. Bill worked at a cracker factory at night and he worked three hours a day, four days a week, for Floyd. Bill could go continuously on only four hours of sleep a night. He was a handsome man in a mutt dog kind of way. At 6 feet 2 inches, he stood out in a crowd. He had a solid look to his frame and a kind face with a square chin and a broken nose. He could talk and talk. He spoke in a soft deep tone on any subject. A stranger might strike up a conversation with Bill and talk for an hour and never receive anything in the way of fresh information or fresh thinking. Bill would just take whatever anyone said and repeat it back to them in a convoluted manner and it seemed like conversation. Floyd didn't hire Bill for his deep insight into life. The same poor souls who wasted an hour talking to Bill usually had a good set of tires to drive on.

The price conscious river crowd loved the recapped snow tires. Floyd preferred his men to move them up a grade to increase the profit margin, but in the end Floyd was happy to sell as many retreads as his men could mount all day long. Some dealers didn't like selling retreads. There were too many stories of caps coming off and causing wrecks. The cause of these tread separations was that people were supposed to be running snow tires in the winter months. Then, of course, any fool knows you don't run one half flat at high speeds in the summer. But some people did.

The people who lived on the river bought most of the retread snow tires Floyd sold. These people were handy at keeping old cars going when others had given up on them. They changed cars often and carried their titles with them. They would shop for cars that ran the same size tire, and if the lug nut pattern matched, they were in heaven. The river crowd wasn't afraid to change a set of tires. Many of them could accomplish that task in the dark without making much noise. Doing the same task in the daylight on a pretty day was little more trouble than lacing up a new pair of boots. Every home had a floor jack in the garage or on a slab next to the house. No one locked them up anymore. The teenagers had stolen each other's back and forth so often the thrill was gone. An unwritten truce was called and everyone's jack was safe and handy.

Floyd went back to his desk and peeked through the blinds and watched the money roll in. Yes, he would give the men a bonus—a special bonus beyond the $25.00 check they each received last year—something they could hold onto and remember where they got it. Floyd began to mentally review each employee to try and find some common ground that would direct him to the perfect Christmas gift.

Leon and Brad were veterans of just over a year. Leon had a quick smile and a devilish charm. He sold nearly as many tires as the grown men. Brad was not as successful. His manner was stiff and he looked sullen. He carried a truckload of resentment on his back. Still, for reasons Floyd couldn't understand, some people were drawn to him. His sales were increasing steadily.

Ike had the potential to be his best salesman yet. Al was a good worker and sold enough tires, all things considered, but he needed to smile more. Skip, his other assistant manager, was just a couple of years out of the army and still had that can-do attitude. He set a good example for the younger men. Larry, the horse trader, made his money selling used refrigerators. Still, the customers liked him and he sold his share of tires. Bill was a good man, not likely to become a brain surgeon but steady and reliable.

It was too bad Byron Creed didn't work out. Al could use a break, but the boy just couldn't accept that this was a service station, and that means giving service. That's Al's burden to bear. I hope I don't have to fire Al too. He's got enough problems.

Now what to get the men for Christmas.

CHAPTER THIRTY-SIX

Clay Coal punched the buttons on the car radio. The speaker was brittle and cracked; nothing sounded good. He changed channels often. He was parked at the South County Mall. It was 10:30 on a Tuesday morning, double Eagle Stamp day at Famous Barr. There would be some nice cars to choose from. Clay had pieced together a junker from the salvage yard. The four door 54 Chevy he had coaxed back to life had spent its last few years as a work wagon for a bricklayer. Cement dust coated everything. The man must have carried sacks of mortar mix in the back seat, Clay thought. Clay had to replace the starter with one he stripped from another wreck. The rear end leaked out its oil rapidly, and there was already a large puddle under the back axle.

None of that mattered now. The car had made it and Clay would remove the plate and abandon it. When he left this lot, he would be driving something pretty nice. "Aha," Clay said out loud. A white 1962 Corvette pulled onto the lot. "Good morning, Mr. Big Bucks," Clay said. Everyone who owned anything Clay Coal wanted to steal became known as Mr. Big Bucks. Clay never really considered himself to have a conscience, but still it was easier to assume that the owners of the cars he stole had come by their wealth dishonestly by cheating little guys like himself.

Clay watched Mr. Big Bucks enter the store and looked at his watch and sat patiently for three minutes. The three-minute rule was the professionally agreed upon time to wait before approaching the car. Not all the rich bastards were stupid; some thought themselves pretty clever. Some would enter a restaurant or a store and stop just inside the door out of sight and look back to see if anyone was around their car. Men were most likely to try this defense. Women, on the other hand, were forgetful. They would enter a business and remember something they had left in the car and be heading back to the vehicle just as you're popping the door. The three-minute rule worked for both equally well. After three minutes, they would most likely not be back for at least ten. That would give him plenty of time.

Clay checked his watch and waited. He reviewed his plan one more time. Taking the Vette was no problem; that was the easy part. Getting out of the state with it—there lies the risk. Clay preferred to work at night with a drop off man, taking the car right from the victims' driveway while they slept, striking at midnight, giving himself four to six hours—maybe more—before the car was reported stolen. This was a special order and paid triple his normal fee. He needed the money and decided to take the extra risk.

The three minutes were up. Clay began his approach. People were walking all over the huge lot although none were close enough to see what was about to happen. Clay had a Famous Barr shopping bag swinging from the fingertips of his left hand. He walked jauntily toward the door. He wore dark plastic sunglasses of the cheapest variety, a red Cardinals baseball cap, and a red team jacket buttoned up completely. Nondescript blue jeans and white tennis shoes completed his attire.

When Clay reached the entrance to the mall door, he glanced quickly inside. Mr. Big Bucks was nowhere in sight. Clay looked at his watch again. Four and a half minutes had passed. Clay eyed the lot once more then walked quickly to the Vette. He circled the car like he was checking his tires for a low one. There were no stickers or decals on the windows bragging about the burglar alarm. Thank God people gave a thief a heads up on that or it could be dangerous or, if nothing else, embarrassing. Mr. Big Bucks had apparently not gotten around to having the alarm installed yet. Probably too busy having his hair styled or nails polished.

Clay pulled the slimjim from his shopping bag and slid it down between the door and glass. One jerk. Nothing. A second jerk. Click. The lock was up and he was inside the car with the door closed. A 15-inch rod with a heat hardened wood screw welded to the end was quickly threaded into the ignition switch. Clay had built the small slide hammer himself and was proud of its efficiency. Two pops and the switch came out. With the twist of a screwdriver, the car was started. Now get out of here fast without burning rubber, Clay warned himself.

Clay focused on his driving. Make no mistakes. If he could just get out of sight so that his direction was unknown, he was safe. Even if Mr. Big Bucks comes out a second later, he can't get to a phone, get a report filed and sent out in less than five minutes tops, and that's very unlikely. The odds are still very much in his favor. As Clay likes to say, it's like stealing.

Traffic was light as he had expected. He cruised along with the speed of the rest of the traffic, only a little slower in the slow lane. Four and a half minutes have passed since he left the parking lot of the South County Mall and turned left on Lindbergh Boulevard. The entrance to Crestwood Mall was just ahead. The light at the intersection turned green as Clay approached and he rolled leisurely into the sunken lot. He parked the Vette as close to the center of the lot as he could. A semi-circle of stores faced the lot. The sidewalks were teeming with life.

Clay strolled toward the Woolworth's Five and Dime. There, he knew, was a large restroom where he could change out of his hat, glasses, and jacket without drawing any attention. He returned to the sidewalk still carrying his shopping bag with his tools of the trade and his discarded hat, jacket, and glasses. Now he wore a grey sweatshirt and jeans as he strolled from store to store looking in the windows or stepping inside but always watching the Vette out on the lot. If a police cruiser spots the car, Clay simply walks away. If not, he waits till after dark and heads down Route 66. He'll turn off 66 at Sullivan and take blacktop roads over to Highway 67, then straight down 67 to Arkansas. And he's home free.

Clay had several hours to kill before dark. He decided to do some Christmas shopping. The question of what to do about Byron Creed disturbed his shopping. He found it difficult to get into the Christmas spirit with the knowledge that he would soon be breaking the kid's arms. Byron's time was up. He had disappeared without even making a token payment. Clay was surprised. He knew Al Creed from his childhood. Al had been at the house a few times and played horseshoes with the old man. He thought Al would have offered some kind of settlement. This was a slap in the face and he could not allow it to stand. He might have to bust both of them up.

CHAPTER THIRTY-SEVEN

The bullet wound in Al's side had healed and the normal routine at Floyd's Tire Mart had returned. Ike asked Al about Byron, but Al would only say he couldn't talk about it. Floyd never asked Al about the morning he fell in the driveway. He had heard several versions of the story and assumed they were all exaggerated and mixed up with the story of Ike practicing to be a naked skydiver. Floyd told the story of Ike's fall until everyone was tired of hearing it.

Al worked his shift and pumped his share of gas and sold tires, but everyone noticed how tired he looked. On the nights he closed up, he would wait in his truck on the parking lot drinking beer until Ike or Brad or Leon drove off. Then he'd trudge back to the trailer to talk to Byron. Sometimes he'd bring him coffee, sometimes a beer. He'd open the little door and holler, "You awake, boy?" Al thought by using the same greeting over and over, it would have the effect of jail life where every day is the same.

Byron looked forward to Al's visits and hated himself for it. He returned Al's greeting with, "I'm awake," and scurried to the little door to receive his drink and to talk. Al had some thoughts in mind and would start the conversation with a rehearsed sentence. "Sure I know what's going on with you. The juices are flowing and you think you have to live every day like it's your last. Ha-ha-ha!" Al's gravely laugh rolled up and down the length of the trailer.

Byron, safe in the shadows, couldn't help but smile.

"Ha-ha-ha-ha!" Al continued. The combination of a voice that sounded like a rock grinder and a lead singer in an all boys choir made Al's mocking laughter impossible to resist. Byron stifled a chuckle with his hand.

Al continued. "Now if you were the son of a rich man, there wouldn't be no problem. Why you could just wreck a dozen or so cars, maybe rape you some women, kill a couple of people, including a cop, and old dad would just pay for whatever was needed and that would be that. Well here's the bad news. You were born to poor people."

"Don't I know it," came Byron's sarcastic interruption.

Al snapped his eyes toward the opening and gauged the distance from his right hand to the side of Byron's head. A second later, the impulse was gone. Al relaxed his tense posture, breathed a deep breath, and went on with his lecture. "And that means you have to behave better. Why the price of one crime would break this pitiful poor family." Al let more emotion come through than he had intended when he started the sentence. Now he sat back and smoked, determined to regain his train of thought.

Byron twisted around to his other side, not really interested in Al's philosophy on rich and poor since he only knew the poor side of it. He thought that if he wanted a lecture on rich and poor, he'd want to hear it from someone who had done both—if I wanted to hear that crap, which I don't, he thought. That was the mind set Al was preaching to, the mind of a child in a man's body, unable for whatever reason known or unknown to science to see life as the big picture. Al, with only a limited education, knew for sure that for centuries this very problem had plagued fathers all over the world. "Why those Romans had trouble telling their boys what a mess they were making," Al said with new found conviction.

Byron just blinked and stared. Where Al came up with this stuff and where he was going with it no longer mattered. All he had to do was nod and grunt and Al would keep talking. And it was good to hear someone talk. It beat countin' rivets.

As Al began to run down, there were longer spaces of silence. And in the quiet of the evening, Byron could hear the ding dong of the driveway bell. "How long's it been?" he asked.

Al didn't look up from his stare at the ground. He wiggled his weight around on the stack of tires, adjusting the blood flow in his legs, and ignored the question. "When I was a boy, Dad had saved a little bit of money. I don't know how he did it. But he had put a few dollars away. I was about thirteen at the time and wanted to be a cowboy worse than anything. Dad owned two mules and one was in pretty good shape; the other was all but used up. Dad had his eye on a piece of ground that had a rough old house on it. The fields were terrible grown over, but the dirt was good. Daddy figured he could sell his best mule and with his savings have enough money to buy his own place. Dad had been farming his whole life, but always someone else's ground."

"You mean sharecropping?" Byron asked.

"Don't interrupt me. Well, with the good mule about to be sold, I decided I needed to work on my cowboy skills before the mule was gone. I got me an old piece of rope and rode that mule and practiced my rope throwing. Well somehow the mule hurt himself, pulled a muscle or something. I was told not to ride the mules, but I was so sure I could be a cowboy and not a farmer that I didn't listen. Well, the mule sale fell through and the God damn banker found out that the property was going cheap and told one of his rich friend's and he swooped in and bought it before Dad could get the mule healed up. Dad never did have a piece of ground that was his own. Not long after that, he had a mild stroke. He recovered most of his strength but he was never the same. He give up and started hitting the whiskey and died a year later."

Byron waited for Al to go on, but he just sat on the stack of tires looking at the fire in his cigarette. "What's that got to do with me?" Byron asked.

Al shook his head slowly. He was clearly disgusted that his son was unable to see what should be obvious to even the weakest of minds. "It means that you only get a few chances if you're lucky. Some don't get but one, and you're throwing yours away like you've got a basketful."

"I don't see any chances comin' my way at the moment."

"That's because all you can think of is how mean the world treats you. You got a chance right now to turn your life in a new direction, but you got to want to be somebody. Anybody can be a crook."

"Okay, I get it now. You feel bad about a crippled mule so I get locked in a tin box."

Al crushed out his cigarette in his hand. His skin was so thick and calloused, he barely felt the outer layer of the leathery skin sear. He rose from his wobbly perch and threw his arms to the sky. "Oh, Lord," he began as he paced in small circles around his four stacked tires, "I know I've done wrong and I thank you for my many blessings. I got a good job, I'm married to a fine woman somewhere, I'm in good health . . ." Al coughed. "I got a fine future ahead of me. I know I should be happy with all I've got going for me, but if you could just put a lightning bolt up this boy's butt, I would never bother you again." Al closed the small door and went home.

*   *   *

"You awake, boy?"

"I'm awake."

"So outlaw's your chosen path, is it? Well, let's see now. Can you name me an outlaw that's not been killed or put in prison for the rest of his life. No, you can't. Well, let's say you wanted to be a teacher."

"I don't want to be a teacher," Byron mumbled.

"I know you don't want to, but let's just say you do. Well, you'd need a high school diploma and then a college diploma. But that's too hard. All that studying and reading and test taking. But I bet you that 90 percent of the people that set out to be teachers make it. Now let's look at thieves. Easy money, exciting car chases, no bosses. But one mistake and you're caught or dead. Now let's review. Teachers—90 percent success; thieves—90 percent fail. Now you say you can't make it in a job where ninety out of a hundred do, but you can make it where ninety out of a hundred don't. Son, anyone with that much arrogance can make it easy if he would just swim with the current and not against it."

Byron heard the words, but it was too late. That was his mind set—it's too late. It'll be too hard. This is your fault. You should have come for me. The fear of books, the stubborn fear of conforming, the fear of taking orders from people he didn't like, the will to self destruct, to waste his life, to prove for all to see he had been wronged.

Byron pushed the three main thoughts around and around in his head. It's too late, it'll be too hard, you should have come for me. He threw up a wall, a wall that demanded failure and ruin. If Al would have come for him sooner and trained him to study, it would be easy now, but that's not what happened and it's too hard.

"You think this is torture?" Al asked. "This is nothin'. One day in the not too distant future you're going to wake up from one of the best dreams you ever had in your life, and in this dream you're going to be driving your car on a pretty day with your girl by your side, or you're going to be lying on the beach with all your friends trying to surf, or maybe you'll be walking in the woods when a couple of bluebirds fly onto your shoulders. It don't matter what the dream is, the thing is, it'll be a good dream, a great dream, and then you'll wake up to a concrete ceiling and bars and be shocked back to the fact that you still have three years to do of a five year sentence, and that the two years you just did were the worst you ever thought possible. That will be torture."

"Have you had dreams like that?" Byron asked.

"Hell, yes, everybody does. The brain plays tricks on you and you believe it, and then when you come back to the real world, you better have something pretty good to come back to, cause if you don't, you're going to feel worse than you ever felt in your life and you're going to start crying."

"I don't cry."

"You will, and you'll be cryin' over pain that won't go away."

Byron had heard different versions of this speech many times delivered by a wide variety of people. This time the truth of it hit home and a helplessness took over because he was sure this was his future and he felt helpless to change it.

"Let's talk about something else," Byron said.

"What else you want to talk about?"

Byron thought back to the day at the zoo when the monkey spit in Dwayne's face. "You think your great, great, great grandfather was a monkey?"

"Aah, Darwinism. I remember hearing about that shit when I was a boy. That monkey trial was goin' on somewhere south . . . uh . . . maybe Mississippi."

"Tennessee," Byron corrected.

"Okay, Tennessee. It don't matter. That's something that so many people fell for that reincarnation stuff."

"You mean evolution," Byron said.

"Okay, evolution. It don't matter. The point is, I never believed so many people would give up on a good hellfire preacher for one of them dry as dirt scientists. Why if you listen to an ugly little man paceing back and forth, sweating up a storm about sin and the devil and your eternal damnation, and then compare that to some government scientist with a slide show about frogs, well I just never thought frogs had a chance."

"You believe in God?"

Al squirmed a little and pulled out his fliptop box of Marlboro's. After he had one lit, he noticed Byron giving him the big sad eyes routine and lit one for him. "Yeah, I believe in God the way most folks do—when it's convenient and there's nowhere else to go."

"Don't that make you a hypocrite?"

"No, we was Baptists," Al said.

Byron snorted, trying to hold back a laugh.

"What are you laughing at?"

"Nothing."

"Well, you must be laughing at something." Al showed the leading edge of anger in the tilt of his head.

"No . . . well, yes . . . okay, I was laughing at you. You thought hypocrites was a religion."

"Oh, well, okay, what is it then?"

"It's a person who says things that should be done this way, then the does the opposite of what he tells others to do."

"So it's just a new name for an asshole," Al said, his anger resurfacing.

"I didn't call you an asshole just now. That's just you feeling like one."

Al found a little truth and humor combined in what Byron said. The boy had a quick mind, he thought.

"You think you'll go to heaven?" Byron asked.

Al pursed his lips and looked at the sky. "No, I doubt it."

Byron thought he saw an opportunity to tighten up the screw of guilt. "You think because you locked me up in here they won't let you in?"

"Naw," Al said, "this ain't nothin'. I'll probably get a pat on the back for this. It's other stuff I done." Al suddenly felt sorry for himself and wanted to just give up.

"Well, you deserve to go to hell for putting me in jail without a trial."

"Ha-ha-ha!" Al blared in his rusty voice. A jolt of new found energy rattled through his soul along with the laughter.

Byron hadn't the slightest idea what had set the old man into fits of laughter.

"You . . . ha-ha-ha . . . boy, I got to . . . ha-ha-ha." The lack of sleep was making Al giddy and Byron could say things that were so absurd that Al would need to blow his nose after an attack of silly giggles.

"Boy . . . ha-ha-ha . . . okay, let's . . . ha-ha— . . . examine this . . . ha-ha. A trial is held to try and make sure innocent people aren't punished and guilty people are. You must think . . . ha-ha-ha . . . you didn't do it. There's just you and me here . . . ha-ha . . . Who you talkin' to? I was there. You was there. You was holding the gun that shot me. You think a trial is going to come up with something different?"

"Well, maybe not, but that don't mean I'd be put in jail."

"Son, there's prisons out there full to the brim with men and boys that thought they weren't going to go to jail. And if you keep thinkin' that way, you're bound t join them."

Byron felt the sting of truth in what Al said and grit his teeth in frustration, unable to come back with any clear reason why Al was wrong.

Al's giggles tapered off and once again an uncomfortable quiet took hold."

"I might just get probation," Byron said.

"Let's change the subject. I'm not letting you out until I'm ready, and only I know when that is. You better start making the most of this opportunity."

"This is my big opportunity in life?"

"Yes, it is. It might be the only one you get. There's no bare minimum on opportunity that we all get. Some get more than others; some get none at all. Here's your chance to make up for blowing your high school education."

"Make up for? Who am I making up for? You?"

"No, you dumb shit, you! What do I get out of this except a bad cold and no sleep? You're the only one that can profit from this insanity." Al hadn't meant to use the word insanity and hearing it out loud, it seemed to hang in the air longer than most.

Byron heard it, too, and saw the slight chill it sent across Al's face. "You got that right, you crazy bastard. You're insane all right."

"We're done talkin' tonight," Al said. He popped up from his perch and flipped the small door closed in Byron's face. He could hear a wild cursing as he walked away but paid no attention to it.

*   *   *

"You awake, boy?"

"I'm awake."

"You got to be ready for change."

Byron accepted a can of beer without comment and settled in for lecture number 900. "What kind of change?" he asked.

"All kinds of change. You know you start out to do one thing and it don't work out, you got to be ready to do something else."

Byron decided to toy with Al. "You mean like if you were tryin' for a home run and you hit into a double play?"

"Yeah, that's right. You look at them baseball players. They spend all summer tryin' to make it to the World Series and when they get there, half of 'em lose."

Byron was trying hard to reshape the way he looked at life and that baseball thing almost made sense. But when he thought on how it applied to life in general, it gave him a headache.

Al ran the baseball statement through his brain one more time. He knew there was sound logic there; it just didn't come out right.

"You know you're gettin' crazier every day, don't you?" Byron said.

Al ignored him. "You just wait. We had inches and pounds and everything was all right. Then they come along with millimeters and liters and peters and widgets and gidgets and who knows what else. But you know why they do it? They do it to put the older guys into retirement, that's why. And we ain't done yet. You wait, they'll come up with somethin' new. You just wait and see."

Byron sat riveted to Al's every word.

"The next one," Al continued, "will be some worldwide bullshit so we can all talk together. Well, I tell you, I don't give a shit what some Chinaman or some Arab has to say. Huh, how does that affect me? He's got his goats to herd or somethin' and I've got my own problems. What the hell do I care what he thinks?"

Byron had heard all this before. He never really doubted it was all true; it's just that it failed to have any effect on him. "You're just ramblin', old man. Get to the point. What do you want to talk about?"

"Well, I'll tell you there's another thing. It's those Coal brothers. You have to get shed of them. They're going to take you down."

"They're my friends."

"I know they're your friends. That's the point. You got to get some new friends. Look here, let's say you're a good swimmer—and I know you are—but let's say Dwayne and Gerry ain't good swimmers and in the river of life, they're not good swimmers."

Byron thought about making a smart remark about the term "river of life." Al could see it coming and was ready to snap back when Byron just nodded his understanding and Al went on.

"Anyway, say you're out there in a boat on the Mississippi and it sinks. Now I know you could make it to the closest shore, but let's say the Coal brothers can't. Should you try and help them or strike out on your own?"

"Well I'd try and help."

"No!" Al exploded.

"Why not? They'd help me," Byron replied, sure he had the high ground.

"The reason you can't save them is . . . they're . . . uh . . . carrying stolen auto parts in their pockets and it's weighing them down."

"Why would they put auto parts in a boat?"

"Would you just shut up and listen," Al rumbled. He rubbed his stubbled jaw, letting out a long sigh. "Sometimes a man has just enough strength to save himself. I know on TV and in the movies he always saves everybody, but trying to save Dwayne and Dwight means all three of you go under. You have to let them go if you're going to have a chance."

Byron said nothing. He pictured himself swimming away from his two friends as they struggled in the muddy water. He didn't like the idea at all. "That don't seem right."

"I know it don't, son. It's one of the ugly truths of life you need to understand. There's a time to save others and then there's a time when it's hopeless and it costs you your own life, and for nothing."

"Would you let me go under?" Byron asked.

Al was thoughtful and rubbed at his face again. A few moments of silence before he answered froze Byron's soul. "No, I'd stay with you and help you get that extra weight out of your pockets so you could make it on your own."

Byron's heart leapt and his eyes thickened with tears. He turned away as casually as he could so as not to let Al see his emotions showing. "I got to pee," he said.

* * *

"You awake, boy?"

"I'm awake."

"So you think you're unhappy and you think money's the answer." Al let the statement hang in the air for effect.

Byron rolled his eyes and waited for Al's thoughts on life part 901.

Al pointed to the skyline backlit by the moon. "Look at them cedars, each tree shaped to a perfect spear point. You know I saw in that encyclopedia—the 'F' book—pictures of gardens in France where they clipped the branches off a whole line of trees so that they look like a giant hedge down each side of the road. You know how many full time men you'd have to hire to keep a place lookin' like that?"

"How many?" Byron said a little too quickly.

"More than twenty." Al had no idea how many men worked on a French farm, but twenty sounded like a lot to keep a tree hedge looking good.

"So what?"

"Well, you didn't have to pay no one to keep them cedars pointed. So whatever it costs that duke or earl or prince to keep his trees pruned, you're that much money ahead."

"Where is it?" Byron asked.

Al became frustrated. He got up off his stack of tires and began to pace. "Aw, shit, you don't want to learn nothin'."

"I just asked where my money was I saved."

"Well, it's in the vault at Fort Knox, I guess. The point I'm gettin' at is them rich people never have enough money either. They're always plotting and swindling each other and hatin' their dads and divorcing their wives just like poor people."

Byron let it lay. He knew there was no use arguing with Al. He'd just get mad and leave. Nothing was said for tense minutes.

"I read some of the 'A' book," Byron said.

Al was looking toward the cedars and the moon. He was glad he was because a grin spread across his face he was unable to stop. "Do you remember any of it?"

"Some."

"You ready to be tested on it?"

Byron stalled for time, unsure of the answer that would lead to getting out the quickest. "I don't know."

"Well, I know," Al said, having regained his composure when he sensed Byron was lying. "I know you're not ready because if you was, you would know it too. But it's good to know that you decided to make an effort to do what you need to do. I also know that you think I'm an old asshole that's treatin' you unfairly. Well, you're right. I am an old asshole and I am treatin' you unfairly. The thing is, it's happening and there's not a thing you can do to change it. And that's just the way it's going to be when the state takes you away and throws your smart ass in prison. The big difference here is I love you." Al cleared his throat and stepped back out of Byron's sight line. He hadn't meant to say that. The fact that he had confused his thoughts. After all, it wasn't a bad thing to say, it was a good thing. But under these circumstances, it didn't seem appropriate. He couldn't let himself weaken.

"Anyway, you read that 'A' book cover to cover and I mean every word of it—who wrote it, who printed it, who unloaded it and carried it off the damn docks. I'm going to ask you three questions, one from the front one-third, one from the middle third, and one from the back third. And you've got to get them all right to get another book. And if you can do two or three or more, that's fine too." Al walked out of Byron's sight rubbing his face in an effort to stimulate his brain into saying the right thing.

"I don't' care if you get the answers by luck. Luck is part of life, too, but the biggest part of life is tryin'."

"So why did you quit tryin'," Byron asked.

"We aren't talking about me right now. We're talking about you."

"Yeah, well I'm tired of talking about me. Let's talk about you. Why didn't you ever come for me?"

Al was caught off guard. His face dropped and his breath went out. He stood motionless for a heartbeat and sucked in a cool lungful of air.

"I'm sorry."

"Whoa, now. Hold on there, Mister. I'm sorry is not enough. That's what you said. I'm sorry. Maybe you're the one that ought to be in here reading encyclopedias."

Al turned to look Byron straight in the eye. The corners of Byron's mouth began to twitch as he fought to hold back a smile. Al suddenly caught the humor of the moment and began his own smile control routine. After an awkward second, they both let go a hearty laugh that lasted through a couple of deep breaths. Then the spell was broken and each player resumed his part.

Al fumbled for the words. "I . . . uh . . . I let you down."

"Well that's fine. Now you can let me out."

"You know I can't do that."

"Why not?"

"Because this is your only chance to think slowly and realize what you're throwing away before it's too late." Al poked at several pockets looking for cigarettes. He fished two out and lit them. "Smoke this slowly. It's all I have with me and this is a long story."

Byron accepted the cigarette and calmly waited for Al to begin. Al had thought about this moment many times. He had never thought it completely through, only thinking of his opening line. After that, it became too painful.

"Well, you know your mother is a whore, don't you?"

"Yeah, so what?"

"When your mother left me, she left me with a lot of debt. I had a single digit at the new quarry. You know what I'm talking about? A single digit is what we called your clock number at the quarry if it was less than ten. Old Dry Coal was the one that give me the tip about the job. He told me that a man was going to open the office out in front of the quarry on August 1. I don't know where he heard about it or why he told me, because for a guy with a big mouth, he didn't hardly tell anyone else. I was working as a day laborer at the time diggin' ditches with a shovel, so I run out and I bought me a truck. I had good credit. And I parked it in front of the quarry office on July 28. I was planning on camping in the truck and being the first in line for a job as a driver.

"Well, there was already seven trucks parked along Baumgardner Road when I got there, but that was okay. I got one of the jobs. Things were slow in the beginning and it was taking all I could make to keep my truck payments up. You know what it means to have a single digit today?"

Byron blew smoke as he shook his head.

"It means full loads and short runs and as many short runs as you can make in a day. It means a new truck every two years and means replacing tires before they blow out. It means living in a nice house and having a nice boat and a nice car. It means pulling into Floyd's on a pretty day in a shiny new tandem and having some other poor bastard fill her up with gas, check the tires and oil, and clean the windows. And while this other poor old bastard is doing that sort of thing, you're standing around drinking coffee and bragging about how many loads you hauled the day before. That's what a single digit number means, and I had one. I was number eight.

"I had me a 59 Harvester single axle. She was a handful to drive, pulled to the right all the time. Couldn't get it out of her. I think maybe the frame was twisted, but she was solid." A gleam came into Al's eyes as he remembered the truck much better than it actually had been. In his mind, she was bright and crisp. In truth, she was dull and crumpled on all four corners. Al held on to his daydream for a second and then came back to his story.

"Well, she needed tires and the work was slow. It was taking all I made to keep the insurance paid and make the payments on her. You have to be at the quarry every day to keep your number. You could go on vacation if it was scheduled, or you could be out for repairs, but not for more than two weeks. After that, you lose your number.

"Well, Interstate 55 was on its way and there was going to be all the work a single digit could do for as far as the eye could see." Al paused and drifted off to that dump truck driver's paradise he had created for himself. And in a flash, he was washing soap off the hood of a brand new Ford tandem parked on a concrete driveway in front of a new ranch home. And right next to the one he was washing was its twin only in black instead of red. The driveway was clean and smooth and a man could lie down and put a couple of shots of grease in a tie rod end without grinding gravel into his knees and elbows. And there was Rayleen bringing him a sandwich and a beer. She was wearing that sun dress of hers, the one that fit so well. She loved to wear it when she wanted to tease him. It was a thin cotton jumper covered with flowers and the flowers were huge and grew and blossomed in the curve of her hip and in the swell of her breast.

"So what happened?" Byron asked.

Al came back from paradise bitter and disgusted at the woman who had ruined his life. "She sold it," he said.

"Your truck?"

"Yes, your truck," Al replied with a sarcastic whine. "Sorry," he grumbled, "I just get so damn mad when I think about what could have been. I swear

I'd have killed her if I saw her. I couldn't go after you without committing murder. I didn't have the money to hire a lawyer. I talked to one and he said it wouldn't have changed much. There wasn't much chance of getting my truck back unless I spent a lot of money I didn't have."

Byron shifted around, unfolding his legs and switching sides. He said nothing. He wanted to get comfortable. Al was going to tell it all and he was mesmerized by the story, the story that was his life, the things of life that took him from his father as a young boy. The whole truth and why he was where he was today. Then in a flash, Byron took note of where he was and before he could fight it off, his mind concluded that this story would not explain why he was locked in a trailer. That was Al's doing.

Up until now, his whole life had been filled with whispered half truths told by his mother to her boyfriends. Mom never made up complete lies; there was always some truth to what she said. She just always played like she was holding up her end more than she was. Byron knew this from his own experiences. There were times when she was supposed to pick him up from somewhere and never showed. She would later say he had given her the wrong time and throw a big fit about him making sure he had the time right from then on.

"So you got a single axle and you got a single digit. Then what happened?"

"Well, like I said, things were slow and the front tires were shot and she needed brakes real bad. It was gettin' real dangerous to drive her, so Rayleen says, 'Why don't you work at Floyd's for a week or two, get the truck fixed, and make a little extra money?' Oh, that was just a dandy idea," Al mumbled with mock enthusiasm. "And I never give it a thought. Rayleen and me weren't getting along real well. I should have seen something, but I didn't. So the truck was over at Zeigler's all ready to go. Rayleen called Ziegler on a Friday night and tells Leo I'm going to pick up my rig on Saturday morning before they open. She tells Leo to put the keys behind the rear tires and I'll drop by and pay him Monday.

"So Leo's a good guy and I charged work with him before, so he says okay. Hell, he thinks he's doing me a favor. Now she had already struck up a deal with one of her barfly buddies to buy the truck. Well, it turned out that this fellow wasn't really a bad guy; he just got suckered in by Rayleen. She had told him she was a widow and needed to sell her poor dead husband's truck right away and needed cash to go see her dying mother. She sold it so cheap this guy couldn't pass it up. She took him over to Zeigler's after they'd closed and signed over the title to him. And this feller, he took my truck to Texas. He knew he could make $2,000.00 on her just by driving her down there.

"She wasn't home when I got in that night. That didn't make me suspicious. She'd been staying out all night about once a week at that time. I knew she was whoring around." Al paused and puffed at the cigarette he wasn't enjoying. The humiliation he felt wasn't that she'd pulled one over on him by selling his truck; it was that she was running around on him and he was willing to put up with it. He got back to his story.

"Well, when she didn't come home all weekend, I started to worry and I started looking at all her usual spots. Monday morning, I had to get my truck and be at the gate to keep my number. When I get over to Leo's, he hands me a bill for $500.00 and says he thought I already picked up the truck. I wrote Leo a check—that bounced. She had cleaned out the checking account. I went down and talked to the quarry boss and he gave me an extra three days to get a truck and get in line. Well, it wasn't no use. There wasn't any money anywhere. Rayleen had stopped making the house payments and the truck payments and the insurance payments and I found out I owed money all over the place. My credit was ruined. I was three months behind on the house and they was going to foreclose. Then since Rayleen had let the insurance expire on the truck and the bastards wanted to put me in a high risk bracket . . . do you know what high risk dump truck insurance costs? If you can get it. Well, you don't want to know.

"I couldn't get no one to lend me enough money to get a new truck or a used truck and get myself out of the mess I was in. I been at Floyd's ever since."

Byron soaked in the story. As little waves of truth washed over him, they each deposited a little more understanding about Al, about Rayleen, and about himself.

"You remember when you was working at Floyd's," Al asked. "Jess Taylor and his boy both had them new GMC's. Well, Jess was number 14. I was number 8. That could have been me and you. We would be hauling all we wanted of the good runs and we would just let the crappy runs go to the next in line. Hell, on nasty old days, we would just hang around the house and change oil and do tuneups on the rigs. I bet if you had been raised around them, you could have been a real good truck mechanic."

Byron glowed at the praise. He was sure Al was right. Hell, yes, he could. He could do a valve job on one of them trucks and still have time to put a big engine in one of the Mustangs he would own with all the money he was making hauling rock.

Both the men stared off into their own blue collar, redneck heaven.

"You know what I'd do," Byron said. "I'd build a motor. I'd bore out a 351 and bolt in a wild fuckin' cam, and it would be suckin' gas through a four barrel Holley and blowin' fire out a set of open headers."

"What you gonna put that motor in?"

"My Mustang. A yellow fastback."

"You got more than one?"

"Hell, yes, I got me a slick convertible with an 8-track tape deck. That would be my pussy car."

"Your pussy car?" Al asked.

"Hell, yes, all the money I'm making, I can afford two cars. I might start collecting them. I think they may go up in price someday."

"Oh, bullshit," Al said, "they're making them by the thousands. A things got to be rare to go up in price." Al began to cough and went into a two minute spasm. When he stopped, all red faced and out of breath, it was back to business.

"I got to go. You need to get reading if you want to get out sooner rather than later. But if you don't, well that's up to you. It's your decision. I'll tell you this." Al held up a blood filled finger. "I'm impressed with you, boy. You showed me just how hard headed you can be. I told you how you could be out days or even weeks earlier if you tried and all you had to do was read and remember. But not you, by God. I got to hand it to you. You'd rather rot than learn anything. I'll have to admit you are one of the stubbornest people I have ever met, and I've met some stubborn ones. Now as bad as that's working for you right now, it could be turned into a valuable tool. If a fellow starts out to do something and won't let anything stop him, he can't be stopped. You think about that while you're pouting."

"I never said I wasn't ever going to learn anything," Byron spit out.

"No, you never did, but you sure put yourself in a bind by not thinking about what would happen next when you did something. I can't stand around here all night. I got to get some sleep. You read your book or don't. It's your choice."

"How much longer you going to keep me here?"

"We've been over that already."

Byron knew the answer but stalled for time. He was tired of being alone. As much as he hated Al for what he was doing, he needed company, he needed it bad, and the slight trembling in his voice and the watery eyes that were a blink away from running down his cheeks told Al of his misery. What kind of monster are you, Al thought. That was the question that came back again and again.

Would the guard in the Jeff City prison stay and talk to a crying first timer or would he laugh and cuss him and expose him for his weakness to all the others?

Al paced around, looking for the answers. "I got to go get some cigarettes. I'll bring back some coffee."

"Could you leave the door open?" Byron asked.

But Al wasn't born yesterday. "You want out worse than anything in the world right now, don't you?"

Byron's heart leapt at the chance that Al had softened. "More than anything," he replied.

"So if I leave this open and someone was to come by, you wouldn't yell to them to get you out. Don't answer. You'll just be forced to lie. Not that I blame you. In this case, you'd be a fool not to tell as many lies as necessary to be free."

Al paced in small circles. "Do you think you'd be able to talk your way out of prison?"

"Never mind," Byron said. His hope dropped and his anger rose. "Close the fuckin' door." He pulled back from the opening and Al could hear objects being kicked or hurled the length of the trailer. He started for the truck after closing the small door. As he was almost out of hearing range, Byron's voice carried the single word, "Dad?"

Byron hadn't called him dad for some time now. It had been "Hey, Al" or "Hey, Old Man." Al hadn't minded the disrespect. He knew the first day when he showed up at the house that Byron had been living a rough life and was used to getting away with being rude and informal. The fact that he had not been there as a dad to the boy was justification to give him some leeway in the manners department. Maybe that was a mistake, he thought. Maybe I should have been firm at the start. Maybe he wanted someone to take control of his life. Maybe he was beggin' for it.

Al reopened the door. "What?"

"Would you bring me another light bulb? This one's out."

"Is it out because it's burned out or is it out because you broke it by throwing a fit?"

"I broke it throwing a fit."

"Okay. If I bring you another one, are you going to break it?"

"I don't know," Byron said in a sullen voice.

"Well, you're being straight with me. That's something. Yeah, I'll bring you back a light bulb."

*   *   *

The NEW STANDARD ENCYCLOPEDIA labeled CIVIL WAR to ENGLISH came with the replacement light bulb. Byron had not opened it and decided he would not ever read anything Al wanted him to. There were pictures in the book he was sure of that, all the books had some pictures. But he made himself a vow not to look at them. His arm itched inside the cast. He used the can opener to cut away the cast. Slowly ever so slowly he scratched at the plaster and cloth. Inch by inch hour by hour he carved until the arm was free. He made a sling out of a bath towel. The arm began to throb and Byron wished he had left it alone. The swelling in his knee had all but disappeared and the throbbing of the arm soon subsided. His brief concern that the arm may have to be amputated lifted and he decided looking at the pictures wouldn't hurt. A picture of a diesel powered race car caught his attention and before he could stop he was reading the caption under the picture:

"This car completed the Indianapolis Motor Speedway 500-mile race without stopping for any purpose. Average speed for the 500 miles was 86.17 miles per hour. Fuel cost for the 500 miles was $1.53." Byron processed the information in slow waves of understanding. There was no date on the photo. The car looked old like maybe from the thirties. His interest continued and he read a short article about Rudolf Diesel. He also learned that cork was nothing but tree bark, a fact that astounded him. He wanted to discuss these new discoveries with Al. Then his short visit to happy land was over and he was back in the trailer and mad about it. He would not tell Al about the wonders of the Diesel engin or where cork comes from. He would not ask him if he knew that the X15 was powered by liquid oxygen and ammonia. He would not ask him about the availability of liquid oxygen in this area. He would not allow Al any satisfaction, but he reasoned that as long as Al didn't know about it he could read the books.

CHAPTER THIRTY-EIGHT

The nightmares continued. Tonight it was Al in the trailer. The fear and the panic and the doom left him shivering in the cab of the old Ford. The blower motor was screaming again. Al slapped the dash, not too hard, no harder than necessary to quiet the annoying buzz. He was now thankful for that worn bearing. It had pulled him out of the wretched dream he was having.

What was the time? Al looked at his watch but could not make out the hands. He twisted the knob on the dash to light up the cab just as a car came by. He snapped the light off again quickly.

Bud Browdy was drawn to the light on Floyd's back lot coming on and going off again too quickly. Al waited and listened. He could tell by the sound of the car's motor that it was slowing. He heard the thump of tires as it pulled into Floyd's lot crossing the rain gutter on the edge of the highway, and then the bell began to ring and the ding-ding told him the car had turned around in the lot and was coming back. Al craned his neck to get a glimpse of the car at his earliest opportunity.

"Damn!" Bud said out loud. Bud needed sleep. He was tired and wished he hadn't seen the light, but his own curiosity mixed with his sense of duty, compelled him to investigate. He turned onto Floyd's lot and swung the big car around to have a look. He knew that he should radio in his location and what he was doing, but he hated talking on the radio. All those code numbers sounded silly when he said them. He didn't know but a few of them anyway and the ones he knew didn't apply to this situation.

"Damn, it's a cop," Al said out loud. What to do, what to say. It's too late to think. Just relax, Al told himself.

The headlights of Bud's car filled the cab of Al's pickup. Al looked straight ahead. His stare put his eyes directly on the trailer. To look anywhere else would appear strange, so he closed the eye being blasted by the light and waited for the next move to be made by the new arrival.

Bud recognized Al Creed just by his silhouette—the way the bill of his Zephyr cap tilted a little, the way the crown was crumpled. And the hard features of his nose and lips jumped out the way Washington's profile on a quarter jumps out and you know in an instant who it is. What was Al doing here at this time of night? Why did his interior lights come on for only an instant? Bud left his car running with the headlights shining through the passenger window of the pickup. It was three o'clock in the morning and Bud just wanted to go home. Sixteen to eighteen hour days had become normal lately and Bud promised Martha he would get more rest.

As he walked around the back of the faded old Ford pickup, Bud shone his flashlight into the bed of the truck. A spare tire, more than half worn out, on a rusty rim, two crushed beer cans, and nothing else.

Bud wanted to keep his attitude light and friendly until he could get a handle on what was going on. "Workin' late, Al?"

Bud's congenial approach and soothing voice put Al at ease. "No, I just love them tires so much I can't stand to be away from 'em." Al shifted his gaze to the mountain of rubber carcasses behind the station.

Bud chuckled a little at the smart ass answer. "You need to come up with somethin' better 'cause I want to go home." While not delivered in any official tone, it told Al that one smart ass remark was enough.

Bud waited for Al to speak again. He was learning quickly that asking too many questions often gave a suspect something to hang his hat on; but if you just said nothing, the less than brilliant criminals would talk in circles and fall all over their rapidly contrived lies. So far Bud had not run across any brilliant criminals, so this method of interrogation had worked well.

Al's mind froze. What was he doing there? Ten seconds ticked by. Sheriff Browdy stood absolutely motionless. With each second, the tension grew. "I been sleepin'. I closed up tonight. I had a hard day, drank a few beers, and fell asleep," Al said.

"Well, it's a good thing you woke up. I bet a dollar to a donut there's rust holes in the floor of this old girl." Bud patted the hood like he would pat a horse.

Al saw through the gesture and knew he was checking the temperature of the motor. The hood was warm. "Well, I guess we both need to get home to a soft bed," Bud said. As he started toward his car, he turned. "Oh, Al, would you mind lookin' at these front tires? I think one is wearing on the edge."

"You mean now?"

"It'll just take a second." Bud wanted Al to climb out of the cab. A man Al's age who's been in one position for a long time would be stiff and slow getting out.

Al climbed out of the cab. The door squawked on rusty hinges. Bud watched him casually out of the corner of his eye. Bud just learned two things—Al had been in the truck for a long period of time; he was stiff and slow moving. The other thing was that Al was hiding something. He knew this because he knew this type of man. Men like Al who had been to war, paid their taxes, and generally lived by the rules didn't put up with much foolishness from cops, even the sheriff unless they had something to hide. If Al was willing to look at wear patterns without so much as a cuss word, then he was trying way too hard at being a good citizen.

Al walked on creaky joints to the front of the sheriff's car. What's all this about, he thought. This is some kind of trick. But what was Bud up to? Al hated playing these kind of outsmart-the-other-guy games, but he had no choice but to play along. That's it, he wants to see how much crap I'll put up with. "Well, shine your flashlight on your fuckin' tires," Al said.

Bud pointed the light as directed. He knows what I'm doing skipped across Bud's left frontal lobe. "Never mind that. Come on and get in the car a minute."

Al was reluctant to give up his you-can't-do-this-to-me attitude. "For what?"

"Don't get wound up. I just need to talk to you about what's been going on around here and I want to do it sittin' down. Now would you mind doin' me a favor and just go along with what I ask." Bud chose his words carefully. "I still got coffee left if you want a cup," Bud said, retrieving his thermos bottle from the back seat.

"I could stand a cup if you've got enough."

Bud poured his coffee in a used paper cup that had rolled around on the dashboard that was piled with papers and wrappers. The chrome cup that went with the bottle was offered to his company. Al took note of the gesture and dropped his defiant act and leaned back in the comfortable seat, savoring his first sip of coffee. "That's not bad," Al said. Bud grunted his agreement.

"You know, Al, this job has been harder than I expected. Seems like there's been a crime wave ever since I took my oath."

"It has been busy lately," Al said.

"I suppose you've heard of the knife fights that broke out all up and down the river here lately."

"Oh, yeah, I heard twenty different versions of the same fight," Al said.

"I bet you do. Well, I'll tell you, Al, it would sure help if I was to be pointed in the right direction when it comes to picking up some of these bad boys."

"You mean like a spy or something?"

Bud chuckled and coughed a little into his paper cup. "No, not a spy or a rat or a traitor. Here's the way it is. If a few punches are thrown over a pool game or over a baseball bet between friends, I don't have time or money to mess with it. But we got some real bad ones running around that need put away. That Clay Coal is one that I'd like to put back behind bars. I think he's stealing a car or maybe two or three a week.

"Then there's those Bender brothers raising hell, robbing, raping, stealing. I don't know what all. And tearing up every bar on the river. If that wasn't enough, I keep hearing a local bank's going to be robbed. You wouldn't know anything about that, would you?"

"Wish I could help, Bud, but most of what I hear is second or third hand and mostly bullshit."

"Yeah, well I'm sure that's true, but once in a while you might see or hear somethin', and if you do, I wish you'd pass it along."

"I could do that."

"How's that boy of yours doing? I hear Clay Coal slapped him around some."

"He's doin' okay. He's doin' okay." Al wondered if Bud noticed that the sudden mention of Byron had made him nervously repeat himself.

"That's good. You know a girl over at the hospital said he was in some kind of bicycle or maybe motorcycle wreck."

"No, it was a bicycle," Al said.

"Well, young men give their daddies gray hair all over the world."

"I guess that's true."

Bud and Al sipped their coffee in silence. Al fought to control his urge to look toward the trailer. A line of heavy extension cords connected together stretched across the back lot from the station to the trailer. In Al's mind, the yellow and orange cords practically glowed in the dark. From where the men sat drinking their coffee, the cords were right in their line of sight. Al wrestled with whether to make mention of the cords and explain them away or ignore them and hope Bud didn't get curious. He decided on the latter. He had already made one show of nerves when he repeated himself. The best thing to do was talk as little as possible without appearing not to talk. "Damn!" Al hated this be smart and think quick stuff.

"What?" Bud said and Al repeated.

"You said 'damn.'"

"Oh, did I? I was just thinkin' of some stuff I forgot to do." If Bud asked what stuff, Al was screwed. His brain locked up like a set of power brakes on a gravel road.

"Oh, I understand what you're saying. It's been nice talkin' to you. Let's talk some more in the future. I think we got a lot in common."

Bud drove slowly on home thinking about his unexpected encounter with Al. He had promised Lowell Maynard to take a hand in Byron Creed's upbringing, maybe get him out of a tough spot if he had not done anything too serious. Now here he runs across Al and Al's up to something. But what? The two beer cans in the back of the truck had rust on them. They were not consumed that night. Al was lying, but why?

Martha waited up as she always did. She didn't really wait up, she slept on the sofa with the TV snowing its hypnotic hiss hours after the channel had signed off for the night. The big Indian head flickered on the tube, and if you had the energy, now was the time to adjust your picture. Martha had used all her energy for the day and slept contentedly in the reassuring hiss of the big Indian head.

What was going on? Bud thought. A good sheriff could figure stuff like this out in a short time, and he was determined to be a good sheriff. This was the first real mystery he had run into since taking this god awful job. There, he had said it, if only to himself. This was a terrible job. Somehow he felt better just making the admission. He had fought for this job. "Damn," he said out loud, "now you got to do it and do it good if you want to hold your head up."

Bud's thoughts raced around like an ocean full of tiny organisms in his brain, and each tiny organism was a different thought on a different subject. There had been two stabbings in the last month, and in each case nobody, including the victims, had seen anything. Bud could close both establishments down, but they happened to be the two best run bars along the river. This job becomes more impossible every day, he thought.

In the case of the two bar fights that had turned into knife fights, the owners of the bars ran clean, no nonsense establishments. In most of the other shabby thieves' dens that advertised themselves as bars, the patrons were so rough and mean and equally matched, that an unkind word might lead to a killing with no one confident that he or she wouldn't be killed. In such cases, good manners ruled the day. The drinker who couldn't behave well when the liquor took hold generally went to a more forgiving location where the other patrons would only bloody his head and throw him out.

Bud decided he had to quit thinking so much about the small details and look at the job from above, try to get the big fires under control while he put out the small fires. This seemed like a sensible approach. The rest of the drive home, Bud argued with himself over what was a big or a small fire. As he entered his home, the fatigue had taken over. He just couldn't think anymore. He stumbled on tired legs into the house. The big Indian head was playing its single, mind numbing note. Martha was stretched out on the sofa in unconscious bliss. Bud put an extra cover on her and went to bed.

The next day, Bud had the best plate of scrambled eggs he could remember. Martha made her usual eggs and ham, but Bud had forgotten to eat the day before and in his opinion, these were much better than usual. He discussed the previous day's events with Martha like he always did. Explaining things to her always seemed to simplify the problem. When he told her about his encounter with Al Creed, she took special interest. She was, of course, aware of Bud's promise to Lowell Maynard to look out for the boy.

"What's he like, this Al Creed fellow?" she asked.

"Well, he reminds me of me a lot. He's about eight or ten years older. From what I've heard, he's never been in any serious trouble. They say he used to run the river bar circuit and had a few punches thrown his way and threw a few himself, but never started a fight. Those who know him, think of him as a good man with nothin' much going for him in life but a strong back. And it's not as strong as it used to be."

"Why would you say he reminds you of yourself?"

"Well, we both grew up country poor and went off to war and come back home to a place where a small farm couldn't make a living anymore. We didn't know how to do anything else."

"You made something of yourself. Why can't he?"

"I guess you're right. It's just that if it weren't for you encouraging me all the time, that might have been my fate—to work away my life at a dreary job that should be a startin' place for a young man, not an ending place for an old man."

Martha was intrigued by the whole Lowell, Al, Byron triangle. "You say the motor was warm, that he hadn't been driving, that he wasn't drinking.

So why would someone sit in a truck all night?" Martha cleaned her kitchen with slow, robotic motions. Her mind was running over the problem with slow considered calculations. She would pick each possible situation apart, piece by piece, until she was sure it was wrong before moving on to the next one never to return.

Bud saw her mind working in her eyes. She would get a faraway look and her movements become slow and precise. He had a sudden fear she would solve the riddle first and began to run back over the events again and had the answer first. Bud's mind ran at a much faster pace and he envisioned reasonable possibilities in a flash and dismissed them just as quickly, only to return to them again and again.

"Had the truck been there all night?" Martha asked.

"There was frost on the tires so he had been there at least a couple of hours."

"Is there any scenery there?"

"No, nothin' to look at but a storage trailer and a mountain of junk tires."

"Could he be hiding from someone?"

Bud thought the question was absurd and rolled his eyes when Martha wasn't looking. "No, he couldn't have parked anywhere that wouldn't have been harder to see."

"Ooh," Martha said. "He's not worried about being seen."

Bud was starting to tire of Martha's detective work and wanted to read the paper for a few minutes before the phone started to ring. He looked up from his paper to the phone on the wall. That phone was about to ring. And then it did. He didn't think he had supernatural powers; the phone rang every morning at 8 o'clock. The only calls made to his home before 8 must involve officer down or something equally important. That was the rule. Eight o'clock and no sooner for regular stuff.

Bud looked at his watch on the way to the phone. Eight o'clock on the button. He thought, Couldn't it wait five minutes just one day?

Ten minutes later, Bud was on his way to Hillsboro. A lunch mob had gathered and Millie was flustered. Rhonda was at a doctor's appointment and wouldn't be in for another hour. The body of Todd Boman was found in a ditch along the Meramec bottom road. Wilber Boman, the young man's father, and a group of concerned citizens were demanding action.

When Bud pulled into the parking lot, he could see two of his deputies holding back a dozen men from entering the courthouse. The deputies had their billy clubs at the ready and looked to be only moments away from swinging into the mob. Bud approached unnoticed from the rear. "Hey!"

he bellowed. His voice cut through the murmur of the crowd. "I got one question for you men and I want a one word answer." The shuffling and talking stopped. "Did you men come here to beat up my deputies?" His eyes searched the faces of the men in the crowd and each one shriveled a little under his stare.

"No," came a mixture of voices.

"Okay, let's go inside and talk about what's on your minds without all the yelling." Bud walked slowly toward the door of the courthouse. A path in the crowd opened before him as no man wished to block his way. That was the natural command Bud had over men. He seldom cursed or raised his voice. He had an aura about him that most men recognized. An energy surrounded Bud that said, I will be reasonable but will tolerate no resistance to a reasonable request. Bud had earned this reputation in the short time he had been on the job.

The first time Bud was called to Jenny's in Fenton, one of the rougher bars along the river, Mark Mayfield had just shot his brother in the nuts and was refusing to be put under arrest. When Bud came to scene, Mark was sitting alone at the end of Jenny's bar. Deputies Brown and Skaggs had their guns drawn. Mark Mayfield would reach for his beer every few seconds in quick jerky motions. Next to his beer mug lay a .38 revolver. The excited deputies demanded he step away from the bar and put his hands up, to which Mark taunted and jeered, "Shoot me, you pussies." Wild eyed patrons watching the event snickered under their breath.

Bud assessed the situation at once. "Good work, men," he said. "Can you hear me all right, Mr. Mayfield?" he asked.

"Yeah, I hear you," Mark said, not looking up.

"I need to talk to my men first, then I'll be talkin' to you."

"Take your time," Mark said, drawing a few giggles from the gawking patrons. Mark laughed a drunken laugh that was meant to mask his fear.

Bud turned his back to Mayfield and stood between his deputies, being careful not to block their firing line. "I'd like to thank you men for the fine job you've done," Bud said, his voice loud enough for all to hear.

Brown and Skaggs hesitated for a moment when Bud offered his hand. "Thanks, men," Bud said, shaking each man's hand. "Okay, here's what we're gonna do. Can you hear me okay, Mr. Mayfield?"

"Yeah, I hear you."

"Fine. Okay, I'm going to go talk to Mr. Mayfield. If he moves toward that gun, you shoot the hell out of him." The deputies nodded their understanding.

Mark Mayfield stiffened, his stomach turned to ice, his breath came in short gasps. Bud turned his attention to him. "I'm unarmed," he said, opening his coat. "I'm coming over to talk." Bud strolled casually across the floor toward the end of the long bar where Mark Mayfield sat motionless, staring straight ahead. "I hear you shot your big brother in the nuts," Bud said as he stood next to Mayfield.

"He had it comin'," Mayfield said, refusing to look in Bud's direction.

"I'm sure he did, but we can't allow people to shoot each other in bars where someone else might get hurt," Bud said in a sympathetic voice. "Now I'm going to have to arrest you or my deputies will shoot you. Now you don't want that, do you?"

"Don't matter to me," Mayfield said. There was a tremor in his voice that gave away his phony bravado.

"Okay, then, let me buy you one more beer before we start." Bud moved his left hand toward his rear pants pocket where his wallet would normally be carried. Mayfield was drawn into the idea of one more beer before he died just a little too deeply. When his fog covered brain came to the conclusion that something was wrong, Bud's hand was already on the handle of a lead slapper. Mayfield's hand started toward the gun, but it was too late. Bud brought his arm up so quickly no one in the shadow filled bar saw it clearly. There was a blur of motion, a muffled thump, and Mark Mayfield slumped backwards off his bar stool into Bud's arms. Bud lowered Mayfield to the floor, where he lay motionless. There was a collection of sighs of relief that filled the room as the deputies holstered their pistols and the patrons murmured among themselves.

Bud had only been on the job for two weeks when the nut shooting incident, as it became known, occurred. He was at once accepted by the deputies as someone to follow into battle.

Bud ordered the mob to the basement and went to his office to be updated on what the hell was going on. "Millie," Bud said, "when's Rhonda gonna get here?"

"She'll be here in twenty minutes," Millie said. Millie was her usual self, overly frustrated and so nervous she made other people nervous.

"Call downstairs and tell Deputy Pratt to come to my office." Bud went to his desk slightly ashamed of the giddy feeling he was experiencing. He had his first murder case and he had to get it right. He knew from his reading that most murder cases are solved in forty-eight hours or they're never solved.

Deputy Pratt was clearly shaken. His face was drained of color and his eyes seemed to be looking off into a memory. "What were you doing when you found the body?" Bud asked.

"Fuckin' off."

Bud blinked his astonishment at the deputy's boldness. He looked closer at his man, coming toward him and giving him a hard stare. Brown didn't notice. His mind was fixed on the scene that had so startled him that he could hardly focus on the present. "Deputy Pratt," Bud said. Bud was shaking the man's shoulders when he came back to the here and now. "Let's try this again. I've got a roomful of angry men that I have to calm down. I need to know some information. You were driving around down on Meramec Bottom Road fuckin' off and what happened next?"

"I was west of the interstate—maybe a mile—and I thought I heard a gunshot."

"You thought you heard one or you did hear one?"

"Well, it turns out I did hear one, but I wasn't sure at the time."

"Why weren't you sure at the time" Bud asked.

"Well I had the radio on pretty loud."

"The dispatch radio was too loud?"

"No, uh, I had the . . . I had the FM radio playing some music."

"What kind of music?"

"Rock and roll."

Bud filled himself up with a huge lungful of air. "Mr. Brown, if I knew exactly what song you were listening to, I might be able to establish a time of the murder. That might come in handy somewhere down the line."

Deputy Pratt had a sudden realization about how the sheriff was going to proceed and he didn't want to be the goat. "Sorry, Sheriff, the song was 'Only the Lonely' by Roy Orbison. I had it turned up all the way."

"Okay, we'll check the time with the radio station. Then what happened?"

"I drove on west toward where the shot came from. I didn't see a car or a truck, but I heard one. I had turned the radio off and had the windows open and I heard a strong running motor winding out for all it was worth."

"Uh, huh," Bud said. "Go on."

"Well, I didn't think I had a chance of catching up to whoever it was, so I slowed down and started scanning both sides of the road. And I probably would have missed him except he had on those light brown work boots with all white soles. You know the ones I mean?"

"Yeah, I'm following. Go on."

"Well, the bottom of that boot almost glowed when my spotlight hit it, so I pulled over and I just knew I was going to find a body." Deputy Pratt slid back into his trance momentarily, then jerked his head lightly, and locked wide eyes with Bud. "I never seen nothin' like that before. All the dead people

I ever saw was dressed nice and looked peaceful. This was horrible. It was poor little Todd Boman. I knew him since he was a baby. He was shot in the head. There was no doubt about that. But what was worse were his arms. They were both stuck out like Christ on the cross, but instead of being palms up, they were palms down, twisted back toward his shoulders. He didn't have on a shirt and you could see the skin all twisted where the bones were broke and the arms were bent the wrong way."

Bud saw the pain in this man's face. He knew Brown would be seeing that scene for some time to come. "Okay, Deputy Pratt, take a minute and push that picture out of your mind. The boys tell me you got a real nice ski boat. Is that right?"

"Yes, sir."

"What color are the seats in that boat?"

Deputy Pratt shifted on his feet. He was close to breaking down and crying and Bud wanted to spare the man the embarrassment. "Pink and green," he said.

"You got a pink ski boat?" Bud asked with mock skepticism. "How's she run?"

Deputy Pratt now realized he was being steered away from his emotional meltdown. "Thanks," he said. He hitched his belt around and squared his shoulders. "So then I called dispatch and went back to the crime scene and shone my flashlight around lookin' for clues. I didn't get too close and I didn't touch anything."

"That's fine," Bud said.

"So then when the ambulance showed up and everybody, I just come back to the courthouse."

"Okay, that's all for now," Bud said. He made his way to the squad meeting room in the basement of the courthouse. He had promised angry men waiting for him there answers and he had none. The boy's arms being broken the way they were made anyone familiar with the local roughnecks think of Clay Coal. He had broken several arms and had often promised to break both arms of men who pissed him off. He would tell his victim that he was sure that "a no-good bastard like you don't have anyone who loves you enough to wipe your ass, and after I break both your arms, you'll have to scoot across the rug like a dog with worms until they mend."

As Bud entered the meeting room, the conversation abruptly stopped. A metal chair screeched as it was skidded in front of the nervous leg of a man shifting to get a better look at Bud Browdy and hear the information he would share. Bud moved to the podium and cleared his throat. "Mr. Boman, I'm sorry for your loss." No one said a word or moved a muscle.

Bud scanned the group of about twelve men. He recognized all but a few.
He knew their names, he knew where they lived; they were just like him. They
had been to war and seen the terrible things that men do to other men. They
had come home and started their families and put all the ugliness behind
them, and now here it was on their doorstep. Bud felt the heavy responsibility
of the job once more. What would he tell them? The truth? That he had no
idea of who had done this or why it had happened?

"Who did this? Who killed my boy?" Harold Boman said.

"We've got several clues and leads that we're following up on," Bud said.

"Was it that Clay Coal bastard?" Harold asked.

"I've got no reason at this time to believe it was Clay Coal. He is someone
I'll be talking to as soon as we can locate him."

"That no-good bastard needs killin'," Harold said. The rest of the room
agreed.

"That may be true, and if he done this he'll get the gas chamber for sure.
If anyone should happen to see Mr. Coal, call my office and I'll pick him up."

"What if he don't want to come?"

Bud recognized the voice but couldn't place it. He leaned forward and
stretched his neck. A path cleared between him and Lowell Maynard. The
question wasn't delivered with innocent curiosity of a stranger new to the idea.
It was asked with a sharp edge meant to cut at Bud's credibility. If anyone
else had asked that question in that tone, Bud would have come down hard.
When he didn't, the others in the room all concluded that Lowell enjoyed
a special place in the sheriff's eyes. Bud at once felt anger and remorse. He
hadn't followed through on his promise to check on Byron Creed. He felt he
had let down a friend, so he let the cut go.

"When I find him, I'll take whatever steps are necessary to bring him
in," Bud said.

CHAPTER THIRTY-NINE

The first few flakes were floating to earth when Al and Ike finished rolling out the display tires. The weather had been cold for several days and clouds still hung low as they had all week. Today the sun was going to shine brightly according to the radio weatherman.

Ike had heard the forecast just as he pulled onto the lot twenty minutes ago. The radio had said sunshine by noon and a light dusting of snow. The sun came out at ten o'clock; the day was bright as summer. The snow had fallen steadily, the flakes growing in size. Ike slurped a swallow of coffee as he passed by the radio inside the station on his way to get change. The man on the radio, Biff Anchor of KLOW, was embarrassed that he had missed badly on his forecast of the night before. He now was sure this would be a major snowstorm with up to twenty-four inches of accumulation.

Floyd saw what was about to happen and got on the phone for help. All his employees were needed. This could be the biggest day in his tire-selling life.

Ike had never seen anything like this at his young age. The flakes were large as quarters and wet and when they touched your skin, they melted quickly. The concrete road and the asphalt drive were frozen from three days of zero temperatures. The first small bits of ice that had fallen this morning protected the surfaces from the sun's rays. Now the snow was piling on top, daring the sun to do its worst.

Floyd made his calls. He was thrilled that all his men could see the opportunity for his business and had given up their own plans to readily come at once. "What a crew," he began to say repeatedly all day.

It appeared to Ike that everyone in Jefferson County thought that snow had somehow been eradicated from the environment. Here it was the end of December and no one had put on their snow tires or bought the new tires they knew they would need. The tire changing machine was working nonstop, each man taking a turn peeling off old carcasses and replacing them with fresh, shiny black rubber treads that promised trouble-free driving even in the deepest snow.

Floyd had thought ahead last summer. He could see that a day like this might come. He was going to be ready when it did. He had tripled his usual order for snow tires from KNL Distributing. The last two mild winters had left KNL with their warehouses full of snow treads. With the radial tire catching on with the public, KNL needed space and sold cheap. Floyd filled the basement and the two trailers parked out back of the building.

It was a Saturday, the day before Christmas. The gas pumps were always crowded on a Saturday morning, so the first rush didn't seem unusual. Only the first rush never stopped. At nine o'clock, the first of the help arrived. The islands were full. If a customer wanted regular gas and was waiting for a pump to clear, the men were to offer a three cent discount on premium gas if that pump was open. Floyd was not going to pinch pennies today. Keep 'em moving was the slogan for today.

Every jack and jack stand had a car or light truck perched on it. People were standing shoulder to shoulder in the waiting room. Many of the newcomers had to stand by the tire changer or outside. Four cars were in the air with six in line to be next. The phone was ringing every five minutes with worried customers frantic to get snow tires. Floyd assured all who called they would get their tires on today even if it took a little longer than usual. The routine was simple. Once the sale was made, get the wheels off the customer's car. That was sound business practice and had a calming effect on the customer. Seeing their cars with no rear wheels took the matter completely out of their hands. Up until that moment there was still the nagging worry that they had purchased the wrong tires or had paid too much. Now it was too late and they only had to wait.

The vehicles with missing rear wheels were all staggered down the driveway. There were no inside racks. This was Floyd's Tire Mart. Keep the overhead down and the cars moving. It was much faster to use roll around floor jacks and bumper jacks than to pull the cars in and out of bays. There were no air ratchets either. A four-way lug wrench spun by an experienced handler was just as fast and didn't drag an air hose that could leak or freeze or tangle in someone's feet. One man was kept busy shoveling snow so that the jacks could be rolled and drug up and down the driveway.

At eleven o'clock, Sally Geiler, who worked at the Meramec Deli, came in with a box full of meats and cheese and bread. Floyd cleared off a plywood table used as a tire display, spread newspaper for a tablecloth, and laid out a sandwich table that left nothing to be desired. The coffee pot was kept fresh and the soda machine door was open wide for all to enjoy.

The snow kept coming. At twelve thirty, sixteen inches of snow layered the lawns and fields and back roads and frozen ponds and windowsills all over Jefferson County. The pumps were busy and it was good planning by Floyd again that his tanks had just been topped off yesterday afternoon.

The men were working in rhythm like never before and astonishment was the word of the day because the cars and trucks just kept coming.

Floyd was making most of the sales and wasn't wasting much time doing it. He showed folks the type of tire best suited for their vehicle, tallied the numbers, and asked for the sale. The buying frenzy was infectious and with the snow falling at record pace; those that normally would have kicked, bounced, and rolled and spun tires, then complained about the price before committing to the sale, were put off guard by Floyd's urgency to make a deal. "If that's too much on a day like this," he would say, "just think how much it's going to look like when it's warm and sunny. Ha-ha-ha. But sooner or later, you got to have 'em, and in a couple more hours, you're going to need them real bad. So have a sandwich and a soda and I'll take another $5.00 off. How's that? And I'll have you ready to go in thirty minutes." That usually pushed the deal over the edge.

"Ike, get two 825-14 Remingtons All Weathers and put them on Mr. DeClue's Impala," Floyd said.

"Got it," Ike said. Ike stopped what he was doing and carried the tires up from the basement. He put the tires next to the Impala that had no hope of being ready to go for at least an hour and a half.

At two thirty, the basement was but empty. There was a short stack of 200-15s, used only on VW Beetles, left in a dark corner. The rest was bare. No one could believe it and all the men took a quick jog to the bottom of the steps to see for themselves. The tire changer ran nonstop. When one man was tired or needed to pee, someone was there to keep the changer running.

The freshly inflated tires bounced on the old wood plank floor and dust rose up from the seams. Tires were rolled out the door and aimed down the drive to a waiting receiver. The cars and pickups were supported by jacks, jack stands, used wheels, and cut off chunks of railroad ties. The men manned the pumps, they shoveled the drive, they moved tires on and off at a pace that amazed themselves. Floyd orchestrated the symphony with short, curt sentences. The vehicles were reshod and sent down the road with the efficiency of a circus tent being raised. Everyone knew his job.

The green rope of woven pine bows arched on the face of the old stone building and white flakes of ice piled upon itself along the top of the green rope and spilled off the sides. The flakes of ice drifted down in a never ending supply. Every surface displayed its own variation of white topping. The flat surfaces rolled and dipped into frozen waves. The tops of the pumps grew into hedgerows of white triangles.

Shoveling the drive was a fight in itself. One man shoveled continually. Brad proved to be a world class snow shoveler. Keeping the drive clear was an important job and although it was shared by everyone, Brad shone at the task. He shoveled snow like it was his personal enemy. He worked at a pace that made seasoned laborers raise an eyebrow.

Brad had struggled at other aspects of the job and had never mastered the operation of the tire changer. The changer worked on air pressure and was controlled by a foot pedal. A two-inch thick steel pedestal protruded from the triangle base. When the pedal was pushed, the pedestal would turn. If a slotted tire iron was placed on top, the tire iron would turn. If that tire iron was wedged against the wheel, a tire would be peeled off. Brad could wrestle a set of tires on and off if given enough time and no one was killed by a flying tire iron which had a tendency to go spinning across the room when Brad was changing tires. He was not a very good salesman either. He made a good effort and took orders on a few sets but never sold a tire on its performance or its good looks or its financial good sense. When the madness started, Brad saw that he could be of the most help moving snow.

All the men knew this was a special day, a day that would be talked about over coffee and cigarettes and beer and campfires for years to come. Brad wanted to be part of the story that would be told and retold with a different slant of each man's own experience. He set his mind to the idea that the story of the big snow on Christmas Eve 1964 would never be told by anyone without reference to the boy who shoveled snow all day long. Ike tried to relieve him twice. Brad declined. Ike ripped the shovel from his hands and tried to run, but Brad was too fast and took it back. Floyd ordered Brad to take a break and get some food. Brad asked for a sandwich and coffee to be brought out, but he would not come in. Brad bent to the task he had set for himself. He switched arms on the shovel to balance the load of fatigue on his body, pitching snow to his right, then turning and pitching snow to his left. He worked steadily, hour after hour.

Floyd pulled Ike off his job at the bubble balancer and sent him out with a thick ham and salami and cheese sandwich and coffee. "You tell Brad if he don't stop and eat, he's fired," Floyd said.

The customers in the changing room and in the showroom had become part of the play. There was a shared sense of fraternity on that day. The whiskered men in their fedoras and their ball caps, the harried women in a tugging contest with small children, the insurance salesman waiting for his Turino, someone's mother or maybe grandmother calmly waiting for her Impala wagon to come down off the jacks. Twelve vehicles in all at the height of the madness. The two sets of jack stands, four chunks of cut off railroad ties, and a wide variety of old rims and concrete block combinations, along with the rolling bumper jack and the monster floor jack had a dozen snow covered chariots suspended in the air.

No one complained. The atmosphere was electric with the expended energy of competent men working at a single task in perfect coordination. Tires bounced on the floor, the changer clanged and whished, and the chorus of men's voices carried each act's progress or lack of to a customer's ear who was listening with acute interest. "The Turino's ready."

"I need 7-75s for the Falcon."

"Who owns the Galaxy?"

"You want those whitewalls out."

"You brought me Remingtons. This car gets Goodrich, you moron."

Floyd would break into the chorus if the opportunity was right. "Hey, quit calling him a moron. He hasn't reached that level yet."

The workers and the customers formed a temporary performer and audience relationship. Biting insults were hurled back and forth between the men as they maintained a blistering pace. The customers watched the movement of men and tires in unison like fans at a tennis match. When the boy shoveling snow was sent a sandwich and an ultimatum, all attention followed the sandwich's flight.

Floyd watched to see Brads's reaction, as did all in earshot of the order. Brad laid his shovel against his hip and took a large bite out of the sandwich. Ike could be seen explaining Floyd's order and pointing toward the showroom. As Brad struggled to grind the food small enough to swallow, he noticed all the faces in the showroom looking his way. He gripped the rest of his sandwich in his teeth and sent his middle finger toward the sky and began again to pitch snow on an ever increasing pile. Floyd let out a howl and slapped his leg. The waiting customers enjoyed the rough and tumble humor of the moment as well. Ike returned with the news that Brad would come in when he was damn good and ready. A new tremor of grunts and giggles filled the room.

The stream of cars and trucks continued to slide up to the pumps with no letup in sight. The gas flowed and the tires rolled. At four thirty, the huge tank of regular gas was gone. Floyd ordered that premium would be sold at regular price. The snow continued to fall. At seven thirty, the driveway was empty. The last car pulled out with a new set of rubber and the men at Floyd's Tire Mart let out a collective sigh. A few more cars came in for the last of the gas and then the day was over. Floyd hit the lights and the men slumped into chairs or stacks of used tires or to the floor. Floyd was beaming. His happiness was infectious and he paced around the showroom shaking hands over and over. "What a day," he said again and again. "What a day. Boys, we did something here today." He turned off the pump lights and locked the door. Floyd's Tire Mart was officially closed on Christmas Eve. No more gas would be pumped, no more tires mounted.

There was a joyous flow of energy in the room. The holidays were here and each man in the room was better off this year than last. The rumors had flown all day long about the boxes of Browning shotguns stacked in the office with a bedspread draped over them. Two quick peeks, one by Brad and one by Ike, confirmed that there were enough boxes to provide for every employee. Floyd glanced around the showroom with a smile stretched tight. He took note of each man with a smooth sweep.

Al could be heard in the office punching numbers into the adding machine and the machine grinding away at its job. Skip Boman, the man next in line for Al's job, was walking around stacks of tires shaking every hand in the room. Larry Williams was looking at the swap board and comparing it to the small black book he carried at all times. Ike and Brad and Leon sat closest to the stacks of shotguns still covered by the bedspread. The three boys all agreed, in a not too subtle conversation, that Floyd was the best employer in the country.

Floyd made a short speech about loyalty and trust and thanked everyone as a group for the fine job they had done all year. Then he passed out pay envelopes, each with a man's name on it. The envelopes came with a handshake and a sincere smile. The checks inside represented an extra week's pay for each man. Those who worked more, got more. Nothing could be simpler than that in Floyd's mind. He was held to no union contract language to do this for his men; he just knew it was the right thing. Too many employers lose dollars trying to save nickels—another one of Floyd's sayings he thought he had made up. Everyone helped himself to a deli sandwich and a beer. Even the boys, as they were known, were allowed to partake of a beer on Christmas Eve at Floyd's Tire Mart.

Al poked the adding machine for the last time and the numbers generated onto the paper matched perfectly with the bank deposit. Al was still amazed and thrilled whenever the numbers matched on the first try. Two nights a week, they might; most nights took several attempts. Al had a system he had developed for those nights when the money and the numbers didn't match. He would do the numbers two more times and then simply add or subtract from the money to make the match. He would take the extra money and place it in a cigar box hidden in the back room. The system worked well because there always seemed to be more money than tickets.

Al came down into the showroom and made his own rounds shaking hands, slapping backs, and making toasts with cold beers. For Al, this was not only a Christmas party; it might well be a going away party. And now that the time had come to open the door on Byron's cell, Al felt he might be stepping into a cell himself. Perhaps by this time tomorrow. But it was too late to change anything now. He had imprisoned his son and tonight he was going to release him and take whatever came next.

It was Christmas Eve and Al felt the spirit of the holiday in a way he had forgotten. Not only was he willing to show kindness and charity to his fellow man, he was willing to do the same for himself. The long days of pumping gas dead on his feet from lack of sleep, the long nights sitting in the truck staring at the trailer, the thinking and worrying each day on the course of action he had taken was now over. In a few hours, Byron would be free and the matter taken completely out of his hands. He had nothing to do but relax. The Johnny Carson Christmas show would be on tonight. He relaxed with the knowledge that he was free falling with no way of going back. The chute would open or it wouldn't. He could lean back, take off his shoes, put his feet up on the sofa, watch Johnny and Ed in their tuxedos welcome the beautiful people of Hollywood, and listen to them sing Christmas classics. Who was on or what they sang made no difference. It was a comfort to him that the world he had abandoned fourteen days ago was back. The sameness of it all was what Al was seeking—the world before he became a hostage taker, a kidnaper, a prison warden. That was the world where watching Johnny Carson was like coming back home after a long and exhausting trip.

"Well, men," Floyd said, taking the floor, "I need to be getting home to my family and I know you all do too. Al, would you start handing out those boxes stacked in the corner over there." Floyd was beaming with excitement. He knew the men were going to be thrilled. The stack of boxes was a poorly kept secret. Everyone knew they were getting a Browning shotgun or rifle, but only Al and Floyd knew the content of the boxes. Floyd had left work early three weeks ago to make the long drive to Springfield. Bass Pro was the Missouri distributor of Browning guns and had the largest inventory of Superposed shotguns in the Midwest. Superposed was Browning's trade name for its over and under line of shotguns. Floyd opened boxes for two hours, picking out the handsomest shotguns in stock. Each gun was examined for matching bore end and stock, fit and finish. Each one was a work of art. Satin blue steel with just a touch of gold on the trigger. The heavily checkered fore stock varnished to a high gloss matched perfectly with the butt stock the grain of the wood flowed into the engraved receiver and out again into the butt stock.

Ike was the first to get his box open and put the shotgun together. He held it up at arms length admiring its classic lines. All the other men stopped stone still for just a moment looking at Ike's gun, then resumed in unison their own unpacking and assembly with a new sense of urgency and fear, fear that their own weapon might not be as beautiful, but each was. Floyd had a box to open too, but he waited until everyone else had theirs assembled. Then he opened his own with as much thrill and surprise as anyone. He, of course, knew what was in the box, but he had not picked one especially for himself. He had made sure all were excellent and was eager to see which particular piece of wood and steel artwork would be his own.

Al drifted off into dreamland. He was standing outside the trailer on the deck. He would open the door and Byron would be standing there with a blank expression on his face. And Al would present the shotgun to him, and he would smile and Al would say Happy Graduation.

The boys were discussing a quail hunt that was in the planning for sometime next year and were arguing about who would bag the most birds. "You couldn't hit the side of a barn if you were standing in it," Brad said.

"Well, who the fuck are you, Annie Oakley?" Ike replied.

Shotguns were being pointed all over the ceiling, firing at squirrels, quail, clay bird targets, ducks, and rabbits. Each man felt the heft and swing and decided that it fit like a glove. All were sure their next hunting trip would be highly successful. Most hadn't gone hunting in years and probably wouldn't for years to come, but tonight they were all living that life of comfort and joy depicted in the Field and Stream magazines. Each man over thirty was now sitting in a overstuffed chair by the fireplace, his trusty shotgun disassembled on the coffee table, all his gun cleaning tools handy to his reach. And over on the kitchen table, fresh meat being prepared by his lovely wife, who is so proud of him she just might be in the mood tonight.

Larry Williams is standing by the trade board. He knows he'll be able to trade this shotgun easily and through a series of trades, make enough money to buy it back and have an almost new color TV to boot.

Sheriff Bud Browdy swung the Cadillac into the parking lot at Floyd's Tire Mart a little too fast. The traction on the drive wasn't as good as he had gotten used to on the highway and when he hit the brakes, the big car went into a smooth controllable slide. His trajectory would put him right in front of the main entrance, give or take a foot or two. Bud had been sliding around all day. He had been all over the county dealing with one family crisis after another. Twice he had had to be pulled out of a ditch and both times he had to phone in his predicament from the home where he had just threatened to put folks in jail on Christmas Eve.

Bud had taken the role of domestic dispute negotiator. When a squad car pulled up in front of a home where emotions were running hot, it tended to take things up another notch. But when Bud pulled up and casually walked to the door, he had a presence of fair play and understanding. He had a calming voice and always looked for positive things to talk about.

Bud pushed harder on the brake, which is what people do when all four wheels are already locked up and they're still sliding in a direction they don't want to go. There was a three foot wide path shoveled all the day to dry salted blacktop right in front of the door. The rear wheels hit the dry spot and stopped; the front end swung around and stopped leaving the car parked perfectly parallel to the showroom. Bud slammed the shift lever into park and stepped out in one motion, trying to convince all the eyes watching from inside that this was all part of everyday skilled driving on his part and he knew exactly where the car would come to a stop.

Floyd and his men had been watching with interest from the moment Bud's headlights announced a car had turned onto the drive. Then when the car started sliding and rolling the bell hose under its tires and the bell ding, ding, dinged fifteen times in rapid out of control rhythm, everyone's eyes were glued to the approaching disaster. When the car righted itself and came to a stop at the front door, a chorus of cheers and expletives rolled across the room. Everyone began talking at once.

"Holy shit!"

"Whooee!"

"Damn that was close!"

"That's the sheriff."

"Show him your shotgun."

"You'll never take us alive."

A chorus of laughter broke out. Bud could hear the jeers and see the party going on inside and had to turn his head and fake a cough to get the embarrassed grin off his face.

"Come in, Sheriff," Floyd said. He held the door open wide and made a formal motion with a half bow beckoning the sheriff in.

Bud had no wish to pour cold water on what was obviously a great party, the kind of party he wished he was a guest at right now. "That's some fancy driving, Sheriff," Floyd said. "Get yourself a cup of coffee or a beer and a sandwich."

"Well, to tell the truth, that sounds just right. I ain't had nothin' but black coffee all day."

Bud began to pile ham and cheese and pickles on rye bread.

"What's the roads like?" Al asked. Al's gravely voice came out from behind a stack of tires.

"Oh, they're passable." Bud didn't suspect any foul play on Al's part, but the fact that everyone in the room was holding a shotgun and Al probably was too made Bud finish his sandwich sooner than he normally would have.

"What brings you by here on Christmas Eve?" Floyd asked.

"Well, I got business in the area and I seen your lights on," Bud said with a mouthful of ham and cheese and pickles tucked into his cheek.

Al rose from his chair with his new shotgun held casually across his chest and the barrel nestled in the crook of his left arm. For less than a second their eyes met across the room. Bud could see there was more than casual concern in Al's face, and Al knew he had just received an appraisal of his threat level. He didn't know what a threat level appraisal was, but he knew when a man made one on another man and what it means. He knows something, Al thought. His heart began to beat a little faster. No, don't panic, he told himself. He's just pokin' around. Al smiled. Don't let your face show anything. His brain worked feverishly. He didn't want to go to jail now; he was so close, so close to completing this crazy plan he'd put together in a drunken stupor. No, that don't sound right, Al thought. He was prepared for arrest and jail tomorrow or the day after, but not now. Keep smiling. Talk to Ike, he thought.

"Ike," he said, slapping the young man on the back. "Think you'll be here next Christmas? We'll probably get two or three of these, you know, because things were slow this year." Al had made the remark to Ike loud and boastful.

Ike had a quick wit and immediately shifted gears. The boys had moved off into a private huddle right after Bud Browdy and the old guys started their discussion of weather and road conditions. "Not if I have to work twice or three times as hard," Ike said.

The party came back to life and the insults began to fly around the room. Any screw up or embarrassing moment was fair game now and stories were told on each other, and each one got a bigger laugh than the one before. Al and Ike both took a beating over the naked skydiving incidents, as they were known, but each had a big laugh about the other's fall and no one in the room escaped the jabs except the sheriff. Any embarrassing stories were all exaggerated until the truth was only lightly scattered into the story.

The time a woman showed her tits to Larry Williams when he asked for the $2.00 she owed for the gas, she calmly leaned toward him from her car seat and pulled down her blouse, exposing her ample breasts. Larry, in the sober, no-nonsense manner he was known for, said, "Thank you, ma'am, I still need $2.00."

Ike turned toward Al and whipped the snaps open on his work shirt, arching toward Al with his head thrown back. "Thank you, ma'am, I still need $2.00," Al said, taking his voice up a couple of notches. "Is that how you said it, Larry? We need to practice that."

Everyone, including the sheriff, turned to someone and said, "Thank you, ma'am, I still need $2.00." Larry turned red because of the attention directed at him and laughed like everyone else even though he couldn't see where the joke was in his actions.

Leon, in a show of bravado, spoke up to draw the sheriff into the round-robin attack. "Sheriff Browdy, didn't I hear somethin' about a hot day, a picnic, and cold beer?"

The sheriff was visibly taken aback by the remark. Then after considering the situation and the boy's age, and the fact that he could see the effects of the beer in Leon's watery eyes, Bud decided to ignore the lack of respect shown by this teenage boy and play along. "Well, you could have heard somethin' like that. Oh, yeah, I remember now. I was wanting to talk to you about a motorcycle chase we had last summer. Some kid led my deputies on a wild chase where some innocent child might have got run over. The suspect cut through yards and corn fields and tore the front end out of two of my squad cars. Cost the county over $400.00 to put them cars back in service. I'm sorry I got off the subject. What was you wanting to talk about?"

"Nothing, sheriff. I can't remember now. I don't think I'll ever remember it again."

The room had gotten quiet and now that Leon was back pedaling, a low rumble of laughter began to rise up. "That's probably a good thing," Bud said. "Oh, you know that story about the motorcycle rider? Well, I'll probably forget that myself. That is, if I don't have no more trouble out of him. Merry Christmas." Bud toasted Leon across the room.

Leon toasted him back with a smile and a look of submission, admitting that he wasn't ready to play cat and mouse with Bud Browdy

"Well, this has been fun, but I got to go," Bud said.

"Glad you stopped by," Floyd said.

"There's just one more little thing," Bud said. Al's heart jumped again. Damn it, he was almost out the door.

"If I could talk to Al somewhere private for a second before I'd go."

"Sure," Floyd said. "Al, Sheriff wants to talk to you. Use my office, Bud."

The men began taking their shotguns apart so they could be put back in the boxes.

"Al, there's been some thievery going on around here and my sources tell me them Coal brothers might be in on it. They also tell me your boy Byron spends a lot of time with them Coals."

Al was still holding his prize shotgun in one hand and a cigarette and beer in the other. He listened motionlessly. When the sheriff stopped, Al shook his head slowly. "Sounds like you got good information to me," he said. "I guess you want to talk to Byron."

"When do you think I might be able to talk to him?" Bud asked.

"I imagine you'll be able to find him pretty easy tomorrow or the next day. Hell, he might even contact you. He's mentioned a couple of times in the past couple of weeks that he had somethin' to tell you."

"So you've seen him? He's around?"

"Oh, yeah, he's around. Anything that's happened since the tenth of this month, though, he's clear of, I can guarantee that."

"You been keepin' a close eye on him?" Bud asked.

"I've been watching him night and day."

"I understand he hasn't been seen by anyone lately," Bud said. "I also been told he's not living in your house with you."

Al was tired. He had worked a long day and consumed three beers in the last hour. This battle of wills and wit he fought with Bud Browdy, a man renowned for being smarter than he looked, was taking his last bit of air and a sinking feeling started to overtake his will to hold on. He took one more grip at hope and did some mental calculations that would burn up the motor in the adding machine. No one has been watching my house night and day, so what's that mean? It means he's bluffing, Al concluded.

"Yeah, he's not been outside much. I believe he needed time to think," Al said.

Bud took note that Al was choosing his words carefully, a red flag that he was hiding something. Damn, I'm good, he thought. "I hope you're right. I don't like to see boys go bad, and there's a very thin line between those that go bad and those that someday get elected sheriff, if you follow me on that."

Al nodded his head.

"I'll help him out if I can," Bud said, "if he's not in too deep. But whatever I can do for him would be easier if he comes to me."

"Next time I see him, I'll tell him just that," Al said. "As far as this thievery you're talking about that's happened lately, I know for a fact he wasn't in on it. Nothing that happened since December 10, up to and including today, can be tied to Byron. I'm absolutely sure of that."

"I'm glad to hear that." Bud naturally wanted to ask Al how he could be so sure, but he let it go for now.

In the showroom, the men had put their shotguns back in the boxes and with a final Merry Christmas were heading out the door.

"Go on home, Floyd, I'll lock up," Al hollered through the doorway.

"Thanks, Al, I got to get going. Merry Christmas."

Bud was drawn to the swivel chair by a subconscious urge relayed by a tired body and when his weight dropped into it, it just naturally swung toward the window. Bud stared past heavy eyelids at the large flakes of snow that just kept coming down. How deep was it going to get? All day long it had been falling. He just assumed it would stop at somewhere between two and twenty inches. What if it didn't? The thought came to Bud like a small electrical shock. In all the thinking he had done prior to his election, never had he thought about his duties in case of a snowstorm. He needed to call somebody and find out what the record snowfall was for Christmas Eve. Bud felt he needed to call somebody but couldn't think of who.

"Are we done?" Al's voice cracked across the room, bringing Bud back from his daydream.

"Yeah, I've got to get going. You tell Byron to call me the day after Christmas."

Al released a long breath as Bud Browdy's car pulled out of sight. Rough hands rubbed a tired face. It was time to get Byron out and Al must face him and take whatever beating Byron delivered. And Byron had promised to deliver plenty. Wow, that boy was hot them first couple of days, Al thought. He shuffled his way around the showroom turning off coffee pots, grinding out cigars, and turning lights off until he was out the door.

The walk from the driveway to the trailer proved to be much more strenuous than Al had prepared for. His boots were wet and though he struggled in waist deep snow and his body temperature came up quickly, his feet were freezing. He stomped his feet on the landing trying to get some circulation in them. Byron heard the noise coming from beyond the big doors. Al fumbled with the latch. The snow and ice held tight to the rusty metal. Byron remained still, afraid he might break the spell if he said anything or made any noise. Then one of the big doors opened, cold air rushed in, and Al stood in the doorway silhouetted against the white background of snow.

"You awake, boy?"

Byron jumped to his feet and was at the door in three long strides. He pushed past Al and stopped in the knee deep snow that covered the landing. He was out. He breathed in the crisp night air and looked around in wonder at the thick layer of snow that covered everything. Now he began to feel the cold seep through his socks. His shoes were somewhere in the trailer under a pile of blankets.

"I left my shoes inside."

"So go get 'em," Al grumbled.

Byron looked back into the trailer and then at Al. "You don't trust me, huh?"

Byron didn't reply, but he didn't move.

"Okay," Al said, "I'll go warm up the truck and wait for you there. We may have to push the truck to get going. You're gonna need shoes."

Al worked his way down the steps and trudged along the path he had made back to the truck. Byron watched him go, still unable to re-enter the trailer. His feet began to ache from the cold. He stepped into the doorway and brushed the snow from his socks. He gazed around the trailer at the empty cans and cardboard boxes and dirty clothes, trying to locate his brogues. Then when he had them spotted, he ran to them, snatched them up, and ran back to the doorway, where he hopped on one foot while he pulled them on. He did the same with his coat and then he stepped outside and gave the interior of the trailer one last look before pushing the door closed.

When he got to the truck, Al had brushed enough snow from the windshield to see the road. He had kicked a path in front of each of the tires to get the truck moving and was sitting behind the wheel smoking and waiting for the heater to warm up.

Byron stood next to the door but didn't get in. Al rolled down the window and waited, looking forward.

"What now?" Byron asked.

"Same thing." He turned and looked at the boy. "You got to work to eat. Nothing changed out here. I hope somethin' changed in that head of yours, but that's all I got to say about it. You done your time. It's over. But you got to stick with the plan and stay out of trouble. I can't watch you day and night and if you want to go wrong, I can't stop you."

Byron began to dance a little and pat his arms across his chest as the cold and disappointment hit him at the same time. "That's it? Work to eat, stay out of trouble? I thought you had a plan."

"Well, I did," Al said, trying to maintain his dignity. "I had a plan. This was it. It's over. I never said it was a good plan. It was just better than your plan."

"I never had a plan," Byron burst out.

"I know. That's the point."

"You mean you locked me up in there for . . . how long was I in there?"

"Thirteen days." Al put the truck in gear and pulled forward a few inches. "You comin'?"

"No, I'm not comin' and you're not leavin' until you tell me what this is all about. You told me you had a plan and I bought into it. I did the work, I read the books, I stayed locked up."

"You didn't stay locked up, you were locked up. There's a difference. That was part of the lesson. Things will happen to you that are out of your control. You didn't stay locked up, you were locked up. And when the State locks you up, you stay locked up until the State decides to let you out. And as for the studying and reading, well you were just preparing yourself for that GED test you're gonna take someday. Without a high school diploma, you close so many doors you hardly have a chance. I've given you a chance. I made you do things you couldn't do for yourself. Now the State will help you get a GED too, but it will cost you a lot more time than I used. You'll be there for years. I did it in thirteen days. Now I know I was wrong, and I'm sorry."

"Sorry! Now you're sorry? Well sorry ain't gonna get it, mister. Go on, get out of here, I'll do my talkin' to the cops. Then I'll be the one sorry, sorry I had your big fat old ass thrown in jail. Go on, get out of here." Byron's eyes were starting to blur and his speech began to tremble just a bit.

"Byron, Byron," Al said, "come on. Get in the truck. The phone at home still works and I got a hot meal in the stove. You can eat some turkey while you're puttin' me in jail."

"Aw shut up." Byron turned away and wiped his nose on his sleeve. His childish emotions told him to stomp off in a fit. His much improved, clear headed thinking convinced him that stomping off in knee deep snow in the cold and the dark on Christmas Eve with an empty stomach was not a good plan. He trudged around to the other side of the truck and climbed in. He rubbed his hands together and wiggled in the seat.

Al pulled out on the highway. The old truck sputtered as it picked up speed. After they had gone a mile or two, Al flipped on the heater blower. The warm air began to circulate throughout the cab. As Al made his turn onto Sycamore Lane, he hit a pothole he had been missing all year. The shock rattled the truck all the way to the frame. The heater motor began to make its own grinding whine. Al was just about to slap the dash when Byron's hand popped it and retreated back to his side as if the arm had acted independently of the rest of his body. Byron kept his eyes out the window looking at the Christmas lights.

The mashed potatoes were lumpy and the pork chops were tough, but Byron ate heartily and didn't complain much. "I thought you said we was having turkey."

"Turkey, pork chops, what's the difference?" Al croaked.

"You know you're still goin' to jail," Byron said.

"Yeah, I know." Al ate lightly, only poking at his food, trying a few small bites before pushing his plate away and tilting his chair back with his cup of coffee in one hand and a cigarette in the other.

Byron took note of Al's frozen moment in time and realized that this was the way he would always remember him—tilted back in his chair with his smokes and his coffee. Byron assumed Al would get at least thirty years for what he had done, which meant he would die in prison. This view of him would be the one he remembered.

"Santa Claus left you something in the living room," Al said with only a slight smile at the corners of his lips.

Byron chewed on his pork chop and considered Al's remark. Al had gotten him a Christmas present. Some sort of joke was probably attached to the gift. Maybe a lunch box or a tool box. "I don't want it," Byron said and resumed eating.

"Well, it's there if you change your mind."

"I won't."

"You sure?"

"I'm sure you can't buy your way out of this. You took away two weeks of my life and I ain't ever gonna forget it."

"I suppose you're right. If you're not able to turn your life around, then it was a waste of time," Al said.

"Who says my life needed turning around?"

"Well, you tried to rob Floyd's and you shot me. You coulda killed me or Ike. That don't look like you were going along very good." Al took a long drag on his Winston and blew a smoke ring toward the ceiling. "I think I'll fix that ceiling if I have time."

Byron couldn't deny the truth of Al's statement and had spent long hours in the bean bag trying to justify his actions, and could not. But the whole failed robbery episode seemed so long ago, and he had pushed it from his mind after just the first two days in the trailer. After that, he had concentrated on how unjust the world was to him and how much he hated Al. And now when the botched robbery was retold in a just-the-facts kind of way, it did sound pretty dumb.

"You let me worry about the ceiling," Byron said, pointing a fork full of mashed potatoes at Al.

Al raised his eyebrows. "Oh, you going to take the payments up on the place while I'm away?"

"Don't worry about it. You won't be coming back. You're going to be gone a long time."

"How long do you think I'll get?"

"Twenty years would be my guess."

"You think so?" Al blew another smoke ring and watched it drift away. He showed no sign of worry. Byron wished he would try to talk his way out of it, but he didn't. He just looked tired. Not the kind of tired a good night's sleep will fix. He looked the kind of tired very old people get who have given up on life, the ones that would never take their own life but if a large tree would drop squarely on them, that would be all right.

Al watched the smoke ring rise and come apart. There was the chance Byron wouldn't call Sheriff Browdy, but he put no hope in it. The future would come without any input from him, and that was the way he wanted it. Trying to change what he saw as the future had worn him out. The future could take care of itself. Al Creed was out of service and not likely to come back. He had given it his best shot and was content to accept whatever lay ahead.

"You really think I could be a good mechanic?" Byron asked.

Al made no movement to indicate he had heard the question.

Byron gnawed on some bones that promised another bite of meat. "I bet I could pass the GED and go to Rankin Technical School."

"I doubt it, boy. Rankin don't take just anybody." There was no conviction in his voice. He was telling what he believed to be the truth, but not putting any thought in his answers. Everything that happened to him and Byron from here on out would probably be bad and getting worse.

"I bet I could. You saw how many of those books I could read in a day and remember it too."

"Well, that was good, but you're talkin' about Rankin. A man that gets papers from Rankin goes to work wherever he wants."

"How long does it take to get your papers?" Byron asked.

"Two years if you pass everything on the first try."

"I bet I could. That reading and remembering got a lot easier once I got used to it. How do I find out about going to Rankin."

"There's some application forms in the drawer over there," Al said.

Byron looked in the direction Al was pointing, then turned his head back slowly with a look of sudden insight. Al watched his face slacken and his head drop slightly. Then his eyes shot straight at Al. Al's grin revealed every tooth in his mouth, the grin spread as tight as the muscles would stretch, and Al's head bobbed up and down in rapid little strokes to let Byron know that he had been trapped.

"You had it all figured out."

"Not all of it. Hee-hee-hee." Al laughed like he had pulled the perfect practical joke. He was truly tickled with himself. Byron shot glances all around the room, not sure how to react.

"I went through all this so you could get me to go to Rankin?"

"No, you went through all this so that you would want to go to Rankin."

"I'm not sure I do now."

Al came up out of his chair with a sober face, and the speed of the movement sent the kitchen chair over backwards, slapping the linoleum floor. Al held the moment for a split second and laughed through the shock that ran through Byron. Then laughed again and began a little dance, shaking his butt and waving his arms and laughing at the spectacle he was making of himself, and laughing at Byron for walking right into the trap.

"Don't even start that kind of talk. It won't do you any good because I didn't push this on you. This was a decision you made after long consideration."

"Maybe I'll change my mind," Byron said. He was starting to feel blood race through his veins.

"No, you won't. Ha-ha-ha. You know why you won't? Because you crossed over. You came out of that trailer smarter than you went in, and you can't undo that. You're stuck with it." Al laughed again. "You got smart, and there ain't nothin' going to change you back except maybe a square kick from a big mule. Ha-ha-ha-ha."

Byron was unable to watch Al pranced around the kitchen without cracking a smile. He tried to summon his anger and outrage. This wasn't right. Al needed to go to jail. But even as he said it to himself, he knew he was different. He couldn't deny that truth. The world looked different. How much it had changed in just a couple of weeks. "I may just call the sheriff first thing tomorrow. You won't think it's so funny then."

Al was still laughing. He was howling. Al's howling and stamping around the various rooms in the house turned from flamboyant marching to hula dancing to doing the twist, which sent Byron into hard fought laughter.

"You ain't gonna call the sheriff because you're cured. You don't think the way you used to. You'll never be able to think that way again." Al stopped his gyrations long enough to catch his breath and came face to face with Byron. "You're healed." Al placed his bare paw of a hand on Byron's head. "You're healed," he repeated.

Byron slapped the hand away. Al took no offense. "Okay, okay, I'll let you be, but this is a new day. Don't you see, you decided. You want to make something of yourself. I didn't think it would work; but no, you were sure of what you were capable of. You can't deny it; you got smart, and it don't go away. You got your thinking hat on now and you can't take it off. You're gonna be thinkin' about everything you do. And you won't be able to stop. You're hooked on thinking, and the more you try to make it stop, that's just more thinkin' you'll be doing. And you'll always come back to the same truth."

"What truth is that?"

"The truth is, you were lucky enough to be born in the best country on earth. You read all them books and you took your time and thought about all those people in all those places on earth. People who had truly hard lives and had to scratch and claw just to live. And after you read and thought of all that, you figured out that you got it good. Then that started you thinkin' again that this reading and remembering ain't all that hard. Then you thought, why I could do this or that, or I could fly an airplane, or I could do anything that only requires reading and remembering. And that's the one truth. You can't ever give in to that other life you had planned because it just don't make sense anymore." Al put his hands on his hips.

Byron worked hard at coming up with an argument that would shut Al up. Then he realized he was doing the thinking that Al had predicted.

"You're doing it again," Al said.

"What?"

"You're thinking."

"I am not."

"Then what are you doing?"

"I'm just . . . aw, shut up."

"Ha-ha-ha. I knew it. You lookin' at this all wrong, boy. You won, not me. You're the one that's going to benefit from your new found intelligence. I get nothing out of it except the privilege of paying your way through school."

"You get out of going to jail," Byron said, with the certainty that he had just regained lost ground.

"So do you," Al replied.

Byron was dumbstruck and stammered and stuttered and twisted in his chair. "I might still go to jail."

Al chuckled, shaking his head. "I can see this is going to take a few days to sink in that the only way you win this argument is to go to jail." Al turned and hobbled toward his TV chair. "Bring in those Rankin papers and let's see if we can find a western on TV."

Byron watched Al hobble into the living room, turn on the television, and drop out of sight into his TV chair. He considered his next move. His stomach was full, and with Al settled in his chair, the sofa would be all his for the taking. He could hear the electronic voice of Dean Martin. He hadn't seen a television screen in two weeks. The flickering light on the walls of the living room looked like an old friend calling his name. He went to the refrigerator and grabbed two cans of beer. He gave in to the belly full of warm food; he gave in to the empty sofa; he gave in to the soft light of the television; but he had to make a point. He stood next to Al's chair. He cradled one of the cans in his elbow while he opened the other. After a long swallow from his can, he handed the other to Al and waited for his reaction.

Al received the offering with a role of his eyes. "If you're gonna drink it, it wouldn't hurt you to buy a case now and then."

Byron didn't acknowledge Al's remark and was drawn to the sofa and the Dean Martin Christmas Special with equal force. Sixteen ounces of cold beer put the finishing touches on a long ordeal. He watched with half interest in what was said and done on the Dean Martin Christmas Special. He just felt so good to be there, he even liked Al being there. His whole world seemed to be brighter and full of promise. He was out of the trailer, never to go back. He had no fear of Al now. There was a finality in Al that said, The next move is yours. And although he had spent a thousand hours planning Al's demise, he just wasn't interested in that now. The soft tones of Dean Martin singing Christmas classics made his chest swell in a way that said he was home.

CHAPTER FORTY

Lou Ann Coy met Clay Coal at the parts counter at Broadway Ford, the largest parts house for Fords in the Midwest. Mechanics, tow truck drivers, drag racers, car dealers, anyone that needed a part for a Ford right away came to Broadway Ford. In Lou Ann's case, the largest Ford parts house in the Midwest was on the same city block where she lived with her father and three sisters. They lived in a small, two bedroom apartment over the top of a corner drugstore.

Mr. Owens had lived in the apartment above his store with his small family and a small income until both his income and his family had grown and it was time to move to larger quarters. Mr. Owens knew Lou Ann and her family's situation. There was always someone sick in Lou Ann's house. After her mother died, her father spent the family savings on a grand funeral. Benton Coy had almost no education. He could read a street sign and little more. He had long ago come to terms with his lack of intellect. The one thought that held his pride together was that he was smart enough to know he wasn't smart and would need to consult others in the case of important decisions. Fortunately, no important decisions came along.

Benton worked as a janitor and never missed a day. His meager income barely kept the family going. Lou Ann tried helping out with a job of her own, but after a couple of weeks her father begged her, with tears in his eyes, to resume her duties as mother, housekeeper, referee, disciplinarian, cook, shopper, doctor, spinster. Lou Ann swallowed her hurt and only cried once a week softly to herself. Her father was right. Without Lou Ann to ride herd on the sisters, they began to stray rapidly. Lou Ann still had a voice of authority over them. Benton had given her full range of control. He would not listen to complaints about her rules or methods. He had dumped a huge burden on a young girl and he beat himself up on a daily basis for doing it. The chore he had laid upon his oldest daughter would be daunting at best and totally impossible if he second guessed her mother's role.

Benton still made a few decisions, the kind only a man could make. He was spared most manly decision as he was important decisions, but he made at least one manly decision he was sure was right. He decided he was owed one cigar and a pint of brandy every week. He would take his tobacco and booze, along with the kitchen radio, to the basement of the building. There among the cardboard boxes and assorted signs that promised relief for everything you could have, Benton Coy smoked his cigar, drank his brandy, and tuned the radio to his heart's content. It was his only gift to himself. He took his pleasure every Sunday evening, then on Monday morning he started another week of ten hour days. On Friday, he gave his paycheck to Lou Ann.

Benton Coy missed his wife. He missed her guidance. He missed her optimism. Life had always gotten better every day after he had married his lovely wife, Hallie. Then when she died, life got worse every day. In the near dark of the quiet basement storage room, with the soft music of Patsy Cline singing to him from far away, he felt close to Hallie and would have conversations with her that might last for hours.

Lou Ann was a looker and had boys buzzing all around her. She was going to start dating when she turned sixteen. She dropped out of school and for a while the boys came around, but she shooed them away, along with her sisters' boyfriends. Trying to maintain order around giggling girls and obnoxious boys was an almost impossible task. No one but family was allowed in the apartment, was one of Lou Ann's many rules. Many strictly enforced rules followed. Lou Ann was hard on her sisters, as she was hard on herself. Several unimpressive boys pestered her for years trying to wear her down. The word on the street was that she was a lesbian because she wouldn't go out with anyone. The truth was she was tired most of the time and her responsibilities advanced her maturity to the point where she found the boys who called on her silly with their big talk and childish attitudes toward life. She would give them a few minutes of her time, then coolly dismiss them.

The day Lou Ann met Clay Coal, she was putting an alternator on a neighbor's car. She knew nothing about cars. She had watched old man Smith do some work in the garage they shared. Her family didn't have a car, so Mr. Smith used both sides. For this, he paid them $10.00 a month. At night when the weather permitted, Lou Ann would go out to the garage and watch Mr. Smith work on someone's car. He only did small jobs; his years of bending over fenders had taken their toll. Still he couldn't stop completely. He would help out people he knew just to have something to do and to add a little extra to his Social Security check.

If asked, Lou Ann would say she had no idea how a car worked; but she could replace a starter, an alternator, a water pump on the older cars. When Mr. Smith died, he left his tools to Lou Ann and she took over the repairs on Mrs. Smith's car and a few others.

As Lou Ann waited at the parts counter for a starter, she gazed around the room at all the men and boys gazing at her. All would look away if she made eye contact. No one wanted to openly stare at the beautiful girl in the tight jeans. Lou Ann was a tall girl at five foot ten. Her dark eyes and high cheekbones suggested some Indian blood several generations back. She was large breasted with proportional hips and long legs. She carried herself erect and with a quick smile showing beautiful teeth—she commanded the stage. None felt worthy to look at her directly.

When Clay came in, all eyes shifted, as they always did, to the latest arrival. When Lou Ann looked straight into Clay's eyes, he looked right back. The others in the room were also caught up in the silent drama and watched with disillusioned envy. Clay walked right up to Lou Ann and they inspected each other without concern for the onlookers.

"How'd you like to go out with me?" Clay asked.

"I'd like that just fine."

CHAPTER FORTY-ONE

Ramona Gillman's butt was only a couple of inches wider than the butts in Vogue at the time. She was not large breasted or blessed with soft beauty and kind eyes. She was, though, blessed with muscle tone you could strike a match on anywhere. Ramona drank too much. Her husband, Luther, drank too much. Her daddy and his daddy drank too much. Nobody expected there to be trouble.

Ramona was making the rounds at a bar called the River's Edge. The crowd was large and the air was festive. Every table was full; extra chairs had to be brought in from the back room. The whole of the interior, wall and ceiling, was covered with knotty pine planking. The tile floor and the pine walls showed the damage and the depth of the latest flood. The waterline on the wall reminded the customers that had they been there during the flood;, they would have been sitting in waist deep water.

Ramona flirted at every table she passed. Luther was at the bar with his daddy and hers drinking beer and talking baseball. Ramona sat on laps and hugged necks everywhere she went. She was twenty-eight years old and at the top of her game. Many of the women she called friends only tolerated her behavior, not wanting to deal with her flashing temper. Ramona had been known to make a fist and hit as hard as any man her size. When not prone to fighting, she was the life of the party for women and men. She would take up collections for the jukebox and taunt and tease any man who wouldn't cough up a dollar. She would spontaneously start up sing-alongs. She would drag people to the dance floor and in general make sure she had a good time no matter what she had to do. That good time she was looking for could come in the form of a new romantic conquest or a hair pulling fistfight in the middle of the dance floor. Either way, she went home exhilarated with the total focus of everyone there. And that's what it was all about.

Luther was in over his head and knew it. Ramona was a loose cannon that had him by the balls. Her wild antics and behavior translated to the bedroom with equal zest. He knew in his soul this could not go on forever, but he was unable to pull away. The scene had been played out many times. The fact that his father and hers were both here only changed the script on the outer edges. Ramona would find a victim, using her own methods, which could not possibly be explained. She liked men and she liked other women's men the best. Stealing a dance or a kiss or a cheap feel with a spoken for man allowed her to show her sexual power to Luther, to the other women, to the stupid male she chose, and to everyone in the room who followed the game. The fact that some bitch might object to her rubbing her breasts all over her man just made for a new opportunity for Ramona to show that she was the dominant female in Jefferson County.

Luther checked his watch. It was nine thirty. The evening was progressing at a normal rate—Ramona was coming into her own.

The door opened and Lou Ann Coy stepped into the room. Luther, along with most of the men in the room, let his eyes drink in the view. She was new and that, along with her striking good looks, made her very interesting. Luther thought he might do a little flirting of his own. Of course that meant this new girl would have to get beat up by Ramona, but that wasn't his concern.

She was still standing by the door. Maybe she was looking for a girlfriend she was supposed to meet. Luther was about to offer his services when Clay Coal came in and put his arm around her.

Luther Gillman saw Clay and Lou Ann in the mirror as he was eating peanuts and drinking beer with his daddy and hers on either side. The older men didn't pick up on the situation right away but noticed Luther stiffen slightly on his barstool. This was going to be bad, Luther thought. He had been down this road before, but this was going to cost him some pain. Sooner or later, Ramona was going to cause a fight. Luther could tell by her energy level even before they arrived that it was going to be one of those nights. He was not a large man at five feet ten and his build was thin and lean. As far as anyone knew, he had never won a fight but was skilled enough to come away not too badly hurt.

Luther had trouble following the conversation at the bar which was dissecting the Cardinal's pitching staff and debating the worth versus the cost of each pitcher. He always sat in the same place at the bar and from his position, the mirror in front of him on the wall showed most of the room. Ramona knew the corners Luther couldn't see and would drag men out of his sight for a quick kiss and a butt pinch.

Luther followed Ramona's movements in the mirror. He watched her flitter around the room, laughing and flirting, loving the spotlight. If he could escape a fight with Clay Coal and just get in a scuffle with someone else, that would be enough. Ramona, of course, would have to get at least one good lick in on somebody even if it was just a passing whack on the way out the door. This was the price to be paid to be married to Ramona. Once he got her home and the rage of violence wore off, the passion began and it could last off and on for several days. Luther watched and waited. She was full of herself tonight, and the anticipation of their lovemaking made the beating he might receive from Clay Coal a necessary possibility.

Clay Coal swept the room in a single gaze. Ramona Gillman was there. That meant Luther was there somewhere. Ramona was on the dance floor dancing with everyone at the same time. Dewey Coogan and a group of old timers were at a big table in the corner. Dewey was standing on his chair waving like a fool. Clay guided Lou Ann to their table. He knew it would be an evening of one old story after another about the good old days on the river, about how this old timer was alone with Clay's daddy, old Dry, when the boat caught on fire. Then someone would tell how old Dry and him caught a twenty-five pound catfish and cooked it and ate it the same night, and how no one would believe how big it was because they ate the damn thing.

Clay had heard it all before, but didn't mind hearing the stories again and again. He wanted this girl to like him and he wanted her to know he came from a good family. She would hear the bad things about him soon enough.

Dewey Coogan started another story. "Then there was the time good old Dry drank a case of beer while slalom skiing the length of the Meramec all the way down to the Mississippi. And everyone on the river had heard about the bet and would dice around Dry waiting for their chance to pull up alongside and give him a fresh beer. The bet was to drink a case of beer between Moss Hollow Bridge and the mouth of the Mississippi, skiing on one ski the whole time. Well, the bets started right here," Dewey said. "I got pictures right here." Dewey Coogan carried a Polaroid camera everywhere he went and everywhere he went, something happened worth taking a picture of. Dewey carried his pictures in his car and when his money ran low, he would drag out a couple of pictures, tell a story that would last an hour or so, or as long as the bottles of beer were placed in front of him. "I got a picture of you standing over that Creed boy with a big rock held over your head. You want to see it?"

"Not now," Clay said and when Lou Ann wasn't looking put his fingers to his lips to shush Jim.

"Well, Dry was a bottled beer man himself," Dewey said. He would often get off the subject and need to be reminded of the story he was telling. He was a loud talker and was easily heard at his table and beyond.

The party raged on around them, but at Clay and Lou Ann's table, all ears were tuned to Dewey Coogan's tales of yesteryear. "Why old Dry was sitting right there where Luther Gillman is sitting now," Dewey said. Luther saw all the eyes at the table look in his direction and thought for a moment it had started and that he had somehow missed the signs. When they all looked away again, he cast about the room, looking for Ramona. He saw her next to the pool table leaning over a pocket giving the shooter a view down her blouse to try and make him miss his shot. Luther studied the situation. If this was the guy he ended up scraping with, that would be great. The fellow was about the same size as him or maybe a little smaller. The fellow missed his shot; Ramona did her victory dance and gave the guy a hug, laughing and howling and having a great time. The pool shooters girlfriend wasn't having a great time. She sat at a table with another couple and shot daggers at Ramona. Ramona saw the look and smiled demurely in the girlfriend's direction. Luther ordered another round of beers for his father and himself and leaned forward on the edge of the bar, stretching his shoulders to loosen up. It wouldn't be much longer now.

"Well I was right here the night the bet was made," Dewey Coogan said. "But you know, I don't think nobody knows how the argument got started, but old Dry, he stands in the middle of the floor and says, 'I can drink a case of Budweiser from Castlewood State Park to the Mississippi on one ski. And I got $500.00 that says so.' Well, hell, everyone in the place wanted in on that, and in them days the river was jumpin' with boats and word went around and everyone on the river wanted to send out a boat with a fresh beer as old Dry passed by. Well then all the distributors wanted in on the thing but said it wasn't fair for Dry to drink only Budweiser. He had to drink a Stag or a Falstaff or a Black Label or whatever they was selling." Dewey stopped to take a long swig and catch his breath.

"Now Don Cox was gonna do the pulling, and he had a brand new Johnson on a fourteen foot Starcraft and thought he was king of the river. Well that damn motor would foul a plug if you just laid it on the boat. I always liked those Evinruds. I had one one time that . . ."

"Jim, what happened to Dry and the bet?" Lou Ann asked. Lou Ann had heard the story before, but never from start to finish and never told by Dewey Coogan, who knew it better than anyone.

The tale of the ski bet had worked its way up to South Broadway and beyond. Most people thought it was a tall tale and Lou Ann was amoung that crowd, but here she was out on a date with the son of a legend and hearing the tale from people who were there.

Clay tapped his foot to the jukebox playing a Patsy Cline song. Lou Ann considered for a second asking him to dance but knew he wouldn't; he just wasn't the kind.

"Oh, yeah, the ski bet. Well old Dry stood on the dock at Castlewood State Park. Don Cox had his boat idling with the ski rope tight pointing downstream. Dry was handed a beer, but wasn't allowed to take a drink until he was on the water. He wasn't wearing no life jacket, just a pair of cutoff painter's pants with strings hanging down past his knees. He had the cloth liner out of a hard hat—the kind they wear in the wintertime to keep their ears warm—he was wearing that on his head, and it looked like one of those fighter pilot hats they wore back there in the war. I got a picture of him right here."

Dewey produced a badly worn picture of a thin man with a big smile holding a ski rope in his left hand and a bottle of beer in his right. The picture showed him at the edge of a floating dock with the river in the background.

"Old Dry could ski and he could drink, but that was going to be twenty-four miles of skiing and twenty-four beers of drinkin'. A tall order even for old Dry." Dewey took another long draw from his bottle of beer, and as he drained it, he looked at the brown glass bottle with mock disbelief at its empty condition. Lou Ann caught the hint and went to the bar to get another round.

Lou Ann had been watching Ramona Gillman's antics all night. She had made such a spectacle of herself you couldn't ignore it. Now as she crossed the warped, often flooded floor, she made a sudden decision. She was going to sucker punch Ramona Gillman. Lou Ann was startled by her own thoughts. She was not used to drinking, but she had only drunk two beers. She couldn't be drunk, she thought. But yet she was certain that punching Ramona was the right thing to do.

The area of South St. Louis known as Dogtown where she had grown up had produced a crop of gravel dancers that would match up well with these river rats. Lou Ann did not see her bare knuckle fighting as a sport the way some did. She saw it as a necessary evil. Riding herd on three sisters in the rough neighborhood had propelled her into the roles of peacemaker, counselor, and enforcer. She didn't enjoy the enforcement role, but she conceded that hardheaded fools understand your point of view much better when they are lying on the ground on their backs bleeding.

Lou Ann hated a bully. Her sister, Debbie, had taken a bad beating from a bully once. There had been people there to stop it but they didn't. Lou Ann swore she would never let that happen again. She made boxing gloves out of old socks and rags and tape. The three sisters sparred and wrestled and learned. Lou Ann's ability to hold her own enhanced her reputation as a lesbian.

Lou Ann gathered up eight bottles of beer and made her way back to the table. Dewey had halted his tale of Dry Coal's legendary stunt until the fresh beers arrived. "So what happened?" Lou Ann asked as she passed the fresh drinks around the table.

"Well, old Dry he gives Don the go sign," Dewey began. "And Dry almost falls the moment he hits the water. Oh, I tell you everybody's heart skipped a beat because at this time the money had gone up to $1,000.00. All the beer distributors had wanted in and now it wasn't a bet at all, but a challenge. I was right there the whole time and I don't know when it changed. Dry started out making a bet with any takers, and the next thing you know, he's gonna get $1,000.00 if he makes it and it don't cost him nothin' if he don't. It was the damndest thing I ever saw. I tell you old Dry, he could strike up a deal in hell to get the place air conditioned.

"Well anyway, boats were lined up all down the river and each bar had a lottery or contest to see who got to deliver a beer to Dry as he went by. It was the biggest thing to happen on this river I ever seen," Dewey said. "It was the Saturday after the Fourth of July, 1956. It rained heavy that year on the Fourth, and everyone had their party washed out. So knowing that old Dry was gonna make his run a few days later, most folks on the river just rescheduled their celebration. Half the bars on the river had a little firecracker stand with leftover inventory, and they was sellin' cheap and givin' it away since a lot of it got wet. Them damned kids. I'll never forget, up there along Winter Park, a bunch of kids set up bottle rocket launching pads. They must have had a hundred beer bottles stuck in the bank packed full of bottle rockets. I near peed my pants, I was laughin' so hard. Old Dry was caught completely off guard and froze up when the first volley came in. They was lightin' 'em off ten at a time with blow torches made out of hairspray cans. I swear, there must have been 200 bottle rockets in the air at the same time. Lucky for Dry, the river is wide around there. So Don swings to the far side.

Well, them boys, bein' the sons of the greatest fightin' men on Earth, they had another bank of rockets ready and waitin' on the other side. They had changed the trajectory and lead the boat a little so that they was comin' right in on Dry now. He was hit with a couple, but he hunkered down till they was out of range. I think that day may have been the most fun I ever had at one time. I saw folks I hadn't seen in years. People come from all over and set up parties in every backyard on the river. All the bars had big crowds. Two or three boat dealers had big tents set up. There was a cloud of barbeque smoke from all the grills. Music blared from every party, and the songs they was playin' lifted your spirits as we went by. I was in the closest boat behind Dry but not too close incase he went down. The VFW had a big tent and flags all over. They was playin' a John Philip Sousa marching song. I don't remember which one, but it was a good one. The Elk's had a tent and they was playin' Boogie Woogie Bugle Boy. I remember that one for sure, and there was a bunch more I can't remember."

Clay enjoyed hearing Dewey tell of the old days and his dad. He had heard it all before, but Dewey had a way of making each retelling a little different depending on how many empty beer bottles sat in front of him. Clay listened to Dewey, but his eyes were on Ramona. She was up on a table now dancing and about to fall. The table was wobbling and the fact that she hadn't fallen yet indicated she had very good balance or she wasn't that drunk or she was incredibly lucky.

The barmaid was hollering across the floor for Ramona to get down or she would be thrown out. Nobody in the bar took that threat seriously, especially Ramona. She was about to peak. She had danced and drunk and worked herself into an aerobic and alcohol induced sense of indestructibility. Old bleached blond had been giving her the eyeball ever since she showed her tits to that bonehead boyfriend of hers. Like she would want that skinny jerk anyway. She already had a skinny jerk. Who needs your skinny jerk? Not that I couldn't take him if I wanted him. That was the nature of the thoughts that ricocheted around in Ramona's head as she jumped to the floor with amazing grace all things considered.

Clay Coal was not alone in watching Ramona, and he privately speculated about her next move. Lou Ann tried to divide her attention between Dewey Coogan's story and the dance floor where anyone with good observation skills could see trouble was brewing. Lou Ann followed Ramona's gaze and saw the young chubby blond girl in the corner of the room was getting Ramona's attention. She was the skinny pool player's girlfriend. The girl vaguely resembled Debbie, Lou Ann's little sister. She had a round face and big innocent blue eyes that were about to be blackened by Ramona. Lou Ann had witnessed this scene before. A little more eye contact and then the rookie would confront Ramona about her behavior. She would expect Ramona to be taken aback by the insult and hurl back an insult of her own. This was probably the first time she had come across anyone like Ramona.

Lou Ann was finding more and more reasons to blind side this Ramona girl. She had come across girls like her before. Ramona Gillman would put herself in a good position to deliver a quick right to the soft round face of the little blond girl. Just as blondie was about to scream an insult but before the "ut" of you're a slut or the "itch" of you bitch could clear her lips, she would be down.

Lou Ann's attention was drawn back to her own table as Dewey Coogan asked her a question. "So how long did the first beer last, do you think?"

Lou Ann shrugged her shoulders. "Ten seconds," Dewey said, his eyes wide, his face red, looking from face to face around the table daring anyone to doubt the facts.

"Ten seconds!" Lou Ann said in mock disbelief, knowing it was just the right thing to say to keep Dewey Coogan's enthusiasm in high gear. Dewey Coogan was the most entertaining storyteller she had ever met; and he kept everyone crying with laughter with that half lie, half crazy storytelling talk that could entertain you for hours when you were in the mood for it.

"That's right, ten seconds. Old Dry chugged her down. You see, Dry had given this some thought. A thousand dollars was a lot of money at that time. Old Dry, he figured that there was no way his stomach was big enough or would stretch enough to hold twenty-four beers, so he had to get the exhaust system up and running right away so it could keep pace with the intake system. Most of the spectators thought that was a flawed plan. Many thought he should pace himself or he'd be too drunk to ski in a matter of just a few miles. Well, old Dry, he could drink and he could ski. He knew what he was doing," Dewey said as he reached for his beer.

Lou Ann heard a chair screech across the floor and turned her attention instinctively to Ramona. The chubby blond girl had stood up too fast and knocked her chair over. Her eyes were locked on Ramona, who was slow dancing with her boyfriend. The glassy eyed young man was unsteady on his feet as he cut across the small dance floor. Ramona spun him around and pushed her breasts tight up against him and forced him to dance. The song was a slow one and Ramona embraced him like a lover.

As the outraged blond girl made her way toward the dancers, Luther Gillman spun around on his bar stool. He saw it was time to move in. The skinny pool player might be a match in size but was in bad shape at the moment.

Clay had been watching this drama unfold and knew the final act was about to be played out. He had no particular like or dislike for Luther Gillman and didn't know the pool player or his girlfriend at all. Whatever happened next was no concern of his.

Lou Ann rose from her chair and moved across the floor so quickly that Clay looked back to where she had been just a second ago to make sure she wasn't still there. Ramona had her back to the blond girl but knew she was there. She had a tight grip on the girl's boyfriend but was ready to make her move. She stopped shuffling her feet to the music and centered her weight on the balls of her feet. She had long ago kicked off her shoes and her bare feet on the tile floor gave her excellent footing.

The chubby little blond girl was right behind Ramona now and was giving her boyfriend a what-the-hell-do-you-think-you're-doing look. Ramona felt the boyfriend tense and with her back still turned, she lowered her arms down to the sides of her dance partner's hips. The moment the name calling started, she would push off, bend down, spin, and come up with a smashing right hand to the side of sweet cheek's head. This move had worked well against Nancy Bell last summer, a much bigger woman and a seasoned gravel dancer.

"Who the fuck do you think you are, you cheap river slut?" Blondie finally got out over her outrage.

Ramona had tightened her grip on old skinny butt's hips and began her move. She shoved hard on the young man's hip bones, sending him sprawling backwards. The laws of physics sent her backwards as well, and she stepped back, bobbed down, and spun. She tightened her right hand, making the fist into one solid chunk of knuckles. The target was in sight. Little Miss peroxide would be taught that if Ramona wanted her man, it was best just to let her have him.

The stupid snot was just standing there with her arms folded under her tits and a scowl on her face. Ramona's right would come to rest where the jawbone meets the skull, a favorite spot for her to strike because of its devastating effects and its lack of trauma to the fist. Her right arm had just begun its arc when a stunning blow split her lips. Ramona's knees crumpled and she hit the floor on her back. Lou Ann Coy looked down on her for only a moment, didn't say a word, and turned and walked back to her table.

Luther stared in disbelief. He had watched the whole thing from his place at the bar sitting between his two fathers, who were still discussing baseball and not making much sense. This was not right. Luther had been all prepared to move in on the pool player after Ramona smoked the girlfriend. A couple of good hits on him as drunk as he was, and he and Ramona would be out of there and she would go to work on him as soon as they were in the truck. Luther was pissed. He started toward Lou Ann and Clay Coal stepped into his path. Clay stood relaxed with a pleasant smile on his face. Luther stopped a few feet away. His chest was rising and falling, moving gushes of air in and out. His fury showed in his face, and his jaw muscles worked, bulging in his face. He was stone still, unable to think of what to do now.

"Pleasant evening, isn't it," Clay said.

Luther didn't reply but altered his path toward Ramona, who was being helped up. She dabbed at the blood dripping down her lips. "Who the fuck hit me?" she asked, spraying tiny droplets of blood on the good Samaritans who had helped her to her feet.

"That girl over there," came the reply from several people at once.

Ramona looked in the direction that was pointed out in time to see Clay Coal and his latest whore go out the door. Clay and Lou Ann tromped down the wooden steps to the mud and gravel parking lot, giggling like fourth graders with stolen candy.

"What'd you do that for?" Clay asked. "You don't know any of those people."

"That little blond looked like my sister, and she got sucker punched once and I wasn't there."

"Girl, if you're gonna bust heads everywhere we go, we'll run out of bars before our third date."

CHAPTER FORTY-TWO

L̲ou Ann wanted to go home. Clay argued that the night was still young and he could find her a stringer full of women to punch out if she was still in the mood. "No, I did wrong," she said. "I just want to go home."

The long drive back to the city seemed short to Clay. Lou Ann could talk. She had saved up years worth of thoughts; and she told Clay about all her dreams, her dreams about what kind of life she would have with the man she married. At first Clay became a little nervous with this kind of talk, but Lou Ann made it sound so simple and comfortable and fun. Mostly he didn't have to say anything, just toss out an "uh, huh" now and then.

Clay accepted an invitation to go upstairs for coffee. He didn't really want any coffee, but who could say where it might lead. He glanced at his brogues. Small chunks of dried mud flaked off the edges as he crossed the kitchen floor of Lou Ann's apartment above the drug store. The bits of mud no larger than peas demanded Clay's attention. Lou Ann's voice found its own pathway to his brain and he liked to listen to her talk. She gushed out a warm, soothing confidence that pulled him toward her like a slow moving current.

But now Clay's eyes returned to the bits of dirt boldly displaying their squatting rights on the clean floor. Never before had he cared if he dirtied a floor. At his home, his mother had given up on a clean house. She would often say that the place was just a notch above filthy, but it was the best she could do.

Clay's mother was stricken by Dry's death. She tried to exert some control over the boys, but she couldn't keep up. She worked at a purse factory and hardly missed a day, but the loss of Dry sapped her strength and there was nothing left at the end of the day. She paid the bills, managed to keep one old car running, and put food on the table; but the boys were getting away from her as she no longer had the will to pretend she had any control. She stopped scolding; she stopped picking up after them. Rita did enough to get by and little more.

In Lou Ann's kitchen, under a bright overhead light, everything sparkled. The countertops were worn, the porcelain sink was chipped, the linoleum floor had the top layer ground off in all the high spots, yet it all shone, shone from the labor of the girl on the other side of the table. Clay looked back to Lou Ann. He tried to absorb in his memory every detail of her face. Her brown eyes sparkled, almost emitting their own light. Her face was round and slightly impish, her smile was completely at home and was barely able to hide large white teeth that fit perfectly with her nose and chin and eyes.

Clay only half listened to what Lou Ann was saying. She was telling him about her father and sisters and her life up until now, and he knew he should be paying closer attention. He only wanted to gaze upon her and drink in her loveliness. To be sitting in her home drinking coffee at two o'clock in the morning was not the way any of his other dates played out. On any other occasion, he would be in a motel room or in the back seat of his car feeding his lust with girls who knew who he was and what he was and expected nothing more.

Lou Ann talked and talked about everything. She told him right up front that she hadn't finished high school and seemed to be terribly embarrassed about it. She swore she would finish if she ever got a chance, and Clay believed her. Clay believed everything she said. Lou Ann didn't promise much. She had no high ambitions; she only wanted to live a better life than she was living now and answer only to herself for a while. She was used up with helping others. She wanted to live free. Not that crazy kind of free, she made clear so that Clay would have no misunderstanding. She wasn't about to trade a moment of total abandon for years of repercussions. That was the speech she had delivered to her sisters so often they mocked her every word when she was out of the room.

"So are we going to fuck, or what?" Clay blurted out, interrupting Lou Ann in mid-sentence.

Lou Ann laughed a teasing laugh. "You bet we are. Right after we're married."

"Hah!" Clay said. "Married. Who said I was getting married? And if I did, that I would marry a skinny, ugly girl like you. If I was going to marry anybody . . . now who said that?"

"Well I just said it. Aren't you paying attention? Or maybe you're still staring at the dirt you left on my clean floor."

"What dirt?" Clay asked.

"Right there," Lou Ann said, pointing in the general direction but never taking her eyes off Clay.

"Oh, did I track that in?"

"Let's forget about the dirt. Let's talk about our wedding," Lou Ann said.

"You're crazy. I'm not gettin' married."

"Never?" Lou Ann said, flashing her teasing smile.

"I don't know about never, but not for a while."

"What are you waiting for? I'm ready to start living my life now," Lou Ann said. "I've waited long enough. I passed up more than a few cute boys while waiting for you."

"I don't expect you passed up anything while waiting for me."

"But that's all over. Here I am and I'm the one that's right for you. I knew it the moment I saw you."

"You did, huh? What makes you so sure?"

"Clay, darling, Mother Nature has been pushing me to make a baby since I was fourteen. I have fought her off and prayed I'd have the strength to hold on until you come along. Now you're here and I want to do it right. I want to completely surrender myself in my wedding bed without guilt or hesitation. I want to wake up in that wedding bed in the arms of the man I'll spend the rest of my life with."

"Damn, girl, just listen to you talk. You should be writing poetry or something."

"I know it might sound crazy to someone like you, but that's what I want and I deserve it, I've earned it, and I'll not settle for less."

"What do you mean someone like me?" Clay asked.

"Well, I just mean someone who's had more and different experiences than I have. You have lived a more fast paced life, haven't you?"

Clay sat mesmerized looking into Lou Ann's eyes. His mind raced down a list of possible responses. Lie to her, do whatever it takes to get in her pants, just grab her and force yourself on her. No, just tell her the truth about yourself. No, she'll run away. Tell her some truth and lie about the rest. No, she'll find out eventually and never trust you again. What do you care? You just want a piece of ass. No, I want her. You're nuts. Why do you want her? That's right, I don't need her. There's plenty of girls in the world. Not like her, there's not. Stop it, stop it, stop it!

Lou Ann looked serenely across the table at Clay. She could tell there was a battle going on in that cute head of his. He was twisting his lips unconsciously and cocking his head from side to side.

"This is 1964. Girls don't wait until they're married anymore," Clay said. After he said it, he wished he hadn't. He sounded like he was begging, and he was.

"Some girls wait, some don't. It's always been that way. This one's waiting," Lou Ann said.

"What about a free sample? It's not unusual to receive a free sample before making a commitment."

"Clay, darling, if we was to start hugging and kissing and rubbing each other, there'd be no stopping you. Now you know that's right. And then it would turn ugly, and what we have now would be ruined forever. What I feel about you now is pure and clean and clear. I don't want to lose that."

Clay struggled to find an argument that might tip the scales in his direction. "How do I know them are real?" he asked, pointing to Lou Ann's breasts.

"What, my boobs? You want to know if my boobs are real?"

"Your bra might be stuffed with toilet paper for all I know."

"So I guess you want to squash them to make sure. No, I've already told you what would happen if we headed down that road. Okay, I want to be fair with you." Lou Ann popped to her feet and in an instant had her breasts exposed shamelessly. She shrugged her shoulders and they moved across her chest in perfect unison, and then they were gone.

Clay became aware that his chin had dropped and his mouth was open and casually tried to regain his composure. "Well, those look real, all right," he said.

"You might as well take a look at the rest of the package," Lou Ann said, slowly turning and posing, her tight blue jeans outlining a world class butt.

Clay was drawing deep breaths as he watched Lou Ann's playful posing like one of the models in the Playboy magazine.

Lou Ann sat back in her chair, keeping the table between them. "Now it's your turn," she said.

"My turn?" Clay was clearly startled. He had been with several girls, although not as many as he had led people to believe. His reputation as a bad ass street fighter had to be accompanied by one of a big time lover. It was part of the code. Grabbin' and squeezin' and humpin' in the dark when he was drunk with a woman who was just as drunk was an easy and natural thing. Not much thinkin', no tricky talking. Just get it done and go home.

This looking into each other's eyes across a table in a bright room, this wasn't right, he thought. "I'm not gonna twist and bend or expose myself. I've got standards," Clay said.

Lou Ann laughed hysterically. She twisted in her chair, pointing at Clay. Clay couldn't hold on to his indignation under Lou Ann's assault of laughter. Damn, he loved to watch her laugh, he thought.

"Okay, maybe my standards have slipped a little."

"Slipped a little?" Lou Ann blurted out, still caught up in a giggle spasm. "You're a car thief; you got no standards."

Clay stood up quickly, knocking his chair over backwards. He gave Lou Ann an intense but less than honest look of anger. She didn't buy it, not one little bit. "You ain't mad. Why you're having one of the best times you ever had."

Clay was caught and he knew it. He picked up his chair and started for the door. "Clay," Lou Ann said. Clay froze in his tracks. "If you can spare the time, I'd like to kiss you."

"I guess I could spare a minute," Clay said. He had his back to Lou Ann. He willed himself to face her. He was confused. He could beat the hell out of almost anybody in the county, and this girl was telling him what to do, and he liked it. "Don't just stand there; come on over here."

"You come over here," Clay said. He needed a victory of some type. He hoped she would come to him, but if she didn't, he was sure he would go to her.

"Oh, I was right. You're the one for me," Lou Ann said. She began a slow, sensual walk across the kitchen floor toward Clay, who still had his hand on the doorknob that led to the back stairs. Lou Ann placed a hand on each side of Clay's face and pulled him slowly toward her soft, pouting lips. The kiss had just begun when Clay felt the presence of someone else in the room. He opened his eyes and with his lips still attached to Lou Ann's gave a hesitant wave to an old man standing in the doorway across the room. The man was small and thin and gray and bent. He stood still, waiting patiently for his oldest daughter and her boyfriend to come up for air.

This was not the first time Benton had interrupted one of his younger daughters in various states of undress. The hugging and the pawing would stop and the red faced participants would readjust bra straps and tuck in shirts and zip up flies and rush for the nearest exit. Benton seldom had to say a word. He would tell Lou Ann about what he had seen and ask the boy's name. It seemed to be the fatherly thing to do. Lou Ann would tell him that she was aware of the situation and the boy's name didn't matter—he wouldn't be around long enough to make it worth remembering.

Benton had faith in Lou Ann's judgment. He had dumped the responsibility of being a mother onto his oldest daughter's shoulders and as bad as that was, he would not make it worse by questioning her handling of such things, but this was new. Lou Ann had a fellow pinned against the door and was kissing him like she meant it. Benton decided he had been polite long enough and needed to get on with his routine. He wore a faded flannel housecoat over faded flannel pajamas, old worn dress shoes with the laces removed and holes cut in the sides to give his little toes extra space served as slippers.

Benton shuffled across the kitchen floor, careful not to step on the small chunks of dirt in his path and receive a scolding from Lou Ann. The heels of his slippers slapped tap, tap, tap as he walked. The coffee had to be made and the lunches had to be bagged and the floors at the grade school needed buffing, and this was basketball season and the entire gymnasium would have to be cleaned and polished before the first home game tomorrow. The seasons at the grade school became as much a part of life for Benton as it was for the students. Holidays and sports and plays and open house nights each presented Benton with a different set of challenges. He was completely at ease with himself. The resentment he had felt about his place in life had vanished long ago. He was a janitor and that was all he would ever be, and he made the decision one day many years before to be the best janitor Washington High School had or ever would have.

Lou Ann could hear Benton rattling around behind her, but she was in no hurry to pull away from her man. Clay could stand awkwardness no longer and made the first move. "Is that your dad?" he whispered in Lou Ann's ear.

"Yeah, that's Benton. Benton, this is Clay. He's going to be your son-in-law." Lou Ann flipped the remark over her shoulder, never turning her gaze from Clay's eyes.

Benton nodded at Clay again. "Looks healthy," he said.

"Oh, he's healthy all right," Lou Ann replied, giving Clay a wicked grin.

"What's the young man do for a living?"

"Oh, he's a car thief."

Clay tensed and shot lightning bolts from his eyes. Lou Ann saw for a second the violence that lay beneath the surface. She saw the pointed tip of rage and then it was gone. Clay was now embarrassed for giving Lou Ann such a menacing look and pretended to be examining the decor, unable to look at her.

"Well that's not right," Benton said. He continued with his well rehearsed morning duties, seemingly unfazed by anything said or done.

"He just retired from that line of work," Lou Ann said.

"Oh, well that's good news. Is that right, Clay?"

"Yes, sir." Clay reflected on the fact that he couldn't remember the last time he had called anyone sir without being forced to. This was all happening too fast. I'm not retiring from anything, and why am I calling this old fart sir? Get out of here. I have to get out of here, Clay thought.

Lou Ann enjoyed Clay's confusion, the way he twisted and shifted and looked away from her and then back again. She had him on the hook, and although he jumped and flopped and fought the line, each time he looked in her eyes she took several quick turns on the reel.

"What are you going to do now?" Benton asked.

Clay couldn't think. This just couldn't be right. He had always had a lie on the tip of his tongue, but now a lie wouldn't form. He didn't want to lie, that was even stranger because she would know and she would be disappointed in him, and he would hate himself if he disappointed her. Get out of here, he thought again.

"I haven't worked that out just yet."

"There's good money in aluminum siding," Benton said. He stopped his robotic movements and turned his attention toward Clay. With all his personal power of persuasion packed into his posture and with a professional salesman's delivery, he repeated his advice, "Aluminum siding."

Clay was locked into a stare with Benton. Benton had his head tilted at an odd angle. The seconds ticked by and Clay suddenly understood that the old man was prepared to remain frozen in place for eternity if necessary waiting for Clay to acknowledge his agreement on the subject of aluminum siding.

Lou Ann was motionless also and had quit breathing. Tick, tick, tick. Clay became aware of a clock on a shelf. He hadn't heard it before, but now the ticking was crisp and clear. Still, no one was moving or breathing but him. "Yeah, aluminum siding might be something to look into," he said. Then the world started spinning again. Benton went back to his dish rattling and cabinet door slamming; Lou Ann was breathing and running her fingers along his neck just below the hairline like nothing had happened. This is too weird. Get out of here, Clay thought. "I got to go" he said. He turned and was out the door quickly. Then his head popped back in for one more touch of his lips on hers.

Lou Ann and Benton waited and listened to the clomping of Clay's heavy brogues descending the back stairs. When they were sure he was gone, they exchanged knowing grins and stifled chuckles. "You got that boy so confused, he'll be putting his shoes on the wrong feet."

"Well how about you with your aluminum siding pronouncement? When we did that time stop, he didn't know whether to poop or go blind," Lou Ann said. She gave Benton a hug and kiss on the cheek.

"So this is the one," Benton said.

"He's the one all right. I knew it right away."

"Where did you meet?"

"At the Broadway Ford parts counter."

Benton nodded his head in understanding. "I'll guess he was buying a new ignition switch."

Lou Ann gave Benton a beaming smile. Her face was flushed and she was giddy with excitement. "He's all done with that, and I'll see he don't get started again."

Benton could not remember ever seeing Lou Ann so happy. She had always put on a good smile when a smile was the proper emotion at the time, but now Benton realized he had never seen her truly happy since she was a small child and still had her mother. "Be careful not to let him drag you down," he said.

"He's not draggin' me anywhere. I'm doing the draggin', and I intend to drag him up. He's got it, Daddy; he could be anything he wants to be. He's smart and he's confident and he's good looking. He could be president if he went to college, but all I want him to do is look at his possibilities. Once I get him to stop and look around, he'll see that I'm right. Like I say, he's smart."

Lou Ann was bouncing around the kitchen unable to get her thoughts in order. She would reach for a cereal bowl, set herself at the table, then bounce up again, go to the refrigerator and look over its contents, not seeing anything but Clay—the way he walked, the easy way he moved, the solid firmness of his neck and shoulders. Lou Ann wanted this boy; she would have him. She was never so convinced of anything before. The waiting was over. Life begins right now. She would be married before Christmas. She saw flashes of the future—the small house they would live in, the bed they would make love in, the cart full of groceries she would buy at the IGA and not add up the cost as she shopped, but get what they needed and be able to pay without worrying about having to put something back.

Lou Ann pulled herself from the trance of the refrigerator light and ran to Benton for a hug. "I'll be leaving soon," she said.

Hearing the words out loud sent a tremor through the hug and neither one knew who trembled. The hug lasted longer than Lou Ann or Benton expected. Releasing it would be like the closing of an era that would never be again.

CHAPTER FORTY-THREE

Clay Coal used a small portion of his brain to operate the car. With that portion focused on the twin yellow lines that curved and arched under his headlights, he reviewed the evening and the events that led to it. He could see her at the parts counter when they first met. He had felt something, something more than the normal lust. Every fool has heard the phrase "Love at First Sight." Is that what's happening here? No, I don't believe in that crap. What's so special about her? Clay tried to compare his vision of Lou Ann with the other girls he knew. In his mind's eye Lou Ann had a glow about her that made the others look dull and drab. He wanted her so badly he began to dream wild unlikely scenes—standing at the altar wearing a tuxedo, Lou Ann in a white dress with a thin veil over her face.

The steering wheel jerked in his hand and Clay whipped the car out of a shallow ditch and back onto the road. "Tuxedo, I ain't wearing no tuxedo," Clay murmured out loud. Then he realized that by refusing to wear a tuxedo, he was accepting the idea of marriage. The car dropped into the ditch again. Clay put Lou Ann away for a while and focused on driving. Why was he going so fast? He didn't know, but he had to.

The Meramec River bridge was coming up soon and the shoulder of the road disappeared down a steep embankment. The fog was much thicker this close to the river. Only the surface of the road gave any hint as to where he was. A speed bump, the result of a poorly laid pipeline, rattled the car to its frame. Clay knew where he was. He pushed through the fog using all his senses. He pulled at the wheel slightly. He could feel the acceleration as the car dipped into the valley. When he felt the suspension bottom out and the road begin to go up again, he pulled harder to the right. The yellow lines would curve here and go past the swimming pools. In the summer, he would always honk his horn at the hundreds of swimmers splashing in the twin pools. Everyone did.

Clay honked the horn. The sound echoed back off the water and the face of the concrete building. The sound of the horn echoing back widened the smile on Clay's face. He had not noticed himself smiling until he tried to smile and couldn't stretch it any wider.

His thoughts drifted back to the kitchen. What's with the old man and the aluminum siding? he thought. Were they messing with me? Damn, that kitchen was clean. I bet she can cook. She's full of life. She'll try to run your life. Who cares, you're not doing such a good job. You'll have to get a job. A drop of adrenalin shot to his brain. I wouldn't mind being an airline pilot. She could be my stewardess. Ditch digger is more likely. Hard work and low pay, barely getting by, driving a station wagon with fake wood paneling down the side. She a real virgin? She's awful flirty for someone who's never done it. What if you hurt her? You haven't hurt anyone yet with that little dick of yours. It's normal size. How many times have you done it? I've done it enough. No one's complaining.

Clay's thoughts were racing. Marriage, where would he live, what would he do, swimming pools, girls in string bikinis, Lou Ann in a string bikini, untying Lou Ann's string bikini.

He should have slowed down. He was going too fast for the conditions but couldn't fight the need to push faster. Something was driving him to tempt disaster. He was close to the river now and the sound of his glass packed mufflers cracked across the water. Clay gripped the shift lever and dropped her down to third gear just to hear her roar. He wound out third and slipped her back to fourth. The weeds were making a scratch whish along the bottom sides of the car as it left the road. Now with total clarity, Clay realized what it was that frightened him. He was scared of work.

The front wheels were off the ground, then the hood dropped out of sight. Clay was weightless now, and in that moment he could see his mistake. It was all so simple. He was afraid of work. Lou Ann wasn't. She made it look easy. All his life, every decision he ever made concerned the avoidance of work. Now he was going to die. What a fool he had been. And then the front bumper plunged into the soft river bottom soil and Clay slammed into the steering wheel.

He was back in prison, standing in the yard. There was a fog in the prison yard, but through the gray curtain a small group of men came into view and Clay moved closer to hear them talk. He didn't want to be seen, but he needed to hear them talk. The conversation was about cops and how stupid they were. The absurdity of such talk hit him like a bright light in the face. Men wasting their lives away declaring someone else stupid.

Then the fog thickened and blocked out sight and sound. Then cold consumed him and shivers shocked him awake. The taste of blood in his mouth and sharp pain in his ribs when he took deep breaths told him he was no longer dreaming. Cold brown water filled the car to the top of the seats. The door opened with an extra shove and Clay waded toward the road. He followed the path the car had made and was amazed at the route of near misses that threaded through huge sycamore trees. Dancing by death's front door made even the most cynical stop and consider his own understanding and belief of the truths of life and death.

Clay stopped and looked at the water-filled ruts that led toward one tree after another, twisting away before impact. He had no memory of the wreck past the point where the hood dipped out of sight and he was drifting through a cloud. He had a strong understanding of cars. He knew how they worked and why they handled good or handled bad. He knew why a car would slide on some turns and not on others. He knew that an off camber turn at the top of a hill was the worst. All the forces were working against you. He knew that a car plowing mud at the speed he was going could not turn that sharp, but there was the truth, and as the early morning light improved, the evidence became more disturbing. He had been spared. No, it was just luck. No, you should be dead. That car would never make those sharp cuts without washing out in the mud. Clay analyzed the ruts and mud, the distance from the roadway to the touchdown point. Clay's ribs ached with every breath and his lips were thick and numb. The sun was high now and still he studied the scene. At last his cold wet feet demanded he start moving.

Clay trudged up the bank to the asphalt and looked back once more, then hobbled toward home. He had a lot to think about. This was the damndest day he would ever have. He trudged along on the empty road one wet boot after the other, gravel grinding underneath, and with each step a small jolt of pain in his ribs. He tried to sort out the change in course his life was taking. What was it about Lou Ann that made her so special? Everything. Clay reviewed a list of character traits that he thought other people ought to live up to, and in every one, Lou Ann was grade A+. She was beautiful, she was sexy, she walked on water, she could rise up and fly if she chose to.

Clay halted his rhythmic thump, squish, thump, squish. A car was coming. He would thumb a ride. The car was going the wrong way. Thump, squish, thump, squish continued mile after mile. If he would have died in the wreck, no one would have known for days or even weeks. His mother wouldn't start a search; he often stayed away for a week or so. Lou Ann would come, she would come looking for him, and she would find him too. It may be too late by then to do him any good, but she would come, and she would find him. And if anyone said anything bad about her or that she wasn't good enough, he'd pound them in the head until they thought different. Clay felt his anger rise. The thump, squish, thump, squish stopped. Who was he mad at? He wasn't mad at Lou Ann; he loved her. The thought slipped by unfiltered. You love her? You just met her. You just think you love her. Isn't that the same thing? Thump, squish, thump, squish.

Clay marched on, and the struggle to understand the workings of the universe and how it all could come together so neatly continued. Yesterday at this time he didn't know a girl named Lou Ann. Now he had to find a job. Clay stumbled as he came to a sudden stop. He waited and nothing happened. As long as he could remember, the contemplation of taking a regular job had sent a wave of nausea through him. The dread was the same as having a long car trip end and discovering that you forgot something and have to go back. He hated that feeling, but it didn't come. Not this time.

CHAPTER FORTY-FOUR

"I want you to let Byron Creed alone," Lou Ann said. The words came across a little too harsh. She tried to pull back, but it was too late.

"You givin' me orders?" Clay asked. His words had an edge to them too, and he wished he would think a little longer before he spoke.

The afternoon had started so well. Now they were both wet, cold, and angry. Lou Ann sat on the very tip of the bow of Clay's boat with her back turned. She was as far from him as possible.

Clay turned on the running lights. A thin mist had formed inches off the water and the red and amber boat lights made a soft glow around Lou Ann's naked back. Clay stood by the outboard motor, still breathing hard from the labor and the passion that had just taken place. When he had suggested a boat ride, Lou Ann had agreed at once. She had very little experience with boats and was a poor swimmer, but she had complete faith that she would be safe with Clay Coal.

Clay blamed himself, as he knew he should, for the ugly situation he was in now. It was his fault, but it wasn't. No, it was. She just looked too good.

Lou Ann had been watching for Clay's arrival and came bounding out to his car the moment he stopped in front of her apartment. She wore well fitted, snow white, bell bottom hip huggers with a wide red belt. Her top was a loose fitting red and white striped halter without a bra. She had red leather sandals, a matching purse, red toenails, a red plastic bracelet on her left arm, and matching red lipstick on her beautiful lips. Never had the sight of a girl had such an effect on Clay Coal.

The drive to the river was torture for Clay. Lou Ann sat close to him on the bench seat of the '57 Chevy. Lou Ann asked about the Impala and Clay lied. His pride wouldn't allow him to admit that he was so in love with her that he had daydreamed himself right off the road and into the Meramec, the second car he had lost to the river this year. He told Lou Ann he was having the front end aligned. This, he rationalized, was not a real lie; the front end no doubt needed a lot of work, ending with a wheel alignment.

Lou Ann talked and talked. She told him of her plans for their future. Clay tried to listen, but when the need arrived to shift the transmission from third to fourth, or fourth down to third, Clay's right bicep brushed Lou Ann's left breast.

"I paced all day yesterday waiting for you to call," Lou Ann said, giving Clay a playful smooch on the neck.

"I slept all day. I was real tired for some reason."

Lou Ann's left hand rested on Clay's right thigh. The weight of her hand changed slightly, a constant reminder of its presence. Clay shifted to third gear, picked up speed, and came back to fourth. The breast was heavy and warm against his arm.

"I think we should buy a tow truck," Lou Ann said, "after we're married, of course. It just makes sense."

Clay heard the words "tow truck" above the wind noise of the open windows and above the music coming from the radio and nodded his agreement, but wasn't sure what he was agreeing to. His mind was on the buckle of the red patent leather belt. He was thinking of where they would boat ride. The slough was the place. He would stop the motor and drift in the quiet solitude, and there he would have his desire fulfilled.

The plan was going well. Clay and Lou Ann twisted and writhed in a lovers' embrace. Clay could tell she wanted it as badly as he did. She was asking him to stop, but her words were soft and breathy. She pushed his hands away, using only a portion of her strength. But when he tried to get that damn red belt unbuckled, she took them both over the side. The strings on her halter top had mysteriously come untied and it was lost when they hit the water. One of Lou Ann's sandals was lost in the water and the other she threw at Clay before taking her seat on the bow. The shoe boomeranged around the side of Clay's head and went to the bottom to join its other half.

"What's Byron Creed got to do with this?" Clay asked. Just the mention of another man's name arched Clay's back and he knew at once she was cheating on him with Byron; but as he spoke, he saw the lunacy of his reaction and was amazed at his own muddled thinking.

Lou Ann said nothing. Clay could hear her choked down whimpers as she sat hunched over hiding her bare breasts. Those weren't the tears of a child wanting attention; those were the tears of a girl deeply hurt. Damn, if anyone else ever hurt her like this, I'd pound the bastard to death with my bare hands, Clay thought. He hammered his fists on his thighs in a weak attempt to punish himself.

"I'm . . . I'm sorry." Clay waited for a harsh rebuke.

"I know," Lou Ann whispered.

At once Clay's spirits soared. She didn't hate him. She was saying she understood. Say something, you idiot, he thought. "You want my shirt?" Clay pulled his t-shirt over his head in a rush to make amends. The wet cotton stretched and twisted and rolled and finally came off. He worked to unknot the shirt and present it to Lou Ann before her forgiveness faded and turned to anger. He worked his way slowly toward the bow. He moved and shifted his weight with care not to rock the boat. With females, you never know what's going to set them off.

Lou Ann sniffled and wiped at her runny nose. She had regained her composure but felt tired and drained of will. What's the use? she thought, I should have just did it. "That was my only outfit," she said.

Clay was right behind her now with a wet t-shirt as an offering. Unsure of what to say or do, he said nothing. Kneeling now close to her, he could see droplets of water from her hair running down her backbone, disappearing in a shallow groove behind the red belt. The red and amber lights made her skin glow in the near darkness. He twisted the shirt, wringing the water back into the river. Lou Ann craned her neck to watch. Clay put all his strength into twisting the shirt, his arms and shoulders and chest rippling with corded muscles under a thin layer of tan skin.

"You mean those were the only shoes and shirt you got?" Clay asked.

"No, that's not what I mean. I mean, this was the only complete outfit I ever bought myself where the shoes and purse and belt and bracelet and lipstick all matched. And I went out all excited and paid way too much for it just to look good for you." She began to tear up again.

Clay twisted on the shirt some more. Lou Ann turned to face him, their knees touching. She made no attempt to hide her breasts and took the t-shirt from Clay before he twisted it to pieces. Clay looked to the right and then to the left as if he were surveying their exact location on the river, but with each sweep of the darkening shoreline, his eyes rested on Lou Ann's breasts a little longer until his gaze came to a stop in the middle of her chest. Then Lou Ann had the shirt on and the white cotton clung to her and her cold nipples made sharp protrusions on the white surface.

"Let's have a talk," Lou Ann said. "I thought I could handle this. I know how men are, but I thought I could be strong enough for both of us. But I can't. I'll leave it up to you. I've waited for you to come along and now you're here, and you're everything I prayed you would be, and if you had been less passionate, I would have been disappointed."

"Prayed?" Clay said. "You prayed for me?"

"Well I didn't know your name back then, but you're the one, and I've been praying to God to keep you safe ever since I met you."

Clay reluctantly shifted his gaze to Lou Ann's eyes. "Were you praying for me the other night after I left?" he asked.

"Just as hard as I could."

Clay gave the matter some quick thought. He wanted to focus his attention back to his lust, but this new information couldn't be ignored. If God guided my car around all those trees, why didn't he just keep me on the road in the first place? Clay thought. Clay was comfortable with that argument for now and his thoughts went back to the buckle on the wide red belt. Was it a fake buckle? It has to come apart somehow, he thought.

"Clay, honey," Lou Ann said, "I don't have a thing to bring to this marriage but my honor. Please don't take that from me when I'm so close to the finish line. This is a promise I made to God and to myself."

Clay was thrown off track again. "What kind of religion are you? You're not Catholic or Jewish or some other weird religion, are you?"

Lou Ann gave him a quizzical look. "No, but if I was, what difference would it make? What do you have against Catholics and Jews?"

"Nothing, I guess. It's just all those candles and fancy clothes and stuff. Seems kinds of silly."

"I don't know what religion I am. I feel like I got the kind of religion that has a good chance of getting me to heaven as the next guy."

"You're not going to try to drag me to church, are you?" Clay asked.

"No, you're not ready for church yet. I'll need a few years to work on you. Then it won't sound so bad." Lou Ann grinned.

"Well, we'll see about that."

"I do want to take our kids to church and Sunday school. You don't have nothin' against that, do you?" Lou Ann said.

"Kids. How many kids?"

"Three."

"Why three?"

"Oh, I don't know. It's bigger than a small family and smaller than a big family. It just seems right."

Clay was thrown off track momentarily with this talk of religion and kids; but then his animal instincts, stimulated by the visual delight within his reach, brought him back. He could grasp her by the shoulders with strong hands and she would not be able to escape.

"What are you thinking about, honey?" Lou Ann asked.

"Nothing."

The frogs were in full voice and became even louder in an awkward moment of silence.

"I never said I was marrying you," Clay said.

"You never said you weren't." Lou Ann was happy again. Her eyes were puffy from crying, but her smile brightened the night. "Honey, could you just hold on for one more week? We could get married next week. I don't see how I could put it together any faster."

Clay considered whether he had any other plans for the next week, then became frustrated with himself. The question is not whether you have time, you idiot, it's whether you want to marry this girl. Clay's lips twisted and his head cocked slightly.

Lou Ann could read the signs and knew that the wheels and gears were turning at a frightful speed in that cute head of his. "Honey," she said.

Clay was far away in thought. Lou Ann placed her arms around his neck and pulled her face close to his. "Honey, I never let a boy get any further than I have you, so I don't have any experience, but I've read all about it and I want to try all of it with you."

"Okay," Clay blurted. It was done. The decision was made. He felt a great burden lifted. Never had he felt such high expectations for the future. "I think I will marry you, and one more week won't kill me."

CHAPTER FORTY-FIVE

Things were happening too fast for Dwight and Dwayne Coal. They never expected their big brother to marry; they expected he would always live the life of a vagabond, doing what he liked, eating, sleeping, drinking, and screwing as the mood struck him. They were disappointed that he was selling out for a piece of ass. Then they saw Lou Ann.

Clay had dropped in two days ago with Lou Ann at his side to meet their mother. The brothers were watching TV in the darkened living room and were able to comfortably stare at Lou Ann without being noticed.

Lou Ann feared Clay's mother didn't like her at first. Loretta was making beans and wieners when they came in. The kitchen was no different than any other day, with small stacks of dirty dishes covering every flat surface.

"Mom," Clay said as he came in. Lou Ann trailed behind him holding his hand. Loretta didn't turn from her work. She was glad Clay had come for a visit and maybe he would have supper with them, but more than likely he had come home for a quick change of clothes and a shower. Then he would go off into the night, drinking, fighting, stealing, and maybe even worse. But what could she do? She kept a bed for him, although he rarely slept there; she washed his clothes if he left any. Where he slept most nights was a mystery to Loretta. When he first returned from prison, he stayed with them for two weeks, then he began to not come home a few nights. Loretta waited and listened for the sound of his approach night after night until her health began to fail from worry and fatigue and guilt. Then she had to quit worrying and accept that some day a knock on the door would come and a policeman would deliver the news of Clay's death or his return to prison. Loretta felt ashamed of herself for not praying for prison over death. She couldn't help but feel that maybe if he died in some tragic way, his brothers might stop their hero worship of him and his way of life. She couldn't bear to lose another son to prison, yet their destinies seemed unchangeable.

"Mom, Mom, this is Lou Ann. We're getting married Saturday."

Loretta turned, expecting some sort of joke. Her jaw dropped and she was frozen in amazement at the sight of Lou Ann by Clay's side. The look on Clay's face said that this was no joke.

Clay ordered the brothers to get off their butts and meet their future sister-in-law. The twins fumbled with handshakes, then Lou Ann grabbed each one for a hug. Her large soft breasts pressed against the boys and they fell instantly in love.

Loretta became conscious of her kitchen and picked up a small stack of dishes, held them in their hands for a moment looking for a place to hide them, then returned them to their original position. "Clay, you should have told me you were bringing company home."

"She won't be company for long. We're getting married Saturday."

"Saturday? What's the rush?" Loretta stole a glance at Lou Ann's belly.

Clay and Lou Ann saw her eyes shift and enjoyed a laugh. "No, she ain't pregnant. We ain't even screwed yet." There was a hint of pride in Clay's voice.

Loretta slapped Clay on the shoulder. "Don't talk like that in front of the boys."

The twins turned red and shuffled and twisted with embarrassment.

The next few days passed quickly. There seemed a constant stream of people coming and going from the Coal house. Loretta darted around the kitchen cooking and baking and cleaning. She had a smile on her face constantly and hummed an old song about sitting under the apple tree. Dwayne and Dwight could not remember seeing their mother so happy. They wondered if she was like this all the time before their father's death.

Clay and Lou Ann went shopping for their wedding clothes. Clay had accepted his obligation to wear a coat and tie if that was Lou Ann's request; but Lou Ann, ever conscious of the need to be practical, went a different direction. They bought new Levi jeans and brogues from the J.C. Penney store and bowling shirts from a guy Clay knew. The shirts had a satiny look and feel. The body was shiny black and the short sleeves, collar, and pocket flaps were sky blue. They were beautiful. Over the left front pockets, their names were embroidered. Across the back, in the same sky blue thread, the shirts read: Coal Brothers Towing. Fast Service, Reasonable Prices.

On Friday, the day before the big event, Lou Ann came to the house alone. She had insisted that she and Clay not see each other until they made their vows. Clay became angry and sulked saying there was no need to deprive himself of her company for even a day. In the end, Lou Ann got her way and Clay agreed he would not lay eyes on her again until the wedding.

Loretta had left the house early for an appointment at the Best of Curl beauty salon. The boys called it a poodle perm. She would be in a chair wearing a pink plastic turban until noon at least. Dwayne and Dwight had always discussed everything since they were able to talk, but they did not talk about Lou Ann. They talked about Clay getting married and about the tow truck business and about the possibility of stealing cars with a tow truck, but not a word about Lou Ann. Both had secretly formulated a plan to impress Lou Ann with their manliness and to be in a position to comfort her should something tragic happen to Clay.

Dwayne paced around the yard picking up sticks and rocks and throwing them at the river as he waited, always maintaining a view of the road so as to see Clay's car with Lou Ann behind the wheel. Clay never let anybody drive his car, but he let Lou Ann drive it. Dwayne thought, If I had a car, I'd let Lou Ann drive it.

Dwight stood at the kitchen door peering down the road and dreaming of ways he might rescue Lou Ann from certain death, and her gratitude would turn to love. Something would have to be done about Garry. Dwight hadn't worked that part out yet.

Dwayne heard the popping of gravel as a car approached and could see a cloud of dust coming this way. Dwayne removed the screwdriver he carried in his back pocket and squatted behind an outboard motor clamped to a sawhorse. The motor had been striped of all usable parts long ago, but to the untrained eye Dwayne appeared to be fixing it. From his position, he had an excellent view of the stairs and he was hidden, with only his eyes showing above the motor he pretended to work on. Women like men who can fix things, Dwayne thought.

Dwight came out of the house and without showing any notice of Lou Ann's arrival, climbed atop the railing at the corner. He did a high wire walk to the house and proceeded to clean leaves out of the gutter. If all went as planned, Lou Ann would scold him for taking such a risk but admire him for doing necessary maintenance even if danger was involved. She would say he was crazy to walk that shaky railing. He would say, It ain't nothin'. Heights don't bother me none, and Lou Ann would suddenly realize a newfound respect and sexual attraction for him she had not noticed before.

Lou Ann had her head down. She carried Clay's new jeans. She had washed and ironed them inside out the way Clay liked. She had missed the high wire walk completely and seemed not to notice Dwayne hiding behind the outboard motor. She wore a red sleeveless t-shirt with a deep V collar, the cloth stretched tight across her bosom. Her matching shorts were cut high and her thigh muscles rippled under smooth, silky white skin.

Lou Ann attacked the stairs with vigor. The weather worn boards flexed with each step. An object in motion tends to stay in motion; an object at rest tends to stay at rest. The rules were being tested. Dwayne and Dwight were willing observers.

Dwight arched and twisted, holding the gutter with one hand. He gained an excellent view down Lou Ann's shirt. He thought for a moment one might actually bounce out. Dwayne had a side view and the shifting and shaking of muscle and fat did not disappoint him. At the top of the stairs, she stopped. She looked at the jeans she held in her hands and seemed not to notice Dwight pulling a handful of leaves from the gutter and pitching them into the air to drift lazily to the ground. She seemed to have made up her mind about something, and she turned her attention to Dwayne, still half hidden behind the outboard motor.

"I know what you're doing and it's not very nice," Lou Ann said.

Dwayne wilted under her gaze. How cruel the world was. She's scolding him while Dwight's still stealing peeks down her blouse.

There were a few moments of awkward silence, then each boy denied his own personal lechery but was quick to point out his brother's guilt. "Look, boys," Lou Ann began. She was having trouble finding the proper words. "I don't ever want to come between you and Clay, so I'm not going to go running to him every time one of you . . . you walking boners . . . says or does something out of line. But I will bang you in the head with something hard enough to lay you out if I have to."

Lou Ann waited for a response. Dwayne tried to run the calculations as to what would be a reasonable amount of pain to suffer in trade for what offense. He decided he needed more information. Dwight felt his shame much deeper. She would turn on him any second now and there was nowhere to hide. A change of subject was needed, and quickly.

"Dwayne still wets the bed," Dwight said.

A dark cloud drifted across Dwayne's face and Dwight knew he had gone too far. Dwayne took the blow hard. Yes, he had peed in the bed, but it was over a year ago and he could explain that. He was overly tired from a full day of swimming and skiing. He was a sound sleeper and that was all. His mistake was drinking a sixteen-ounce RC Cola just before bed. That night in his dream he was standing on a railroad trestle watching the brown water slide past far below; and like he had done many times in his waking life, he sent a golden arc of pure relief down to join the river and eventually the sea. The fact that there was a sliver of truth to Dwight's accusation only deepened the wound.

Lou Ann gave Dwight a disgusted look. "Get down off that railing before you kill yourself. Are you crazy?" She turned to the door and was gone.

Dwight jumped down in time to get a whiff of her perfume hanging in the air where she had stood. His chance to tell her that heights didn't bother him none was lost for now, but she had said he was crazy and that was something. So he breathed in her scent and grinned with satisfaction. He had already forgotten the dagger he had plunged into Dwayne's back. Dwayne had not forgotten, and he willed lightning bolts to shoot from his eyes and turn Dwight to a smoldering cinder. He was unsuccessful, so he threw the screwdriver and the Philips point struck Dwight in the forehead just above the left eye. Dwight dropped to his knees from the blow. He put his fingers to his head, fully expecting the screwdriver to be stuck in his skull. He felt relief that it was not. Blood dripped off his eyebrow onto his cheek. His rage began to grow. Just an inch lower, he thought, and the eye would have been lost. Dwayne had to pay for this.

Dwight pulled himself to his feet, holding one hand to the wound, and started down the steps. Dwayne came to meet him. The years of lingering arguments and halfhearted unresolved fights had left a bitterness between the brothers that had to be settled one last time. Hormonal drive combined with cruel immaturity and repressed anger brought out a viciousness that neither boy thought himself capable of. Somewhere buried very, very deep in the brain, a cluster of primal cells promised the victor mating rights with Lou Ann.

Dwight came slowly down the steps, holding his left hand over the eye and the wound. In this matter, he could look through his fingers as he appeared to be unsteady on his feet. Dwayne didn't buy it. He was sure Dwight would lunge at him when he came within range. Three steps from the ground, Dwight did just that. Dwayne was in mid-step, and although he had been expecting a move, he had underestimated the distance his brother could soar as he came over the railing. He had vicious look in his eye and he was clearly trying to hook his left elbow around Dwayne's neck and slam him to the dirt.

Dwayne pulled back, but not enough. Dwight had managed to grab hold of a handful of hair, and he held tight, his weight whipping Dwayne's head around. His body had to follow or his neck would break.

Dwight, holding the hair with a death grip, was pulled offline and unable to break his fall. He landed with the kind of flat-out belly flop usually reserved for old fat guys at the swimming pool. Air huffed from matching lungs and the brothers lay writhing, desperate for air.

Lou Ann had witnessed Dwight's aerial assault and as she stepped out the door, the sickening thud of human flesh pounded to the ground caused her to grimace with pity. She waited with a clear view from above to see if both boys would recover their breathing. They did.

"See you boys at the wedding," Lou Ann said. She came down the stairs in her usual brisk stride and paid no attention to the groaning bodies lying in the dirt coughing and wheezing.

The brothers, in their pain, managed to get a look at Lou Ann's shapely butt as she walked to the car.

CHAPTER FORTY-SIX

L ou Ann Coy admired herself in the mirror. She felt the bride's power and inhaled its radiant warmth. They could not start the wedding without her and she would come out when she was ready. "Come on, it's time," her youngest sister, Debbie said, coaching her from the door. Debbie couldn't sit still and didn't understand that it was the bride's duty to make everyone wait just a little bit. Her sisters stuck their heads in every few minutes to tell her it was time.

Lou Ann was in the restroom in the basement of the Hillsboro Courthouse. The facility had been built when indoor plumbing was in its infancy and the exposed pipes supported that fact. The walls were the rough stone of the foundation. They had been painted so many times all the sharp edges were smooth with a quarter inch layer of government green. The whole room, minus the porcelain, could have been flooded in green paint and had the excess drained away, and the effect would have been the same. She played with her hair just to give her hands something to do. She had never been so happy. She smoothed and squared her shirt again and again. She turned and admired her butt in the snug fitting Levis. The brushed leather brogues were a perfect fit and did something to increase her confidence. Perhaps the ankle support or the broad base, she thought. A weird thing in a woman's shoe and something Lou Ann had never experienced.

She felt good about her wedding clothes. She only primped to make this time last as long as possible. She knew she would never be this happy again. The future loomed so huge she could not comprehend its possibilities. Like the distance to the stars, her mind could not expand enough to take it all in. She was free at last to live her own life. She would be married within the hour, and tonight she would find out what all the fuss was about.

Clay paced in the hallway. He wasn't nervous. He reminded himself of that fact as he walked back and forth. He stopped as he paced for a quick drink each time he passed the water fountain. His mother and brothers sat quietly on the wooden benches that lined the hallway. Life moves at half speed in a courthouse, Clay knew. But with his mind racing at double speed, he felt that he could do a back flip in an instant if he wanted to. His mother whispered something to his brothers and they all looked his way and giggled. His brothers wore new brogues and new scratchy Levis and blue cotton t-shirts that almost matched the bride and groom's bowling shirts. Over each of the boy's pocket, their names were printed in black Magic Marker. On the back of the t-shirt, in bold letters, the words Coal Brothers Towing had been painstakingly blocked out and filled in with black Magic Marker. The boys had spelled the word "Towing" T-o-e-i-n-g. Loretta had pointed this out to Clay when they first arrived, but they snickered and kept it to themselves.

The whole world seemed to be in on the joke, as countless people at the courthouse saw the mistake and muffled a laugh. Clay knew his mother and brothers were enjoying his situation. He smiled back at the brothers and said, "I got a good joke for you too," pointing a finger of each hand at them like leveled six shooters.

"What's that?" the boys asked in unison.

"You just wait. You'll find out," Clay said as he paced away.

"What's he talkin' about?" Dwayne asked.

"Nothing," Loretta said, "I'll tell you later."

Loretta felt a sort of warmth and satisfaction. Just a few weeks ago, she was certain Clay would come to a bad end and now she was just as certain that everything would be better. Dwayne and Dwight would add more gray hair to her head, but with a new role model—a businessman instead of a car thief—to look up to, she was sure it would be easier.

Lou Ann's father and sisters were twenty feet down the hall on a bench of their own. Benton wore blue cord pants that were sharply creased, a white shirt, a blue tie that almost matched the bowling shirts, and black patent leather shoes. He stood as straight as he could. His hair was white and freshly cut. A generous application of Brill cream held it in place. He chewed on his pipe and pretended to be in deep thought. He watched the people as they passed by and enjoyed the anonymity of being in a strange place full of important people. No one knew him here; he could be anyone, maybe a lawyer collecting his thoughts before fighting a big case. Men in suits carrying briefcases offered a greeting as they passed by. "Good afternoon," they would say.

Benton would nod slowly, accepting their politeness and reply, "And to you, sir," with the stiff formality of a retired judge from a fine old family.

Lou Ann's sisters rolled their eyes and pretended not to know the strange old man standing next to them. They wore new Levis, blue cotton, button-front blouses crisply ironed that almost matched the bowling shirts, new white canvas tennis shoes substituting for the brogues.

The two sets of siblings attempted to examine each other without being caught. They failed. The brothers were not ready to give up their dream of having Lou Ann someday, but the sisters had some of her qualities and Clay didn't have to die to make that dream come true. The brothers arrived at the thought at the same time and without verbal communication, they quit trying to hide their interest in the Coy sisters, as they came to be known.

Dwayne saw himself as a young Tarzan at home in his environment, needing nothing but a loincloth and a knife. He would walk to the water fountain on the balls of his feet, ready to pounce on any enemy at any moment. Dwight would not be outdone. He combined a John Wayne walk with a James Dean hip cock when he reached the fountain. On his return trip, he turned his back on the sisters and squared his shoulders and cocked his head before strutting back to the bench.

Benton and the girls saw the shirt's message clearly for the first time. Their eyes widened slightly as they turned to each other and then to Loretta. Loretta smiled demurely and nodded her understanding. The sisters slapped their hands over their mouths and raced to the restroom to tell Lou Ann. Benton's ears picked up the high pitched laughter coming from the restroom and smiled at the ceiling. Dwayne and Dwight didn't seem to notice.

The doors to the meeting room opened suddenly and Clay flinched. The sounds reverberated off the block walls and the tile floor. Finally the meeting was over. People filed out slowly, talking loudly. Clay thought for a second that someone might need his head punched in. He focused his attention on a heavyset short man with a ruddy complexion. This room was supposed to be his. He had made arrangements with Judge Parker. This room boasted a piano. The courthouse lady had said she'd play it for them. This meeting was supposed to be over forty-five minutes ago. Clay felt sure that the fat guy with the red face was the cause of his aggravation. The man passed by never noticing the brewing anger on Clay's face. Clay took a deep breath and the moment passed.

Judge Parker came into the hallway and motioned the group inside. Benton pecked on the restroom door with a single knuckle. "We're ready to start," he said softly as he opened the door a crack.

The wedding party stuttered to their places. Judge Parker motioned for the elderly lady at the piano to begin. Molly Layton began her piano lessons after her retirement. She took Judge Parker under her wing when he was young and fresh out of law school. When he later became a judge, she worked in his office until near blindness forced her into early retirement at the age of seventy. She still goes to his office, but only three days a week. She brings donuts and makes coffee. Her piano teacher meets her here Mondays, Wednesdays, and Fridays. The county lets her use the room and the piano and even put the deal in writing as part of her retirement. Molly Layton is a good student and works hard at her lessons, but stiff hands and bad eyes make for an uphill battle. The lines and the notes on the sheet music smear into wavy black streaks; she must memorize everything. Molly bangs away at the keys and although it's a little slow and there's an odd note now and then, everyone recognizes the Wedding March.

Benton and Lou Ann wait in the hallway and exchange a nervous laugh at the piano player's expense. "What's she gonna play on your way out?" Benton asks.

"I don't know. She said she only knew a handful of songs. I told her to just play something happy and upbeat."

Benton smiled and nodded. He was stalling. He gave Lou Ann an eye-to-eye look like this was the last time he would ever see her. She patted his arm. "I want my daddy hug right now. I don't want you to fall apart on me in there."

The two embraced and the tears gushed down their cheeks. Lou Ann squeezed too tight and Benton couldn't breathe. His face turned red before Lou Ann released him. Benton began to cough and Lou Ann began to laugh, then Benton began to laugh. Molly Layton banged away at the piano and Clay Coal twisted in the wind.

Benton walked her down the aisle and made the handoff and took his place. Judge Parker read the vows. Lou Ann spoke in a soft, clear voice while looking directly into Clay's soul. Clay gulped as he tried to speak and his first words hung in his throat and when he forced them out, they were much too loud. The wedding party suppressed a giggle. Then it was over and Clay and Lou Ann kissed and without being prompted, Molly Layton attacked the piano, doing her rendition of a Little Richard song entitled "Good Golly, Miss Molly." Her vocals were equal to her keyboard work and the wedding party fell to pieces.

CHAPTER FORTY-SEVEN

Hollywood Beach offered all of the best amenities—a wide, gently sloping ramp that led to a deep hole, a long clean beach sheltered by huge sycamores, and the two-storey concrete block bar and grill sparkling with fresh paint, pink and green being the colors of choice. Hand-painted life-size pictures of sharks and mermaids and frogmen carrying spear guns adorn the exterior walls. On the inside, the ground floor bar offered cool, dark retreat on a hot summer day during the week; but on the weekends families picnicked, boated, and fished. The picnic tables are made of concrete bolted to small islands of concrete that jut out of the black sandy silt left by the last flood. The tables are bright red and glisten under strings of white, used-car-lot lights. No one under twenty-one is allowed on the grounds after 7:00 p.m. The kids go home and the jukebox is turned up.

On a perfect Saturday night when the temperature drops to a refreshing eighty-five degrees and the soft humid air blows across the bow of a fiberglass ski boat, there's a magnetic pull that reels in the members of the Meramec Yacht Club. And the boats chug in and the new boats are examined and praised, and the old boats are berated for being too small. Ex-patriots of the river look for old friends in the place they'll most likely find them—the Hollywood Beach Bar and Grill.

Sixteen boats are tied up along the shoreline, ski boats mostly. One pontoon and three jons round out the selection. The parking lot overflows with cars and pickup trucks, many parked haphazardly along the road. The wedding party had not yet arrived, but the celebration that started around noon was cruising along at a high rpm. The newcomers that didn't arrive until the 7:00 p.m. start of the party did their best to catch up.

Dorris Bueford, the owner of the resort, made an emergency phone call to the AJ liquor store for two more barrels of beer. Clay Coal had paid for one, but it was almost gone. Dorothy would pay for two more as a wedding present. The grill was doing a record business in hamburger sales and she felt she would probably break even.

The bride and groom were to arrive at eight o'clock. Lou Ann sat so tight up against Clay he was afraid he would squirt out of the truck if the door popped open. Clay had spent the hours since their wedding installing a pair of air horns on their tow truck. He had other things on his mind, but Lou Ann insisted they wait until after the reception. "After all, we've waited this long," she argued. Clay pouted a little, but then set to work on the truck to make the time pass quicker. He began blowing the air horns the moment they turned onto Meramec Bottom Road. The blast of the horns bounced off the river and carried over the sound of the jukebox even with its two extra speakers attached.

The party guests heard them coming a mile away and in an act of spontaneous merriment, the boaters rushed to their boats and blared their horns in response. Clay gave the horn three short blasts and the boaters returned the call. Clay put a little rhythm in his next blast and the boaters matched his tune. When the next beat became more complicated, the boaters lost their unison and everyone began blaring away in total chaos. The new used tow truck containing Mr. and Mrs. Clay Coal, decorated in crepe paper flowers, rolled into the middle of the party. The horns continued and the guests covered their ears and then without a cue, everyone stopped at the same time and the sound echoed and rolled down the river and faded away. Then a second of near silence hung in the air until Little Richard sang out "Good Golly, Miss Molly" from the jukebox with the two extra speakers.

Dwayne and Dwight were forced to dance the hokey-pokey with Debbie and Sara. They wore their t-shirts inside out. Benton and Loretta chaperoned their children as best they could. They found there sons and daughters sneaking drinks from unguarded beers. Scoldings proved unsuccessful and the teenagers grew bolder as the party cruised into the night. They dumped cup after cup of illegally obtained beer, but the place was awash in the stuff.

Loretta and Benton examined each other with the thought of a possible romance, but they each concluded that the other was too old and ugly.

Dwayne pulled a willing Debbie behind a tree and kissed her. The beer had led him to dancing, which he had never done because he was too cool.

Then the dancing led to thirst and then more beer and more dancing, and the cycle spiraled out of control. They were trading tongues when Benton tapped his shoulder. "I believe the party's over there," he said. The startled couple meekly skipped back to the bright lights hand in hand.

Lou Ann held court at the bride and groom's table. If one more ugly old man comes up to kiss the bride, I'll scream, Lou Ann thought, but she didn't; she carried on like a trooper. And after a few cold beers and a plate of mostaccioli, she melted into a soft dream where she tried to absorb everything and store it away. She looked for Clay; she looked for him every few minutes, and if she didn't see him right away, a tiny panic happened. She knew this need to keep him in sight would diminish. She knew the day would come when she would be glad to have him out of the way and out from underfoot, but that day would come soon enough. Tonight, she would enjoy her madness.

Dewey Coogan came to the bride and asked to have his picture taken standing next to her. Lou Ann agreed but only if he would tell her the rest of the ski bet story.

Dewey began the tale and a small group gathered like children at their grandfather's knee listening to a reading of "The Night Before Christmas." Dewey started off good but got off track and began repeating himself. Lou Ann tried to help him along. "Yeah, yeah, you told me all that," she said. "The last I heard was that Dry had made the bet and took off from the dock at Castlewood State Park and chugged his first beer. Then we had to go," Lou Ann said.

Dewey brightened and said, "I'll say you had to go. You poked a stick into a hornet's nest. You watch out for that Ramona Gillman. She's gonna hold a grudge."

The group of listeners grunted their agreement. "She's too lazy to come looking for you, but you ever run into her again there's gonna be trouble."

"Thanks for the warning." This was about the twentieth warning whispered to Lou Ann today. They all wished her the best on her wedding day and then told her about Ramona Gillman's big talk of what would happen the next time they met. Each one believed they were breaking the story and then when they found out they weren't, they were disappointed. "Okay, enough about Ramona Gillman. Get back to the story."

"Well, he was working on his eighth beer when he cut in toward the bank at Cheryl's Seaside Lounge. You know Dry had promised Cheryl he would and he narrowly missed the dock, and in fact come much closer than he had planned. As a result, he had to cut hard at the last second to keep from coming aground. The hard cut produced a huge spray of water which drenched the spectators who had been promised a close-up look at the main attraction. Well, they got one," Dewey said with a laugh.

"Well then little Margie Walters, the youngest skier on the river, handed Dry his ninth beer. You know she was only eight years old? Well then them chase boats of Bluff City Distributing and Grey Eagle Distributing and Broadway Distributing followed as close as prudence would allow. They had a spotter in each boat and he declared if Dry was drinking or spilling most of the beer passed his way. Well, the judgin' was fairly loose, you know, 'cause no one wanted to disqualify Dry unless it were a flagrant violation of the rules. Dry, after all, was on a slalom ski and there would naturally be some spillage, so when Dry tipped back beer after beer, a little would run down his neck."

Dewey stopped talking and drifted off to a long ago, faraway thought. Lou Ann used the break to look for Clay. She scanned the scattered groups of people standing, dancing, or reclining in straining lawn chairs. A pathway opened by magic and Lou Ann had a direct sight line to a group of young people. Among them were her sisters and her brothers-in-law. Dwayne stood apart squirting lighter fluid on his lower lip. He blew the fluid across a lighter and caught his brother's hair on fire. Lou Ann started to rise but then she saw Clay giving chase and the brothers, apparently unhurt, moving quickly among the guests with fear in their eyes and she knew everything was under control.

Lou Ann nudged Dewey back to the present with a question. "So how far along is old Dry now?"

Dewey came back to life and carried on as if he'd only taken a deep breath. "Well, when he come to the Bridge Bar and Boat Ramp, Dry had his fourteenth beer delivered to him by old Gus Walters. Gus was the great grandfather of little Margie Walters, and he was the oldest skier on the river at that time. Gus was eighty-nine and looked every hard year of it. He came along Dry for a beer drop. He was steady on his skis and smiled through missing teeth at the reception of boat horns and cheers and applause. Then he looked confused, and when his boat towed him up next to Dry, he forgot to make the handoff and instead began drinking the beer and waving at the people. Dry was beginning to feel the effects of fourteen beers and was less steady on his slalom than he knew. He had known Gus for many years and had spent many a night discussing world problems until the last call was made. He knew right away Gus was confused. He had seen the expression Gus now wore many times. No one paid attention to Gus's lapses into dreamland and after the first few times it happened, made no mention of it to him. Dry needed to get the next beer soon. Even as slow as they were skiing, he was running out of river. The race was to the mouth of the Mississippi and Dry figured he was about four beers behind schedule.

"Gus didn't respond as Dry tried to coax the beer from him; he just smiled, waved, and took another drink. The way Dry figured it, he needed that beer but he must not cause Gus to fall. Dry leaned forward on his ski, reducing the drag, and began to pull in his ski rope until he was several yards ahead of Gus. Old Dry lowered himself down into a tight ball and cut under Gus's tow rope and drifted back until he was even with Gus. With a quick snatch, he had the beer from Gus's hand. Gus looked hurt. Here he was, skiing along, waving to friends he hadn't seen in years, and some bastard pulls his beer from his hand. 'Hey,' he blurted out over the sound of the outboards. 'It's okay, it's me, your old buddy, Dry,' Dry says. Gus hollers back, 'Hey, you tell this boat driver to pull over there. There's some people I want to see.' 'I sure will,' Dry says. Dry waved at his boat driver, Don, to give it the gas and swings back under Gus's rope. His knees wavered as he stood up straight and he wobbled hard before regaining his balance, but he held on. 'Take him in,' Dry shouted as he sped by Gus's tow boat and motioned to Don to start the switchback pattern so as to give him more time. He leaned back on his ski and dug a deep trench in the water. The brown water peeled away on both sides of his ski and a warm yellow rivulet ran down his leg. Dry had held his water as long as possible and now its release was a pleasure that has only a few rivals in life.

"There had been talk weeks before the event about the need to answer nature's call, a call that was bound to make itself known when drinking beer after beer. Several of the sponsors were unsure they wanted to associate with a situation that had only one answer. Dry consoled their concerns and gave them a short lecture on river etiquette. 'It was,' he said, 'the height of bad manners to be standing on the shore and for no other reason than to see the water splash relieve yourself in the river. On the other hand, if you find yourself far away from land and it is very inconvenient for yourself and for others to get you to land, your fellow boaters, fishermen, and skiers see no need for you to suffer.' All agreed that was the truth of the matter and that if nobody spoke directly to the issue, people of manners would pretend not to realize that there was an issue.

"Dry's stomach churned and for a few seconds threatened to put a stop to the insanity, but then it settled down and accepted its duty. The long slow weave of the boat from shore to shore gave Dry some time to refocus his attention and bolster his resolve. Old Dry heard the commotion at Earl's

Landing before he could see it. The crowd had been advised that Dry was about to come around the bend and had begun to cheer and sound their boat horns. Clay Coal was fourteen at the time. He stood on the floating dock as close to the edge as he could get. In his right hand he held a stag that Dry would snatch as he swept past. He had his left hand in his pocket as part of the bet. Dry had several side bets, alleging that he could swoop in, pitch his empty bottle high in the air, snatch a fresh bottle out of Clay's hand, and Clay would catch the empty with the same hand. The good time gamblers along the river had learned to consider long and hard before making a wager with Dry Coal, but in this case they wanted to see it done and wanted a dog in the fight. With a dozen different wagers ranging from $5.00 to $20.00 riding on the trick, Dry stood to make or lose $230.00. If he didn't win his bet, he had to win the challenge to pay off his losses or lose face along the river. Dry would find the money somewhere and cover his bets, but it might take awhile and he didn't want it said that you had to wait for your money when you wagered with Dry Coal.

"The floating dock at Earl's Landing was little more than a loose wooden sidewalk bobbing on barrels. It sat right in front of the mouth of a slough and if Don Cox swung in too deep, he wouldn't be able to get back out in the channel without putting way too much slack in the ski line. Dry would lose speed and if he didn't fall over, he would be jerked so harshly he would dislocate his shoulders." Dewey Coogan stopped the telling of the tale here for dramatic effect. He tipped back an empty cup of beer also for its dramatic effect.

While someone went to get Dewey a beer, Lou Ann looked for Clay. She stood on her bench and could see him. He had the tow truck started and all the lights on and had a concrete picnic table suspended from the winch. A large group of men of all ages oohed and aahed at the spectacle. Lou Ann returned to her seat. Dewey refreshed his voice and continued.

"The approach was the key," he said. "Don, the boat driver, needed to get Dry next to the dock, but only just within reach. Dry shocked himself back into focus. He had one chance to make the exchange and if he could pull it off, it would be a profitable day no matter what else happened. He shifted the empty into his left hand as he approached the dock. He could see Clay clearly now standing by himself out on the edge. He held the bottle of beer between two fingers and a thumb by the very top. Dry held the empty by the neck and pumped its weight like a man about to pitch a horseshoe. Closer and closer he came. He had never tried this before, but he had thrown many an empty up on the beach with great accuracy. Now he made his final calculation and sent the empty bottle skyward. Almost straight up went the throw.

"Dry had allowed for his own movement across the water to carry the bottle forward. Now that it was in the air, there was no reason to look at anything but the fresh beer Clay held, and Dry cut his ski hard and stretched to his limit before whisking the fresh brew out of Clay's grasp. Clay stepped back and his right hand shot to the sky and the bottle made a slap and came to a stop in his palm. Dry cut his skis hard again to his right. Now there was too much slack in the line. He put the bottle in his front teeth and raised both arms straight up. His speed was slowing, his ski running deeper in the water, cutting a brown curve of failure. The watchers began a whispered sigh. Then the slack was gone and Dry was whipped forward, his uplifted arms showing hard corded muscle under a thin layer of sun baked skin. And then he was up again and skiing confidently.

"Dry waved to the crowd and made a teasing bow, the kind he had seen French guys in silk stockings make before a king. The dock watchers erupted, the boat horns sounded, Clay waved the empty bottle proudly for all to see, spinning in both directions at once, his feet bouncing on the dock quickly in short rapid strokes. He nearly hovered. The joy and pride he felt at that moment would never be equaled.

"Dry began working on the fresh brew. It was a Stag and it was warm and flat. Clay had paced with anticipation and held the bottle with both hands, sucking the chill and the bubbles right through the glass. The pleasure of a long draw on a cold beer had vanished eight beers ago and this warm flat Stag was a battle only the brave of heart could face. It was common knowledge that Stag was an excellent choice when it was fresh and cold on tap at twenty-five cents a glass in a cool, dark tavern on a hot sunny day. This wasn't that beer. Dry swallowed in big gulps. His stomach, already stretched to new limits, stretched again.

"Don resumed a slow weave from bank to bank. Dry leaned back on his ski and watched the sky disappear and reappear as he skied deep into the shadows, then back across into the bright warm sun, then back under the light blocking canopy again. Reality began to slip away. He became hypnotized by the repetitive sights and sounds and the pull of the rope. Back and forth for how long he didn't know. Dry knew every mile of the river, but beer and fatigue were taking their toll. He had no idea of his location. He began to relax too much. His stomach protested every bump. He wouldn't make it. That much became clear. Even in his beer-soaked brain that message got through. He couldn't drink another beer. He barely held on to his stomach now.

"'If you say you'll do something, do it.' That was the advice he had always given the boys. He would have to add 'and have a backup plan' to his next lecture. With all his bragging and bravado aside, he had considered what he might do in the event of failure. Now he had to act if it wasn't too late. 'Straighten her out and go slow,' Dry hollered over the din of outboard motors. When Don had settled on a course down the middle of the channel, Dry began gathering ski rope until he pulled himself up close to the boat. 'Where we at?' he shouted. 'We're comin' up on the Highway 21 bridge,' Don said. 'Take me in close at the Peters ramp,' Dry said. Don smiled a knowing smile. 'You sure you want to?' he asked. 'It's now or never,' Dry said, recapturing his confidence. 'I'm going to do the gainer. I think I need to be going around 45,' Dry said. 'You got it,' Don said. 'Get me there in a hurry,' Dry said as he drifted back to the end of the rope.

"Don gave it the gas and the spotter boats and the watcher boats, all trailing happily along, pushed their boats to full throttle and the roar of a drag race involving forty boats put a charge in everyone's heart. A freight train of ski boats rushed down river three and four abreast. Don was proud of his boat and relished the opportunity to show what she could do. Dry tried to shout but could not be heard. He wanted to wave his arms and get Don's attention, but he could do nothing but hang on.

"Year after year, the boats had gotten lighter and the outboards increased in size and horsepower. Dry had skied behind them all, but it had been a while since he had gone this fast. He cut to the side, jumping the wave made by the wake. Out on smooth water now, he hunched his back and bent his knees and let the ski have its head. The shoreline floated past and Dry recorded its passing in quick still shots like an erratic slide show. The legs began to quiver. He couldn't control his ski at this speed much longer.

"The bridge came into sight, Don backed off the throttle, and Dry straightened his aching legs. Dry made a circling motion with his arm and Don understood he wanted him to circle the ramp. The title wave of ski boats caught up to their quarry. When they saw Dry circling the ramp, word spread from boat to boat: He's gonna do the jump. Dry had lost the challenge. There would be no prize money. But worse than that, he had failed to do what he said he would do. Now with his strength gone and about to throw up, he had one last chance to carve out a place in history. Okay, so he couldn't drink a case of beer while skiing thirty miles of river. He had consumed eighteen beers in twenty miles and then done a gainer off a twelve foot ramp. Let someone top that, Dry thought. It never occurred to him that no one would care to try.

"Dry still held an empty bottle in his right hand and waved it toward the grandstand of boats positioned for a good view. The traveling audience waved back, many of the watchers having consumed a good number of cold beverages themselves. Some considered going over the jump too, but saner minds prevailed. Dry pointed to the ramp and Don knew he was ready to make his run. He pulled him three hundred yards upstream above the ramp and made a slow, wide turn and lined up his run. He watched his speedometer—30, 35. He looked back at Dry. Dry looked strange, not in the normal strange way of a wiry, middle aged man with a huge beer belly wearing painter's pants cut off and made into shorts and a canvas hard hat shell that appeared to be an aviator's cap. Nothing strange there. It was his face. Don saw the squinty eyes and pursed lips and the tilted head of determination.

"The ramp was close now. He would need to lean back at the last moment. The ski would have a lot of drag when it hit the ramp. Then, when he's almost off the top of the ramp, he needs to hold the rope low and whip his head and shoulders back and let the pull of the rope take him through a back flip. Now he's off the ramp. His head drops back and he feels his ski come up and over, but then his rotation stalls. Did he start the flip too late? Was he holding the rope too high? Should he have been going faster? The answer could not be found in the brief second he had before dropping into a fifteen foot high, thrity-five miles per hour belly flop. The slap of flesh striking the water could be heard over the murmur of idling outboards and the boisterous crowd went silent.

"Don cut hard and returned to the crash site. He shut off his motor and came alongside Dry's lifeless body. Gripping a strap on the aviator's cap, he lifted Dry's head out of the water, then pushing him up and down a few times to gain momentum, he flopped him over the side of the boat. Dry's body weight balanced on his stomach, and the stomach gave up its contents, including a large serving of river water. Don pulled him into the boat and Dry coughed and retched for a long time. When he stopped and rose from his knees, a bright red glow could be seen on his face and chest and belly and thighs and shins. The chase boats all came over and everyone was so happy that Dry wasn't dead, that they said he should have the prize money anyway for putting on such a great show. So they gave it to him."

Dewey Coogan tilted back his empty cup. Someone handed him a whole one.

"Well that was a good story, Dewey, and worth the wait," Lou Ann said. "Has anyone ever tried to match it?"

"No, no one's tried. A couple of guys talked about doin' it, but it was just talk. They never give her a try," Dewey said with a forlorn look. "I was right there. I was in a fast boat and we was the second boat to see that Dry wasn't dead," Dewey said with obvious pride.

"She's on her way." The words floated across puffs of cigarette smoke from one small group of guests to the next. No one knew where the news had come from, but it spread like a grass fire in a high wind.

"Let's go," Lou Ann said.

"I'm not gonna let some girl run me off from my own party," Clay replied.

"We're not running. We were gonna leave soon anyhow. Let's just go and leave sooner. I don't want a brawl on my wedding night."

"There won't be no brawl," Clay said.

"Well I guess this is our first argument. We haven't been married five minutes and now we're havin' our first fight." Lou Ann pretended a childish pout and rolled big puppy dog eyes at Clay. "They say marriage is a compromise. I'll make you a deal. You leave with me now and we'll go to our room for an hour, and if you want to come back, we'll do her," Lou Ann said as she gave Clay's butt a hard swat. "But I don't believe you're gonna want to come back."

Clay fought to control a grin and lost. A telltale protrusion under each pocket of Lou Ann's bowling shirt proved that the night air was beginning to chill. "Let's go to our room," Clay said. He had reserved a room at the Holiday Inn which featured a round bed and a big console colored TV with remote control. He wasted no more time on polite goodbyes. With a wave and a shout, holding hands, he and Lou Ann began a brisk walk that became a lazy run before they reached the cab of the tow truck. As their taillights disappeared into the night, the reception guests went back to the serious business of draining a half barrel. When Ramona Gillman didn't appear at three o'clock, the party broke up and everyone went home slightly disappointed.

CHAPTER FORTY-EIGHT

Rhonda Long sat on a gray metal folding chair at the end of a long line of rectangular tables in the basement of the First Baptist Church. The high pitched squeal her chair made echoed off the tile block walls as she adjusted her butt to the unforgiving contours of the chair. "Miss Polly, you can send in the next student now." Rhonda's voice carried easily to the stairwell, where an unlikely group of men and women, all below thirty years of age, waited in silence for their interview.

Byron Creed walked loose jointedly across the painted concrete floor and stopped a few feet from Rhonda's chair. Rhonda had her head down marking papers with a red pen. Byron waited nervously to be acknowledged. The sight of the red pen chipped away at his resolve. Red pens always brought trouble. When at last Rhonda looked up, she gave the boy a long critical gaze. "Have a seat," she said. "Your name?"

"Byron Creed."

Rhonda peeled the corners on a stack of papers, stopping periodically to wet her fingers on her tongue. "There you are," she said, pulling Byron's application out and placing it on top of the stack. Now she studied the form intently, slightly shaking her head at parts, looking up into Byron's eyes, then back to the paper. When at last she was satisfied that she had absorbed all the information the application had to offer, she sat back in her chair and inhaled and exhaled a deep breath.

"Mr. Creed, are you aware of the fact that the GED course I teach is not affiliated in any way with the local school district?"

"No."

"Do you know that you will not receive any sort of credit for taking this course?"

Byron twisted, confused. He adjusted his chair and an ear piercing squeal startled him and he felt like a bug under this old woman's intense gaze. "No, I didn't know that."

"Did you understand this course to be free?"

"Yes." Byron's teeth clenched. He suspected this was some sort of shakedown and his anger began to rise. Al had filled out the papers. The way the old man explained it, he just had to come to this church and sit in the basement for two hours on Tuesday and Thursday nights for a few months and they would give him a diploma.

"Okay, let me explain this to you. And I need you to follow along because I don't like to repeat myself. I present the material that you will find on the State issued GED test. It is up to you to learn and remember enough of this material to pass the State test." Rhonda paused, giving Byron the bug look again. "I do this for free as a service to my community and as a service to my church. If you notice, most of the students waiting out there in the stairwell are twenty-five or older. That seems to be the age where it becomes obvious that a high school diploma is necessary if one is to improve one's place in life. You, Mr. Creed, are barely seventeen." Rhonda put her cold stare on Byron, daring him to say anything in his defense. Byron, not knowing what to do, held her gaze, determined not to blink. Silence seconds ticked by and Rhonda released her grip.

"Mr. Creed, as a non-profit group, we are free to turn away any student application without reason. I am going to go against my better judgment and accept you as a student on certain conditions. Do you have any money?"

Byron shook his head.

"Stand up and empty your pockets on the table, please."

Byron's face became defiant. She has no right to demand this; she's acting like a cop; I won't do it, he thought, but said nothing.

"Please, Mr. Creed, don't take too long to make up your mind. My students have a ninety-six percent success rate on their first attempt to pass the State test. They have a one hundred percent success rate on their second attempt. That's because I drill it into them without mercy." Rhonda paused for a second to let that sink in. "If you agree to my terms, I'll drill it into you without mercy."

Byron stood and emptied his pockets on the table. From his right front pocket he produced his Case two-bladed pocketknife and a short stub of a pencil. From his left front pocket, he laid out a quarter, a nickel, a penny, and a rubber band.

Rhonda examined the items and reached for the pencil. "I assume you plan to use this to take notes, fill out forms, answer test questions?" She dropped the pencil to the table and it clicked from end to end and seemed much louder than normal, as the clicking increased in speed until it became a hum, and then the silence returned. "Do you have any identification?"

"No," Byron replied, now humbled by the pitiful contents of his pockets.

"Mr. Creed, do you have a driver's license and forgot to bring it or do you not have one?"

"I don't have one."

"Mr. Creed, if you accept my terms, I'll see to it that you get one."

Byron smiled. "Oh . . . okay, what terms?"

"Mr. Creed, I don't like my classes disturbed. You will have to exhibit perfect behavior. May I see your pocket knife." Rhonda extended a hand, but not as far as she could have. She forced Byron to reach across the table to place the knife in her hand. "Have you owned this knife long?"

"Yes."

"How long?"

Byron looked toward the ceiling tile. A long plane of white cardboard hung in brown metal frames. "Eight years," Byron lied. It seemed important that he had had it for a long time.

"Eightyears? It says here that you're seventeen. Are you telling me that you were given this knife when you were nine years old?" Rhonda opened the larger of the two blades, the swept back point looking more sinister than usual.

"Why are you asking me all this?" Byron asked.

"Because I need to know if this knife is worth more than its face value. Who gave you this knife?" Rhonda raked her thumb across the blade testing its sharpness.

"Uh . . . uh . . . this uh . . . Indian . . . old man."

Rhonda rolled her eyes with impatience. "Okay. Here's what I'll do for you, Mr. Creed. I usually receive $50.00 in advance from a student under the age of eighteen. If that student comes to every class, completes all assigned work, and passes the State test, I return their $50.00 along with a $50.00 check donated by the church as a graduation present. In your case, I will hold this pocketknife and if you fail to meet my requirements, it will become mine to keep. Do we have an understanding, Mr. Creed?"

Byron's mind swirled with pictures of fast cars and hot girls and money to spend. "What if I need my knife?" he asked. It seemed a reasonable question as the words rolled off his tongue, but now being pinned by this old bitch's gaze, he wished he had said nothing.

"Mr. Creed, if you need to stab someone, come and tell me and I'll go with you and hold them while you do the stabbing. And when we're all done, I'll hold the knife until you need it again. Is that fair?"

Byron hesitated before answering. "Yes."

"Okay, classes start at seven o'clock. I lock the door at five minutes past seven. If you are late, you miss the class. If you miss two classes, you are out for good. Do we understand each other, Mr. Creed?"

"Yes."

"Be here a week from tonight with two pens and two pencils and a spiral notebook. One more thing, Mr. Creed. If you succeed in passing the State test and go on to bigger and better things, at some point you will realize that you no longer have to take crap from mean old women like me. That should offer some extra incentive, don't you think?" Rhonda smiled, enjoying her position.

"Yes, ma'am. Thank you for being so mean."

"My pleasure. Miss Polly, send in the next applicant, please."

CHAPTER FORTY-NINE

Sheriff Bud Browdy's unmarked police car swayed badly in the corners. The power was there. The big motor never seemed to be working hard. He just pushed the pedal and the big four-barrel opened its throat, making a roaring rush of air and gasoline. The old sheriff had bought himself a brute, only he wanted the soft ride, willingly sacrificing the good handling the car was capable of. That was something Bud had promised himself to fix when he got the time.

Bud topped the hill at eighty miles per hour and the weight of the big car became nothing as its suspension topped out, its tires barely maintaining contact. Then the road flattened out and Bud felt the jar of the impact all the way up his spine, the steering became mushy, and the car changed lanes with a mind of its own. Bud regained control of the car and slowed to a more reasonable speed. After a few deep breaths to settle his nerves, he reached for the radio. "Dispatch, this is Bud. Put Rhonda on."

"This is Rhonda," came a voice crackling back.

"Are they still there?" Bud asked.

"Yeah, I just got off the phone with Squeaker. He said they just bought another pitcher. Looks like they'll be there for a while."

"Thanks. That's where I'll be," Bud said. He hesitated, still not used to radio manners. "Okay, I'm done now," he said into the microphone.

"Out, Sheriff. You're supposed to say out."

"Out, Rhonda."

"Out, Sheriff."

Bud could hear Rhonda laughing before she released the button on her mike. He had begun sharing his thoughts with Rhonda more often. She could listen quietly and keep the facts straight and offer good simple advice that went straight to the root of the problem.

It was Rhonda's suggestion that he run the Bender family out of the county. "Run 'em out of town," were her exact words. "That's the way my great granddad used to do it. The ones that were dirty but hard to catch like this Bender family. The old man knows the trade, knows the crooked judges, and taught those boys of his how to hot wire a car before they could walk. You ain't never gonna catch him red-handed," Rhonda had argued.

Bud knew she was right. Still he was not ready to cross that line. That was, until the last county council meeting. The fat asses on the council demanded that the car thieves that had settled in the county be brought to justice. No one wanted to hear about manpower problems or unpaid overtime or radios that didn't work. Bud had gotten so red in the face he had to storm out of the meeting to keep from slamming someone to the floor. That's when he decided to take Rhonda's advice.

Carl Bender and his two boys, Carl Jr. and Jeff, were at Squeaker's Tavern. Bud had put out the word to a few of the tavern owners he felt he could trust to call his office if all three came in together. Now he was on his way to run them out of town. "What the hell are you doing?" he said. He liked to say the opening thought out loud. He felt it made his mind sit up and pay attention. Now he ran the list of all the things that could go wrong, and after every review of the list, he added a few more possible bad outcomes.

On the good side of the list, there was only one item: He could scare the old man enough that he would take the boys and start up business somewhere else. But on the bad side of the list, if a fight broke out and he was forced to use his gun, the whole thing could blow up in his face. This is crazy, he thought. Of course a fight's going to break out. These stupid rednecks will have two or three pitchers of beers down by the time I get there and all three are known head kickers. Bud continued to argue himself, but his car stayed on course for Squeaker's Tavern.

Bud turned off the highway at 141 and sped down Highway 61-67 toward the river. The lights of Floyd's Tire Mart came into view and Bud glanced at the cars and trucks on the lot. A rusted hulk of a tow truck caught his eye. The truck was so ugly he assumed it was being towed off for scrap. Standing next to the scrap pile was Clay Coal. Bud hit the brakes and the squeal of his tires turned every head. He swung the car onto the lot and it rocked to a stop. Seeing that all eyes were upon him, Bud grabbed the radio microphone and pretended he was talking to someone. He watched Clay and Clay watched him. Bud waited until Clay had topped off his gas tank and paid the kid before he stepped out.

"Clay, can I have a word with you?"

Clay hesitated for a second before walking toward Bud's car. "What's this about?"

"Nothing bad for you."

"I already talked to the cops about the Boman boy," Clay said.

"I know. You're clear on that. This has nothing to do with you in a bad way. I just want to talk to you for a moment. I might have a proposition for you." The proposition just jumped into Bud's mind. Clay had a tow truck. "Come around and sit down for a moment so we can talk private."

Clay came around the car, still suspicious. He shuffled a pile of papers over far enough for him to get in and close the door. Bud stared out the windshield, looking at nothing, scratching his chin and neck and head just behind his ear. He was about to make a foolish offer and was trying to talk himself out of it, but he also believed he could make it work.

"So, Bud what'd you want to talk about?" Clay had put a little too much attitude in Bud's name. Bud stiffened and slowly turned his attention to Clay. Clay felt he was about to have some sort of confrontation, but then Bud softened and just showed a tired expression.

"You mind if I call you Clay?"

"No, I don't mind."

"And you can call me Bud."

Clay sensed Bud was trying to be nice and decided to be nice too. "What can I do for you, Sheriff?"

"Well, son, we can help each other. Sorry, some people take it wrong when I call them son."

"Don't bother me."

"Well, here's the deal, and it just came to me so I haven't got all the details worked out. But I could use your help, and in return for this help, I'll clean your slate. Any cars you've stolen up to right now, you're clear on. Nothing is going to come back and bite you in the ass. You start out tomorrow not having to look over your shoulder anymore."

"I'm not looking over my shoulder now."

"Well you should be. And you're about to find out that I'm going to start using new techniques to gather evidence."

"New techniques?"

"Yes, sir."

"What kind of techniques would that be?" Clay asked.

"The ass kicking kind."

Clay smiled at Bud, a soft smile but unafraid.

"I got no reason to trust you to go straight except that girl of yours seems to be heading you in the right direction."

"What do you know about my girl?" Clay asked, showing his willingness to defend Lou Ann's honor.

"I hear things, and in this case I hear she's smart and pretty and got you wrapped around her finger."

Clay tried to get puffed up, but with Bud giving him a big possum grin just across the seat, he couldn't hold his frown. "Yes, she's got me."

"Well, son, don't fight it. Just let her lead."

"Lead? Lead where?" Clay asked.

Bud laughed. "It don't matter cause you're gonna follow her wherever she goes."

Clay laughed. Then it struck him that Bud must be in a tight spot.

The conversation dried up. Bud fumbled with the radio dials just to kill time. Clay waited patiently, knowing Bud needed him more than he needed Bud. Finally he asked, "What's this proposition you mentioned?"

"Yeah, I was getting to that. The County has a contract with Earl Blick to tow cars that are impounded or abandoned or wrecked. I don't care much for Earl he's a sheriff Wells holdover." Bud paused for effect. "I could give that contract to you, and with it in hand, the bank would loan you enough money to buy a new tow truck, and you and Lou Ann would be in business." Bud grinned.

"Who says I need a new tow truck?"

"Is that your truck, your only truck?" Bud asked, pointing to the wreck across the yard.

"Yeah."

"Well then you need a tow truck."

"It could use a paint job." Clay tried to defend the truck. He was beginning to lose his patience but maintained a civil tone. "How'd you know her name?" he asked.

"Who's name?"

"Lou Ann's."

"I hear things."

"Why would you do this for me and what do I have to do, give you some sort of kickback on every tow?" Clay suddenly felt dirty. Stealing cars was clean compared to official corruption.

"No, nothin' like that. It's . . . well, it's . . . I've got to put the Benders out of business, and I can't seem to do it with evidence. They're too smart or I'm too dumb. Either way, I've had enough, and I'm gonna run 'em."

"What's my part in this?" Clay asked.

"I might need a little help to keep from getting my ass kicked or having to shoot someone." Bud couldn't look at Clay. He felt ashamed of himself for reasons he couldn't understand. Damn, Clay Coal held no high moral ground over him.

"You got deputies?" Clay asked.

"They mostly run to the puny side, but if you take enough of them . . ."

Bud and Clay shared a chuckle. "Yeah, I could, but I don't want to get any of them involved. They got sick kids and mortgages and cars that won't run. This could get 'em fired—after I'm indicted, that is. Besides that, they can't keep their mouths shut." Bud took a breath. He hadn't intended to spill his guts like he had.

"When do you want to do this?"

"Right now."

CHAPTER FIFTY

Unlike most of the Meramec River bars, Squeaker had his bar on the lower level of a two-storey concrete block building. The bar flooded more often, but Squeaker had a system for removing the things the water would damage, and the things that were left, made of concrete or metal or plastic, he would wash down and be open for business two days after the river returned to its banks. The bar smelled of fish and mold and stale beer.

Two old timers sat at the bar drinking draft beer out of glass mugs and looking bored. Squeaker stood behind the bar made of glass blocks wiping the stainless steel top. Carl Bender and his sons, Jeff and Carl Jr., were huddled around a small table at the far end of the bar. The table was covered with empty glass pitchers and half filled mugs of beer. Carl Bender spoke in a soft tone, giving instructions to his boys on what should be done first thing the next day.

"Strip them two Mustangs first. I want the heads, the carbs, and the intake manifolds pulled off first thing. I got them sold. Take the hoods and front fenders and doors over to Valley Park and put them in the big shed."

The door opened and Carl's eyes shifted toward the new arrivals. When his eyes widened, Jeff and Carl Jr. turned in their chairs to see what had the old man's attention. Bud Browdy strolled through the open door wearing a big smile and carrying a small souvenir Cardinal baseball bat. "How about those Cardinals?" he said to everyone in the room.

Squeaker caught Bud's eye and tilted his head toward the Benders. Bud didn't show any reaction to the signal, but he was thinking, You dumb ass, of course I see 'em. They're the only other people in the place.

"Give me two frosty mugs of your finest fifty cent draft," Bud said.

"You drinkin' with both hands tonight, Sheriff," Squeaker asked, putting the mugs on the bar.

"Naw, my buddy Clay will want one. Where is he?" Bud looked over his shoulder toward the door. Clay stepped into the light. He too carried a souvenir bat. He scanned the room with a quick sweep of his head, and when he saw the Benders, he tensed and his jaw tightened. Bud thought to himself, Damn, he's good!

Bud had given Clay instructions not to start anything and to follow his lead and not look surprised at anything he might say. Clay turned to close the door behind him and snapped the deadbolt lock closed. He tucked the bat under his arm and pulled the nearest table in front of the door. Clay had everyone's attention. Carl's two sons looked at Dad for advice. "Steady, boys," Carl said in a calm voice.

Bud and Clay strolled side by side toward Carl's table, a beer in one hand and a bat in the other. "Bring these boys another pitcher," Bud said with a big smile.

Clay didn't have a smile. He looked focused on the job at hand.

Carl Jr. came out of his chair and grabbed a pool cue that was leaning against the wall close by. He made no move to raise it; he just held it with both hands like he was waiting for his next shot. Jeff got to his feet and moved around behind his father's chair. "You boys go to the ball game together?" Carl asked.

The question brought out snickers from his two boys. The picture of the hard boiled sheriff and the barroom brawler car thief sitting together at the ball park seemed unlikely.

"That's right, we did," Bud said. "We been hanging out a lot lately. We found that we have a lot in common." Bud grinned broadly. "In fact, we've become real close. Ain't that right, Clay?"

"Yeah," Clay said, his eyes focused on the middle of the table, not looking at anyone but seeing everyone. He had pulled out a chair and put his foot on it. He sipped his beer with his right hand and dangled the little bat in his left, his left elbow resting on his knee.

Squeaker lowered a fresh pitcher of beer to the edge of the table with an outstretched arm and scurried back behind the bar. "Drink up, boys," Bud said. "Enjoy your last pitcher of beer in Jefferson County."

Carl Jr., feeling well armed leaning on his pool cue, understood what the sheriff was saying and decided to show off his complete knowledge of the law. "You can't make us leave," was the complete sentence on its way out, but the dull thump of Clay's bat striking the middle of his forehead stopped him at "You can't." Carl Jr. clutched at his head with both hands and the pool cue he was holding struck the concrete floor with a crack. Clay maintained his position. No part of him had moved except his left arm, that was now resting back on his knee with the small bat dangling loosely in his hand.

"That wasn't called for," Carl said to Bud.

"That was nothing. If you ain't gone in two days, you could end up like that Boman boy, dead in a ditch on the side of a dirt road." Bud sipped his beer, giving Carl Sr. a steady stare. Carl wanted to say "You can't get away with this" but decided against it with a glance at the little bat. Then the meaning of Bud's threat became clear. Was he saying he was responsible for the Boman boy's death? Everyone knew the boy had both arms broken. Carl looked up at Clay Coal hovering over him in easy striking distance. Clay maintained his frozen position, looking blankly at the table full of pitchers and mugs, his peripheral vision seeing everything.

"If you start tonight loading doors and hoods and motors, you know just your best crap, I think two days is plenty of time, don't you?" Bud said.

Carl didn't say. He was trying to think. There must be a way out of this.

"Okay, then, we've got that settled," Bud said. "In two days you'll be gone. If not . . ." Bud leaned in close and spoke just loud enough for Carl's ear. "If not, one of these boys is going to come up missing. Then the other one. If you're still not gone, I'm going to make you disappear." Bud leaned back in his chair and sipped his beer, looking over the mug with the coldest expression he could muster.

Bud readied himself for an attack. To threaten to kill a man's son was a bold and reckless move and Bud felt the shame of it as he said it.

Carl studied on the situation, his anger rising rapidly. He could kick out with his left leg and send Bud over backwards. Look at that bastard, he thought, leaning back on the hind legs of that chair grinning at me like a possum. He rubbed at his neck and twisted in his chair and rubbed his head so everyone would know he was thinking. He pursed his lips and rolled his eyes and stole a glance at Jeff. If Jeff would tackle Clay Coal and take him to the ground, Carl Jr. could pick up that pool cue and put him down for good. All eyes were on him now. He rubbed his mouth with his left hand while he looked at his son Jeff. With his index finger crossing his nose, he wiggled it slightly as he pointed at Clay. Everyone in the world except Jeff picked up on the signal. Carl was forced to repeat the hand across the face wiggle of the finger move again. Jeff finally understood. Clay turned his head toward Jeff. His face was blank and his eyes were empty. There was no fear or anger or excitement, just focused concentration.

Damn, he's good, Bud thought.

Jeff wanted to be someplace else. Carl watching the whole plan crumble, decided to save Jeff from a knot on the head. "Okay, you win," he said.

"You made the right choice," Bud said. He popped up out of his chair. "Well, this has been fun, but we gotta go. Clay, you got anything you want to say?"

Clay ignored the question and made no move to leave. "Okay, then, I got a big day tomorrow and so do you. So let's get out of here, Clay." Clay didn't move.

"This ain't what we said we was gonna do." Clay's voice was sharp and clear. A moment of frozen time slipped by.

"Clay, we gotta go," Bud said, putting an edge on his voice.

Clay whipped the little bat around and shattered an empty pitcher, sending a hailstorm of glass toward Carl Jr., who was still holding his forehead. Clay strutted toward the door, and as he walked, he measured his steps. When he reached the table blocking the door, a snap kick with his right leg sent the table pinwheeling across the floor and then he was out the door.

Bud turned toward Carl and his boys smiling. "I guess we'll be going now," he said.

Clay twisted in the front seat to watch the door until they were out of shotgun range. Bud worked the steering wheel frantically. He had not thought out the getaway and had parked nose first in the small gravel lot. Now he worked the shift lever from Drive to Reverse, back to Drive, then Reverse, then Drive, Reverse one last time, then Drive and hit the gas.

Clay slammed off balance into the dashboard of the big Cadillac, then back to the seat. He braced himself for the next set of jolts. "You didn't have this part figured out, did you," Clay said.

"No, I didn't."

Now the gravel flew and the dust boiled up and they were down the road and the tavern was out of sight. Clay began to snicker a little. Bud suppressed a laugh then gave up trying to be serious. "Holy shit!" he shouted.

"Ha-ha!" Clay boomed with laughter. "That was fun. Let's go back and do it again."

Bud jerked the wheel and hit the brakes in a mock determination to return.

"Hell, I'm game," Clay said.

Bud complimented Clay on his handling of the situation and Clay remarked on Bud's evil smile. "Man, when you told the old man you were gonna kill him, then leaned back smiling, man you were scaring me."

"I thought Carl would try to kick me over," Bud said.

"And you was ready for that, weren't you."

"Oh, yeah, I was watchin' for the first twitch of his boot. He might have tried it, too, if old Jeff wasn't so dumb."

"Yeah, be a waste of money to send that boy to medical school."

CHAPTER FIFTY-ONE

A light rain sprinkled on the windshield of Bud Browdy's car. He turned off the motor and sat quietly surveying the small farmstead. The gravel road went right up to the front door of the old two-storey farm house. Bud concocted a lie to tell if Luther or Ramona Gillman came out of the house, but nothing stirred. As he looked about the yard and approached the house, he shook his head with disgust. The old house had sad charm and the yard and the outbuildings had once been kept neat and weed free. Now the place smelled of diesel fuel, discarded oil cans littered the ground, a lowboy trailer sat atop a flower bed, its border of small stones scattered, weeds grew tall in the fence lines, and gates hung crooked on broken hinges. The covered front porch that extended across the house had rotten underneath and sagged in the middle.

This had been a pretty little farm, Bud thought, just twenty or so years ago. He had never been here before, but he had been to many like it. He imagined a woman with lots of energy had lived here; remnants of a half dozen or so flower beds long overtaken by nature poked out of the wet grass. Bud envisioned an old woman in a faded cotton dress with a sun bonnet loosely shading her face holding her long strings of gray hair out of her eyes. She was breaking her back in the early morning sun. She would have only the time she could steal from the daily chores to work on her flowers, but after years of labor she would have a yard she was proud of, and then her time is over and her husband's passing not far behind, and her children have moved away, and the neat little farm becomes valued only according to how many bedrooms it contains and goes up for rent.

Bud had seen dozens of places like this and still it pulled on his heart to see something that could have been easily saved, the hard work having already been done, just let go.

Bud went to the front door and knocked, waited, and knocked again. There was no sound inside or any movement at the windows. He stepped down off the porch and strolled to the back of the house. Beer cans were underfoot in the tall grass, worn out fan belts hung from fence posts, wrappers and boxes from food and auto parts lay everywhere in various states of decay. Bud surveyed the scene, feeling foolish for coming. What did he expect to find? He had no search warrant and nothing to justify a request for one. But still something bothered him.

Dale Boman hauled water all over the southern end of the county, so when a look at the route sheet showed Luther and Ramona Gillman as one of the stops, something just twitched in Bud's mind. Bud had never met Luther Gillman, although from what he had heard, he felt he knew him. Luther's daddy had built a small excavating company into a prosperous business. As a child, Luther learned to operate a backhoe while other boys his age were trying to master a two wheeler. Luther lived in his father's shadow, never quite measuring up.

Rhonda knew all about Luther and Ramona. Their exploits had become an ongoing topic of conversation among Rhonda and her lifetime network of friends living in this end of Jefferson County. Bud trusted Rhonda's assessment of the stories she'd heard. Based on the teller of the tale, she graded the stories by percentage points—fifty to ninety-five percent accuracy. She said the things she could tell Bud about Luther and Ramona were about ninety-five percent accurate. Ramona had a wandering eye, as Rhonda put it, and Dale Boman was a good looking boy with raging hormones. Luther Gillman was acording to Ronda's sources a barroom brawler, but was he a killer? The tails he'd heard of Ramona's flamboyant behavior could lead to a killing. The murderer of the Deputy was most likely the same man that killed the Boman boy. Bud felt sure he was right about that but right now he could not explain why even to himself.

Bud felt there might be something to see out here; he just didn't know what. He wandered away from the house and walked down a worn path that no doubt had led to the old outhouse. The raindrops became larger, Bud increased his stride in spite of himself, and at the end of the path a shed roof hanging precariously off the side of a small barn offered shelter. He ducked under the rusted tin roof at a fast trot. Part of the roof was caved in; the part that was left provided poor shelter for a pile of junk.

An old wringer washing machine filled with Hollywood magazines, its legs dissolved into the dirt, took center stage. Around the washer, decades of junk were stacked in layers like a canyon wall, each layer telling the year of its deposit. The bottom layer of old Buckets and horse-drawn farming implements was covered by early electrical appliances with cloth covered cords giving away their age—a radio with a big round dial and the speaker missing and an iron that heated itself.

Bud scanned the pile of junk, vaguely intrigued by the story it told of changing times. There was a slight movement in the shadow he caught out of the corner of his eye. When he looked harder, the outline of a coiled copperhead appeared where he had not seen it before. The snake was there all along—Bud was sure of that—and the thought that he had not seen it from five feet away sent a chill wind across his nerve endings. He began to examine all the likely snake hideouts and discovered three more copperheads minding their own business. The snakes were all large for copperheads, around twenty-eight inches. They were no doubt eating well on mice and baby rabbits, he thought. "Damn, the place is probably full of them," he said out loud just to hear his own voice.

The rain continued to hammer on the metal roof just above his head, and Bud decided against a run for the car. He would be soaked and forced to go home for dry clothes, losing half a day and all his momentum. He felt if he left here today planning to return later, he would no doubt become overrun with each day's new emergencies and never make it. He felt he had put a tourniquet on everything just to slow the bleeding, never closing a wound. He had run this thought by Rhonda and she accused him of watching too much of the "Dr. Ben Casey" show.

The rain let up and all but stopped suddenly and Bud left the cover and circled to the opposite side of the small hay barn. As he passed the main section, he peered in the open doorway, not wanting to get within striking distance of anything that might conceal a snake. One of the large doors was missing and the other hung forlorn by a single twisted hinge. The loft area held nothing, its floor boards having been stripped for some long forgotten project deemed more important at the time than having a floor in the hayloft. Maybe the doors, he thought.

The dirt floor was surprisingly clear of debris. The walls were bare wood, aged and gray, but no harness chain or triple trees or bridles hung on the large rusty pegs that protruded from every post. The place was very clean and except for a rake a shovel leaning together in the corner, it was empty. Bud couldn't deduce anything from this abnormality but thought it curious. Why would the Gillmans let their yard go to hell yet keep this part of a snake barn so clean? Bud's spirits inched up a notch.

"Damn," Bud muttered out loud. He suddenly realized that this was the kind of work he had wanted to do all along. He was doing detective work and there was something amiss here. He could feel the energy in the air. His close encounter with the snakes and the electric currents of the storm seemed to aid in his perception. His mind relaxed and absorbed everything. The joy he felt at the opportunity to solve this mystery was slightly intoxicating. Was that wrong? Bud questioned his motives. This is fun, he thought. He could feel that ten-year-old boy he thought he had left behind coming back. Hours of practice with wooden guns hunting robbers . . . all that work as a child began to pay dividends. Bud felt at home in this scene he had played out a hundred times. Was that wrong? he thought again.

Bud moved on to the other lean-to roof area. This space did not contain as much junk as its twin but instead sheltered an old Buick. The car sat on the dirt, its tires and wheels missing, with the borders of rusted metal and pitted chrome ringing the lower edges. Bud subconsciously speculated on its age—probably a late thirties to early forties model. The long hood, the high turtle shell roof line, a backseat big enough to dance in. Bud picked his steps carefully, trying to avoid the deepest puddles, and inched forward, cupping his hands under the glass to get a better look at the backseat. It was empty. The cushions were gone; the dirt was working its way up through the gaping brown holes in the floor. The dirt was packed and smooth.

Bud stepped back and observed the ground around the car. There was no clear pathway worn in the rough stubble. A clump of fescue close to the back door rose out of the earth with decades of persistence. In the middle of cow pie sized clump, the blades of grass were withered and bleached. The dead grass matched the place a foot would land every time a person entered or exited the back door of the old car. Lights began to flash in the deepest recesses of Bud's brain. There's something here. A good detective just knows when there's something out of place, he thought. His gaze swept the wall and the underside of the shed roof. There it was—just a few inches of electrical wire arched out where it turned and went behind a board and down the wall to seemingly nowhere behind the car.

Bud walked back to the center section of the barn and stepped inside. A workbench with an old vice bolted to a corner protruded out from the wall at the spot opposite to the old car. The area underneath the bench that would normally be a shelf loaded with paint cans and coffee cans full of nails was not there. Instead, the space was closed in with boards nailed vertically side by side from the bench top to the dirt floor. Bud used his lighter to get a closer look at the nail heads used under the bench. They still had a gray metallic shine not covered with rust like all the others.

There's a room or something like a room under that bench. The thought came gracefully to Bud's mind. He was solving mysteries, and he was good at it. His confidence began to pick up speed, and he was well on his way to pronouncing himself a genius when he regained control. "Don't get too far ahead of yourself," he counseled in a low whisper. "Let's think about this a second," he said out loud. "There's a room hidden behind that car. Someone's been using that old car to enter and exit that space. There could be a booby trap set. Then there's the snakes. You don't have a flashlight. It's completely illegal. If I use my lighter for a flashlight, I could blow myself up. You really want to go bumbling around in the dark under that bench? What will you find? A body? Naw, I doubt that. What will you find that would make it worth the risk? A murder weapon?"

The conversation was over. Bud instantly knew any man that went to this much trouble to hide his lair had something to hide. He felt sure it was a he. Only one woman in a million would step foot in this snake riddled barn. Anticipation took control and Bud nearly broke into a run getting back to the old car. Then he stopped and took a deep breath. Okay, look for booby traps. No, he's sure of his hideout. The way it's hidden and the snakes, no one would come across this by accident. Okay, then, don't look for booby traps.

Bud opened the door. He stood back, looking inside from various angles. The front seat was still in place and the dark space under the seat looked like the kind of place he would hang out if he were a copperhead. The driver's door wouldn't open; the door handle was light and felt disconnected from the linkage. Bud found a thin tree limb and peeled away the branches until he had a coach whip sized shaft. He poked around under the seat and felt movement transfer back to his hand. He dropped the stick and put his face to the driver's door window.

The evil looking head of the snake moved lazily onto the floorboard area on the passenger's side of the car. Bud watched with chilled fascination. The snake just kept coming out from under the seat and when at last its tail came into view, Bud estimated it to be four feet long with a girth the size of his forearm. The big guy coiled into his new location and seemed content. Bud considered killing it. He could get the shovel out of the barn and chop down over the front seat, but if he missed taking the head off on his first try, he would have one big pissed off snake back under the seat. He could try and shoot it. Still, that shot would need to be perfect and firing his .357 service revolver inside the car would be painful as hell to his ears and the ringing would reduce his hearing for the rest of the day.

Bud paced a few steps looking around for someone who might offer a better idea on the situation. He had only a reasonable fear of poisonous snakes. He had killed dozens in his life, although they were much smaller than the ones he had seen here today. He glanced at his watch; it was almost 12:30 a.m.; someone was bound to show up here soon. In the construction trade, when the rain hits, you go to the bar or you go home. Bud was hoping Luther Gillman would be at a bar right now, but if a piece of equipment needed work, he might pull up to the house at any moment. Bud felt he could wait no longer. He must enter now or leave. He moved into the car. The barn wall was in shadow. He fired his lighter, extending his arm forward. He found what he was looking for, a pair of hinges that betrayed a hidden door. He worked his fingernails into the groove that outlined the doorway and it sprung open.

Bud crept forward with his lighter, straining to see into the cave-like opening. He lowered the flame to see the ground around his feet. A moment of panic raced up his spine; he was frozen in a stooped over, crouched position. His right leg began to cramp and he knew he must move fast before it locked up completely and he fell to eye level with his buddy in the front seat. In or out, you gotta move now. He decided to retreat, and who could blame him was the thought that consoled his bruised ego. One last look. He extended the fire into the darkness a little further. The white plastic coating of electrical wire illuminated itself in the tiny light. The Zippo lighter was now getting hot in his hand. His eyes traced the glowing line to where it disappeared into the darkness. He stretched and inched further. Now his left leg began to remind him that he had a bad knee. He'd all but forgotten about the knee; it hadn't bothered him for years, but now it was saying, Do you remember this? and a familiar pain returned.

There it was—a light bulb. Bud pulled the chain and a stone stairway appeared below him. He let the lighter fall—it was hot, too hot to hold. It clattered down the stone stairway into a storm cellar. Bud recognized the common style at once. The barn had been built over the old storm cellar. The space was brightly lit and clear of debris. He felt confident enough to drag himself into the stairwell, where he could at least stand up straight.

From the look of the rock and the skill with which it had been laid, the cellar was old, much older than the barn. The stairway ran parallel to the barn wall. Luther had simply built a workbench over it and enclosed the walls around the bench. At the bottom of the steps was a doorway. Bud's curiosity conquered his fear and he proceeded down the steps. Another chain came into view and when he pulled it, a small room appeared in a flood of bright light. The floor and walls and steps were made of field stones the size of suitcases hand stacked with a splash of mortar just to fill in the holes.

Now an image of the man who lived with such a woman as the one who built the flower beds sprang to mind. He would have been tall and lean, burned brown, and with slightly rounded shoulders. There would been talk of Indian blood in his ancestry. The high cheekbones and excellent teeth would have lent credit to such talk. His father and his father's father had all lived off the land successfully and each generation had passed on the lessons learned and the mental attitude and physical ability to work ten hours a day, six days a week for as long as it took.

The ceiling appeared to be made of metal road signs advertising soda and beer and cigarettes. The exterior would have been layered with steel and rock and mortar and then covered with dirt mounded like an ancient grave.

A subtle scratching sound came from within the small room. The floor was no more than six by nine feet but the ten-foot foot high ceiling with its bright colored signs made the room feel bigger. Along one long wall, crude shelving was built. A bench wide enough to lie on ran the length of the other side. At the time of its construction, the family would have had only candles for light and might have had to spend the entire night here until it was light enough to see if another storm front was moving in. It would be unpleasant, but safe; it would take a hell of a storm to suck a body out of this hole, Bud thought.

The shelves were littered with magazines of naked women. Coffee cans labeled with strips of tape with names printed on them lined the shelves. Beer bottles formed huddles everywhere and an assortment of hubcaps hung from nails hammered in between the rocks on the walls above the bench.

Bud moved slowly toward the coffee cans—the source of the scratching. The cans had ventilation holes poked around the top ring. A square of plywood with a fist-sized rock on top of it formed a lid. Bud read off the names written on the side of the cans out loud. "Elizabeth, Marilyn, Connie, Annette . . ." Bud shuddered at the thought that there might be body parts in those cans. No, those are movie star names, he thought. There's no girls missing by those names. There's no girls missing at all. Maybe they're not from around here, he argued with himself. He shook off his mental argument, annoyed at himself for wasting time. He needed to find whatever there was to find and get out.

Bud picked up the can labeled Elizabeth, gauging its weight. With the board and rock removed, he guessed its weight at only six or eight ounces—not enough for a large snake, at least not one big enough to come charging out the moment the lid was removed. Still, Bud placed the can in good light and slid the board and the rock across the top of the can just enough to peek inside. "Hah!" he let out with relief. White mice—a mother and her babies. A moment later he was repulsed at the certain knowledge of their purpose. "Damn, he's feeding the damn things." Bud's voice came back to him in an unfamiliar tone bouncing off the cave-like walls. That's why the snakes are so big and why so many big snakes can all co-exist in such a small area. A fleeting desire told him to run up the stairs, dive through the back seat of the Buick, do a forward roll, come up on the other side, and run. He pushed it down. He quickly examined the remaining cans. One was empty, the other two contained a mother and babies. Another can was labeled Luther and held what looked like a larger male mouse.

Bud wished for a law that would allow him to jail creeps just for being creeps. "Hell, that would make it too easy," he mumbled softly to himself. He scanned the cell-like space one last time. There was nothing to see. He had risked being snake bit and given himself nightmares for years to come for nothing. With one last desperate hope, he examined the hubcaps that hung on the walls for decoration. There were six of them, ornate in style like the cars they came off of. He removed them from the wall gingerly. He expected some kind of deadly spider or scorpion to live on the backside of each one. There was nothing but cobwebs and dust. There was only one left to examine.

Bud looked at his watch again. He had been here too long; he was going to be caught. He turned to the steps, then turned back. "What the hell," he said. He was thinking, If you're going to do a search, do a complete one. The weight of the last hubcap instantly told him there was something there. His rational mind told him it wasn't a copperhead coiled inside the hubcap hanging on the wall, but his nerves were shot, so when he felt the weight, he dropped the hubcap to the floor and stepped back with a jerk.

The hubcap made an ear splitting clatter on the stone floor. The revolver hidden inside bounced once and lay at Bud's feet. He stared at the gun. He felt pride at his detective skills and shame that he came so close to leaving without checking everything. He made a vow to himself to never again think about giving up on a search until every last rock had been turned over.

Bud raised the revolver from the floor on the blade of his pocket knife. It was a Smith & Wesson .357, the same standard issue pistol he carried on his hip. Now what? The thought struck him hard and eased the glee he was feeling only a second before. He lowered himself to the bench, unconcerned now with the reptiles and insects. He had a murder weapon; he was sure of that; he had never been more sure of anything. And then the thought came to his mind that it was worthless if he took it out. Time slowed; the urgency to get out was gone. Bud still held the gun swinging from trigger guard on the end of his knife blade. He had solved one of the biggest murder cases in Jefferson County history, and if he didn't do some hard thinking now, he would sink the case and look like the incompetent fool that half the county believed him to be.

And then there was Martha to consider. He couldn't let her down again. She's had faith in you so long, he thought. Don't fumble it again. A plan began to form, and as it took shape, a grin stretched its way across Bud's face. Now he felt time again and the need to move quickly ruled his actions. He examined the open end of the cylinder without getting his fingerprints on the gun. The bullet noses were gray lead wadcutter's. He laid the gun down on the bench and examined his own revolver. The guns were identical. He opened the cylinder on his weapon and removed a cartridge. It was copper jacketed. Bud considered, then dismissed, switching the rounds. There was no way of doing it without leaving his prints all over the murder weapon. Even if he had gloves, he might smear Luther's prints just enough to make them inconclusive. He would have to take the chance that Luther would not look closely at the weapon before he threw it in the river, where Bud felt sure would be its final resting place. Still, it was a big chance.

There's no other way. Bud settled his internal dispute and placed the dangling revolver on the shelf. There were scuff marks on the end of the barrel. Bud slapped the barrel of his pistol into the wall. Several more times he slapped the barrel onto the rock surface. He placed it on the floor and kicked it and ground it with his boot. The marks would be similar to the murder weapon in their location but fresh in color. Bud squeegeed his rough hands over the wood shelves and rubbed the dirt and dust on his hands all over the gun. He compared his work to its twin. It would have to do.

With his plan in mind, Bud's confidence roared back to life. This would work, he thought. He placed the forged pistol into the hubcap and replaced it on the nail where it had hung. The murder weapon was then transported on the knife blade to the furthest decorative hubcap, where Bud gingerly lowered it into its new hiding place. Now it was time to go. The near panic was on him again. This time he embraced it. He needed an adrenalin surge right now. His instincts were screaming at him to get out.

Bud pulled the chain on the bare light bulb. His legs found long forgotten power and he reached the top of the stairs in three strides. He stopped and adjusted his stance to that of an NFL linesman's and pulled the chain on the other bare bulb and headed for daylight. His left hand stabbed at the ground for balance as he tried to run in a low crouch. His fingertips raked the top of the snake's broad back and Bud knew at once what he had touched. His ankles and toes flexed like compressed coil springs and then he was out in the open, stretched out like the TV Superman two feet off the ground. Then he was on his belly sliding across the mud and the wet grass and loving it. He pushed to his feet and did a little dance, checking his legs for bite marks. There were none. "Holy shit!" he shouted.

Bud found a stick long enough to push the hidden door closed. There were no snakes to be seen. He closed the door of the Buick and walked briskly to his car, stopping twice to shiver along the way. He dropped exhausted into the luxurious comfort of the Cadillac's big seat. His desire to get away from this place took precedent over all other thought. He calculated it would take twenty seconds to turn this big boat around. Too long, he thought. He put her in reverse and poured on the gas. He then realized he had never tried to drive the car fast in reverse. This came to him just after he creased a large walnut. Not too bad, Bud thought. Probably won't be able to see it from across the street. He over-corrected and did similar damage down the other side. He slowed her down a little. Now he was out the driveway and on the blacktop. He slammed the shifter into Drive and released the breath that he had unconsciously held.

As Bud rounded the first curve, Luther Gillman's dump truck came into view. Behind the truck, a lowboy trailer carried a backhoe. Bud raised his hand to his face pretending to scratch his head. Luther tipped back the last drops of a can of beer just as he came close enough to possibly recognize Bud. The vehicles passed each other with Luther being none the wiser.

CHAPTER FIFTY-TWO

Rhonda Long tapped her foot impatiently as she blocked the doorway to Bud's office. Rhonda didn't have time for this. She had a stack of papers to go through—things that must be filed today. Lives would be changed, prisoners would spend extra days in jail, court dates would be mailed too late, bureaucratic snow would turn to avalanche. She didn't have the time or patience to walk a new kid lawyer through the system.

"How much money has your client paid you so far?" Rhonda asked.

"I don't have to disclose that information," the young man said.

"Well let's just say it's $100.00," Rhonda said. "So you put $50.00 of that money in your pocket and you take the other $50.00 down to Dr. Kelso. He does the dental work for the inmates at the jail. He'll fix your client up with some new front teeth and everyone will be happy. I'll call him and work it all out."

The kid in the cheap suit hesitated. Rhonda didn't allow him time to recover his thoughts. "Say, how long did it take you to fill out the paperwork necessary to file this suit?"

"About two hours."

"All right, then, that's $25.00 an hour. That's more than I make and a damn good start in the law business," Rhonda said as she closed the door, leaving the young lawyer in the cheap new suit on the outside. She went back to Bud's desk, where she had set up a workstation. Bud didn't like it when she took over his desk, but he never told her not to. Bud had been short with her lately and she wondered if she had put too much trust in this man. She concluded he deserved the benefit of a doubt for now. His fights with the county commission made for spicy gossip in the courthouse. The story going around lately about Bud beating up the Benders with baseball bats, and hiring thugs to help him, just put gas on the fire. Rhonda didn't ask about things. Bud told her all she needed to know without putting her in a position where she might perjure herself.

Rhonda was moving through the papers, picking out the high priority items to go in their own stack, when Bud burst in. He was wet, covered down the front in mud and grass stains. His jaw was set and he didn't smile, but there was humor in his eyes.

"I suppose there's a story to go with this scruffy appearance," Rhonda said.

"Yes, there is, and it's a dandy. One of these days I'm gonna tell it to you, but first you tell me something. If I request a search warrant to go search Luther Gillman's place, how long would it be before his daddy heard I was coming?"

"Well if I call down to the assessor's office and pretend to be confused and blurt it out before realizing I've got the wrong number, his daddy will hear about it before the judge does."

"Start the ball rolling," Bud said, "while I come up with that thing—you know, that thing."

"You mean probable cause?"

"Yeah, I'll need a minute to get me some of that."

CHAPTER FIFTY-THREE

Luther Gillman struggled to get out of the covers. He was tangled in quilts and sheets and Ramona's arms and legs. He grit his teeth at the annoying, off key ring of the wall phone. He had meant to take it off the hook before he went to bed, but now he remembered that Ramona had been eager to get started and had thrown him into bed before he could accomplish that task. It had been a full night of drinking, fighting, and fucking. He remembered now.

"Hello!" Luther shouted into the receiver.

"Luther."

Luther recognized his father's voice. "Yeah," he replied.

"Luther, don't say a thing. You just listen. The sheriff is coming out to your place today with a search warrant. Now I don't know what they're lookin' for, but I know if it's not there, they can't find it. Anything you got hid over there, no matter how well you think it's hid, you get rid of it. And if it's not there, they can't find it. I'll be over there to be sure they don't pull no tricks and I'll have my lawyer with me. And I want you gone. Don't come back until you hear from me."

Luther hung up the phone, pulled on his pants, and trotted barefoot and shirtless down the footpath to the barn. At the car door, he checked for snakes he might step on, but seeing nothing, he moved quickly to the cellar. He stuck the hidden gun into a pillowcase and came out quickly. He ran back to the house to get his truck keys. Ramona had not changed her position in the bed since he left. He gazed at her half-nude body and thought about using her again before she recovered. Her knuckles were cut and small droplets of blood stained the sheet by her hand. A bottle of pills, open and spilled, lay on the night stand. She had loosened some teeth last night in a short fight with a big girl. She took her down in four quick jabs, and Luther sucker punched her boyfriend, a small dim-witted looking fellow with oily hair and Elvis sideburns.

Luther dismissed the idea of getting a quickie with Ramona, deciding she'd still be there, probably still unconscious, when he returned. The old man had been insistent that he move fast so he pulled on some more clothes and ran to the truck. Five minutes later, he stood on the bank of the Meramec where the channel was deep, and swinging the pillowcase around and around his head, He took comfort in the splash it made when it hit the water in a deep spot.

Elmer Gillman and his lawyer, Clinton Blum relaxed on chrome kitchen chairs they had carried out to the front porch. They sat at the far edge on each end of the porch at Luther's residence. Elmer owned the house; Elmer owned the cars, the trucks, and all the equipment. Luther received a small salary and most of his bills paid. Elmer, being a shrewd man, had foreseen a time in the future when his only child, Luther, would part ways with that crazy whore he had married, and when that day came, she was not going to leave with half his business.

The center of the porch sagged to the point that the chairs were unstable if moved closer together. The roof line sagged to match the floor. Elmer cradled a pump shotgun across his lap. He could hear the small parade of cars coming twenty seconds before they came into view. The sheriff's Cadillac appeared first, followed by two county police cars.

Bud suddenly realized he had made a potentially disastrous mistake by bringing his sheriff's car back to the farm. He could see the scraped bark on the trees he had hit. The scrapes would match perfectly with the creases down each side of the car. He would have to admit to being here earlier after telling the judge he had not. He could not turn back now. That would arose even more suspicion. He came to a quick decision. A good many people in the county considered him stupid because they understood stupid and ignorant to mean the same thing. Bud played to this assumption when it suited his purpose. He stopped his car fifty yards from the house. He stepped out of the car, giving instructions and hand signals to the cars behind him.

"You boys pull up on each side of me and we all stay together as we approach," Bud shouted.

Elmer and Clinton exchanged looks reading, What a pitiful shape this county is in with this pitiful fool for its sheriff.

The cars continued forward in a tight formation. Twenty yards out, they stopped. Bud barely had room to get out Elmer and Clinton didn't try to hide their amusement. "You need some help gettin' out of your car there, Sheriff?" Elmer said.

Bud was equally amused, knowing that no one would see the scratches down each side of his car and that before the day was done, he would have the last laugh. "No, I'm okay. I just got to squeeze through here. Uh . . . what you got the shotgun for?"

"Snakes," Elmer said.

"Oh, and I see you brought your lawyer. Is he here for snakes too?"

"He's for a different kind of snake."

Bud laughed and Elmer laughed, each sure they had outsmarted the other.

The sheriff, the citizen, and the lawyer paced in the yard while the three deputies conducted the search of the house. The weather, the baseball Cardinals, the river, and the price of gas were all topics of conversation while they waited. "So you say there's a lot of snakes out here," Bud offered, trying to fill a slow, silent, awkward spot.

"Yeah, I've seen a few. Didn't have nothin' to kill 'em with at the time," Elmer said.

"Yeah, that can be frustrating."

"We're done here, Sheriff," Deputy Pratt hollered from the porch. The deputy stood on the front porch straddling the low spot.

"Find anything?" Elmer asked.

The deputy didn't respond. "Did you find anything?" the sheriff said.

"A little bag of pot and some pills."

"Put it back," Bud said. He let his head droop just a little and turned and walked toward the barn. Deputy Pratt knew better than to ask him a bunch of questions.

Elmer and Clinton smiled at each other. They sensed he was beaten. They assumed he was offering the drugs as an apology.

Bud made his way to the barn. He stood five yards out facing the junk yard side, waiting for the others to catch up. Under the shed roof, in uneven, shaky piles, a history of rural life revealed itself. Layered by the decades, tools, appliances, catalogs, furniture, and radios, all were put together in a single layer of time, and each layer came closer to the present. Bud fumbled with the button on his shirt pocket. He won the battle just as his deputy came to his side.

"How do you want to handle this?" Deputy Pratt asked.

"Station yourself along this line and be ready with your shotgun." Bud held two small packs of firecrackers, the red paper torn back enough to expose the laced fuses. Bud's Zippo produced a large yellow flame. He tossed a pack of the firecrackers toward each end of the shed. The three deputies and Elmer Gillman held twelve-gauge pumps at the ready. The crackers began to pop. Two snakes and a rabbit streaked out of the junk pile. Shotgun blasts churned the dirt. The snakes and the rabbit crossed paths and then crossed again. The men pumped shell after shell into their guns, chasing after the snakes and trying not to hit the rabbit. In the end, everything got away.

"I guess I'd go hungry if I had to depend on you boys to bring home supper," Bud said. He circled behind the group, shaking his head. The shotgunners, without saying a word, tried to blame each other. Their looks challenged the others with the question, Why didn't you hit something?

Bud went to the other side of the barn. He fished out a cigarette and gazed off toward the horizon, showing no interest in the search. Deputy Pratt appeared at his side feeding fresh shells into his shotgun. "We gonna search through that junk?" he asked.

"Let's do that last," Bud said. "You and one of the men check out the barn and what's left of the loft. I'll search this shed. Send your other man around to me and make sure he's got a working flashlight and a fully loaded shotgun." He appeared detached. He looked off and smoked and paced like a man unsure of his next move.

Elmer sensed that something was wrong. Bud kept looking his way, taking quick mental snapshots. Elmer saw pity in Bud's eyes; he knew now the pity was for him. All of Elmer's internal organs hardened at once. No measure of logic could explain his complete understanding of what was to come, but he knew that he was beaten. The slow thinking, no-nothing sheriff felt pity for him. He would take his son, but take no pleasure in it. Elmer felt some relief; he had done all he could, but now it was over and there was nothing left to do but watch. He would not interfere; he would not kill for the boy.

Deputy Peters reported for duty. He covered Bud's back while waiting for him to finish his cigarette. He was a tall, thin man with tight fitting skin on his face. His eyes were dark and sunken and his nose and chin were sharp. He carried himself in a military manner. He had no idea what was going on, but he knew that at this moment in time he had Bud Browdy's back.

Bud flipped his cigarette into a puddle and relieved the deputy of his shotgun. He approached the old car warily. From the driver's side window, he could see his old friend coiled on the floorboard on the passenger side. The door handle was missing. If he entered the car from the rear, he would be in an awkward position trying to take aim across the seat. He opened the rear door slowly; the snake seemed unconcerned. Bud moved back to his position at the window on the driver's side. He chambered a round into the gun. He took a step back and quickly raised the gun to his shoulder and blasted out the window. With planned precision, he stepped forward with the gun still at his shoulder and tipped the barrel through the window. He sent a load of No. 4 shot into the area where the snake had been. Without looking to see if he had been successful, he scurried to the back door and dropping to his knees to get low enough to be most effective, he sent three more loads of No. 4 shot under the front seat. The big snake could be seen on the passenger side floorboard twisting and writhing, its white belly turned up and around and over again. One by one, the deputies and the citizen and the lawyer and the sheriff all watched the snake go through its death throes with a mixture of fascination and disgust.

"Sheriff, there's a strange looking workbench in the barn," Deputy Pratt said.

"What's strange about it?" Bud asked.

"Well, it looks like it has a storage space underneath, but there's no door; it's sealed off."

"Where would that bench be," Bud asked, "if you was lookin' at it from out here?"

"Right around the back door of that old car," Deputy Pratt said.

"Would you take your flashlight and examine the barn wall where the lines up with this door," Bud said, pointing to Deputy Peters.

The other deputies felt a twinge of relief that they weren't asked. Peters hesitated for only a second then proceeded with the task like a soldier marching into gunfire. He duck walked his way to the barn wall. In a few seconds he hollered out, "There's a door here and there's a lightbulb and a set of stairs."

Bud leaned into the car door. "Go on down the steps and check it out. I'll send in Mr. Brown to help you."

The two men were gone only a few minutes, but Elmer Gillman counted every heartbeat while he waited. He had told the boy to get rid of anything that might hurt him. He didn't want to believe he was guilty of anything serious, but if he was, would he have had the good sense to get rid of any evidence knowing a search was coming? Yes, yes, he would. No one could be that dumb. Elmer battled his doubts as the seconds dragged on.

"We're coming out." Deputy Pratt's voice carried from the cellar. The two men emerged from the car. Deputy Pratt held a revolver swinging upside down on an ink pen.

Elmer Gillman turned white right before everyone's eyes and crumpled to the ground-dead.

CHAPTER FIFTY-FOUR

Luther awoke shivering. There was a heavy dew and Ramona had pulled the blankets and the tarp off him in her sleep. He adjusts his position and re-covers himself. The boat begins to rock, making manmade noises and the night sounds along the river quiet just a little. He turns onto his back. The sky is clear, the stars are the same, his life is forever changed. His father is dead. Each time this reality bursts into his consciousness, his breath is chopped short and his eyes well up and fat tears roll out.

He is on the run. He has only a little money. Ramona is driving him crazy. He could bash her in the head right now and push her into the river and be done with her silly ass. The thought of killing her brings on a reaction that surprises him. He had, of course, thought of killing her in the past, but only out of anger. When the anger passed, his desire to kill her passed as he knew it would. But now, her death may become a necessity, even serve a purpose. The thought of killing her for real excites him. Luther had no illusions of going to Mexico with a sack of money and living like a king. He had no problem, however, convincing Ramona of that plan. She was eager to go anywhere. The week they had spent together on the river moving from one hiding spot to the next, living on lunch meat sandwiches and beer had taken a toll on their relationship.

Luther Gillman knew his chances of escape were slim at best. He had to have money. He stayed in the area hoping to get some money through his father's attorney. The bastard wouldn't help. He advised that Luther give himself up and accept a life term in exchange for a guilty plea. "The bastard,"

Luther whispered to himself. If I'm killed or plead guilty, there's no trial. None of what should have been my inheritance is spent to defend me. He wants me dead. That would make it even easier to milk Dad's estate until it's gone. That's why he told me he could get me life. If he had really wanted to lure me in for my own good, he would have said he could get me a ten year deal. He would explained it real sweet so that it made good sense. That's what he would have done if he had my best interests at heart.

The sudden possibility of killing the lawyer, too, sent a jolt of pleasure across the curve of his brain. The two men he had killed in the past had only been fun in the memory of the act. The killing of the deputy came as a surprise even to Luther. He had confronted the man about his involvement with Ramona and only struck out when the bastard sneered and turned his back on him. The next thing he knew he was emptying the deputies own gun into his back. He had not been sure he could do it even the second time. When he killed the kid water hauler, he had intended to just put a scare into him. But in the end the desire to kill overcame reason. Now he was free to enjoy the preparations. Ramona was dead for sure, but not until the last. He would use her and keep her high, but always keep her close, and if he had only a few minutes before he was to be killed or captured, he would have a little fun with Ramona. After all, this was her fault.

Luther felt the full weight of his ugly thoughts. A hopeless depression pushed the violent sexual daydream to the side. There were now just two choices in his future—death or prison. The number of days left until he had to make that choice was growing short. He considered his options. He had his truck; he had a boat; he had a rifle. He had to have money to run. He must have enough not only to get him down the road, but to get him re-settled. Pulling a holdup locally would improve his chance of success, he thought. He knows the roads and he knows who has the money. The plan begins to form. He'll need to hit more than one place to get enough money to do the job. A string of three works best.

Luther watches the stars move across the night sky. Everything's the same as it was just six days ago. Yet nothing in his life would ever be the same again. The anger and the need to make others suffer returned. The sheriff needed killing. He planted that gun. But the lawyer said the ballistics proved it was the gun used to kill the deputy and the Boman boy, and Luther's were the only fingerprints on the gun. How did he find that gun in the river and replace it so fast? Even if he had somehow watched him throw it in, even if he had Mike Nelson waiting in the weeds, he could not have recovered it and taken it back to its hiding spot before his father and the lawyer got there.

The answer came slowly and with it, his desire for revenge grew. The bastard planted the gun I pitched. The bastard cheated. He can't do that. He set me up. I voted for him. His fury increased. There's nothing lower than a cop that don't play by the rules, he thought.

The number of people he wished to kill before his luck ran out kept growing. Like a host making out a party list, Luther had at first tried to keep the party small, but when he thought about it, money was no object, and the more people you have around you who need killing, the larger your total score will be. He would find a way to make the sheriff come to his party. A new plan began to form. Win, lose, or draw, no one in this county would ever forget his name.

CHAPTER FIFTY-FIVE

Al Creed examined the steering cables on his just purchased used boat. They'll need replacing and they're hard to get to. He was glad he didn't have to do it. "This is going to be a pain in the ass," he said to Byron. Byron worked on the motor and nodded his head.

"Yeah, I looked at 'em yesterday. They won't be that bad. I can do it."

Byron scraped carbon off the top of the outboard motor's pistons. Al had picked up the little rig cheap, a deal set up by Larry and his notorious little black book. Byron took one look at the motor and just knew the prop was too big. He took some measurements and made some calls and was proved right. He also assumed that a two stroke motor working at too much load would never reach its proper rpm and therefore be carboned up in the combustion chamber. He was right again.

Al reclined on the boat's red vinyl seat with a mug of coffee in one hand and a cigarette in the other. He soaked up the early morning spring sun, the sun that never lives up to expectation. It hits you with a spotlight of instant heat only to fade too quickly. The sun popped out again and Al looked straight into it with his eyelids painting a crimson landscape that flowed like lava down the side of a volcano. He accepted his good fortune like a convict accepts his last meal. No matter how good the meal, you know things will take a turn for the worse soon.

Al reflected on his life and concluded that yes, that has been the pattern so far. Byron's transformation has been the most miraculous thing to ever happen in his life. He is sure that something bad must happen to keep the universe in balance.

Byron passed his State test on his first try. His high school equivalency diploma hung proudly in the living room above the television. Byron would start a two-year course at Rankin Technical School in the fall. He wants to be a diesel mechanic. Al said the words in his mind—a diesel mechanic. Had the boy been a piano prodigy and pledged to become a concert pianist, he could not have been prouder. Al beamed his joy and pride toward Byron. Byron felt the energy and looked up with bored eyes. "You just gonna sit there with that sappy smile on your face all day?" he asked.

"I can if I want to." Al grinned back.

"I'd like to take this boat out before the river freezes." Byron pitched the cylinder head into the boat in mock frustration.

Al cackled softly, unwilling to let the moment pass too quickly. His grin widened and his satisfaction deepened. "I'm glad to have you here, son," he said. They had talked very little about the time Byron had spent in the trailer. The subject was at first too painful for Byron to ponder. It brought on nightmares and moodiness. Then at some point any discussion of the trailer days, as they had come to be known, took its toll on Al more and on Byron less.

"Glad to be here," Byron said. His words were stuttered and unrehearsed.

Al would not let go. He held on to every second of this time and place.

"If you keep sitting around looking at me with that silly grin on your face, I'm gonna put you in a home. I swear I will. I'm gonna find a nuthouse that will take you, and I'm gonna find one that looks just like the inside of a trailer."

Al cackled with contentment. Byron would be all right. There was no mistaking the sounds. There was a new force propelling him; a will to succeed replaced the defeatist attitude that Byron had lived by just six months ago. Would he have come this far on his own if just given a little more time? This was an ongoing debate in Al's subconscious mind. He could not be happier with Byron's behavior. The boy was going to make out all right with or without him, Al believed.

"You're the one that said you could fix it," Al said.

"I can fix it all right, but I thought you were gonna do more than just sit there and take pretend boat rides while watching me work."

Al enjoyed the banter. "Okay, how about I cut the old cables out and get them out of your way. Will that be enough work, Captain Bligh?"

"That'll do for now, you scurvy dog."

Al grunted to his feet, at last ready to do a little work.

"Who do you think paid my tuition at Rankin?" Byron asked.

"Hell if I know, and don't care. I know when something good in life comes along, you better take advantage of it. I would have paid for it, you know. I'd have found a way, but it would have been hard and I'm gettin' tired of hard. If someone else wants to pay for it, then it's okay with me."

"Well I'd kinda like to know who I'm indebted to," Byron said.

"Hand me them bolt cutters and I'll tell you again how it works. The sheriff, he comes by the station last Friday night and he don't even get out of his car. He just pulls up to me and says that a business group in Arnold has picked you to give their scholarship award to this year." Al snipped a cable with the bolt cutters and the outboard snapped around. Byron pulled his hands out before they were smashed.

"Did he say what business group? Who are these people?"

"That's just it. They don't want you to know. They just want you to do well. I don't know, probably live by some code—maybe the Boy Scout code. I'm sure that'll work. If you want to show your appreciation to whoever's doing this, I'm sure the Boy Scout code will do. So there you go, you just have to live your life according to the Boy Scout code and your debt is paid. How's that?"

"I can do the honest and the helpful stuff. It's the courteous and friendly that's tough. You see, I haven't had a good role model."

Al squeezed the bolt cutters and the outboard slammed back. Byron pulled back, again saving himself from a smashed finger. Al held the bolt cutters up in a menacing pose ready to strike down on Byron's head. "You saying I'm not courteous and friendly?"

"Oh, shut up and get out of there before you fall," Byron said. "I mean it—I'm gonna start looking for a nuthouse if you don't straighten up. As soon as I'm out of school, I'm putting you away, old man."

"Well that'll be fine with me. I doubt there'll be much left of me by then." The statement had a sobering effect on the light mood. The cancer growing in his throat made the future a difficult thing to plan. When at last he had to have it cut out, he would lose his voice box. The diagnosis was clear; the day would come when he would never speak normally again. He would postpone that day for as long as possible. He was having trouble swallowing lately. Was the cancer growing again or was it just a regular sore throat?

"What are you going to do about your throat?" Byron asked.

"I had it looked at. It's gonna be okay." They both knew he was lying.

"When are we gonna go get me a car?" Byron asked.

"Not till August. The longer we wait and save, the better car we can afford."

"August. Three more months." Byron picked up a ragged copy of a shop manual. He thumbed the pages to find the chart he needed. "I don't know if I can wait that long."

Al didn't reply. He had resumed his position in the sun in the boat, watching his son decipher the confusing charts and tables and the number degrees before top dead center and a bunch more crap no one could understand. Byron could read it and understand it. Al swelled with pride. How things had changed between them in such a short time. He looked around in all directions for the house that would surely drop from the sky and crush them both.

"I could get you one now, but all we could afford is a six cylinder, but if we wait, what with the money you make at Floyd's and what I can put in, we could get one of those big old fire breathers—maybe a 427 with three deuces on top."

Byron was sucked into the daydream momentarily. "Would you shut up." He threw the shop manual at Al. He blocked his head with his arms as the book fluttered past.

"And you'll need lots of tires. You'll burn a set off every week. Course I'll pay for them too. And rubbers. You'll need lots and lots of rubbers always. Always keep the glove box full of rubbers."

Byron climbed into the boat. Al retreated to the open bow, holding a boat cushion up in defense. "It's better to have 'em and not need 'em than need 'em and not have 'em." Al continued his taunt.

Byron sparred with Al, trying to get a clear shot at his shoulder. Al used the foam cushion like a Roman shield. He ran out of breath quickly and surrendered, taking a punch to the shoulder. "Ow," he said as the punch hurt more than he expected.

"What's this about me working at Floyd's?" Byron asked.

"Oh, didn't I tell you? Floyd's gonna give you another try."

"No, you didn't tell me." Byron cocked his arm for another punch.

"Don't, damn it! That hurt."

"Oh quit your whining. You didn't bitch this much when I shot you."

"That's because you're a crummy shot."

CHAPTER FIFTY-SIX

"Why do I have to go?" Ramona asked. Ramona pouted in Luther's boat. She wouldn't look at him. Luther stood in the weeds on the bank of the Meramec where it cuts its path through the little town of Fenton, Missouri. Up the bank and across the road, a nightclub called The River's Edge had two outdoor pay phones that cannot be seen from the road.

"I just want you to come with me, that's all," Luther said.

"You promised me a motel room. I been sleeping and eating and fucking and shitting in this god damn boat for a week. Now you better do something quick." Ramona's voice carried well and had an edge that could force the Pope to tighten his fist.

Luther carried a Winchester lever action 30-30 close against his leg. The gun was hidden to the casual eye. He hefted its weight and took comfort in the knowledge that her time would come soon. "Please, honey, just do what I ask. I'm gonna get us a whole house. I figured out a place we can go and it's a big house with hot showers and clean sheets and a refrigerator full of food."

Ramona's mind plodded through the fractured memories of the past week. Her brain had been awash in whiskey and pills. She was having trouble separating dreams from reality. She had stopped drinking yesterday and had only three pills last night. She was thinking clearly now. Her lack of sleep took a higher toll on her reasoned thought process than she knew. The prospect of a hot shower and a clean bed made her want t shout out Who do I have to kill? Instead, she just said, "Okay."

They were both bug bit and sun burned. Ramona scrambled up the bank, scraping her bare legs. "Huck Finn can kiss my ass," she shouted at Luther.

"You think you could be any louder?" Luther scolded.

"Aw, there ain't nobody around."

"Walk on this side of me." Luther took her by the arm and they crossed the road. No cars came past.

"When we going to the house?" Ramona asked.

"Soon as I'm through here. Keep an eye on the road while I make this call."

Ramona reluctantly did her job. She glanced over Luther's shoulder and watched as he slid dirty fingers down the pages of the phone book. He stopped his search at the Sheriff's Department. He dropped a quarter in the slot and dialed the number. Ramona tried to make sense of his actions but could think of nothing. She knew he would not be giving himself up. She also knew it was time for her to go. The reasoned thought did battle with the selfish need. She would stay a little longer, at least until she got a hot shower and a clean bed. She did not look forward to a future in the hands of the sheriff's department. She would, of course, say she knew nothing of the two murders and there would be no proof to say she did because she never did know for sure, but yet she knew. She would say he forced her to come with him. They had committed no crime together so they would have to let her go. But how long would they keep her and how many times would she be questioned, and without her whiskey. She pulled a pint bottle out of her back pocket and took a snort to ward off bad luck.

If Luther doesn't produce this house, he's going down, she thought. I'm not spending another night on that boat, not ever. She visualized her plan. He'll turn his back on me again. He keeps that rifle close. He thinks he's holding me. She saw herself swinging the six foot paddle that lay in the bottom of the boat. She saw herself with a two-handed grip on the end of the paddle the way she held a splitting maul in her youth. She saw the edge of the paddle striking the back of Luther's neck as he leaned over the side of the boat.

"Hello," Luther said into the receiver. "Could I speak to the sheriff, please."

Ramona is shaken from her daydream. She took another snort from her bottle as her curiosity peaked. Luther was using a fake voice. He was calling the sheriff using a fake voice. Ramona took another snort trying to make sense of his actions.

"Okay," Luther said. "Could you give him a message?" Luther covered the receiver and coughed a little. He continued with the raspy voice he'd been faking. "Tell himAl Creed called and Floyd has got a new set of radial tires for the sheriff's car. He can try them out and see if he likes them. Tell him to come by the station tonight about 7 and we'll put them on for him—for free that is."

Rhonda Long scribbled the information on a note pad. "Okay, I'll tell him," she said.

Luther hung up the receiver. He turned and Ramona was in his face. "That was the worst fake voice I ever heard. That didn't sound at all like Al Creed's voice. I've heard Al Creed's voice and that was a bad impersonation." Ramona stood firm, glaring into Luther's eyes. She had the absolute certainty of her position that can only be acquired with whiskey poured into a tired, empty stomach.

"So," Luther said, "not wanting to create a scene." He pushed past her and walked toward the boat.

Ramona was wrong and confused much of the time. She so seldom had the opportunity to rub her rightness into his smug, I-know-everything face that she could not pass on this occasion. "Whatever you got planned ain't gonna work. You know I'm right on this. That did not sound like Al Creed." Ramona cocked her hip and jutted her jaw. By god, she was right about this and demanded that Luther humble himself to her superior intellect.

Luther steadied his impulse to swing up the rifle and fire. The gunshot would not attract much attention; people often shot from their boat around here. He could drop her in her tracks the way a buffalo drops in the movies. Maybe if she said one more word, his indecision might go the other way. Luther could not say. He knew he was close. "Honey, it don't matter. The gal I talked to has most likely never met Al Creed, but the sheriff has, so she'll give him the message and she'll say that the guy had a gravely voice. And the sheriff will say, 'How do you mean?' And the secretary will say, 'He sounded like he needed to cough something up.' And the sheriff will say, 'He sounds like that all the time,' and then they'll both go about their business and my plan will work."

Ramona took another snort from her pint bottle. "Damn," she said softly. She had thought sure she had him this time. So she made a new demand. "Tell me the plan or I'm not moving."

Luther was at a crossroads again. She still cleaned up good. If he could just stand her until he could get her showered and get a couple of Qualudes down her, he could ride her one last time and then kill her and dump her out on the side of the road, maybe somewhere in Oklahoma. I bet they got some back roads in Oklahoma, he thought.

"Baby, if you'll just trust me a little longer, we're going to a real nice house right now."

"Who's house?" Ramona demanded.

"My old man's lawyer's house."

"He's gonna let us use his house?" Ramona asked.

"He's not letting us use it. He won't be home."

"How do you know he won't be home?"

"Because the last thing I said to him was to stay close in case I needed him. And because I know he's a crook and he wants me dead or in jail, I know he's left town and won't be back until he thinks it's safe."

"But what if he didn't leave? What if he's still home?"

"We can find that out in about thirty minutes."

Luther could see he had hit a soft spot. The thirty minute estimate cut through the fog of Ramona's thinking. She could comprehend thirty minutes. That was only six songs on the jukebox. She took another snort. She could be standing in a hot shower in the time it takes to hear a couple of Elvis tunes and a Patsy Cline hit or two. "Okay. Are we going to the truck right now?"

"Right now," Luther said.

CHAPTER FIFTY-SEVEN

Luther cruised past the lake house nice and slow. He had his arm out the window and the radio playing. He was just an average Joe driving by the lake. He made Ramona crunch down on the floorboard. "How long I gotta stay like this?" she asked.

"Just till we get around the corner." Luther had no idea whether they would attract more attention as a couple or as a man alone, but he enjoyed putting Ramona on the floorboard. He had been to this house with his father years ago and remembered the lot was heavily wooded on the north side. The greedy bastard had purchased two extra lots to protect his privacy. Probably stole them, Luther thought. He turned off the road onto an overgrown gravel driveway of the adjoining lot. "Okay, you can get up now," he said.

"I can't. My leg's asleep. Come around and open the door."

"Okay."

"Are you coming? Hurry up. This hurts."

"I'm coming." Luther circled the truck, stopping at the tailgate. He waited for Ramona to plead again.

"Damn it, Luther, hurry up!" Ramona screeched.

When Ramona was limber enough to walk, they picked their way through the trees and brush to the edge of the freshly mowed lawn. The lower level of the home was exposed on three sides. The north end offered concealment and a large window. They would be exposed to neighborhood eyes for only as long as it took to cover a hundred feet of grass.

"Put your head on my shoulder and your arm around my waist," Luther said. He held his rifle vertically behind his back. "Okay, let's go—fast. But not too fast."

They reached the cover of the house and Luther examined the window for wires or switches. He broke the glass with the stock of his rifle the way he had seen done a thousand times. He opened the window and they easily climbed through. They listened for any movement upstairs. The room was covered in knotty pine planks—walls and ceiling. Thick, green shag carpeting covered the floor. An eight-foot bar of knotty pine and behind it large shelves laden with every type of the most highly prized alcoholic beverages imaginable stood at the far end of the room. A sitting area with a TV on a rolling cart and a steel-framed sofa and chair with bright orange broadcloth cushions completed the room. A set of stairs broke the two rooms apart.

Luther was confident he had been right in his assessment. He jogged up the stairs and made a quick search of the house. "Come on up," he shouted from the top of the stairs.

Ramona eagerly complied. When she reached the top of the stairs, she searched out the master bath and locked herself in. She started the hot water running into the tub before dropping her pants and taking her position on the porcelain throne.

Luther went to the kitchen. He looked for a little tray or a bowl or a board with hooks on it or a small drawer. On top of the refrigerator, a large porcelain bowl looked empty. He raked his hand into it and scooped out a set of keys. He ran to the garage. A freshly waxed Buick Skylark sparkled under the bare bulbs of the garage. He rushed to try to keys. He found one that fit. The motor turned over once and came to life. It idled so smoothly, Luther revved the engine to make sure it was still running. The odometer read a little over eighteen thousand miles. His spirits began to rise. With a new car that wouldn't even be reported stolen for a few days, his plans suddenly seemed possible. Maybe he wouldn't have to die. He could rob Floyd's and kill the sheriff and get away with it. The thought of success was tempting. There are still a lot of things to go wrong, his inner voice cautioned.

Ramona finished her business and swooned in the luxury of tissue paper. She heard something. No, she could feel more than hear the sound of a car motor being revved up. The tub was only a third full and her curiosity drove her to search for the source of the vibrations. She tiptoed down the hallway wearing only her bra and panties. Above the home's thermostat, another plastic box filled with switches and lights decorated the hallway wall. She took casual notice as she passed and speculated it was only some kind of intercom system. God forbid these rich pricks would have to holler down the steps to say it was time to eat, she thought.

Ramona found her way to the garage. Luther was walking around a shiny new car kicking the tires like he was thinking of buying it. "Come in here and fix some food while I take my bath," Ramona said. She scratched at the bug bites that dotted every crevice of her body. On her way to the tub, she strolled through the formal living room. The sofa felt like velvet, the curtains like silk, the carpet is new and thick and soft. Ramona did a twirl around the room, doing her best impersonation of Julie Andrews in The Sound of Music. She came out of one of her spins at the front door. She flamboyantly took hold of the door knob and swung the door open in time with a waltz playing in her head. She gazed out on her castle grounds, closed the door, and spun away to the royal bathtub.

As Ramona danced down the hall, she saw the two red lights in the intercom box were now flashing. She suddenly remembered that she was almost out of whiskey. The well stocked bar in the rathskeller should solve that problem. She would bet a million dollars there was a bottle of Crown Royal on one of those shelves behind the bar. The image of herself in a hot soapy tub nipping on Crown Royal caused her to change directions. She could hear Luther in the kitchen looking for food. She crept down the steps and there it was—a quart of Crown Royal in the decorative decanter. She uncorked the bottle and took two large swallows. She sighed with relief, suddenly thinking, Luther might not want me to have this, he might try to take it. Drink it down now. You're just gonna go sit in a tub. What can it hurt? Luther may want you to drive. Fuck Luther. She took two more large swallows.

Luther began shouting her name. "What?" she shouted back.

"Where are you?"

"I'm downstairs."

"Hey, was those lights in the hallway flashing before?" Luther yelled down. Ramona sloshed down another drink.

"Well, were they?"

"I don't know." Ramona took one more slug just for good measure. She would go to her bathtub now. She was steady at the bottom of the stairs. She gripped the handrail tightly. One foot at a time, she coached herself. When she reached the last step, her heart rate had reached a thousand beats per minute. She was zooming.

The telephone rang and Luther dropped his rifle, his nerves on edge. It rang again. He couldn't think. They must have tripped an alarm. He answered the phone after the third ring. "Hello," he said in his most jolly voice.

"This is Viking Security. We have an alarm light at your residence. Is everything okay?" the voice asked.

"Yes, everything's okay. I'm just over here cuttin' Mr. Blum's grass. He's a nice fella and he give me a key to let myself in so I could get a Coke. I was supposed to turn the burglar alarm off first and I forgot."

"I'll need the four digit code to cancel this alarm," a droning, bored, female voice said.

"Yeah, I got that wrote down in my wallet and it's out in the car. I'll go get it and call you right back." Luther hung up the phone. "We got to go," he said to Ramona.

Ramona ignored his demand and staggered away. "I'm taking a bath." Her voice was weak and her words were slurred.

Luther knew at once she was smashed. His composure came apart and he flew into her swinging two open hands. Ramona's balance and reflexes were shot. She suffered half a dozen hard, popping slaps. She aimed a kick at his crotch but missed by a mile. She could see herself now on the floor being slapped and beaten. Her nose bled onto her upper lip. She could do nothing. She curled into a ball and covered her head. Luther stepped over her and went to the bathroom. He came back with her purse. "Go get in the car," he ordered.

Ramona whimpered on the floor. The world was spinning faster than she could ever remember it spinning. Her hurt and sorrow and anger swam in a pool of blended whiskey liqueur. Luther pulled her to her feet by her hair. She did not try to resist. Luther gripped her arm and guided her to the car. He pushed her into the backseat and ordered her to lie down. He raised the garage door and drove slowly away. Ramona sniffled for a few minutes and then passed out. Her breathing was ragged and she snored and belched and gagged and coughed.

Now might be the time, Luther thought. He could just drive out on a back road, drag her out of the car, shoot her, and drive away. She had become nothing but a liability. He considered which back road might fit his needs when the beautiful neon lights of a Dog & Suds drive-in restaurant appeared. He would eat and think.

CHAPTER FIFTY-EIGHT

Floyd's Tire Mart celebrated its fifth year anniversary. The celebration took place three months early of the actual date so as not to miss the spring tire season. The pump islands and the face of the stone building gleamed in fresh white paint. The streamers of multi-colored, triangular shaped flags formed a canopy over the driveway. Along the edge of the drive, a snow cone cart and a popcorn cart and a hotdog cart and a fountain soda cart attracted much attention. Each cart was separated from the next by huge stacks of display tires.

The whole crew was called upon to handle the crowd. Byron Creed was added to the crew that very day. Floyd, Brad, and Ike gave him the cold shoulder at the start. Leon had agreed to give Al's troubled son another chance. There was still a mystery about the events the day Al went home sick and Ike and Al were rolling in the drive with their pants around their knees. Floyd was sure he would hear the whole story eventually. He was willing to wait. As far as he could tell, he had lost no money and business was better than he had ever dared to hope for.

People say the boy has straightened up, Floyd mused on the situation while watching Byron fuel a pickup. The other boys don't like him, but we'll see, Floyd thought. If he does his job, he'll get along.

Brad begins the day on the tire changer. He has slowly and patiently mastered the art of peeling tires. His short, stocky build is an advantage. The steel wheels clang and rattle as they are dropped onto the spindle of the changer. The floor shakes and dust arises when they are bounced out of the door ready for the lug nuts. Brad pushes pedals and twists the stripper bar and flips them over and wrestles them until they accept air, and out the door they go.

"Twelve tires in less than an hour," Brad said. The boys were standing in a loose group out on the driveway.

"Not bad," Leon said, "for a moron."

Brad accepted the compliment. He had expected nothing less. "How's the new boy doing?" he asked.

"Who, oh, you mean deadeye?"

Ike was within hearing range and stifled a laugh, making a snorting sound. Each boy made his own attempt at restraint. The momentary lull in the action was over. Cars were coming into the driveway like planes dropping onto the deck of an aircraft carrier.

Byron had heard the question and answer and squeezed away a grin of his own. They were all pumping gas and washing windshields across from each other, avoiding eye contact. Ike and Byron worked on opposite sides of a Chevy wagon. As they wiped away the bug juice, their hands stabbed together. "Sorry," Byron said.

"Sorry about what? Robbing me or shooting at me?"

The hubbub of barefoot children running from cart to cart, squealing in anguish over spilled snow cones drowned out their conversation.

"I never shot at you," Byron said.

"Well that's not much comfort when you're handling guns, deadeye," Ike said.

Brad and Leon cackled from the other side of the pump. Floyd saw and heard part of what was being said. He walked closer to the scene and in his most businesslike demeanor said, "I need two men to pull the rear wheels off that Ford pickup when you get caught up."

"Me and Brad will get it," Leon shouted.

Floyd turned to go, then stopped like he had a new idea. He turned back to Leon and said, "No, I want you and . . ." He looked from man to man as if he were picking his daughter's prom date, then with a stab of his hand, he pointed at Byron and said, "Deadeye." He had no idea what the name referred to, but it sure made the boys laugh. Byron would be Deadeye from now on if he makes it, Floyd thought.

The last car of the last rush ding-dinged off the lot. Al Creed shuffled into the showroom and wasted no time attaching a cup of coffee and a cigarette to either hand. He had by now heard Byron referred to as Deadeye a dozen times. Even a customer used the name when pointing at him. It was too late to ask the boys not to call him that. He would have to plead ignorance as to its origin.

There were four mag wheels stacked next to the changer. Floyd would want him to mount them. The changer was not designed to mount these new fancy wheels and pry bars and flashlights and crawling on your knees to see and pushing from your knees and twisting your neck and back were all requirements to mount the tires without busting the wheels.

"Mags." Al spat the word out like a nasty taste in his mouth.

CHAPTER FIFTY-NINE

Bud Browdy left his office at 6:30 p.m. It was not unusual for him to be working so long, but lately he had been trying to get home earlier. He no longer felt the need to take care of every detail; he was a success. His crime-solving abilities were the talk of the county. Car thefts were down and bar fights were down. He would not only be re-elected, he would probably win by a landslide. That's what everyone else says. Bud believed them. If that wasn't enough, Martha was pregnant. Glory be! he thought. Bud had had the body work done on his sheriff's car and tomorrow he would drive Martha to St. Louis in a freshly painted Cadillac. And if all this wasn't enough to make a man happy, he was on his way to have new radial tires put on. The story was that these new tires turn every car into a sports car. Bud was very excited and ver happy about the baby too. He had heard you could drive just as fast on wet roads as on dry ones with radials.

Luther Gillman's name popped into Bud's thoughts. Since the day Elmer dropped dead, Luther's name had been his constant companion. The last few days he had thought about him less. The boy was on the run. He'll most likely be picked up in Texas or California worn out and hungry.

They say you don't even need snow tires—that these radials even go in the snow. Floyd's Tire Mart came into view. The place had a carnival atmosphere. Cars and pickups waited their turns on the side of the road to get to the pumps. Four cars balanced on jack stands covered the north end of the lot. The pumps were covered and a constant stream of children and adults scurried from the drive with bags of popcorn, hotdogs, and paper cups of soda.

Bud parked at the northern edge of the lot and walked toward the circus. Byron caught his eye and he was once again reminded that he had promised to keep a lookout on the boy. The boy looks like he's doing fine. Another good job I did, Bud thought.

Luther Gillman parked just south of the blacktop. He could easily spot the sheriff's car from this distance without being noticed. The moment he recognized it, he idled the stolen Skylark around the back of the station. He needed to be in place when the sheriff discovered he had no free radials waiting for him. The movement of the car awoke Ramona from her stupor. "Where are we?" she grumbled.

"We're on our way to Mexico," Luther said. "There's a chili dog and a root beer in this bag up here if you want it."

Luther parked the car and took the keys and the rifle. "I'll be right back," he said before running off.

This must be the big plan, Ramona thought. She wasn't sure of her location. She watched Luther jog along a high plank fence to the back of a long, low building. She could hear the ding-ding of the driveway bell and guessed that this was the tire place. At the moment, she didn't care. She rubbed at the deep red ditch that ran across her face, the result of sleeping on vinyl seats. She still wore nothing but her bra and panties. She examined herself to see if Luther had used her in her sleep, a practice she found disgusting, but still it was better than being awake.

Ramona clutched at the paper bag containing the root beer and chili dog. The bag slipped, and as she caught it, she squeezed too hard and the plastic lid popped off. She stretched over the top of the front seat to reach the glove box where a napkin might be found. A big, blue, double-action revolver reflected soft light from the glove box light bulb. Had it been a cottonmouth with fangs displayed, it could not have startled her more. The gun was not the worry—it was what she might do if she picked it up. She moved her hand toward the weapon slowly, her cowardly side pleading with her to leave it alone, to do nothing that would interfere with her supply of whiskey and pills. Her defeated side berated her for what she had become and demanded that she put the gun to her head quickly and put an end to this.

Luther Gillman believed his luck had changed. When he had called the courthouse that morning, he had no knowledge of the big anniversary celebration going on at Floyd's. He only knew that Floyd pumped a lot of gas and there was a lot of cash in small bills lying around. He also knew Al Creed worked there and could be used to set the trap. He had watched for Bud's arrival long enough to see that Floyd's was doing at least triple its normal business. He took that as a sign that either god or luck or the devil had not abandoned him.

Luther steadied himself outside the back door of the tire showroom. He peered in through the corner of the window in the top half of the door. The cold currents of revenge stiffened his neck and shoulders. He anticipated the look of shock and helplessness on Bud's ugly face, the look his father must have worn when the planted gun was brought out. He knew his father's last thoughts must have been, I told the stupid fucker to get rid of the evidence. He could plainly hear his father's voice saying the words over and over again.

Al Creed entered the showroom from the driveway. He was followed by Bud Browdy. "Well I know I didn't make no calls. Maybe Floyd knows somethin'," Al said.

Luther slid in the door just after they passed and in three quick steps he was right behind the sheriff. He swung the short rifle overhand and brought the barrel down across the back of Bud's head. He intended only to stun the bastard, but if he struck too hard and it killed him, it was no big deal. He would just give his revenge speech to whoever happened to be there.

The blow sent Bud lurching forward. He plowed into Al and they both went down. Floyd heard the grunts and thuds of falling bodies and came to the office door. A thin, dirty, greasy man pointed a lever action rifle at his chest. Al recovered enough to see what was going on. He couldn't believe it; he was being robbed again.

A tooth grinding pain screamed in the back of Bud's head. The brain could focus on nothing but the pain. Al helped Bud to a sitting position. Bud's hands covered the spot where a knot was beginning to rise. "That's just fine. Keep your hands right there," Luther said. "You get the money out here and put it on the counter."

Floyd moved fast. He had paid handsomely, he thought, for insurance for just this occasion. The sooner he gets the money, the sooner he's gone, he thought. He saw his priorities very clearly. He dumped an armload of small bills wrapped in rubber bands on the counter. "The money clips," Luther said, pointing the rifle at Floyd and Al. "Now call the others in." Luther directed the order at Floyd.

Floyd went to the door and called each man by name. "Come in here right away," he shouted.

Byron was first through the door and he comprehended the situation at once. He turned to Al for confirmation. Al shrugged his shoulders. One by one, the men came in, unable to see the gun toter until it was too late. "Money clips on the counter and get over there with the others." Luther repeated the phrase several times in a sing-song fashion. "You." He pointed at Al. "Get him on his feet and don't get near his gun if you want to live. Sheriff, you just keep those hands on your head."

Al raised Bud to his feet from one side; Floyd helped from the other. Floyd stood closest to the handgun that Bud wore on his right hip. He could not help but look at it and think what if. "Go ahead," Luther dared him.

Floyd shook his head. "Take the money," he said. He hoped that he had sent a message to his men not to risk their lives over this.

"Put it in a bag," Luther said. He liked working with Floyd. He was fast and efficient.

"Okay, here you go," Floyd said, placing a brown paper bag full of money on the counter.

Luther ignored Floyd's offering. He held a hard stare on Bud Browdy. "Clear a path," he ordered with a wave of the gun. He wanted a full length view of Bud Browdy. He wanted to put a round in his gut. "You cheated. You would have never caught me if you'd played fair."

"You're right. I shouldn't have done that," Bud said. The time had come; he must go for his gun. The crazy bastard was about to shoot him and from fifteen feet away, he wouldn't miss if he didn't move. To move in any direction meant using other people as cover. If you are shot, the others will be at his mercy. The debate in Bud's mind covered various ethical points of view and would have made a thick, dry book, and it all took place in Bud's mind in less than a second.

The irony of his impending fatherhood being cut short just like another failed business venture did not go unnoticed either. He made a decision; he would go for his gun, but before his brain could push the go button, Ramona Gillman stepped through the tire room door wearing only a bra and panties. Dark eyes peered out of blackened sockets. Crusted blood ringed her nostrils, wild stalks of hair stood out in all direction. She whipped up a pistol in a two-handed grip, the tip of the barrel almost touching Luther's head, and fired in one smooth motion. Luther Gillman's picture tube went out. A hollow point exits the barrel of a three-inch .357 at 1300 feet per second. Sound travels at 1180 feet per second. Luther's brain was turned to mush before the sound waves entered the air.

Everyone jerked at the harsh crack of the gun in the small room. Bud was the first to recover. "Put the gun on the floor."

Ramona did not hesitate. She laid the pistol down and stepped back. "I figured shootin' him when I did would get me some special consideration."

"You figured right, honey. Saving my life will get you a free pass every time. How can I help you?"

"I don't want to go to jail right now. Could you get me a motel room and some food?"

"Hell, yes, girl. I'm sorry you had to do that, but I'm glad you did. You haven't killed anyone else, have you?" Bud asked.

"No."

"I didn't think so. So you get some rest and I'll have a deputy take you to a motel and get you a hot meal and set outside your door just in case you need anything. Then tomorrow we'll work out your story. Is that all right?"

"Okay," Ramona said.

"Where's everybody at?" The voice came from out on the driveway. Mr. and Mrs. Clay Coal strolled in with big smiles and snow cones. Clay recognized the serious look on Bud's face before he saw the body.

Floyd, and the rest of the men, shuffled around not talking. Larry and Bill left the room like they might be sick. A large pool of blood made a perfect circle around Luther's head. Lou Ann swept the scene and when her eyes locked on Ramona, she knew what had happened. Ramona's gaze fell to the cherry snow cone Lou Ann held. "I haven't ate on it yet. You can have it if you want."

Ramona accepted the offer. She seemed to be only half awake, with lost eyes.

"Al, would you get on the phone and get a couple of cars on the way. I'll go get on the radio and let 'em know what's going on," Bud said. "Honey, you better come with me." Ramona looked for somewhere to put her snow cone. "That's all right, honey, you can bring it with you." He placed one of Floyd's raincoats around her shoulders and led her out.

Clay looked around at all the glum faces and decided he was not going to allow this to ruin his day. "If anyone wants to see a brand new, bright red tandem tow truck, I got one parked right out here," he said.